Includes Bonus Story of
Honor Bound
by Colleen L. Reece

Desert Moon

SUSAN PAGE DAVIS

BARBOUR BOOKS
An Imprint of Barbour Publishing, Inc.

Print ISBN 978-1-68322-085-5

eBook Editions:
Adobe Digital Edition (.epub) 978-1-68322-300-9
Kindle and MobiPocket Edition (.prc) 978-1-68322-301-6

All scripture quotations are taken from the King James Version of the Bible.

This book is a work of fiction. Names, characters, places, and incidents are either products of the author's imagination or used fictitiously. Any similarity to actual people, organizations, and/or events is purely coincidental.

Published by Barbour Books, an imprint of Barbour Publishing, Inc., P.O. Box 719, Uhrichsville, Ohio 44683, www.barbourbooks.com

Our mission is to publish and distribute inspirational products offering exceptional value and biblical encouragement to the masses.

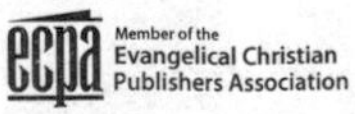

Printed in the United States of America.

Chapter 1

September, 1911

She couldn't have Arizona unless she shared it with Adam Scott. That was horribly unfair.

The stagecoach rolled out of Flagstaff, and Julia Newman leaned eagerly toward the window to see every landmark along the dusty road toward Ardell, the tiny mining town she thought of as home. Some would call this land bleak and unforgiving, but Julia loved Arizona. She'd longed for it during her two years away.

She ignored the three male passengers for nearly an hour. She'd already appraised them and dismissed them, having pegged them as a businessman, a rancher, and a miner. Harmless, but uninteresting compared to the scenery rolling by.

When they came within two miles of the town, the road climbed steadily. Not long now. Would her brother, Oliver, be waiting when she stepped down from the coach?

Julia had come most of the way from Philadelphia on the railroad, but Ardell depended on the old-fashioned methods of transportation. She wasn't sure the town had ever seen an automobile. Wagons and teams hauled ore to the railroad head, though Oliver said the president of High Desert Mine, where he worked, was seriously considering trying out a truck. They weren't sure it could take the steep ascent to Ardell and the main mine. More dependable in these mountains was the stagecoach that toiled up the trail twice a week with mail, passengers, and once a month, the mine's payroll.

Julia drank in the cloudless sky, so perfect and so vibrantly blue in the dry, cool land. She anticipated each vista, watching for the huge rocks that stuck up out of the earth without warning and the low plants that managed to grow in the harsh climate of the high desert. This was home.

Unfortunately, it was also Deputy Sheriff Adam Scott's home—but she wouldn't think about him until she was forced to.

The wind tugged at her hair until she was afraid it would pull her hat right off and fling it across the chaparral. With reluctance, she withdrew her head from the open window and set about fixing her hatpins more firmly.

The man sitting on the seat opposite her made no pretense of looking elsewhere. He had the mien of an investor going up to see Mr. Gerry at the mine. That or a banker, which she couldn't imagine up here in the mountains, but he was too well dressed for most of the occupations common in Ardell. He watched her with a smile on his lips. Julia avoided making direct eye contact. Had he been staring at her the whole way? She oughtn't to be grooming her hair in the presence of gentlemen, but she didn't want to lose her hat, and she didn't want to forgo the view, either.

One of the two other men sat beside her—a rancher who must have come to the area since she'd been away to teach school in Philadelphia. The other sat in the far corner, on the seat with the banker type. Dressed in a flannel shirt and denim pants, the bearded man had slumped in the corner as soon as the coach door was closed, then shut his eyes, opened his mouth, and commenced snoring. Julia figured he worked at the High Desert Mine, where Oliver was employed as the bookkeeper.

A shout from outside caught her attention.

"Whoa, now! Whoa."

The stagecoach slowed, and the man across from her peered out the window. Julia tried to suppress her annoyance. She didn't want to waste a minute getting home. But the driver, Chick Lundy, sounded as calm as ever, so she relaxed and finished pushing in a hatpin.

A gunshot exploded, outside but a short distance away, and the well-dressed man jerked back from the window. Julia's pulse caught and then raced. Another gunshot sounded, right over their heads. The rancher tensed and pulled out a revolver.

The bearded miner sat up, blinking. "What's going on?"

A couple more muffled shouts reached them but Julia couldn't make out the words. She didn't think they came from Chick or his shotgun rider, Bub Hilliard. The voice sounded farther away than that. The coach came to a halt.

She was about to ask the man opposite if he could see anything when someone outside yelled, "Throw down the guns!" The well-dressed passenger reached inside his jacket and pulled out a compact but lethal-looking pistol.

Julia sucked in a breath as her heart galloped on at full speed. She grabbed her handbag. One thing she'd learned, living in a mining town: Don't ride the stage unarmed. Still, she hadn't expected this today. She'd imagined that Ardell was more civilized by now. It seemed she was mistaken. She drew out her weapon and tucked it discreetly in the folds of her skirt.

"Take it easy, mister," Chick called from the driver's box above her. "You had no call to do that."

The unseen interloper shouted, "Throw down the box, or you'll get the same!"

The same? Julia caught her breath and clutched the butt of her pistol. She felt suddenly hot and a bit light-headed. Several thumps sounded on the roof of the stage. She expected the coach door to be thrown open any second, and a blackguard to order them out. But no one came to leer in at the passengers and demand they surrender their valuables.

A *whump* outside drew her to peek warily out the window. The driver's strongbox had hit the ground a few yards away.

"Drive on now," a man shouted. She thought it was the same voice she'd heard before.

Chick cracked his whip and the coach lurched forward. The passengers braced themselves as the horses strained to start again on the upgrade. Julia clung to a leather strap that hung down from the roof.

An eerie silence swept over them except for the rattle of the wheels, the creak of leather, and Chick's urging to the team. Julia looked over at the professional man. He arched his eyebrows and shrugged. Her heart continued to thud.

"So that's it?" the rancher asked. He looked out the window warily.

"See anything behind us?" the man in the suit asked.

The rancher shook his head.

They continued on for a minute or two, then Chick called, "Whoa, now!" Again the coach stopped, on a flatter place this time.

Two raps came on the roof of the stage. "Hey! You fellas in there. Come help me get Bub down."

The man opposite her opened the door and hopped out, leading with his pistol. The rancher shoved his revolver back in his holster and scrambled over Julia's feet.

" 'Scuse me, ma'am."

She drew back as much as possible and let him pass. The miner blinked at her but didn't budge from his corner. Julia put her pistol back in her bag and leaned cautiously out the doorway. The coach rocked and swayed as one of the passengers climbed up to help Chick. Through the roof of the coach she heard one of the men swear.

"Bad, ain't it?"

"Real bad," Chick said.

Julia held her breath. Everyone loved Bub Hilliard. He was sweet on Edna Somers, who worked at the ice-cream parlor, and they were both saving up to buy a house. Mama had told her about the romance in one of her last letters—before she took a turn for the worse.

"You'll need to make room, ma'am," Chick called. He came into view as they carried Bub, with Chick supporting his head and shoulders. Beyond him, the rancher held up Bub's feet and legs.

Somehow they boosted the unconscious man into the stage. Julia huddled in the corner, holding her skirt as flat as she could while Chick clambered in and hauled Bub farther onto the floor.

"Do you want to put him on the seat?" she asked.

"Naw, you folks would just have to keep him from sliding off." Chick looked toward the two men standing at the doorway. "Anybody got a neckerchief they can live without?"

Julia noticed then that Chick's own bandanna lay on Bub's abdomen, soaked in blood. She sucked in a breath.

"Here." The miner on the other seat started to untie his grubby, twisted neckerchief, but the banker replica was already holding a clean, neat square of a handkerchief in through the door.

"Thanks." Chick took the clean one, undid one fold, tossed aside the bloody cloth, and pressed the fresh one to Bub's wound. "Can one of you fellas hold this on here so I can drive?"

"I'll do it." The man in the suit surprised her. He climbed in and knelt on the floor between Bub and Julia's seat. Chick got out, and the rancher got in, climbing over Bub to get to his former seat.

A moment later the coach lurched and began to roll slowly up the road.

"What happened?" the miner asked.

The rancher threw him a dirty look.

The well-dressed man turned and eyed the miner as if he were a cockroach. "We were held up."

"Nobody took nothing offa me."

"Not unless you work for the mine," the rancher said.

The miner sat up straighter. "What about it?"

"He got your pay."

The miner folded his arms and slumped down in his corner again, tipping his hat down over his eyes.

❧

Adam Scott leaned against a pillar on the porch of the grocery, waiting for the stage to come in. It was late today. Not much, but Chick Lundy almost never drove in late.

As deputy to the county sheriff, Adam liked to make his presence known when the stage arrived in town. If strangers got off, it put them on notice that this town had a lawman, and he was watching out for the people. When all the passengers were acquaintances, which happened frequently, he got to catch up on the news outside the little mountain town.

Sometimes Ardell's humdrum days made Adam restless. They seemed like Sunday school compared to his days with the Arizona Rangers. Long hours in the saddle, occasional outbursts of violence, whether tracking rustlers or busting a mine strike—at least the Rangers always had something to do. Now and then they'd even taken a jaunt over the border to pummel the Mexicans. Since the Rangers had disbanded two years ago, a lot of the corps had drifted around, at loose ends. Adam was glad he had a job in his hometown, but sometimes life in Ardell was entirely too tame to suit him.

"Mornin', Sheriff." Mrs. Whitaker smiled at him as she climbed the steps to the grocery.

Adam touched his hat brim. "Mornin', ma'am."

The sounds of Chick Lundy's horn drifted up the mountain trail. The driver always blew it when he reached the bend in the road. Adam straightened and peered toward the sound. Seconds later, the stagecoach appeared.

The stage was a relic of an era gone by—one of the last left in service. Up here in the mountains, the coaches met the need railroads and automobiles couldn't.

Chick was whipping up the horses, even though they were nearly to the stage station. The coach reached the crest of the hill, where the road flattened out along the main street. Instead of stopping in his usual spot, Chick drove on by, with the horses still galloping. Their manes tossed in the wind of their speed, and foam whitened their sides. That was odd, but it didn't seem they were running away. The driver held the reins in perfect control. It took Adam a moment to realize that Chick sat alone on the box.

He ran after the stage, half the length of Main. Something was wrong—so wrong that Chick Lundy pushed his horses beyond reasonable. Unheard of.

The stage came to a halt in a flurry of dust before Adam's office, a tiny building with board siding perched on the edge of the street. It housed one cell, an office big enough for two men to sit down in, and a back room the size of a wagon bed, with a bunk, a wall shelf, and three clothes hooks in it—Adam's current home.

"Sheriff," Chick yelled as he threw the brake handle.

Adam puffed across the street. "I'm here, Chick. What happened?"

"We got held up, that's what. The robber done shot Bub."

"Is he alive?" Adam asked.

"He was when we put him inside. He's gut shot, though. It don't look good."

A small crowd was gathering, and Adam turned to see who was handy. He spotted Lionel Purdue, owner of the Gold Strike, one of the three saloons in town.

"Lionel, run and fetch the doctor," Adam said.

The barkeep bustled off up the street as more people drifted toward the stagecoach.

"Anyone else hurt?" Adam asked.

"Nope," Chick said. "He didn't bother the passengers none. Just took the payroll."

"He?" Adam asked, squinting up at the driver.

"Only one man," Chick said. "I woulda tried to run right over him, but we was going up a real steep place. He fired first thing and hit Bub. Poor Bub let off a round, but he didn't come close to hittin' him."

"All right," Adam said. "Just wait here for the doctor, and then you can take the stage back to the station and tend to the horses. I'll come over and talk to you again after I see what the passengers can tell me."

The door of the coach opened, and a well-dressed man climbed out. Adam noted he had blood on his hands and shirtfront. "Sheriff, is it all right if we get out here?"

"Yes. Are you injured, sir?"

"No." He looked down at his hands. "Just trying to help the shotgun messenger. My name's Wallace Brink. I'm here to see Mr. Gerry, at the High Desert Mine, and I'll be staying at the Placer."

Adam nodded. The Placer was the one modest hotel Ardell boasted. "All right. I won't keep you long, Mr. Brink. I just want to get everyone's story while it's fresh in your minds."

A swirl of skirt and petticoats announced that a woman was disembarking next. Adam turned and held out a hand.

"Can I help you, ma'am? I'm—" He stared into blue eyes that had flummoxed him before. He swallowed hard. "Hello, Julia."

Chapter 2

Adam turned away after Julia's brief greeting and peeked inside the stagecoach. Three more men were inside, one of them being Bub Hilliard, who lay bleeding on the floor. He recognized Ike Hinze, kneeling beside the wounded man. Ike had a ranch in the steep-sided valley beyond town. The sour-faced man who huddled in the corner was connected to the mine, he was sure.

"The doc's here," Chick called from above him.

Adam turned and looked over the heads of the onlookers, but couldn't spot his uncle. He frowned when his gaze lit instead on Dr. Clyde Browning. Why did Lionel have to fetch the new doc, anyway? He ought to have realized Adam meant his uncle, Dr. Royce Scott, who had served the town for many years. It was bad enough that a lot of folks had forsaken the older physician for the new one, but this was official business. His uncle shouldn't be passed by.

Dr. Browning nodded to him. "Patient inside the stage?"

"Yeah." Adam didn't get any more out before the miner hopped out and Browning climbed inside.

"What's your name?" Adam asked the miner.

"Joe Chesley."

"You work for High Desert, don't you?"

"Yup, I'm a driller."

"Come over here and tell me what happened," Adam said.

"I didn't see nothing."

"Nothing?"

"Nope." Chesley shot a stream of tobacco juice to one side. "We was going along great guns and all of a sudden Chick stopped the team. Somebody hollered, and then a gun went off."

"Only one shot?"

Chesley frowned. "Two. Mebbe three. I'm not sure. I'd been sleepin'."

"There were two shots," Wallace Brink said, stepping closer. "I think our shotgun rider must have fired once, and of course the robber shot him."

Adam looked over at Julia, who had stood by quietly, listening to every word.

She nodded. "This gentleman is correct. The first thing I noticed was a shout, but not from one of our party. It sounded faint, as though someone at a distance was trying to get Chick's attention. Then the coach slowed down, and two shots were fired. One closer than the other."

She looked to Brink for confirmation, and he nodded. "That pretty well sums it up. The driver stopped the coach, and the robber yelled to throw the box down. They threw it to the ground—"

"They?" Adam asked.

Brink coughed slightly. "Well, I assume the driver did. But we didn't know at the time that Mr. Hilliard was shot."

"That's true," Julia said. "I assumed he was fine until after the bandit told Chick to drive on. We went on up the road a ways, and he stopped the stagecoach again. That's when he called for the men to help him get Bub down into the stage."

Adam eyed her thoughtfully. "I notice you both keep saying 'the robber' or 'the bandit.' Mr. Lundy says there was only one man. Is that right?"

"He'd know better than we would," Brink said. "I didn't actually see him."

"Me either," Julia said. "He didn't approach the door or the windows of the stage."

"Did you see any horses?"

Julia and Brink eyed each other for a moment.

"No," Julia said. "Now that you mention it, I didn't see any, or hear any hoofbeats."

Brink shook his head. "Me either."

"I didn't see nothin'," Joe Chesley repeated.

"All right," Adam said. "I'll check with the driver on that. Miss Newman, I know where you live. Mr. Brink, if I need more from you, I'll come to the Placer. Mr. Chesley, are you at the miners' village?"

"Yup."

Adam nodded. "You folks can go."

"Thank you," Brink said. He walked toward the back of the coach, looking up toward the boot, where the luggage was stored.

Dr. Browning and Ike Hinze were lifting the shotgun rider out of the stage.

"Are you taking him to your office?" Adam asked.

Browning shook his head. "Unfortunately, Mr. Hilliard is beyond need for help. He must have passed away during their run up here from the site of the holdup."

Adam lowered his head and let his shoulders slump. Now it was beyond chasing down a road agent. He had to catch the man who'd murdered a friend. He pulled in a deep breath. The crowd was dispersing, some of the people following the men who carried Bub's body toward the livery stable, where the owner made coffins on demand. The rest went off, seemingly to gossip in the saloons or the mercantile, or headed home to prepare dinner.

He caught a glimpse of Julia Newman's elegant form disappearing down the street toward her brother's house. Adam couldn't tear his gaze away until she turned the corner. Why did she have to come back now, anyhow?

Chick Lundy cracked his whip and clucked to the horses. The stagecoach rattled off toward the vacant lot past the smithy, where the driver would have room to turn around. Adam walked toward the livery stable. He'd get Ike Hinze's version and then go and talk to Chick again.

Half an hour later, after he'd questioned Hinze and helped Chick swab out the stagecoach, Adam mounted his bay gelding and rode out to the scene of the robbery. On the way, he thought over what he'd learned about the holdup. One robber. Chick was the only one who'd gotten a look at him, but the others trusted his word, and so did Adam.

Chick had also told him he hadn't seen a horse. The bandit had threatened him, so he'd surrendered the treasure box, but the man hadn't picked it up until after the stagecoach was out of sight. Chick thought he heard another faint gunshot after they were over the next rise. He'd surmised that the robber had shot the lock off the box, and Adam agreed that was logical, but he'd have to see for himself what clues were out there on the trail.

Chick had been so concerned about getting Bub to the doctor quickly and avoiding more violence that he hadn't tried to see where the robber went. He'd lit out for town, which was no doubt the best course.

The robber was long gone, of course. It was easy for Adam to find where they'd been held up—the empty treasure box still sat at the side of the road. The outlaw must have taken the money out and put it into a sack or something before he rode off. Adam looked over the ground carefully and then searched farther afield for evidence that the robber had hidden a horse nearby. Every indicator supported Chick's story of the bandit working solo.

When Adam decided he'd found everything significant, he mounted, carrying the empty wooden box. He left the box at his office and rode out to the High Desert Mine to see the supervisor. Better find out how much money they'd been expecting today.

Leland Gerry came out of his office and greeted Adam.

"Scott, come on in. I just heard. It's a terrible thing. Just terrible."

"I'm sorry about the payroll, Mr. Gerry," Adam said.

They went into the office, and Gerry shut the door. "I won't pretend it doesn't hurt us. But losing a man like Bub Hilliard—well, what can I say? He was a good man."

"He surely was. Now, can you tell me how much money the company had in that treasure box today?"

Gerry gritted his teeth. "I could give you an estimate, but our bookkeeper can tell you to the penny."

"That would be Oliver Newman?"

"Yes. Come on, let's go ask him. He can check the books."

Gerry led him down a short hallway and stopped at an open doorway. "Hmm, that's odd. Newman's not at his desk."

"Maybe he went out to eat his lunch," Adam said. His own belly was starting to feel mighty spare.

Gerry took out his watch and frowned at it. "He should be here now. It's almost two o'clock. Let me send one of our clerks around to look for him."

They walked back toward the entrance to the building. A young man dressed in a white shirt and black vest and pants, with a ribbon tie and paper cuffs shielding his shirtsleeves, jumped up when Gerry called his name.

"Yes, sir?"

"Find Mr. Newman for me and send him to my office immediately."

"Yes, sir." The clerk hurried off.

Ten minutes later, they were still waiting. Gerry paced his office. Adam was past ready to ride back to town. Maybe Oliver was home now.

"Sir, I believe I'll move along," he said. "Oliver's a friend of mine. I can catch him later in town." Adam hovered on the verge of mentioning the fact that Oliver's sister had come in on the stagecoach. Maybe he'd gone to meet her, though Adam had seen no sign of him in Ardell—even though the stage was late. He refrained from suggesting it. He wouldn't want to put Oliver in hot water with the boss.

The clerk came huffing and red-faced to the doorway and knocked cursorily on the jamb.

"Well?" Gerry asked.

"He's not to be found, sir."

Chapter 3

Julia opened the door of the little house.

"Oliver?"

Her voice echoed through the rooms. She stepped inside and set down her valise and handbag. The front room was nearly the same as it had been when she left two years ago. The furniture was the same her parents had had—two comfortable stuffed chairs and a rocker, bookshelves, a side table and lamp, a rug made of braided strips of wool. On one wall, the photograph she'd sent home last year hung in a simple wooden frame.

She ventured to the kitchen doorway. Her mother's cookstove—it would always be Mama's stove in Julia's mind—sat where it had for years, ever since they'd moved to Ardell. Tears threatened her as the memory of her mother working over it came back so strongly she had to look away. Same cupboard, same pine table and chairs, same washstand with a large, enameled dishpan sitting in it. Same flour barrel and coffee grinder.

She'd never expected to come home to this room and not find Mama here. Oliver's telegram a month ago had torn her heart to shreds.

She'd planned to come home, but not until she'd taught another year or two in Philadelphia. With several years of solid experience under her belt, she'd planned to have the family watch for an opening in Arizona, and then she'd return, ready to support herself and pick up life—without Adam Scott in it. The shock of Mama's death had heaved those plans out the window. She'd put in her resignation and continued teaching several weeks while the headmaster found a suitable replacement for her. Finally she'd headed west, knowing the funeral was long past. That didn't matter so much. She needed to go home.

Was she ready to stay here, now that the journey was behind her? She wasn't sure, and seeing Adam today had shattered what little confidence she'd stored up. She couldn't fall back into her old life in Ardell. Of course, it could never be the way it used to be—not with Mama gone.

Julia drew in a deep breath and walked over to the stove. She lifted one of the cast-iron lids over the firebox. The ashes were warm. She took the poker from its peg on the wall behind the stove and raked them over. A few coals glowed orange. The woodbox held ample kindling and some shredded bark and dried weeds. It took her only a minute to lay the foundation of a good fire. She closed the stove lid and opened the draft on the stovepipe. The kitchen would warm up soon. Meanwhile, she'd keep her wool coat on.

After filling the teakettle and setting it on the stove, she went back to the front room and picked up her bags. Weariness swept over her. She hadn't yet admitted her disappointment that Oliver hadn't met the stage. She longed to see him again. Surely he could have taken an hour off from work—but he wouldn't have been certain she'd come today. He would come home as soon as he'd finished his day's work at the mine's headquarters.

She trudged up the stairs. The robbery had wrung the starch out of her. It was all she could do to heft the valise onto her bed and unpack it. She longed to crawl under the patchwork quilt and go to sleep, but her stomach protested. She'd eaten nothing since the sketchy breakfast she'd wolfed down at a stage stop before dawn. Oliver must have something she could eat on hand. She ought to have rummaged through the cupboard while she was down there.

She was halfway down the stairs when someone knocked on the front door. She took the last few steps quickly and walked toward the front window. Maybe Chick had brought her trunk around. From the window she couldn't see the caller, but a bay horse stood out front, his reins trailing in the dirt. She braced herself and opened the door.

"Adam Scott."

"Hello again, Julia."

The afternoon sun sprinkled glints of gold in his thick chestnut hair. His brown eyes gazed so intently at her that she looked away.

"Nice horse," she said.

"Thanks. Can I come in?"

"Oliver's not here."

"I'm sorry to hear that. He's not at the mine either."

She jerked her head around. "What do you mean? He didn't meet me at the stage stop."

"I mean I've been to the mine. He wasn't there."

She eyed him thoughtfully. "Is that. . .significant?"

"It seems to be to you."

"I was disappointed not to see him when I arrived."

"Hmm."

She sharpened her gaze, not liking his manner. "Do you have something to say, Adam Scott? If you do, then say it plainly. You never used to beat about the bush with me."

He gave a rueful chuckle. "No, I didn't, did I? You always said what you meant, too."

She swallowed with difficulty. Facing him for the second time in one day, without the buffer of the other stagecoach passengers, drained her of whatever energy and emotion she had left. "Adam, I'm exhausted. I'll tell Ollie you were here. Maybe he can come down to the jail and talk to you later."

"I'm sorry about your ma."

The unexpected gentleness in his voice tugged at her, and Julia cleared her throat before replying. "Thank you. But you didn't come here for that."

"I need to ask you a few more questions about the holdup."

"Ask away."

"Can't we sit down?"

Julia interpreted his gaze as something between a glare and an entreaty. Could they ever be friends again, after what had passed between them? She had her doubts.

At last she sighed and stepped out of the doorway. "Fine. Come on in."

The hair on the back of Adam's neck prickled as he crossed the threshold of the Newman house. Julia was so beautiful. He could scarcely believe how she'd changed—improved. He couldn't quite put his finger on what she'd gained—sophistication, maybe. He supposed that happened to young women who went East and learned to move in refined society. When he'd courted her, she was pretty—the prettiest girl in Ardell—but half tomboy, riding up and down the mountain trails in her split skirt, camping with her brother, and shooting a bow better than a lot of Indians.

Now she'd gotten so much gentility he wasn't sure he knew how to talk to her. She sat down in her mother's old rocker and waved him toward a cushioned armchair. He sprawled in it as he had a hundred times when visiting Ollie, with his long legs stretched out before him. Suddenly he felt out of place and sat straighter, pulling his legs in and bending them at the knees.

"What would you like to know?" she asked, folding her hands in her lap.

"What did the robber look like?"

"I already told you, I didn't see him."

"Not even when Chick started the stage moving again?"

"No."

"Hmm."

"Stop saying that."

He raised his eyebrows. "A little touchy, aren't we?"

"I don't like the way you come here hmming and insinuating."

"What am I insinuating?"

She glared at him. His stomach heaved, and all kinds of memories that he didn't want to deal with returned. He shouldn't have come here until Oliver was done with his workday and likely to be home. But then, that was part of the puzzle, wasn't it?

"Strange the bandit didn't demand that you passengers hand over your money and valuables."

"Maybe he figured the payroll was enough."

Adam didn't like her ready answer. Either she was still mad at him or she was hiding something. "One of the other passengers told me you had a gun."

"I do. So?"

He shrugged. "A bit unusual for a lady."

"After Papa died, I always carried a gun if I had to go somewhere unescorted. In case you've forgotten, Ardell was a pretty rough place two or three years ago. It seems to have mellowed a little, but I wasn't taking any chances."

Adam had to admit she was right. The Newman family had moved here shortly after the mine opened, and Julia's father had served in the same job Adam now had. The town was rough then, and most men wore sidearms. Oliver got the bookkeeping job at the mine about five years ago—before his father died—and he carried a gun, too, at least on payday.

"Two of the other passengers had guns, that I know of," Julia said. "Have you grilled *them* about it?"

"No. Yes. That is, I asked them about weapons." His cheeks

heated. Why did he let her get to him? One thing hadn't changed—Julia didn't deal well with him in the role of a lawman. Too bad. He would have liked to be able to talk this over sensibly with her. This and a thousand other things. Instead he had to look at her as he would anyone else. She was the victim of a crime. Or was she?

He didn't like the possibilities that flashed through his mind. One robber—a man who obviously knew today was the day the mine's payroll would come. One female passenger packing a gun. He'd never before heard of a stage holdup where the bandits didn't rob the passengers. Could the robber possibly have known who the passengers were—or at least, who one of them was?

She eyed him coolly for a long moment. "You came here knowing Ollie wasn't at the mine. Now you're pressing me about the holdup, when I've already told you everything I know. What's going on, Adam?"

"I don't know what you're getting at."

"Are you implying that my brother was involved in the robbery?"

"I'm only trying to get at the truth, Julia." Her suggestion felt like a slap, but he managed to keep his voice cool. The thought had lurked in the back of his mind, where he didn't have to confront it. Now she'd yanked it into the open—the thought that his best friend had robbed the stagecoach.

Her expression hardened, and her beautiful face seemed a caricature of the young woman he'd loved. Did she despise him now?

"Truth? You've been friends with my brother for a long time, Adam. I won't say anything about our past relationship. Just think about what you mean to Ollie. In every letter he's written me, he's mentioned some aspect of your friendship. He looks up to you in many ways, and he relies on you. But all of a sudden you think he's capable of violence? You don't know Ollie as well as I thought you did."

"Julia—"

She held up both hands. "Stop. Just stop right there."

For a moment, they sat gazing at each other. Adam didn't dare say a word.

Julia's chin rose a fraction of an inch. "Please leave."

Chapter 4

After Adam had left, Julia hurried upstairs. As tired as she was, she couldn't rest. She opened her wardrobe and took out the brown split skirt she used to wear when she rode about the countryside with her brother. In Philadelphia, she'd worn a proper riding habit when she went out on horseback, but this was Arizona, and she was content to slip back into her old ways.

She buttoned a cotton blouse and tied a neckerchief at her throat. Sitting on the edge of the bed, she hauled off her walking shoes and put on her old, worn boots. Last, she topped her ensemble with a warm woolen jacket and her old hat—one Oliver had outgrown and let her have when she was eleven. It fit snugly over her hair, but that was all right. It would stay put. She took her small revolver from her handbag and put it in the deep pocket of her skirt.

The livery stable was less than a city block away, and she strode quickly along the packed-dirt street. She met only a few people, and she nodded at them but kept walking.

Adam couldn't seriously think Oliver robbed the stagecoach. Why would her brother do such a thing? He made a decent salary at the mine. His recent letters hinted at no financial distress. Everything had sounded reassuringly normal until Mama's sudden death. As soon as she'd heard that news, she'd resigned her teaching post and arranged to come home.

But nearly a month had passed since her mother died. What had Oliver been doing in the meantime? Was he more distraught than she knew? He was always a pensive boy, but still she couldn't conceive of him turning to crime. She tried to remember everything she'd heard during the holdup. Wouldn't she have known her own brother's voice? The shout she'd heard when inside the stagecoach echoed in her head: *"You'll get the same."* No, Oliver wouldn't have said that. But she couldn't recall the timbre of the voice—only the sinister words.

Sam Dennis, the livery owner, broke into a wide grin when he saw her entering his barn.

"Well, now! Miss Julia! Welcome back."

"Thank you, Sam. Have you got a horse I can use this afternoon?"

"Surely, but. . . Are you and Oliver going riding so soon? You came in on today's stage, didn't you?"

"Yes, and I want to ride up to the mine."

"Oh, well I guess Oliver's working and you can't wait to see him, eh?"

She didn't disillusion him, but stood impatiently watching as he saddled a lethargic dun gelding. Within minutes, she was in the saddle. She made the horse trot until they were out of sight of the livery then urged him into a lope. Ten minutes later, they drew up before the mine's headquarters. She dismounted and tied the horse to the hitching rail. The clerk inside lost no time in ushering her to Leland Gerry's office.

"Good day, Miss Newman." The older man rose behind his desk. He hadn't aged much, though his hair had a little gray now. He wore the same clothes Julia had always seen him wear—black suit, white shirt, black necktie. While greeting her, he removed the spectacles he'd been wearing.

"Hello. Is it true that my brother is not here?"

He blinked then said, "Yes. No one seems to know where he's gone to."

"Did he come to work this morning?"

"Yes, I spoke to him personally less than an hour after I came in. He didn't mention to me that he'd be going out, but sometimes he does go on errands without my knowledge. Things having to do with mine business."

Julia nodded. "He didn't meet the stagecoach when I arrived, and I assumed he was here." A stack of papers on Gerry's desk caught her eye—campaign posters. One hung on the wall behind him. GERRY FOR SENATE. Arizona wasn't even a state yet, and he was planning his move to Washington.

"I'm sorry," he said. "No one here has seen him since ten o'clock or so. If you'd like to leave Oliver a note, I can show you to his office."

"Thank you, but I know where it is." She whirled then walked into the hallway and a few steps along it to the tiny room that held Ollie's desk, two chairs, and a set of shelves. She found a scrap of paper and a pencil and bent over his blotter to scribble a note.

Ollie, I'm at home. Hurry back.

She added a stylized lizard at the bottom—a rune she'd used for her signature since they were children. Oliver used an eagle. They'd copied the simplified depictions from petroglyphs they discovered when they lived up near Canyon Diablo more than a decade ago. Their father had managed the trading post there for three years, and Julia and her brother had run wild in the desert and loved every minute of it.

She went back out to the dun gelding. Where now? If no one knew where Oliver had gone, searching seemed pointless. She'd check back at the house, but her mind was made up before she reached it. If he wasn't there, she'd ride back down to the place where the stage had been robbed. Adam was right about one thing—that holdup was downright odd. Only one man, no horse, and he hadn't demanded anything from the passengers. Maybe there were some clues down there.

The horse loped willingly back into town. Julia ran into the house. Her trunk sat on the floor just inside the parlor, to the right of the door. They never locked doors in Ardell, and she was glad Chick had brought it inside for her.

"Ollie? Are you here?"

Her voice echoed off the walls and ceiling. Tears sprang into her eyes. Where was he? She refused to worry. Instead, she ran back out to the horse and mounted. The gelding wanted to return to the stable, but Julia forced him to head out of town, down the mountain, along the road toward Flagstaff.

Her thoughts, against her wishes, swung back to the sheriff as she rode. Adam hadn't changed a bit since she'd left two years ago, unless it was to be more suspicious—more antagonistic. She realized how much she'd counted on him taking up some other occupation after the Arizona Rangers disbanded. She'd have happily married him if he became a rancher or a storekeeper or a freighter.

But, no. Adam Scott couldn't lay down the badge. Within weeks after he was done with the Rangers, he'd accepted the offer of a job as sheriff. Technically he was a deputy to the county sheriff—the office her father had once held. But all the townspeople called him "sheriff." Why couldn't he settle down and be an ordinary citizen—one who wasn't hated and cursed and shot at? At the age of twenty, Julia had hoped. She was older now, and she knew he couldn't change. Adam would always need to be a lawman.

And so she'd left—ostensibly to pursue a teaching career. She and Adam both knew she'd really done it to put as many miles as possible between them. She'd nursed her shattered heart at a safe distance from the man she loved but couldn't have.

A mile out of town, and a good deal lower in elevation, she paused. This was the spot. The robber had chosen one of the steepest stretches of the road. The horses had to slow down here. On one side an outcropping of rock rose, with several large boulders at the bottom. Good places to hide. Beyond it, brush grew thick and edged up to a copse of scrub pines. More cover. The other side of the road ran close to the edge of the mountain. Passengers got a beautiful view, but the coach driver had to stay clear of the drop-off.

Julia dismounted and examined the ground. After a moment, she thought she knew exactly where the stage had stopped and located a squarish scuff where the treasure box had hit the ground. A few boot prints showed in the nearby dirt, which must have belonged to the robber.

The road itself was a mess of hoofprints, but no one had seen the robber's horse. He must have had one. She looked around again. The trees were a good fifty yards away. The bandit must have hidden the horse at least that far away, unless he'd had a place in the rocks to keep him out of sight.

She walked toward the boulders and searched the ground between and behind them, and along the edge of the juniper bushes, but all she found was an empty bottle. She held it up for a moment and eyed it with distaste before tossing it as far as she could into the brush. Useless, that's what this trip was. There was nothing here that would tell her who did this.

Maybe Oliver had come home. She ought to go and check. The dun gelding was cropping the short, dry grass at the edge of the road. Julia mounted and headed back up the slope toward town. Halfway there, another horse came around a bend toward her. She drew back the reins and the dun stopped.

Adam stopped his horse, too, for a moment then proceeded toward her. She took in the bedroll and pack tied behind the cantle of his saddle. Adam wasn't out for a brief ride. He planned on being gone a while.

❧

What was Julia doing out here? Adam urged his horse forward, trying to read her face. Impossible—she'd donned a guarded look that might as well have been a mask. In the old days, he'd been able to take one look into her eyes and know exactly what she was thinking. How many other ways had she changed?

"Hello, Julia." He pulled back, and Socks stopped, almost nose to nose with the dun Julia rode. One of Sam Dennis's horses. "Oliver didn't come home yet?"

"Would I be out here alone if he had?"

She had a point. "So, what are you doing?"

"Looking for Ollie, of course."

"Out here?"

She shrugged. "Maybe he rode into Flagstaff to see if I came in on the train."

It wasn't like her to use weak logic—or to lie. What was she really up to? Maybe she knew exactly where Oliver was. He looked her over, more closely, taking in the comfortable old riding clothes she used to wear. This wasn't the proper lady who'd gotten off the stage. She might be taking Oliver information or supplies. Maybe she planned to join him so they could escape together with the loot from the robbery. Adam hated to even think that about his best friend—or the woman he'd loved.

But if Oliver was innocent, why did he disappear when the payroll did? And why was his sister out here in an isolated spot, near where the robbery took place?

"Look, Julia, what's going on?"

"What do you mean?" She blinked those blue eyes at him, so guilelessly that he almost believed she was innocent.

"Ollie knew you were on that stage, didn't he?"

Her eyes narrowed. "I can't believe you just said that."

She turned her horse and clucked to it, going around Socks. As they passed, Socks stretched his neck and nipped the dun's flank. Julia's horse let out a squeal and quickened its steps. Julia flung a dark look over her shoulder at Adam.

He slumped in the saddle and watched her go. How many times would he have to watch Julia ride away from him? He'd had more than enough of that.

He turned Socks back down the trail and determined to forget her. Again.

"Women."

Socks twitched his ears back toward Adam, and he realized he'd spoken aloud. He stroked the bay's withers.

"We were gettin' along just fine, weren't we, boy?"

But Adam wasn't. Life without Julia was gray. The intense color she'd splashed all over it was gone. True, things were more peaceful without her, and he'd gotten used to the calm. He had a lot of friends and few enemies.

Another pain sliced through him. Oliver Newman was his best friend. He couldn't have done this. How could he? Adam knew his friend well—or he'd thought he did.

Oliver had been there for Adam when Julia went away. Even though she was his sister, Oliver hadn't tried to defend her. He'd seemed to be able to look at both sides, and Adam respected that. The Newman kids' father had died in the line of duty when he served as a deputy sheriff. Julia couldn't go through that with a husband, too. Adam had thought long and hard about it, but in the end he couldn't resign his position. He'd honestly felt God had called him to be a lawman. But Julia couldn't accept that. Or maybe she could, but not the two of them together as long as he wore the badge. So she'd gone away to teach.

Oliver had helped him pack up the memories and put them away. Not to forget. Adam could never forget his love for Julia. But he could keep it sealed away in a dark place, like the trunk full of his mother's things that sat up in Uncle Royce's attic. He hadn't opened that for a long time either.

And Ollie had been there to talk things out after Adam came home from a recent trip to Phoenix. He'd gone there to take in a train robber he'd helped the county sheriff catch. He hadn't minded the journey to the capital, though it was hotter than molten iron in Phoenix during July.

Adam had been stunned when the bigwigs in Phoenix had come to his hotel and urged him to run for representative in the new state government. Arizona wasn't even accepted as a state yet, but they were lining up senators and representatives and all kinds of other officials.

He'd thought about it until he got home. Then he told Oliver, and they'd hashed it over—for about five minutes. They both knew he didn't want to spend half the year in Phoenix. He wanted to stay right here and keep the peace in the mining district—which he'd done fairly well until today.

He reined Socks in when he reached the scene of the robbery. Chick Lundy had described it well, and he'd had no trouble finding it the first time he came out here. There had been no rain for more than a week, and it wasn't hard to tell where Chick had stopped the team and they'd stood for several minutes. He'd also found boot prints and a few other scuff marks. Now smaller footprints had joined the mix. Adam dismounted and studied the trail for a few yards beyond. Julia hadn't gone any farther. She'd stopped here and looked the site over again. Why? Had she met her brother here in the short time he'd been gone? He didn't see any other footprints, but that didn't mean anything. Oliver might have met her and stayed in the saddle.

Adam gritted his teeth. He'd only ridden back to town long enough to see Leland Gerry. Then he'd alerted a trusted man and grabbed his gear. Andy Black was going to meet him out here with several other men to help him track the robber. But apparently he'd left the spot unwatched long enough for Julia to look it over—and maybe to communicate with the bandit.

He swung back into the saddle. Did he really believe that? He didn't want to.

Julia was nearly to the outskirts of town when she met four riders. She felt a twinge of unease. In the old days, she wouldn't have been afraid to be out by herself on horseback, so long as she had her gun. But since she'd lived in a city, her ideas about that had changed. Maybe that was part of growing up. She rested her right hand over her pocket, where she could feel the reassuringly hard shape of her revolver.

"Howdy, Miss Julia."

"Sam?" With relief she recognized the livery owner, as well as another of the men who rode with him. "Where are you all going?"

"Out to meet the sheriff. He called for a posse."

"A posse?" Julia looked back down the road in bewilderment. Adam had said nothing to her of this, or even of having a suspect. "What for?"

Bob Tanner, the barber, raised his hat for a moment. "Adam found where someone tied a horse in the trees not far from the holdup, and he called for men to go out with him to track the robber."

"Be quiet, Tanner," one of the other men said.

Julia's stomach curled in dismay. Had the notion of her brother's involvement been discussed in town?

"We'd better get going," Sam said. "Just put the horse in the corral when you're done with him, Miss Julia."

"All right. Thank you." She felt ill as she watched them ride away to meet Adam. When they were out of sight, she turned the dun homeward and galloped for the livery stable. Three more men passed her, heading toward the posse's rendezvous.

She rode into town and tied the dun in front of the mercantile. When she went inside, the owner was standing behind the counter.

"Hello, Miss Newman."

"Hello, Mr. Morley," she said. "I don't suppose you've seen my brother today."

"No, I haven't. He's probably out to the mine."

"Thank you, but I've been there."

"So it's true he's disappeared?"

"I beg your pardon." She didn't try to hide her shock this time—or her outrage.

Mr. Morley shrugged. "Just that folks are saying it's mighty peculiar how Oliver disappeared right when the payroll did."

She stared at him. "Are you implying that Oliver had something to do with the robbery? My brother is as honest as the day is long."

"Have to follow the evidence."

Julia's jaw dropped. "How could you say that?"

Mr. Morley shook his head. "If your brother's found guilty, you'll have to accept it."

"It's more likely he was injured trying to do some good." Julia whirled and went out into the sun again. Two women were coming up the steps.

"Julia, is that you?" Mrs. Tanner peered at her from beneath the brim of her sunbonnet.

"Yes. How are you?" With great effort she controlled her voice.

"Fine, just fine."

"Have you seen Oliver today?" Julia ventured, hoping they wouldn't insinuate that he was guilty.

"Why, no, I haven't," Mrs. Tanner said.

The other woman shook her head, and Julia left them. If they hadn't heard the rumors yet, it wouldn't be long until they did. Just about as long as it took them to get to the counter and speak to Mr. Morley, in fact.

She visited the feed store, the bakery, and the tea shop next to the church, but no one had seen her brother. Nobody else seemed as bold as Mr. Morley, but some of them looked at her oddly, and Julia began to feel like an outcast. As she left the tea shop, she saw an older man walking unsteadily across the street.

"Dr. Scott!" She hurried to meet him. The physician was Adam's uncle, but she wouldn't hold that against him. Dr. Scott had served the little town since before her family moved here, and she considered him an old friend. A whiff of whiskey wafted to her as she took his arm. She looked over her shoulder. Judging from his course, he'd come from the nearest saloon. Oh well. A lot of men had a drink now and then. That's how the town supported three saloons.

"Hello." She smiled up at him.

He stood in the middle of the street eyeing her uncertainly. "Julia? Julia Newman?"

"That's right," she said. "How are you?"

"Oh, not too good."

"I'm sorry to hear that."

The old man took a step toward his house, which was located

on a side street a few yards down. "Well, it's this new young doctor, you know. Since he came to town, I don't see many patients anymore."

"That's too bad." She wasn't sure whether Dr. Scott wanted to retire or not, but perhaps he didn't have much choice. She walked along beside him. "You haven't seen Oliver, have you?"

"Who? Ollie? Can't say as I have."

She saw him to his door, and by the time they reached it, she was certain he'd had more than one drink. "Well, good-bye. It's good to see you again."

He waved vaguely and opened the door.

Julia backtracked toward the tea shop. Oliver had written last summer that the church beside it had a new minister. Maybe he could shed some light on her brother's whereabouts.

She knocked on the door of the little house behind the church. The woman who opened the door looked tired. Julia could see why—she carried a baby, and a little girl tugged at her skirts. The woman seemed older than Julia—at least ten years older, though some of her wrinkles might be due to fatigue.

"Yes?"

"Hello, I'm Julia Newman. Oliver's sister."

"Oh yes, of course. I'm so sorry about your mother."

"Thank you."

"Won't you come in?" The woman stood back.

"Mama," the little girl said.

"Hush, Dorcas. I'll tend to that later. We have a guest."

"I'm sorry to bother you," Julia said. "I just wondered if you or the reverend had seen Oliver today. I came in on the stagecoach this morning, and—"

"On the stage? My goodness!" The woman's face took on new sympathy. "I heard about the robbery. Are you all right?"

"Yes, I'm fine. But my brother didn't meet the stage, and he's not at the house or the mine, so I've been asking around. . . ." Julia's hopes dissipated as she spoke. Why would Oliver have come here? "I'm sorry. I'll be going."

Before she made it to the door, it opened and a short, stocky man entered. His dark hair was sprinkled with gray, and he wore a plain black suit. No doubt the minister.

"Hello," he said, eyeing Julia curiously.

"This is Miss Newman," the woman said. "Oliver's sister. Miss Newman, this is the Reverend Mr. Kepler, my husband." She spoke the words as though invoking respect and reverence.

"Ah yes, delighted." The minister shook Julia's hand.

"How do you do," Julia said. "I only dropped in to see if either of you had seen my brother today. I just returned to town, and I've yet to talk to Oliver."

"No, can't say as I have," Mr. Kepler replied. "In fact, I haven't seen him for several weeks."

"Oh?" Julia found that odd, but decided to keep her own counsel.

Mrs. Kepler, however, was more forthright. "Yes, Oliver hasn't been to services for several Sundays."

"Quite irregular lately," her husband said. "I'm sorry that we can't help you. I must say your mother's funeral went well."

"Oh yes," Mrs. Kepler said quickly. "In very good taste. A great many people turned out. I believe your mother was well thought of in thesc parts."

"Thank you," Julia said. "I wish I could have been here."

"Of course you couldn't have reached home in time," the minister said.

"No. And since I was teaching school and we were near the end of the term, it seemed reasonable for me to finish it out." Julia felt tears coming on. Why must she justify her absence from her mother's funeral? "If you'll excuse me, I think I'll go home and lie down."

She rode home, ignoring the people she passed. As she entered the house a few minutes later, her mind raced. This was nonsense! How could the people have known them so long and suspect as nice a young man as Oliver of being a criminal? She felt as though all her strength had melted like bacon grease in a hot spider and drained out of her.

This was Adam's fault. He was the one who had made a point of Oliver's absence, and now everyone in town suspected him. She wasn't sure she could forgive Adam for that. She thought she'd forgiven him for smashing her heart into little tiny pieces, but now she wasn't sure. The shards had pricked deeply each time she'd seen Adam today.

She walked over to the desk in the front room. Her mother had always kept important papers here, but she didn't find much. A few envelopes, a pen, a few pen wipes, and a nearly empty bottle of ink. Oliver must keep most of his writing supplies at his desk in the mine.

She went upstairs, pulling her hat off. If she were wise, she'd return the dun to the livery and take that nap. On the landing she paused and then turned resolutely toward Oliver's room.

He still kept it neat, as always. His bed was made, with one of Mama's pieced quilts on top. His dresser was bare except for his razor, shaving mug, and soap. Feeling slightly guilty, she opened the top drawer. It was half full of the things she'd expected—socks, underdrawers, handkerchiefs. She was about to close it when on impulse she shifted the stack of neatly folded handkerchiefs to one side. She smiled. Beneath them was a small pasteboard folder.

She took it out and opened the bankbook. Oliver had been making regular deposits to his account at the bank in Flagstaff.

It appeared that he put a portion of his pay each month into his savings. The balance was $174.36. A nice nest egg for a young man.

Oliver did not need to rob stagecoaches.

She tucked the bankbook into her pocket and headed for the stairs, determined to find Adam and talk him out of this insanity.

Chapter 5

The sun lay on the west side of the mountains now, and long shadows met to form pools of darkness over the hillside where Adam and his men searched for clues to the robbery.

"We ought to turn back, Sheriff," Sam Dennis called to him from a bluff above him.

"Not yet."

Rancher Andy Black rode up beside him. "We lost the tracks an hour ago, and this country's too rough. There's no use hunting for them in the dark."

Adam exhaled heavily. Andy was probably right—and he probably wanted to get home to his family. "Gather the men and let's hash over what we've got."

Later, in the twilight, the seven other men circled about him.

"I'm going to stay up here," Adam told them. "I'll try to pick up the tracks in the morning."

Bob Tanner shook his head. "No disrespect, Sheriff, but I don't think you'll find 'em again in these hills. That fella's long gone."

"That's right," Andy said. "He knew exactly what he was doing. Knew Bub Hilliard was a crack shot, too."

Sam pushed his hat back. "I tend to agree, Adam. This man knew what he was up against."

Adam clenched his teeth. What they were saying supported the possibility that Oliver Newman was behind the holdup. Whoever had carried out the robbery knew the stage schedule and the best place to stop the stagecoach. He didn't let his face or his horse be seen, and he knew where to hide.

"He didn't act like most bandits," said one of the mine's foremen.

"That's right," Sam said. "He went out there on foot and left his horse in the trees."

"Yeah, and he didn't confront the passengers," Andy said. "I was on a stage once when it was robbed. That bandit made us all get out and empty our pockets. I lost over fifty bucks that day."

Of all their points, that one bothered Adam most. Why hadn't the road agent wanted the passengers to see him? Was he afraid someone inside would recognize him? If this blackguard was someone local, it only made Adam more determined to ride down the thief.

"You all go on back to town," he said.

"What, you're really staying out here?" Andy asked.

Sam eyed him carefully. "What do you think you'll find?"

"I don't know."

Adam sat on Socks's back until they were all around the bluff and headed back to the trail. He rode his horse down to the creek and dismounted. He let Socks drink his fill and then hobbled him. Enough grass and low brush grew along the creek bank for his horse to graze on. Adam gathered some wood and spread out his bedroll. He pulled a packet of crackers and a can of sardines from his saddlebag. It was full dark before he had a fire going. He sat beside it for an hour, feeding sticks in.

Finally he decided to quit wasting fuel and save enough wood to heat coffee in the morning. Lying back with his head on his saddle, he gazed up at the brilliant sky.

He tried to think about the proposal he'd gotten from the territorial officials. Two men from Flagstaff had approached him before his trip to Phoenix. They'd asked him to meet in the capital with some of the men who were revising the Arizona constitution.

"We need men who don't have their minds made up on some

of the issues," one of the Phoenix politicians had told him. That meant they wanted men who would take *their* side. Their suggestion that he run for a seat in the new state legislature was flattering. He'd even flirted with the idea that a girl like Julia might not mind being married to a legislator.

They'd shown him around, and Adam was impressed with the preparations they were making for statehood. But he didn't want to be in the middle of it. As exciting as it sounded to become a statesman, he didn't want to sit in a stuffy room all day, hammering out bills and arguing with people he didn't like. The Lord had put him out here in the willywacks, as his grandpa Scott would have said, and this was where he belonged.

But he had to be able to do this job right.

"God, you've got to help me. I need to find this robber. He's killed a good man, Lord. I don't want it to be Ollie, but if it is, give me the strength to bring him in."

He remembered how Julia's eyes had flashed when she realized her brother was his top suspect. She was so beautiful, but so far out of his reach now. Adam's chest ached. Part of him still mourned her leaving. If he was honest, that same part of him rejoiced now that she was back. But he couldn't trust that she'd stay.

He gave a bitter laugh. He couldn't even trust her not to abet a robber and murderer, let alone allow him to court her again.

Julia heard horses coming. Why had she headed out here alone with darkness coming? She urged her mount off the trail and into the pines.

"Quiet now." She stroked his withers and prayed he wouldn't whinny when the other horses passed.

The men of the posse rode past her, toward the road that led back to town. She looked for Adam among the riders. Even in the moonlight, she'd have recognized him, but he wasn't there. He must still be out in the mountains, looking for the robber.

When they had passed and she could no longer hear their horses' hoofbeats, she emerged from cover and rode on. She'd found their trail near the robbery site, shortly before sunset. It had been easy to follow at first—that many horses had made a plain path through the brush. They'd split up once they got out on the rough mountainsides, but she'd followed the clearest track and the general direction of the searchers. She ought to have turned back, but she needed to see Adam, to convince him that the man he was trying to trap wasn't Oliver.

The dark mountains huddled over her. Something moved in the bushes, and her horse snorted. She urged him on. The wind made the tree limbs whisper. Night birds called, and the darkness deepened. Her regrets grew stronger, but it was too late to turn back. She must be getting close.

Ten minutes later, she pulled the dun in and sat listening. Maybe Adam was with the men and she'd missed him. Or maybe he'd gone back to town a different way. She'd been foolish not to wait in Ardell. She could have confronted him when he returned. Maybe Oliver was home now, wondering where she'd gone and worrying about her. She ought to go back.

She decided to go on to the top of the ridge before her. By the time she topped it, she'd nearly persuaded herself to give up the search. She peered down the slope beyond and caught her breath. A faint glow showed in the ravine below. She rode slowly toward it. Smoke drifted in the air. When she got closer, she saw a campfire burning in a hollow among the rocks, and she heard the faint trickle of running water, but she couldn't see anyone near the blaze. She stopped her horse and watched the camp spot. What if it wasn't Adam's camp? What if someone else was out here? She hadn't given a thought to the possibility that she might stumble into the real outlaw's camp.

A slight noise behind her made her stiffen and gather the reins.

"Stay right there and put your hands up, mister."

Adam's pulse tripped as he eased out of the shadow of the trees and approached the horseman. Someone had followed him out here into the mountains. It couldn't be one of his men returning. Any one of them would have called out to him as he approached the camp.

Adam had heard the horse when it was still a quarter mile away. Whoever this fellow was, he wasn't trail savvy.

"What do you want?" he asked.

The rider started to lower his hands.

Adam cocked his pistol. "I wouldn't do that if I were you. State your business."

"It's me, Adam. I came to talk to you about Oliver."

Adam exhaled. Relief vied with chagrin.

Julia.

Before she rolled into town, he'd convinced himself he was starting to forget her, but she was making that mighty hard to do.

He walked forward and up to the horse's head. Julia still sat with her hands at shoulder height, letting the reins fall slack on the horse's withers. The dun took advantage of that and lowered its head to browse.

"Put your hands down, Julia."

"You said—"

"I know what I said. You want to tell me what's so all-fired important you had to risk your neck to come and tell me?"

"It wasn't Oliver. He didn't do it."

"Seems like you said that before."

"But it's true. Please, Adam, let me get down and show you something."

"Come on. You might as well have a cup of coffee. I'll stir up the fire."

While he got the brew heating, Julia unbridled her horse and tied it near Socks. She didn't remove the saddle. Adam was glad in a way—that meant she didn't intend to stay long. On the other hand, he'd have to escort her back over the mountain to the road. It wouldn't be right to let her go alone.

When she came over to the fire, he let her sit on the log he'd used for a seat. "All right, have you got some evidence?"

"Just this." She held out a little booklet.

Adam took it and held it up so he could read it by the firelight. "A bankbook?"

"Yes. It's Oliver's. It's proof that he didn't need to rob anyone. He's been putting away money every month, out of his pay."

Adam sat in silence, looking at the figures in the bankbook.

"Well?" Julia said.

He sighed and handed it back. "This proves nothing."

"What do you mean?"

"Just what I said." He reached for the coffeepot. It probably wasn't quite as hot as he liked it, but he poured a tin cup half full. "Look, Julia, you have to understand. Ollie's gone. His horse is gone. The payroll's gone. What else am I supposed to think? Until I find something definite that says otherwise, I've got to assume Ollie's involved in the robbery."

She stared at him with those huge blue eyes.

"Take this." He held out the cup. "Tell me if it's fit to drink."

Julia straightened her shoulders. "No, thank you."

"Come on, Julia. You've got a hard ride ahead of you. At least have some coffee."

She relented and took the cup. After one sip she grimaced. "It's not ready."

"Sorry." Adam picked up one of the few remaining sticks and poked it into the fire beneath the coffeepot. He'd have to gather more wood in the morning.

He wanted to scold her, but he knew it wouldn't do any good. She was already here—as if he didn't have enough to worry about.

"You've got to stop tracking Ollie," she said.

He frowned at her. "Are you saying the tracks we followed away from the holdup site belong to Oliver's horse?"

"No. I'm not saying that at all."

"Then what are you saying?"

She plunked the cup down so hard the lukewarm coffee sloshed on the ground. "I'm saying you need to trust your best friend. Has something happened between you and Oliver that I don't know about?"

"No, nothing's happened."

She stood, gathered her skirts, and stepped over the log. "Then all I can say is, you have a funny way of treating your friends."

Adam stood and watched in astonishment as she marched to where she'd left her bridle and picked it up.

"What do you think I *should* be doing?"

She whirled and scowled at him. "My brother could be hurt. He may have had an accident, or that robber may have injured him. But all you can think about is putting Oliver in jail."

She marched away. Adam followed her slowly. "Julia, think about it. I'm searching for the robber. If that search takes me to Oliver, so be it. And if he's hurt and needs help, maybe I'll find him while I'm looking for this bandit. You should be glad that I'm out here."

A strangled noise came from Julia as she jerked her horse's head up. He hated making her feel this way. Or was she putting it on—hoping to distract him so that Ollie could get clean away while she cried on Adam's shoulder? He steeled himself.

The bit bumped the dun's teeth as Julia pulled the bridle on. She cringed, but the horse opened his teeth and took the bit. She pulled his ears through the crown and buckled the strap under his throat. She couldn't get away from Adam fast enough.

She'd loved this man and dreamed of a future with him. But Adam knew how she felt. He'd all but promised he would leave the Arizona Rangers. Though she considered herself a strong woman, she couldn't abide the thought of losing another man she loved in the line of duty. Adam knew she fretted for him when the Rangers went into a dangerous situation. He'd promised to think it over, and to pray about her request. When he proposed, she'd turned him down. At least she'd told him she couldn't marry him as long as he wore the badge.

Then word came that the Rangers were disbanding. Adam was disappointed about the turn of events, but Julia had rejoiced. She'd hoped he would settle down to ranching and propose to her again. Instead, he took the job of deputy sheriff. That was the last straw for Julia—it felt as if he were shouting at her, "This is who I am. I will never do what you want. I will never be the man you want me to be."

That's when she'd accepted the teaching position in Philadelphia—because she couldn't stay in Ardell and watch Adam make himself a target every time a drunk decided to shoot up a saloon.

Her family members had supported her decision, although they loved Adam, too. Of all people, Mama and Oliver knew why she felt as strongly as she did. Only five years ago, her father had been killed while on duty as a deputy sheriff. They didn't insist that she listen to Adam's pleading. They knew the pain that could lead to. Her mother had approved of her decision to go away—for a while, anyway. "Put some distance between you," she'd said. "If Adam is the man for you, something will change."

But now Mama was gone. Oliver's telegram had shocked Julia out of her complacency. The news of her mother's sudden death made her realize that life was too short to live in loneliness. If Adam Scott insisted on strutting around town wearing a tin star, too bad. She could ignore him. She'd always hoped for a family of her own—with Adam—but now she was reconciled to living quietly with her brother. Adam wouldn't keep that small happiness from her any longer.

The bridle in place, she gathered the reins and put her foot in the stirrup.

"Hold on," Adam called. "You can't tear off alone. It's dark."

She smiled bitterly. "You just noticed that?"

"Well, no, I. . .wait, Julia. Let me douse the fire. I'll ride down to the road with you."

"I can take care of myself."

"I'm sure you can. I'm coming anyway."

Of all the arrogance! Julia considered turning her horse and riding off without him instead of waiting while he tended the fire and carried his saddle over to his horse. In his head, he was probably screaming at her for causing him all this trouble. If he'd wanted to go back to town, he'd have gone with the posse. Now he felt he had to do it because of her.

For Adam, it was a matter of duty. She could see that. So was being a lawman. When an injustice was done, he couldn't sit by and see the criminal get away—like now. The killer must be caught, even if it was his friend. Well, she wasn't going to watch him chase her brother down and ruin his reputation.

"This really isn't necessary," she said as he lugged the heavy stock saddle toward his bay. "I'm capable of riding home by myself."

"No, you're not, and you can't stay out here."

"I should think not. But I'm anxious to get back now and see if Oliver's returned. He may have some logical explanation for why he was gone all day."

They rode in silence for the first hour. Adam went slowly, letting Socks pick his way in the moonlight. Julia followed, hoping the dun would prove sure-footed on the steep downhill places. At last they reached the road, and she relaxed. Adam waited for her to ride up beside him.

"Where do you think Oliver is now?" he asked.

"Home in bed, I hope. Where do *you* think he is?"

Adam sighed. "I don't want to believe it, but I'm afraid he's run for it."

Julia pulled back on the reins, and her horse stopped abruptly. "You make me so mad, Adam Scott! Why aren't you looking at other people who knew about the payroll shipment?"

Adam's low laugh added to her rage.

"The payroll comes every month on the same stage," he said. "The whole town knew about it. You want me to question the whole town?"

"If need be."

"Look, I'm using a process of elimination. Who wasn't around when the stage was robbed? Who stayed away for the rest of the day?"

She glared at him. "You heard that Oliver was away, and you fastened on him like a leech. There could be a dozen other men missing from Ardell and you wouldn't know it. Why? Because you're convinced it was Oliver. But you know Oliver! You, better than anyone else, should trust him. He wouldn't do this, and you know it."

"Do I?"

Julia kicked the horse, hoping to leave the infuriating man in her dust. The dun, however, refused to go faster than a slow jog. She rode along feeling Adam's presence behind her, too angry to speak to him again or even look at him.

Finally they reached the Newman home. She hadn't expected Adam to escort her all the way into town and to her door, but she was too angry to renew her pleas for him to leave her. She rode straight to the small barn behind the house and dismounted. Adam was right there at her elbow when she opened the door.

She didn't need a lantern to tell her the barn was empty. Nothing had been disturbed since the last time she'd checked. She sagged against the half wall of the stall where Oliver's horse should be. After a moment she felt Adam's hand, warm and comforting, on her shoulder.

"I'm sorry, Julie."

She stiffened. He had no right to call her that now. And his touch. . . How could it make her feel all yearny inside when she was so angry with him?

"You'd better go. If anyone sees you leaving here after midnight, tongues will wag."

He chuckled, and she didn't like the sound of it. "That's right. Your brother's disappearance is enough of a scandal. If you want to live in Ardell, you mustn't risk adding another."

She whirled on him, her fists clenching. "How dare you?"

Adam held up both hands in surrender. "All right. I'm going. I've lost half a day in my search for the robber by coming back here to spend the night."

"And that's my fault."

"I didn't say that."

She shook her head. "You didn't have to. I'm sorry, Mr. Sheriff, that I wasted your precious time. I *did* tell you I could see myself home."

"Julia, listen to me." Adam put a hand up to his eyes for a moment. "Look, I did find some evidence, all right? It's not just that he's gone."

Her chest tightened and her throat went dry. "What is it? What are you talking about?"

"I think it's best if I keep it to myself for now, but I found something that made me think of Oliver. I need to prove, one way or another, whether he was involved in the robbery. Can you understand that?"

"No. No, I don't think I can. Unless you tell me what it is you've found that's so compelling—"

"Good night, Julia. I'll drop your horse off at the livery."

He walked out, and she slumped against the divider again. She was too tired to sustain her fury. She waited a full minute before moving, thinking about her brother. What if Oliver had encountered the outlaw? Or what if he'd met with an accident? He might be lying dead in some ravine while she dithered about trying to clear his name.

When she went outside and closed the barn door, Adam and both horses were gone.

She dragged herself across the yard and in through the back door of the house. The kitchen fire had gone out. She decided not to bother to build it up, but went on up the stairs. Without hope, she glanced into Oliver's empty room then went to her own and undressed.

She fell into bed barely able to formulate a mental prayer for wisdom and strength. Adam's deep voice echoed in her mind. *"I'm sorry, Julie."* The words had made her heart leap. She'd wanted to turn and fling herself into his arms. There was a time when she could draw warmth and strength from him. But not now.

She'd just begun to drift into the haze of unconsciousness when a loud hammering on the door downstairs brought her upright in bed, gasping.

Chapter 6

Adam took Julia's horse to the livery stable. All was quiet there, so he unsaddled her mount and turned it into the corral. He took the tack into the barn and left it.

Usually the fun was in full swing at the saloons around midnight, but tonight the street was quiet. Maybe the murder had subdued folks and kept them home this evening. Adam was glad—he wouldn't feel too guilty if, instead of making the rounds, he went to his cot in the jail and slept for a few hours.

As he rode past the intersection, he glanced toward the third house down the cross street. A light shone in his uncle's house. It wasn't in the front room. Someone had lit a lantern in the room where Uncle Royce treated patients.

Adam swerved his horse toward it. He'd made up his mind to ride down the stage robber. If Uncle Royce was up, he might as well tell him of his plans.

He dropped Socks's reins and left him standing in the street. The front door was unlocked, as always. Adam went in and followed the light to the doorway of the treatment room. His uncle had a cupboard open and was taking out some of his medical instruments and putting them into a wooden crate on the table.

Adam cleared his throat. "Hey, Uncle Royce."

The gray-haired man turned and gave him a nod. "I wondered when you'd come by."

"I almost didn't, but I saw your light and thought I'd stop in and see how you're doing."

Royce shot him an odd look. "I'm. . .fine, Adam."

"Thought you might have a patient when I saw the lamp was on in here."

"No, no patient."

"Well, I wanted to tell you that I'm heading out first thing in the morning."

"Heading out? Where are you going?"

Adam took off his hat and scrubbed his hand across his brow. "I'm going after the stage robber, Uncle Royce. You heard about that?"

"Oh, yes." The old man sounded a little vague. He turned back to the cupboard and took out a pair of forceps.

Adam looked over at the desk. A bottle of Kessler whiskey stood on the blotter, with an empty glass beside it. The bottle was still nearly full, and Adam decided not to mention it. The old man wasn't drunk now. If he wanted a glass before he went to bed, why should his nephew interfere?

"Lionel should have called you to look Bub Hilliard over," he said.

Royce shook his head as he put the forceps in the box. "Don't worry about that."

"Well, it was too late, anyhow, but folks shouldn't ignore you, just because there's a younger doctor in town now."

"This is as it should be, Adam." Royce picked up a small metal case and placed it in the crate. The cupboard was nearly empty now.

"What are you doing, anyway?" Adam stepped closer and peered into the box. His uncle appeared to have stripped the cabinet of instruments and packed them all.

"My practice is finished now. I thought perhaps Dr. Browning could use some of these things. Of course, he has a lot of newer instruments, but he might find some of them useful."

"Oh come on, Uncle Royce. You can still see patients."

"Actually, I don't think I can. The time has come for me to retire."

"Well, we'll talk about that when I come back, you hear me? Don't give that stuff away yet."

"I'm too old, Adam."

"Hogwash. You still know how to cure people."

Uncle Royce shook his head. "My time is over."

"Quit that." Adam clapped him on the shoulder. "I'll be back in a few days, as soon as I run down this road agent. You and me will have dinner at the boardinghouse, all right?"

"Sure, Adam. I'll see you then."

"So long." Adam walked out unsatisfied. If his uncle gave up seeing patients, what would happen to him? He didn't want to see Uncle Royce wither away. He'd have to come up with a scheme to get a few of his old patients to give him some business. It didn't have to be a lot—just enough to keep the old doctor interested.

He reached the jail and tried to put it out of his mind. Right now he needed sleep, so he'd be sharp when he went after the outlaw.

The pounding continued. Julia threw off the bedclothes and groped for her robe. With trembling hands, she lit the lamp. As she hurried down the stairs, the knocking was renewed. What news could be so urgent? *Oh please, God, not Oliver!*

"Who is it?"

"Name's Harrison."

Julia hesitated. Did she know anyone named Harrison? On the other hand, would a man intending to harm her announce his name? She set down the lamp, threw back the bolt, and opened the door a crack. Staring at her in the light of the lamp was a grizzled old man.

Julia wished she'd fetched the pistol she'd bought before her trip home, but it was too late now. The old man grinned at her, showing a gap in his upper jaw where a tooth was missing. His mottled beard looked as though it hadn't seen soap and water for months. He yanked off his felt hat.

"Don'tcha remember me, Miss Julie?"

She looked him over, trying not to shudder. "I guess not. Help me out."

"I'm Clew Harrison."

She eyed his face closely, though she didn't want to, and this time she caught a glimmer of a remembered face.

"Oh, sure. You came to Canyon Diablo when we lived there."

"That's right." He slapped his thigh and laughed. "You been there lately?"

"No. Not since my father died."

"Aw, yeah. That was a sad day for you, I'll bet. The Diné sure liked him when he was up there."

Julia's father had served as Indian agent at the Canyon Diablo trading post from 1899 to 1902, when Canyon Diablo was little more than a ghost town. The trading post served the Navajo community, and most of the friends the Newman family made during that time were Navajo, or Diné as the tribe members called themselves.

"I remember when that town had fourteen saloons," Clew said. "Wildest place this side of Tombstone."

"It was pretty quiet by the time my family lived there," Julia said. She remembered climbing about the ruins of the town with her brother. "Nothing left but the trading post now." Most of the buildings had been dismantled and removed on the train to the next spot where the track crews needed a town.

"Yup. I used to haul supplies up there for your daddy."

"That's right." Now that he mentioned it, Julia recalled Clew Harrison coming to their home a few times and stopping for a meal with her family after his business at the trading post was finished. "May I help you, Mr. Harrison? It's very late."

"Oh, I know, and I'm sorry about that. But I got to tell you something."

Julia hesitated. Could this unorthodox visit have something to do with Oliver? She swung the door open wider. "Come in then."

He walked in and looked around at the comfortable room, nodding with satisfaction. "Yup. Your ma was a real lady, and she always kept a snug house."

"Thank you, Mr. Harrison. What—"

"You always called me Clew when you was a little nipper." He winked at her.

Julia swallowed hard, trying to reconcile her vague memories of a kindly freighter with this rather repulsive old man.

"How long was you folks at Canyon Diablo?" he asked.

"About three years, all told. Then my father became a sheriff's deputy here in Ardell."

Clew nodded. "Well, I been working for two years now at the High Desert Mine."

"Oh?" Julia's pulse picked up. "What do you do there?"

"I'm just their general fetch-it man."

"Then you must see Oliver regularly."

"My, yes, he's a good chum. It pays to have a friend in the front office, you know?"

Julia couldn't imagine what good Oliver had done for this man, but she nodded. "Do you know where Oliver is now, Clew?"

He smiled and stuck his hand in his pants pocket, fished around for a few seconds, and pulled out a crumpled piece of paper.

"What's this?" She took it and smoothed it out on the arm of the nearest chair. She caught her breath. Sketched in pencil were several simple drawings. "Where did you get this?"

"Why, your brother, of course."

Of course. The crude figures were symbols she and Ollie had found when they were children, carved in the walls of a cave near Canyon Diablo. Through the rest of their childhood they'd used the "rock writing" as a code. She looked at the old man again. "You saw him. When?"

"This afternoon. The sheriff came out to the mine and told Mr. Gerry about the robbery. While he was there, they found out Oliver was missing. After the sheriff left, Gerry and the other bigwigs were saying that Ollie must have stolen the payroll—and the sheriff would have to catch him."

"How do you know what they said?"

Clew shrugged. "They don't pay any attention to me. I'm just an old man who totes wood for their stoves and sweeps up the bark chips. 'Course, I didn't believe a word of it. Ollie would never do a thing like that. So I went out to the stable and waited for him. Figured wherever he'd got to this mornin', he had to come back sooner or later."

"Did he?"

"Sure enough. He come back about a hour after the sheriff was there. He'd been down to the miners' village. Well, I told him everything."

Julia stepped closer to him, her heart pounding. "What did he say?"

"Well, he was stunned. Couldn't believe they'd think that of him—robbing the stage and killing a man. Why, Bub Hilliard was a friend of his'n."

Julia nodded. The relief that swept over her drained her strength, and she sat down in one of the overstuffed chairs. "Go on, please."

"Well, he wrote this here paper and told me his sister was coming home—maybe today." Clew grinned again. "He was mighty tickled that you were coming, Miss Julie. He told me to get the message to you as soon as you arrived in town, but to do it when nobody else was around."

Julia's head whirled. "But I was already here by then."

"Yes'm. You'd got back when the stage came. I found that out. But you wasn't here."

"That must have been when I rode back to the place where we were robbed."

Clew nodded. "I just hung around town, keeping my head down so to speak. I seen you once, talking to somebody at the store, but Ollie had said not to tell you when there was anyone about, so I waited. I came back here after supper, and you was gone again. Finally it occurred to me to check at the livery. Sam come in after dark, and he told me you'd rented a horse and ridden outta town. Well, I wasn't sure what to do, so I walked over to the saloon."

Julia had to credit him with not drinking himself under the table in the intervening hours. "I'm sorry you had such a hard time finding me. But I'm glad you're here now. Where is Oliver? Can I see him?"

"Don't rightly know. He said he'd keep outta sight and I should just give you that paper. I expected it would tell you where he was."

She looked down at the paper again. The first symbol was a lizard, the one she had used for her name. The last one was his symbol—an eagle. She'd need some time to rack her memory and decipher the runes in between.

"It may at that. I need time to work it out, though."

"Well, I'm sorry things are going so bad for you. Most folks in town seem to think Ollie's guilty, but I know he ain't." Clew shook his head. "I heard Lucas Morley say that boy oughta be hung. It ain't right."

Julia felt weak. What if the angry townspeople got to Oliver before he was proven innocent? She managed to stand, though her knees wobbled.

"Why don't you tell the deputy sheriff that Oliver's innocent?"

"Naw. Adam Scott wouldn't listen to me, no more'n the bosses at the mine would."

Julia wondered about that. She had no idea how Clew was perceived in the community. She did know that Adam had made up his mind about the robber, and the old man might be right.

"Thank you very much for bringing the message, Clew."

He nodded and patted his hat on. "Anytime. And I won't tell anyone else."

"I appreciate that."

She walked with him to the door and bolted it behind him. She went shakily back to her chair and sat down to ponder the message. Her heart refused to slow down. Oliver was alive and in good health, but he was in danger—not from outlaws, but from his friends here in Ardell. She had in her hand the only way to save his life.

For fifteen minutes she pored over the paper, trying to recall the code. She recognized the symbols they'd used for the desert and the trading post. Why hadn't she kept a copy of their code?

She jumped up and hurried up the stairs to her room. In the bottom of the wardrobe was a box of old letters and school papers. She carried it to the bed and rooted through it. Near the bottom she found a couple of coded messages from her brother. Half an hour later she had worked out the new message. She knew where Oliver was—or at least, where he was headed.

Chapter 7

Adam rose before dawn and ate a spare breakfast. He packed a few more supplies in his saddlebags and went out to the stable. He'd thought about the robbery half the night and asked himself, "If I were Oliver Newman, where would I go to hide?"

At first he'd thought Oliver would go to Flagstaff and take a train out of Arizona. He'd go to some city—say, San Francisco or Denver—where he could live in style on the loot from the robbery. Then something else had occurred to him.

The Newman family had lived at Canyon Diablo for a while when Ollie and Julia were kids. Ollie had talked about it a lot. He'd told Adam how fun it was and how he and his sister had grown close there and had secret places to play. They'd had Navajo friends, and they'd been to some places on the reservation that white people usually didn't get to see.

Why wouldn't Oliver go into hiding for a while? He probably didn't intend to kill the shotgun messenger. Now he wasn't only a robber. He was a murderer. That would weigh heavy on him. He'd know Adam would be tracking him, and he'd be declared a wanted man. Lawmen and bounty hunters would go after him. The desert northeast of Canyon Diablo might be just the place for him to drop out of sight.

Julia's pleas to consider other suspects weren't unreasonable—if she was being honest. But he found it hard to swallow that she returned home armed the very day her brother robbed the stagecoach and that she had no connection to the holdup. Inside the coach, with her pistol ready, she could have given Ollie support if he'd needed it. If one of the other passengers tried to shoot the robber, Julia could have dropped him and claimed it was an accident.

Adam saddled his horse with grim determination. He'd love to prove someone else did this. But if he delayed in finding Oliver to investigate other people, his main suspect would get away. No, Ollie had a reason for not coming home yesterday. Whether it was a good reason or not—well, that was something he had to find out.

When he rode past the livery, Sam Dennis was just rolling open the barn door.

"Hey, Sheriff!"

Adam turned Socks in and rode up to the barn. "Mornin', Sam."

"I thought you slept out on the mountain."

"Had to come into town late last night after all."

Sam scratched his head. "Oh. Where you headed now?"

"Same as before. Out to try and find the robber."

"Do you need men to ride with you again? We all want to see you bring that scoundrel in."

"I can handle it." Adam turned his horse and rode out. Instead of picking his way over the mountain paths, he stuck to the road that went to the mine and then down the other side. He'd head as straight toward Canyon Diablo as he could and trust that he'd find some sign of Oliver's presence when he got there.

He pushed Socks as hard as he dared across the high desert. The trail had been a genuine road for a while, with stagecoach service to Canyon Diablo in its heyday. Lately it had been allowed to deteriorate. Not many people rode this way anymore.

The temperatures were cooling, now that autumn was approaching. At night it would be downright cold out here. Adam had been up this way with the Rangers once, and he knew the terrain for the first couple of hours. At the last watering place he knew, he made sure Socks got a good drink. Adam filled his canteen. Even though the air was fairly cool, he didn't want to go too long without water. He wasn't sure how much longer it would take him to get to Canyon Diablo.

He met no one and began to feel a little spooked. He might regret riding into the wilderness with nobody to watch his back. But the hoofprints in the trail told him this stretch wasn't always deserted. In places, sand had blown across the way. In others, he rode on bedrock, between towering cliffs. He always watched the rim for lookouts, but saw no one. Maybe the tales about how the Navajo resented intruders were exaggerated.

Sometime past noon, he trotted up to the trading post. Several Indians lounged outside, smoking in the slim shadow of the wall. Several bundles that looked like raw wool lay nearby. The Navajo eyed Adam closely and turned away. Adam tied Socks to the hitching rail, even though the horse was trained to ground tie. He went inside and squinted in the dim interior. The place smelled of leather, tobacco, and gunpowder.

"Howdy." The trader behind the counter was a big, bearded man. "Help you, mister?"

Adam walked over to the counter. "Howdy. I'm Deputy Sheriff Scott, from Ardell. Do you know a fellow by the name of Oliver Newman?"

"Newman?" The trader frowned.

"His father used to be the Indian agent here some time back," Adam said.

"Oh, sure. Everyone knows about Ben Newman. That was before my time, though. I don't think he's been in these parts a good many years."

"No, he hasn't. Ben Newman passed on a few years back, but I thought maybe his son had been around."

The trader stroked his beard. "There was a man rode past here last night. I didn't know who he was, but he seemed to know where he was headed, and he didn't stop in to jaw with me. We don't get many strangers coming through here—not white men, anyways."

"So he rode right past the trading post?"

The trader nodded. "I was banking the fire, getting ready for bed, and I heard hoofbeats. Figured whoever it was needed something. The Diné know I'll open up for them if it's an emergency, but mostly they come during my regular hours. But this fella wasn't an Injun. And he rode right on by, toward the desert. I figured he was familiar with these parts—that or off his nut."

"How do you know he was white? You said it was dark."

"Not that dark. I saw his profile and his outfit. He was traveling light, but he was definitely not Diné."

"All right," Adam said. "Can you tell me where the Newman family lived when they were here?"

"It's southeast of here. Go past where the old town was."

"Right out front here, you mean?"

"Yep. You'll see a few chimneys and such. Not much left, but you can tell where the town was."

Adam nodded.

"Just keep going along the rim of the canyon, past the bridge. You'll see where the trail goes away from the river. Their place was a couple of miles out. Last time I was out that way, the cabin was still standing."

"Thank you."

Adam went outside. Only two of the Navajo were left, and they were hefting the bundles of wool. They walked toward the door of the trading post. One of them nodded to Adam.

"Howdy," Adam said. He mounted and rode along the canyon rim until he got to the railroad tracks. He left Socks beside the rails and walked a few yards out on the trestle. So this was what had brought the short-lived town into existence. Looking down made him a little wobbly. Clear at the bottom, he could see a streambed, but only a thin ribbon of water lay in it now. He wondered if the Indians had a trail that led down into the deep canyon. The trestle was the highest he'd ever seen, and he marveled at the engineering it took. He turned and walked back to his horse—no use putting this off any longer.

He rode two miles to the southeast. He could easily read tracks on the trail now. Unshod horses, all. That didn't bother him. Oliver had a tough little mustang with hooves as hard as granite, or so Ollie said. He never had that horse shod. Adam wished it were otherwise—that would have made Oliver a lot easier to follow in the Navajo territory. The land was pretty near empty, once you left the railroad tracks and the trading post behind. A few bushes, a few rocks, sparsely vegetated slopes.

When he came to the cabin, he marveled that Mrs. Newman had agreed to live out here for three years. It seemed to Adam an awful place to raise children, yet Ollie spoke of it with fondness.

Adam swung down from the saddle and examined the ground in front of the cabin. The hoofprints were clear. One horse. One man. Boot prints led to the door and back out. The horse's tracks rejoined the desert trail. They could have been made this morning. . .or a month ago.

Adam couldn't resist taking another minute to look inside the cabin. It was as bare and bleak inside as out. Mrs. Newman had brightened it up, no doubt. Seemed she'd always been sewing or cooking when Adam knew her. Their house in Ardell was cozy, and he loved to visit his friends there. It was comfortable and warm. It wasn't at all like the house he'd grown up in, yet it never failed to remind him of his own mother and home.

The cabin's one large room had a loft over half of it. A hole in the wall told him where the stovepipe had been. The two small windows were long broken, and a few shards of glass lay on the floor. A rude bunk was built against one wall, a mere shelf a man could sleep on. An empty wooden crate stood near it, and dust coated everything.

Adam went back to his horse and headed out into the desert. After an hour's riding, they came to a dribble of a stream. Barely enough water ran over the stone in its bed to let him fill his canteen. Socks sucked up a little water, and they went on.

There was no longer any way to distinguish the prints left by the horse at the cabin from the others. That was the thing that bothered Adam above all else. Because the tracks he'd found near the robbery site were those of a shod horse. That horse had waited in the scrub pines and nibbled at the nearby shrubbery and tufts of dry grass. The shoes had left a few distinct impressions.

Still, he reasoned, Oliver could have used another horse for the robbery and then switched to his own. Maybe he rode back to where he'd left his distinctive pinto gelding—the mine, for instance—and no one else saw him trade mounts in the stable there. It made sense to Adam. He wouldn't wear a mask to disguise himself during the robbery and risk having someone see his one-of-a-kind pinto.

The only logical alternative was that Oliver didn't commit the robbery. But if so, why did he run?

Julia neared Canyon Diablo late in the afternoon. She'd taken her time and not pushed the dun. There was no need to rush.

Her memories flowed freely as she came near the ruined town that perched along the top of a ravine cradling the Little Colorado River. The railroad crew had built the tracks as far as the edge of the canyon long before Julia was born—1882, if she remembered correctly. But the materials for the trestle were held up for months. The town had popped up almost overnight and reveled loud and hard while the track crew waited. The following year the supplies came in and the bridge and that section of the railroad were completed.

The excitement of having the railroad come through had lasted only until the building materials arrived, and with the trestle completed, the town had died as quickly as it had appeared.

Julia had bypassed the trading post, instead turning her horse off the trail a quarter mile to the south, so that she wouldn't be seen by anyone near the post. She wasn't sure what to expect at their old home—was the cabin even still standing? The wood might very well have been carried off for other purposes. And if the little house remained, someone else might be living in it now.

She took her time, comparing her surroundings to her memories. After a half hour, she rode up to her old home, the weather-beaten cabin southeast of town. To all appearances, the place was deserted.

She dismounted and dropped the dun's reins. He wasn't much to look at, but he'd proven himself a wiry, persistent mount. She hoped he was an easy keeper, because she hadn't been able to carry much feed.

In the dirt were hoofprints—not surprising. Oliver would have been here. But so had someone else. The shod horse had come recently, its prints superimposed on the barefoot one's. She walked up to the door of the cabin and smiled for the first time all day.

Oliver had left her another message. The lizard sign for her name was freshly scratched on the doorjamb, along with three more signs. Having refreshed her memory on the code, it took her only a glance to read them. Her brother was telling her that he would be at the cave on the full moon—tomorrow night, September the eighth.

The cave was a favorite haunt for her and Oliver when they

were children. They'd discovered it while out roaming on their ponies a few months after they'd moved here with their folks. Their mother forbade them to go to the trading post alone, so they spent their free time playing in the desert. Chores first, then schoolwork, and then long, bright days of riding and stalking and make-believe raiding together.

They'd found the petroglyphs their first summer at Canyon Diablo and had puzzled over them. They'd begun to work out their code weeks before they decided to ask one of the young Diné men to tell them what the pictures meant. Kai came often to the trading post with his father, and all the Newmans liked him. He'd shown Oliver how to make arrows that flew true to their mark, and he'd helped Julia make a quiver from leather scraps.

Some of the signs meant just what they portrayed, and some they had assigned arbitrary meanings. The sun could represent the sun itself or a day. In combination with other signs, it might designate a person's name. Kai and other Diné children taught them dozens of other signs. One of these was the spiral, which symbolized a journey. Oliver had used it in the message Clew brought. He was making a journey to their old place of play. For the cave they used a wide *V* with a line across it just above the peak. They pretended it was a bat, though they weren't sure. There were no bats in their cave, but it had seemed appropriate when they were constructing the code.

The circle of the moon, with a cross for a star on either side, told her their meeting would take place on the night of the full moon. Oliver had allowed her plenty of time to prepare and travel here—more than she had needed, as it turned out, but he couldn't have foreseen that. She wasn't even sure whether he knew she'd arrived in Ardell when he wrote the first message and left town for Canyon Diablo.

But he was alive, and probably in good health. He was nearby, and he'd stood in this spot within the last two days. That was enough to satisfy her for now.

She went to her horse and untied the bundles she'd brought. Food, water, a sack of grain for her mount, and a bedroll. Tied up in the blankets were a few extra clothes for herself and fresh socks and a shirt for Oliver. She'd also brought a sack containing small pieces of firewood and kindling. Afraid to burden the horse too much, she'd kept that to a minimum, but she hadn't known what to expect at their old home.

Inside the empty cabin, she spread her blankets on the bunk. Her parents had shared the narrow bed when the family lived here. She and Oliver had slept on straw ticks in the loft.

Having no broom to sweep out the place and no stove to light a fire in, she decided to make do with things as they were, disturbing the place as little as possible. She didn't want to draw unwanted attention. It was warm enough that she thought her wool blankets and her jacket would be enough tonight—she didn't need a fire. And she could get by without cooking. In the morning, maybe she would have a fire outside. And maybe she would visit the trader. She'd have to decide whether or not that was risky. If Adam had already been there and inquired for her brother, would showing herself matter?

As darkness gathered, she curled up on the bunk and prayed silently for Oliver. He was taking a chance that she would come on time. He wouldn't ask her to make the arduous journey unless he felt it was necessary. To Julia, that said he feared his life was at stake.

Lord, I don't know what to ask. Keep Adam from finding him, unless You have a better way that I can't see.

She thought about Adam, in pursuit of Oliver. Had he stopped at the trading post? Did he know he was in Diné territory now? White men entered the tribal lands at their own risk. She didn't fear that the Diné would mistreat Oliver. He had old friends in the tribe. But what if they found Adam sniffing around on their reservation? He wouldn't get a welcoming party—at least not in a good sense.

Lord, if either one of them needs protecting, I guess it's up to You. I certainly can't help them tonight.

In the distance, coyotes yipped, but Julia was so tired she soon sank into sleep.

The scenery was breathtaking. In the treeless valleys, Socks trotted among the sagebrush and short, dry grass, while above them loomed sculpted rock towers. A mile away, a mesa stood up like an island out of the land. The dark smear on top represented treetops, but Adam couldn't see a way to get up there.

He had never been this deep into Diné territory. He wished he had someone to share it with. Julia came to mind, but he rejected that thought immediately. He would probably never have a chance to share anything with Julia again. Not after he tracked down her brother and brought him to justice.

The next logical companion for a jaunt into the desert was Oliver. But if they shared the journey back, it wouldn't be as friends. Something broke apart inside him. Adam knew that he was losing the best part of his life. If he could never be friends with Oliver or Julia again, what would the future hold? He didn't like the prospect. They'd been a huge part of his life for the last ten years. His own parents were dead. His sisters were married and living far away. The only relative he had left in Ardell was Uncle Royce. The Newmans had filled in for him, as close to a family as he'd had for a long time.

Would he make new friends? Find a new love? He'd never forgotten Julia—never given up on his hope that she'd come back to him. The memories of his time with her—when he knew she loved him—had haunted him, waking and sleeping.

And Ollie. Could he ever be as close to another man? He sincerely doubted it. He and Oliver had shared their deepest thoughts. Why, Oliver even knew that Adam loved his sister with a till-death-do-us-part kind of love. No one else on earth was privy to his feelings about Julia. His chaotic, mixed-up feelings.

She'd gone away hurt when he took the job as sheriff's deputy, and she'd bruised him pretty badly before she left. Now she'd returned angry and cold. What was the sense of hoping? She would never love him that way again.

And yet. . . What if yesterday had been different? What if the stagecoach hadn't been robbed? What if he and Ollie had been there to greet her with smiles when she got out of the stage? She might have felt differently about him then. And he was pretty sure she wouldn't have thrown him out of her house.

He could give up right now and ride back to Ardell. Lay his heart at Julia's feet. Tell her he loved her more than ever and never wanted to be parted from her again.

But that would mean letting the killer get away. And for the rest of their lives, his doubts would hang between them. Oliver had run away after the robbery. He couldn't interpret that as the action of an innocent man. Had Julia known her brother planned to rob the stage? Had they laid plans together through letters? If so, Julia would have burned those letters. She was too smart to leave incriminating evidence lying around.

Unlike her brother.

He reached into his pocket and pulled out the item he'd found near the robbery site. A small thing, and yet it added weight to his suspicions. With a sigh, Adam returned it to his pocket and urged Socks onward. Where did he think he'd find Oliver?

The tracks were lost now. Whenever he found hoofprints, he couldn't tell if they were the right ones. Indians out here traveled the desert and went back and forth to the trading post all the time. Oliver had old friends among the Diné. Was he crossing their land to throw off pursuit? Or had he gone to them for refuge?

Adam rode up a ridge higher than the surrounding terrain and surveyed the wild landscape. In this rocky wilderness, there were a million places to hide. He was in the middle of the loneliest country he'd ever seen, and he didn't like it. Though he hadn't met a soul all afternoon, he couldn't shake off the feeling that he was watched.

Socks snuffled.

"All right, fella, I hear you. You're tired, too." Adam guided the horse down to lower ground. He emptied a canteen of water into his hat and let Socks slurp it up. He'd hoped to find a creek or a watering hole, but in this dry country, it seemed you had to know where to look.

He gave Socks a handful of feed. He wouldn't dare turn his horse loose, or even hobble or stake him out. Losing his mount in this desert would be a death sentence. He tied his lariat to Socks's halter and knotted the other end around his belt. He doubted he'd get much sleep, but he'd know if anyone cut the rope.

Darkness had fallen while he made his preparations for the night. He lay down on his bedroll. In the morning, he would scour this land for a sign of the robber.

Socks tugged at the rope for a while, and Adam tossed and turned, disturbed by thoughts of Oliver's actions and Julia's lovely face. At last he fell asleep, but was jolted awake by a sharp pain.

Chapter 8

Adam jerked upright, scrambling to draw his pistol. At the same time, Socks whinnied and pulled on the rope at his waist, and another sharp kick landed on Adam's side. He froze when he realized several dark forms towered over him in the moonlight.

"Who are you?"

Adam swallowed hard, but his heart was pumping fast. "Adam Scott."

"Why are you on our land?"

He took a deep breath and tried to exhale slowly. The Diné had found him.

"I mean no harm. I'm the sheriff at the town of Ardell. It's up in the mountains southwest of here. We had a murder two days ago, and I'm tracking the killer."

After a moment's silence, the one doing the talking said, "You got a badge?"

His tone was so ingenuous, Adam almost laughed. This man was obviously comfortable with the English language and in asserting his authority.

"Yes." Adam opened his jacket slowly. The burnished star picked up a ray of moonlight. The Navajo men grunted. Slowly, Adam threw his blanket off his legs, rolled to his knees, then stood. "I assure you, I have no intention of harming your people. I followed the man I suspect of killing the stagecoach messenger near Ardell to this area. I only want to bring him to justice."

Socks whinnied and pulled against the rope. From a short distance away, more horses answered. One of the Diné men stroked Socks's neck, but Adam said nothing. He was sweating all over, even though the night had turned sharply cold.

The leader looked around at the others. "Sounds like a reasonable man."

"Believe me, I only want to find this killer and take him off your territory. I don't think you want a thief and a murderer hiding on your land."

The Navajo leader was older than Adam, perhaps forty-five or older. A handsome man, he held Adam's gaze for a long moment, and the others waited in silence.

"All right," he said at last. "Three days should be enough. If you don't find him by then, you must leave."

Adam nodded. "Fair enough. I give you my word."

They melted away into the darkness. One minute they were there, all around him—five or six men, quiet but imposing in their presence. The next they were gone.

Socks whinnied and paced back and forth at the end of the rope. Muffled hoofbeats and a faint neigh reached Adam's ears.

"It's all right, fella. They're gone." He pulled the rope in and patted the horse's face and neck.

But Socks wouldn't settle down. Adam knew he wouldn't get any sleep with the horse tugging intermittently on the rope. He also knew the Diné wouldn't steal his horse or Socks would already be gone. He rummaged in the saddlebags for the hobbles. A few minutes later he was able to lie down with his blanket wrapped around him, but sleep was still far away. How different would this encounter with the Diné have been if Oliver was with him? He wished he could have known this land—and these people—the way the Newmans did.

Socks snuffled about for anything edible, and Adam slumped with his head against his saddle. He'd known the lawman's life would be lonely, but he hadn't expected to be cut off irrevocably from the people he cared for most.

Julia looked all about the next morning, but saw nothing that moved, other than a lizard basking in the early sunlight outside her door. She took her time preparing some corn mush and coffee. She wouldn't go directly to the cave. Why draw attention to it? She'd wait and go there late in the day.

After much thought, she decided to go to the trading post. The new Indian agent didn't know her. There had been several changes in the position since her father held it. Still, she wouldn't risk talking to the current trader.

Instead of going in, she ground tied the dun over a ridge, just a few hundred yards from the trading post. From her position, she could see anyone approaching the post from the distant Diné village she'd visited as a child. But anyone coming along the trail from the white man's part of Arizona wouldn't see her. She climbed up the ridge and lay down on her stomach. She could just see the building. With her hat low over her eyes, she waited.

As the sun rose higher, several Diné people went in to trade. Julia thought she recognized a couple of them. She felt safe now and sat up, but she kept her place off the trail, quietly aloof. She had no doubt they saw her, but none approached her. About an hour after she'd begun her watch, an unmistakable figure rode along the trail on a brown-and-white spotted mustang.

Julia smiled as she stood and walked toward the trail, holding up a hand.

He stopped the horse and looked her over closely then smiled. "Can you be little Julie?"

"Yes, Niyol," she said. "It's me."

"So. You are all grown up." He seemed inordinately pleased about that.

She chuckled. "Yes. And you're not any younger yourself." When she'd lived here, she and Oliver often played with Niyol's half-grown children. Oliver had been quite close to Niyol's oldest son, Kai.

"I heard that your father was killed not too long after you left here," he said.

"It's true. Five years ago now."

"I was saddened by this news."

"Thank you," Julia said.

"And your mother?"

"She's gone, too, just a month ago. She was ill."

Niyol nodded. "Poor Julie. And Oliver, your brother?"

She smiled then. "He's alive. In fact, I believe he is not far from here now. I came here seeking him. Has he contacted you and your people?"

"Not that I am aware of."

"I'm sure you would know if he had. He is riding a paint horse, not shod."

Niyol eyed her keenly. "Is your brother in trouble?"

Julia found it hard to meet his direct gaze. "I'm afraid he is. He's been accused of robbing the stagecoach and killing one of the men on it. But that's not true, and now he may be hiding. I haven't been able to talk to him since it happened, but I think he fears for his life."

"I am sorry—for Oliver and for you."

"Thank you." She stepped closer to the mustang and looked up into Niyol's sympathetic eyes. "Please don't let the trader know I'm here. If anyone else comes looking for Oliver and hears that I am about, they would guess that my brother was near."

"I will not speak of it."

She nodded. "Thank you, friend."

Niyol looked over his shoulder, toward the vast desert. "A lawman camped last night on Diné land."

She caught her breath, though she'd suspected as much. "I'm afraid he's looking for Oliver."

"If we had known about your brother's trouble, we would have run him off." He watched her for a moment then said, "What do you want us to do, Julie? We will help you."

"I want only peace. You see, I know the lawman. He is Oliver's close friend. But now he thinks Oliver has done this thing, and he is convinced it is his duty to find Oliver and take him back to be tried."

"Do you think your brother can stay hidden? He was very skillful when he was younger."

Julia nodded. "I do. This man who is chasing him is a good tracker, but Oliver is better at hiding his tracks. I think he can avoid Adam Scott."

"Scott. He is the man. We spoke to him last night. We gave him three days to complete his business here." Niyol smiled grimly. "He was a little bit afraid of us, I think. But that is what we wanted."

Julia smiled, too, though she felt a tiny bit sorry for Adam. "I'm sure he was, especially if he didn't see you coming. I'm going to meet Oliver tonight, I hope, at the cave of the rock writing. Niyol, if I need your help. . ."

"You let us know. We will help you, Julie Newman. Your family are friends of the Diné."

Tears sprang into her eyes. "Thank you."

"Come to the village any time."

She nodded. Other people came along the trail on horses or

walking. Niyol joined two other men riding toward the trading post. They looked curiously at Julia. She waved and turned to go and collect the dun.

As she mounted and rode toward the family's cabin, she wondered if she had been wise to tell Niyol. He wouldn't tell the trader, but a lot of Navajo people had seen her. No, she decided. For her father's sake—a true friend of the Diné—they would close ranks to protect her as they would one of their own.

Chapter 9

Adam rode in the scorching sun all day, searching for tracks. Whenever he came across the hoofprints of one horse traveling alone, he followed them. Most of the tracks led onto trails where they mingled with thosc of other horses. Once he came upon a cluster of hogans with gardens and pastures around them. He turned Socks around and slipped away quickly.

Early in the afternoon he picked up a lone horse's sign leading northeast. Would that be Oliver's course? Across the high desert and out of Arizona, into Utah or Colorado? Maybe he was headed for Denver after all, or some other town where he could get a train. Adam followed the trail for nearly an hour and came to an isolated hogan. He rode Socks off the trail and hid him in a ravine not far away then sneaked back to a place where he could watch the dwelling undetected.

For a long time he sat watching the hogan. He ate some jerky and took what shade he could from a clump of rabbitbrush. Finally a woman and two children came out of the house and went into one of the nearby fields. Adam watched them as they moved among a small flock of sheep and drove the flock farther away. Oliver's horse must not have made the tracks he'd followed. This family seemed to be going about its normal routine.

Adam hesitated then went back and got his horse. He rode Socks out to the edge of the field and called out. The woman looked back at him, startled. She spoke to the children, and they kept walking behind the sheep. The woman came back a few steps, closer to Adam, and looked at him expectantly.

"I'm Sheriff Adam Scott. I have permission from the elders to be here."

Her impassive face told him nothing.

"Do you speak English?"

She nodded, one quick jerk of her chin.

"I'm looking for a white man. He is wanted by the law, and he might be dangerous to your people. Have you seen a white man in this area?"

"You," she said.

Adam smiled. "No, I mean another white man. He killed a man near Ardell and robbed a stagecoach."

She shook her head.

"All right. Uh. . . May I water my horse here?"

She pointed.

"Thank you." Adam rode in the direction she'd indicated and soon found a well-beaten path to a spring. The watering place was rimmed with stones, and a wooden bucket rested on the ground nearby. He dismounted and carried water to Socks in the bucket. He was careful not to let the horse get too near the spring or to disturb the stones.

He headed back toward Canyon Diablo, not knowing what else he could do. After a while, he noticed some vegetation in the distance, greener than what he'd been seeing. He rode closer and decided it was treetops. He urged Socks toward the greenery, hoping he'd find another water source. He wasn't desperate, but a fugitive would head for water. It might be a good place to find a trace of Oliver.

Several piñons grew along a ravine, and in the bottom were a few stunted cottonwoods. Adam didn't see any surface water, but he'd wager it flowed here in the spring. He dismounted and turned Socks loose to forage on the sparse grass while he rested.

Lord, help me out here, please. Am I foolish to stay out here looking for him? I just don't know what to do now.

After a half hour's rest in the shade, he mounted again and rode back toward the trading post. He wasn't sure he could reach it today, but he'd try. He ought to hit one of the Navajo trails soon, and if it was headed westward, he'd follow it.

As he came over a rise, he saw a rider in the distance, the first human he'd seen since the woman at the hogan. He pulled Socks around and below the skyline of the rise, to where he could barely see over it. He sat still, watching.

The rider wasn't headed toward him, but in a more northerly direction. The horse wasn't Oliver's flashy pinto, but a rather nondescript dun. After several minutes, he was sure it was Julia. She rode the same horse she'd had from Sam Dennis's stable yesterday. No mistaking her for an Indian, even at this distance. She wore the tan skirt she used to wear all the time when she rode—divided into wide, billowy trouser legs—and a light blue shirt with a vest over it. Her wide-brimmed hat covered her light brown hair, but he didn't need to see it to recognize her form and the way she sat so easy in the saddle.

She seemed to know where she was going—no hesitation, no casting about for the trail or the proper direction. Adam eased Socks to the top of the ridge. She never looked back. When she was nearly out of sight in the distance, he set out to intercept her trail. He wouldn't join her. Instead, he would follow—straight to her brother.

&

The area around the cave was exactly as Julia remembered it. She rode the dun into a rocky depression a few hundred yards away so that no telltale hoofprints would lead to the opening. When she'd dismounted, she removed her boots and swapped them for the tall, pliant moccasins she'd left at home when she went away to teach. The boots went into her saddlebags. She hobbled the dun, untied her bedroll, and walked slowly up out of the dip in the landscape.

After pausing and looking all around, she made her way by an indirect route to the opening in the rocks. From a distance, the cave's mouth couldn't be seen, but when she rounded an outcropping of rock and drew closer, it appeared. As always, it seemed to be only a slight overhang in the side of the rock face. Only from right outside the entrance could one tell that it extended back several yards. She drew in a deep breath as the trickle of memories increased to a roaring river.

As a precaution, she picked up a small stone and tossed it inside the cave. Their Diné friends had taught them to give any creatures inside a warning before they entered. All was still. She looked behind her again. An undulation in the low greasewood made her hold her breath and stare for half a minute, but it seemed to be just the wind waving the sparse bushes. She exhaled.

Had Oliver been here yet? Ducking low, she entered the cave and stood still, the light spilling in from behind her. Only the very front of the small cave was visible. She waited for her eyes to adjust then studied every part of the cave as best she could before she stepped forward.

"Oliver?" she said softly, but she knew he wasn't there.

A small fire ring remained near the entrance, so most of the smoke could waft outside. She set down her bundle beyond it and took out the items she'd packed for this moment. Tinder and kindling came first. She opened her tinderbox and struck sparks, working hard to get the cache of wood shavings and pine twigs she'd brought to catch and blaze. Someone had left a few bigger sticks, and she added two to her fire then took one of the three torches she'd prepared. She took another look outside before she lit it.

Holding the torch before her, she examined every bit of the

cave. It extended only about twenty feet into the hillside. At its highest point she could almost stand straight, but not quite. When they were kids, they'd had no trouble at all standing upright in here. Oliver would have to hunch over now.

Satisfied that the cave was uninhabited—with no snakes or other annoying creatures to share her refuge today—she turned her attention to the things left behind by other humans. In a cranny at the back of the cave was more dry firewood and a pottery jar. The design on the jar was one she had found in their code symbols—a repeated diamond pattern signifying rain. The pattern was painted in tan, rich brown, and reddish earth colors. She lifted the lid of the jar and sniffed it. Water. Nearby was a small mound of dry, orange pine needles—someone's bed.

Looking over the walls, she smiled as she found the old petroglyphs—the same as they'd been fifteen years ago. The figure of a horse, pecked into the stone low on the wall, was newer, she thought—at least she couldn't remember seeing it before. The artist had painted it after chiseling the crude outline into the rock. Not Oliver's work. He would not have had time to do anything so permanent. Probably some young Diné had added his mark to the work of the ancients.

She'd seen everything—including the flat stone near the fire pit where they left messages and rubbed them out when they'd served their purpose. Julia turned back to it and held her torch close. The runes scratched on its surface were clear: "Sister—I will come." They were followed by another full moon and Oliver's eagle.

She doused the torch and sat down near the fire ring. The setting sun threw streaks of color over the sandy ridges and dips outside, and the rocks sticking up here and there across the landscape. The air cooled quickly, but she didn't add wood to the fire. The silence hung over the desert until a coyote yipped in the distance. Another answered, and soon a chorus of barks cluttered the evening air.

Julia sat by the cave opening, looking out from the deeper darkness into the twilight. She hoped the coyotes didn't come closer or she would have to move her horse. She didn't want to do that.

She began to pray, first for success in her mission and then for Oliver's safety. Finally her thoughts touched on Adam, and she let out a long, slow breath.

Lord, I don't know what to ask. Help him to find the truth, that's all.

Beyond that, she would leave it up to God to settle things. It was all in His hands, anyway. But she couldn't bear it if Oliver remained under this awful cloud of suspicion—and worse, if he were punished for crimes he didn't commit.

Just when she would have said full darkness had come, a shadow moved outside, and almost soundless steps brought her brother to her.

Julia stood and embraced Oliver, clinging to him without speaking. Her throat ached, and she knew then how much she had feared he wouldn't come. That something would stop him.

"No fire?" he said.

"I had one for a little while before dark. But Adam is after you. I didn't want him to see it. I probably shouldn't have lit one at all, but I needed a torch, and I wanted to be sure no animals came here tonight."

Oliver drew her down to the cave floor, and they sat side by side, legs folded, as they used to do.

"Adam is out here, you say?"

"Yes. He came ahead of me. He went to our house. After that, I don't know."

"Does he know you're here?"

"No."

Oliver reached for her hand. "Clew brought you my message. I wasn't sure you'd get it—or that you'd remember our code."

She smiled. "I had to root out my old journal, but—I'm here, aren't I?"

"You sure are. Jules, I'm so glad to see you. And so sorry it's like this. What happened in Ardell, anyway?"

Julia recounted the events of the last three days, from the holdup to her journey to Canyon Diablo and their old cabin.

"You can't go back, Oliver. Not yet. The people might lynch you."

"I'm really sorry that Bub was killed."

"Why don't you tell me where you were that morning," Julia said. "Everyone seemed to think that, since you weren't at the mine, you must have been out waiting to ambush the stagecoach. But I know that's not true."

"Not by a long shot. I went to the miners' village on business that morning."

She nodded. That agreed with what Clew had told her. Mr. Gerry had built a small cluster of cabins down the mountainside from the mine headquarters. It was about three miles from Ardell, by winding, narrow roads. The miners could live there rent free while they were employed at the High Desert Mine. The accommodations were spartan, but adequate.

"Maybe we can get someone there to back up your story. Who saw you in the village?"

"Ed Rines and his wife. I went down to see Ed. He was injured a couple of weeks ago, and I needed to check on his hours before the accident so I could make out his pay slip. Oh, and Mrs. Halstrom saw me, too, and several children."

"Good. If I can find Adam, I'll give him their names and insist that he talk to them."

"I'm not sure he'd think it was proof, if he's so eager to see me hang. Ed told me another one of the miners was sick, and I went over to see him when I left Ed's place. He didn't have any wood or water in the house, so I stayed to get that for him. By the time I got back to headquarters, the place was in an uproar. Clew caught me at the stable and told me I'd better not go into the office or I'd be in big trouble."

Julia grimaced and reached for his hand. "I'm so sorry. I don't know what's come over Adam, thinking you could be involved in the robbery. He's supposed to be your friend. Did anything happen between you two before the holdup?"

"No. I saw him Sunday, and everything was fine. I can't figure out why he'd think I'd do something like this. I mean, other than being away from my desk at the time of the holdup, there can't be any evidence."

"He says he found something."

"What?"

She shook her head. "He wouldn't tell me. But he's determined to track you down and take you back to town to stand trial."

"I was afraid he'd do that. He can be persistent."

"Yes."

Oliver looked at her for a long moment, and Julia wondered what he was thinking.

"I saw Niyol this morning," she said.

Oliver smiled. "I thought of going to the Diné village, but I decided it was better to leave them out of this."

"Well, I told him you were in a bit of hot water. He said to let them know if we need help."

"That's good of him. He always backed Papa up when there was a disagreement. I'm glad he remembers us kindly."

"So am I. He also said they'd seen Adam. They told him he

could be on their land for three days, but none of them knew at the time that you were the one Adam was chasing."

"We can't do anything about that," Oliver said. "Just keep our heads down."

A quiet step outside startled Julia. She jerked around to face the opening. A dark form blocked the starlight.

"Hello, Ollie," Adam said. "Don't make any sudden moves. I've got you covered."

Chapter 10

Adam Scott, how could you?" Julia scrambled to get up.

"Hold still, Julie." Adam's steely tone rankled her. "Put your hands up. Both of you."

She hesitated, crouching and staring toward him. Of all the nerve, telling her that. She wished she'd kept the fire after all so she could see his face, but with his back to the opening and the sparse moonlight, she couldn't read his expression.

"Take it easy, Julia," Oliver said. "Best do as he says until we get this settled."

"That's good advice," Adam said.

Julia plopped back onto the rock floor. She raised both hands, more in a gesture of futility than surrender.

"This is ridiculous."

"I'm not laughing." Adam came into the cave. As he moved forward and turned slightly, the faint light glinted off a revolver in his hand, pointed squarely at her brother. "Hands behind your back, Ollie. Sorry, pal."

Oliver complied and turned slightly so that his back was partly toward Adam.

Julia seethed inside. A stick of firewood lay at hand. Maybe she could grab it and hit Adam over the head with it while he was busy tying up her innocent brother.

"Tie his hands, Julie."

She stared up at him. "You're joking."

"No, I'm not. And I'm holding a gun."

"Oh, this beats all. You expect me to believe you'd shoot me if I don't do what you say? You big bully. Tie him up yourself."

"Jules," Oliver said. "He's just doing his job."

"No, he's not. His job is to find Bub Hilliard's killer. And whoever that is, I guarantee he's not within miles of here."

"Come on, Julie," Adam said. In the darkness he sounded almost pouty, not at all like the big, bad sheriff.

"Forget it. I'm not tying my brother up. You want to take him back to Ardell and have him lynched, and I won't be a part of it."

"It's all right, Adam," Oliver said. "I won't fight you. If you feel like you have to tie me up, I'll let you."

Adam hesitated. "You won't go for my gun?"

"Nope."

"You got one on you?"

Oliver moved and a moment later, to Julia's disgust, he held his pistol out butt-first to Adam. "Here. It's loaded."

"Thanks." Adam took it and laid it carefully on the floor then proceeded to secure Oliver's hands behind him.

Julia seethed until she could no longer remain silent. "This would be funny if you weren't going to let Ollie hang for something he didn't do and would never consider doing."

"You're next. Turn around."

"You'll have to shoot me first."

"Julie." Oliver sounded annoyed and just plain tired.

"This isn't a game," Adam said.

"You got that right." She glared at him. "I didn't shoot anyone or steal any money. What do you think you need to truss me up for?"

"So you won't run away or—or abet a criminal."

"Ha! As if I'd do that!"

"How do I know you didn't already?"

"She hasn't helped me at all," Oliver said. "I asked her to meet me here, but she hasn't so much as given me a bite to eat."

Yet, Julia thought. She had extra food for him in her bundle.

"I'm talking about back at the stagecoach," Adam said.

"Oh, now you're really making me mad." Julia clenched her fists. "How am I supposed to have helped this dangerous killer?"

"I admit, I'd be interested to know that," Oliver said.

Adam was not to be distracted from his purpose. "Put your hands back here, Julia, and I'll tell you."

"Aw, Adam, tie her hands in front if you've got to do that," Oliver said. "No lady should be this uncomfortable."

"Did I make your knots too tight?" Adam asked.

Oliver sighed. "I'll live. But don't be too rough on her."

"Where's your gun, Julia?"

"What?" Oliver cried. "Julia with a gun?"

"She had one when the stage was robbed, which I admit I found a mite suspicious."

"Oh, you two!" Julia jerked around to scowl at them. "Of course I had a gun. Oliver had told me things were rough along the stage line, and even on the trains. I bought it before I left Philadelphia. Didn't want to travel so far unescorted and find myself in a bad situation. Which I did, it turns out." She grimaced at the irony of finding more danger at the hands of a friend than from the stagecoach robber.

"How do I know you didn't pull that revolver out so's you could help the robber if he needed it?" Adam said.

"Do we have to go through all that again?" Julia crossed her arms. If he wasn't going to tie them, she wouldn't sit there all night waiting. "What part don't you understand yet, Adam? I am not an outlaw. I was not in cahoots with the robber."

"Do you seriously think that, Adam?" Oliver asked.

"Well. . ." Adam hesitated. "All I know is, until I get to the bottom of this, I need to make sure she can't get the drop on me. So where's the gun, Julie?"

"Yonder, in my bedroll." She jerked her head toward her bundle.

"I'll get it after I tie you," Adam said. "Now put out your hands."

She stared up at him.

"Do it, Jules," Oliver said.

She sighed and held out her hands, clasped in front of her. Adam wound a piece of thin rope around her wrists and tied a substantial knot. He went to the other side of the fire pit and began to lay a fire on top of the ashes of Julia's earlier blaze.

"There's more wood in the back of the cave," Oliver said.

"Thanks. We'll stay here the night and leave in the morning."

"Oh, and you think Oliver will be comfortable sleeping like that—with his hands behind him?" Julia shook her head in disgust.

Adam ignored her and carefully placed the few remaining pieces of kindling. "Might as well be warm tonight—unless you think the light will draw unwanted company."

"The Diné already know you're here," Julia said. "Me, too. I'm not sure if they know Oliver's here, but they wouldn't hurt him, anyway."

Adam grunted and rose. "Whereabouts in the back?"

Oliver told him, and Adam struck a match. He found the woodpile and returned with an armful of dry sticks.

"There's rock writing on the wall back there."

"Yeah, the Diné have used this cave for a long time," Oliver said.

"It's not a burial cave or anything like that is it?" Adam looked around uneasily. "Are there any bones in here?"

"No, nothing like that."

"What does it say on the wall?"

Oliver said, "We think it's mostly people's signs. Like when white people carve their initials or write something like 'Adam was here.' There's one part our friends told us is the record of a journey. And there's one that seems to be a picture of a battle."

"That's interesting." Adam knelt by the fire ring.

Julia fretted and fumed while he arranged the wood and lit the fire. At least Oliver hadn't told him how they'd painstakingly chipped their own signs into the wall near the other pictures. Right now she didn't want to tell Adam one single thing. His behavior was beyond horrible. But he went on building up the fire as calmly as if they were all out for a picnic. As the flames caught and flared up, she studied his face. He seemed calm now, and determined.

At last she couldn't stand it anymore.

"Adam Scott, you tell us right now what evidence you think you have against Oliver. If you haven't got any more than a notion that I was in cahoots with the robber because I happened to come home the same day the stage was held up, then you're an idiot."

"Well, thanks. Always nice to get a genteel lady's opinion."

"Cut it out, you two," Oliver said. "Adam, I agree with one thing she said. It would be nice to know what you've got against me. Because I know I wasn't anywhere near that stagecoach that morning. I was down at the miners' village, and several people down there can tell you that."

Adam paused and looked over at him then turned his attention back to the fire. The flames had consumed most of his kindling, and he added a few more substantial sticks. When he was satisfied with the result, he sat back.

"Are you sure? Because Mr. Gerry had no idea where you were."

"I don't usually tell him where I'm going when I leave headquarters. It was a routine thing. The payroll was coming in, and I had to straighten out something before I could issue a man's pay, that's all."

"And that took you all day?"

"Well, no, but I did make a couple of other stops before I came back. Then somebody told me about the stage getting robbed, and they said you were looking for me. I was going to go find you and see what you wanted."

"Why didn't you?" Adam asked.

Oliver grimaced. "I woulda, but this person also told me that you and most of the people in town had a noose in mind."

"That right?" Adam picked up a sliver of wood and broke it in two. "Who was this person?"

"If I tell you, will you hound him all over the territory?"

"That's not fair, Ollie."

"Isn't it?" Oliver turned his face away.

Adam let out a big sigh. "All right, just tell me this: Did you know Julia was on the stage that day?"

"No. She'd written me that she was coming as quickly as she could. She told me what day her school let out and said she'd buy a train ticket for the soonest day she could after that. But she didn't know exactly when she'd get into Flagstaff, or if she'd have to wait a day or two there for a stage to Ardell."

Adam nodded reluctantly. The stage only went up to the mountain town twice a week.

"I've been meeting the stage the last couple of times it came in," Oliver said. "But the robbery happened on payroll day. I had to make sure the books were in order, and the errand to the village seemed more urgent. I figured I'd get back within an hour or two of when the stage came in, and if Julia was on it, she'd be at the house."

"I talked to her that evening, and she didn't seem to know where you were. So how did she know to find you out here?"

"Don't tell him," she said quickly.

"Oh, now *that* sounds innocent," Adam said.

"I *am* innocent. But you have a way of using things against people. This is something between Oliver and me that you don't need to know."

"Well, I disagree." Adam leaned forward and looked past Oliver, glaring at her in the flickering light. "If you two saw each other in town—"

"We didn't," Oliver said. "When I walked into this cave half an hour ago, I hadn't seen Julia for almost two years."

"Then I'll ask it again, as a law enforcement officer. How did you know she'd be here tonight?"

Oliver shrugged. "That's easy. I wrote her a message, and the friend who told me about the robbery took it to her. Meanwhile, I packed some grub and water and headed out of there."

Julia exhaled in relief. Of course. Oliver had understood that it was the code she wanted to keep secret, not the fact that he'd written a message. Oliver always understood her.

"It sounds to me like there would have been time for you to visit the miners' village and then get up to the Flagstaff road," Adam said with a stubborn note to his voice.

Oliver shrugged. "I don't know as I could pinpoint the times when I was at each place, Adam. I'm sorry. I didn't think my life would depend on it."

Adam sat in broody silence for a minute or two. "It's not like I want to think you did it. I know you wouldn't deliberately shoot somebody."

"You got that part right," Oliver said. "So what's this so-called evidence?"

Adam reached into the pocket of his jacket and pulled his hand out clenched. "I found this near the spot where the stagecoach stopped. Right beside the empty treasure box." He opened his hand in front of Oliver.

Julia couldn't see what he held, but Oliver stared down at it.

Something small and white. Oliver's blank expression told her nothing.

"You think that's mine?" he said.

"What is it? Let me see." She wriggled closer to him, pulling herself across the cold stone floor with her feet.

Adam held it out to her, and she raised her bound hands. Into them he dropped a square of white cardboard. She bent close and held it so the firelight shone on it.

"A matchbook?" She stared at Adam and Oliver. "I don't understand."

Chapter 11

"That's not just any matches you've got there," Adam said. "I was in Phoenix in July, and somebody gave me half a dozen of those."

Julia peered at the cover of the matchbook. "Arizona, the forty-eighth state. What is this, some kind of advertisement?"

"Exactly."

"I don't understand. Is it to remind people to vote?"

"Sort of. You know President Taft vetoed our constitution?"

"Yes," Julia said. "Arizona has to vote again."

"That's right. And we hope it will go through this time and we'll be a state. Then the map will be complete, and we'll get all the benefits of statehood."

"But what were you doing in Phoenix?"

"I helped take a prisoner down there for his trial. I had to testify."

Oliver looked at Julia. "I guess I didn't tell you about that. I should have mentioned it in my last letters, but with Mama passing and all, I didn't think to tell you."

"Tell me what?" Julia glanced from him to Adam, but Adam was now looking down, seemingly fascinated by the fire.

"Adam helped catch a train robber last spring, and they held the trial in Phoenix, that's all. But when he got down there, some folks started working on him, trying to get him to run for legislature."

Julia eyed her brother carefully. He probably hadn't told her deliberately, because he knew she didn't want to be told when Adam risked his life on the job. Not that it concerned her anymore. But, yes, it was the type of event Oliver might omit from his letters so as not to disturb her.

"Well," she said at last, "who's this *they* you're talking about?"

"Some politicians," Adam said. "I had to hang around the capital for almost two weeks, waiting for my turn to testify in the court case."

"Oh yes, because you were escorting someone you arrested. Who was it that time? Any of my friends?" Julia's voice dripped acid.

"Julia," Oliver said softly.

"Sorry," she said, but she felt far from repentant. "I believe Oliver said it was a train robber, and I don't think any of my friends qualify as one of those."

"There was a gang of them," Adam said. "The county sheriff headed up the case. He called in all his deputies to help catch them. I was in on it. When it came time for the leader to go to court, they didn't think he could get a fair trial up here, so they sent him to Phoenix. Anyway, it kept me away for a while. I wasn't back when your mama died, and I'm sorry about that. I should have been there for Oliver."

She barked out a laugh. "That's all right, Adam. You can be there for him while I'm in jail. Oops! I almost forgot. You're putting him in jail, too. Who's going to be there for the two of us, I wonder."

Oliver scowled at her. "Really, Jules, this isn't the time—"

"Then when *is* the time? The fact that Adam got a matchbook when he was delivering a prisoner doesn't prove a thing. A lot of people probably have those."

"Except that they don't," Adam said. "When I got them, they were just printed. The men who approached me gave me a handful. They said if I ran for office, they could have a bunch printed with my name on them, so I could hand them out to people. See, as soon as statehood is approved by Congress, we'll have to hold elections, and the folks in the territorial government want to have everything in place for that and have the candidates ready to go."

"And you want to run for state office?"

"I thought a lot about it, and I don't really know as I'm cut out for it."

"All right." She felt like arguing with him and telling him he would make a horrible legislator, but deep down she didn't think that was true, aside from his love of the outdoors. He might be very good at it. Adam was intelligent and usually fair minded—when he wasn't being bullheaded, the way he was now. Belittling him wouldn't get them out of the quagmire they were in. Better to stay calm and rational—something she hadn't been doing this evening. She inhaled deeply. "But how does that prove that Oliver robbed the stagecoach?"

"He gave one to me," Oliver said.

"Oh well, why didn't you say so? That's ironclad proof." Julia wanted to march out of the cave and ride for home. Unfortunately there was the little matter of her bonds and an irate sheriff to prevent her from doing that. "Of all the—" She stopped and gritted her teeth. Once again she determined to keep this conversation civil. "Adam, please listen to me. Does it not make sense to you that lots of people may have received some of those matches over the last month or two? Hundreds of people."

"It's possible," he said, "but not people from Ardell. I'd have known if anybody else from town had been to Phoenix. The only person I know of besides me who's been there lately is Leland Gerry."

Oliver's eyes flickered at the mention of his boss. "Folks want him to go to Washington."

"Yeah, that's what I heard," Adam said. "Senator Gerry."

"Well, there. Those could have come from Mr. Gerry's pocket," Julia said.

"I don't think so."

"Why not?"

The smoke was drifting toward Adam. He blinked then shifted his position. "First of all, Mr. Gerry was out at mine headquarters when the robbery happened. He was there all day, so far as I know. And he was there when I went out to the mine right afterward. He took me to Oliver's desk, and he seemed genuinely surprised that Oliver wasn't there."

Julia frowned. It looked as though Gerry had an alibi. And he was the richest man in town. He wouldn't need to steal his own company's payroll. Still, she couldn't give in too easily. Businessmen had been known to rob their own companies when they had personal debts. "It wouldn't hurt for you to make sure he was there all morning."

After a tense moment of silence, Adam said, "You're right. I'll check on it when we get back."

She nodded, somewhat mollified.

"You know," Oliver said, "I've been sitting here thinking while you two have been taking potshots at each other."

"Come up with anything?" Adam almost sounded hopeful.

"Well, you gave me a matchbook, like you said. It must have been three or four weeks ago."

"That's right."

Oliver nodded. "I used a few out of it. And then one day it was really cold up at the mine. When I got there that morning, Clew Harrison was out at the guardhouse by the entrance—you know where I mean?"

Adam nodded.

Julia started to speak, but held back. Oliver hadn't revealed that Clew had been the friend who'd carried his message to her, and she would just as soon leave Clew out of this. No sense setting Adam off hounding the old man.

"Well, we'd had a frost, and it was chilly. Clew was trying to get a fire going in the little box stove they've got in there. Wanted to warm up and make himself some coffee. So I gave him the matchbook."

After a moment, Adam said carefully, "All right. So where is it now?"

Oliver shrugged. "Beats me. Clew never gave it back to me."

Adam's mind whirled. One question hung there like a black cloud. "Answer me this, Oliver. If you're innocent, why did you run away?"

Oliver chuckled without humor and shook his head. "Like I said, my friend who met me in the stable said Mr. Gerry told you I was missing, and everyone at headquarters seemed to think I was guilty. I was scared they'd hang me. I mean, if they were convinced *you* stole that much money, would you stick around?"

"How much was on that stage, anyway? Mr. Gerry gave me an estimate of five thousand dollars."

"Closer to six thousand," Oliver said. "We have almost a hundred and fifty people on the payroll. The miners don't get paid nearly enough, but it still adds up to a pretty big sum."

"I figured you knew Julia was coming in on the stage," Adam said. There were still pieces he couldn't fit together.

"No, I didn't. Not at first."

"Your friend told you that, too?"

"I asked him to find out. I hoped she'd arrived, but I wasn't sure. While he went into town, I hid out behind the stable at the mine. I was afraid to show my face. He was gone the better part of an hour." Oliver looked over at Julia and grimaced. "I'm sorry, Jules. I was so confused, but I wanted to do the right thing. I almost gave up waiting and went into town. But a couple of men from the mine office went in the stable, and I heard them talking about it. So far as I could tell, they believed the rumors. I heard one of them say, 'I never would have thought Newman would do something like that.' It was enough to make me stay put until Clew got back."

Julia winced.

"So Clew was the friend who told you all about the robbery," Adam said.

"Well. . .yeah."

"And also the friend who delivered the message to Julia."

Oliver glanced over at her. "Sorry. It slipped out."

Julia shrugged. "He would probably have found out sooner or later."

"Well, it seems to me that Clew's in this thing up to his neck," Adam said. "You gave him your matchbook, he told you to hide, and he carried your message to Julia for you."

"You think *Clew* robbed the stage?" Julia stared at him. "He's an old man."

"He's fit enough to clean up things at the mine headquarters."

"I wouldn't think he'd do something like highway robbery," Oliver said. "He's a decent man."

"Well, somebody did it." Adam stood and paced to the cave opening. He stood with one hand up on the natural lintel, staring out over the dark landscape. At last he turned. "So you ran away because you thought you'd be lynched."

"That's right," Oliver said. "I hoped I could get away from you, and maybe Julia could meet me out here and tell me how things were in town—and if you'd found the real culprit yet. If nothing else, I figured she could help me think of a way to prove I was innocent. At least she could let me know when it was safe to go home again."

"And instead, you're trying to get us both hung," Julia said.

"Oh, wait just a minute." Adam was tired of her carping on that issue. He walked over and stood towering above her. "I only tied you up as a precaution."

"Oh, that's right." She glared up at him. "I'm the vicious female robber, and I might take my evil gun out of my pack and shoot you."

"It's ridiculous to think Julia's involved in those crimes," Oliver said. "How could you even imagine it, Adam? Just a few weeks ago you told me you couldn't forget her, and you wondered if you'd ever get over it. And now you think she's a cold-blooded murderess? It doesn't make sense."

Julia's jaw dropped.

Adam frowned at Oliver. That conversation had been strictly private. He hadn't expected Oliver to let it out that he still had feelings for Julia. But it was no wonder she seemed so shocked at the idea. If anyone went by the contact he'd had with her over the past three days, he'd probably say they hated each other. And she more than likely *did* hate him. She surely sounded that way now.

Adam kicked Oliver's boot lightly, just a cautionary tap. "Would you shut up, please?"

Julia hauled in a breath, sounding for all the world as if she were strangling. She struggled to her knees then pushed with her tied hands and managed to stand. "Pardon me, gents, but I'll step outside so you can continue this conversation in private."

She walked out of the cave into the chilly night.

Adam stared after her. "Hey, wait."

She kept walking. He looked at Oliver. Only for a second did the thought gallop across Adam's benumbed brain that he couldn't go out there and leave his murder suspect alone.

"Go get her," Oliver said in a kindly tone, "but be nice."

Adam hurried outside. Julia had gone down the hillside toward where they'd all left their horses, but she'd stopped after going a few yards and stood still. He took a deep breath and walked down the slope to join her.

"Where you going?"

She turned her head toward him and wrinkled her lips. "You're afraid I'll escape and go pull some more robberies? Sorry to disappoint you. I just needed some air."

Adam shoved down the anger she fueled. Oliver had told him to be nice, but she was making it awfully hard.

He walked around her until he was facing her. He stood a little lower than she did on the hillside, and so they looked each other straight in the eyes.

"Do you think Clew pulled the robbery and then set up your brother?"

She sighed. "I don't know. Until yesterday, I hadn't seen Clew in years. So far as you know, is he an honest man?"

"I'd have said yes, but. . ."

"Exactly. You'd have said the same about my brother."

Adam's whole body drooped. Arguing with her was too hard, and he didn't want to continue. "Oh come on, Julie. That's not what I was going to say."

"Oh?"

"No. I was going to say that I don't know Clew that well. Look, I'm sorry about all of this."

"Are you really?" Her voice rose in a plaintive plea.

He hesitated. If he said yes, she'd insist he cut the ropes that held her and Oliver and let them go. If he said no, there would be no regaining her respect in this lifetime. He glanced over her shoulder, up toward the cave. What if she'd drawn him out here to give Ollie a chance to escape? But Oliver sat where he'd left him, in the orange glow of the fire beneath the overhang of rock.

"So," Julia said bitterly, "we're not doing any good sitting out here on Indian land."

"True. We'll head back to Ardell in the morning and talk to Clew. And. . . Julie, I *am* sorry. I'm sorry I latched on to Oliver so quickly as my suspect. I should have at least looked at other people, too. People like Clew. And Mr. Gerry. Probably other people we haven't thought of yet."

"You believe Oliver, then, about the matches?" The reflection of the stars glinted in her eyes.

Adam swallowed hard. "Yes."

She nodded. "If we go back to town tomorrow, can you protect him from the people who think he's guilty?"

Adam squared his shoulders. "I can."

She eyed him doubtfully. "I'm not sure I can trust you that much anymore."

His heart plummeted. No matter what he said, she wasn't satisfied, and she was bouncing him around like an India-rubber ball. One minute he hoped she would forgive him, the next he knew she never would. It was probably best that she'd refused to marry him. A lifetime of this pain was unthinkable.

"I'll tell people I have another suspect now," he said.

She shook her head. "You know what happened to our pa."

"Yes," Adam whispered. He did know—all too well. Ben Newman was working as a deputy sheriff after his stint as Indian agent at Canyon Diablo. He was taking a convicted horse thief to the territorial prison when a band of vigilantes ambushed them, killing both Newman and the prisoner. Julia had a right to be wary of going back to face an angry town.

"Maybe you and Oliver can wait outside of town," he said. "I'll ride in first and talk to the people. . ."

Julia sniffed and tears streaked down her cheeks. She wasn't looking into his eyes anymore. She seemed focused on the badge he wore on his jacket. The thing that had come between them two years ago and still crushed any chance they might have at love and trust and permanence.

"Julie?"

She sobbed, only once, but it broke his heart. Adam folded her in his arms. Her head just fit against his shoulder, and he held her close, like he had two years ago, the night he proposed to her.

"Sweetheart, I'll protect you. I can handle the townsfolk, so don't worry about that." Somehow he would make it happen. He'd gather the town's most trustworthy men around them. No matter how angry the people were, he wouldn't let them lay a finger on the woman he loved.

"How do you know?" she choked out. "When I left Ardell yesterday, folks were demanding justice. And they think that means hanging my brother."

She wept then, in big, painful gulps.

Adam tightened his hold on her, feeling helpless. "We'll find a way to get at the truth. We'll go to Clew first."

She raised her head and looked at him, bleary-eyed.

"That's what we'll do," he said. "We'll find Clew, and if he can't account for his whereabouts during the holdup, I'll arrest him. Then we'll ride into town together, and I'll lock Clew up and call a meeting to tell everyone Oliver is innocent."

She didn't speak. He must not be saying the right thing. What was it he hadn't hit on yet?

"Tell me what you're thinking," he pleaded.

She pressed her lips together and avoided meeting his gaze.

"If Clew's not at the mine, we'll find him," Adam said. "Oh, and I'll ask Mr. Gerry where he was that morning, too."

Still she said nothing.

"Julie, please! I've loved you so long I can't stand this. I'll do anything if you'll just trust me again. I know I made a mistake—no, worse than that. I was just plain stupid. I see that now. All I want is for you to forgive me."

He bent down and peered at her in the moonlight. "Please?"

She stepped back from him, distancing herself by a few inches. He hadn't gotten through to her, and he felt awful, like he'd failed her last test. He would never get another chance.

"What am I missing? You've got to tell me." His voice was ragged, and she peered into his eyes.

In the moonlight, she was tragically beautiful with tears glistening on her face. Slowly she raised her hands. He stared down at them, still tied, clasped together in supplication.

Adam grabbed the hilt of his knife and pulled it from the sheath on his belt.

"I'm so sorry."

He stuck the tip between the strands and sliced through one. She twisted her hands, and the rope fell to the ground. She raised her arms toward him and leaned forward.

Adam caught her and swung her up in his embrace. He held her close, fighting for a deep breath when his chest ached like anything. She clung to him, her arms around his neck, and buried her face in the hollow of his shoulder. She hadn't said she loved him, or even that she trusted him, but this was a start. Now he would have to make good on his promise. He couldn't survive failing her again.

Chapter 12

In the morning, Adam woke to the sound of bacon sizzling. Julia had apparently packed along a small frying pan and enough side meat and oatmeal for them all to make a meal of it. The last of his meager stash of ground coffee beans provided them each with a cup of coffee. Oliver, freed from his bonds the night before, contributed by scrounging up enough greasewood and cottonwood branches to replace the wood they'd used from the back of the cave.

No one talked much as they ate. They packed up everything and rode most of the morning to get to the trading post. While Oliver and Julia watered the horses, Adam went in and told the trader he was headed back to Ardell.

"Did you meet up with Ben Newman's boy?" the trader asked.

"I did. Thank you."

When he strode out into the glaring sun again, Oliver was leaning against the wall, under the eaves of the building. The horses stood patiently nearby.

"Where's Julia?" Adam asked.

"She saw an old friend and went to talk to her."

"You've got a lot of friends among the Navajo."

Oliver shrugged. "Some. This woman is the daughter of a man Julia saw yesterday. We used to play with her. Julia's telling her to let her father know that we're leaving, and that you've also left their territory, and all is well."

Adam considered that and nodded. "I suppose they probably knew already that we were going, don't you?"

"Maybe."

"And I don't suppose they'd have let me leave with you trussed up."

"I dunno," Oliver said. "I'm glad we don't have to find out."

Adam shook his head. How could he have been so cocky as to think he could ride alone into Indian lands and come out again on his own terms? He guessed he still had a lot to learn. He squinted against the sun and spotted Julia moving away from a group of Navajo women. "Here she comes."

He and Oliver untied the three horses.

"All set?" Oliver called as she approached.

"Yes. Look what Atsa gave me." She held out a tiny silver bell. "Niyol makes them for his wife and daughters, and they put them on moccasins and bridles for the trader."

"You told her we're all leaving?" Adam said.

"Yes. She said her father will be glad to hear that we are safe." She looked at Oliver. "They were worried about us."

Oliver gazed toward the group of Navajo women approaching the door of the trading post and waved. One of the women lifted her hand in return.

The air was chilly when they'd left the cave, but now it was so warm that they all peeled off their jackets and tied them behind their saddles with their bedrolls. They rode as quickly as they could without pushing the horses too hard. A couple of hours after their dinner stop, they began to climb into the hills, and by late afternoon were close to the High Desert Mine.

"What's the plan?" Oliver asked.

Adam drew Socks to a halt, and the others brought their horses up closer to him, squeezing in on the trail.

"Where are we most likely to find Clew?" Adam asked.

"Either the guardhouse or the stable, unless they've got him off working on something." Oliver stood in his stirrups and peered up toward the mine buildings.

Adam could see the roofline of the headquarters and one end

of the stable. "Do we want to let him see you? I mean, if he was involved in the robbery, he might count on you taking the blame. But if you show up. . ."

"If I show up with you, he can't lie to you," Oliver said. "I mean, with me standing right there, he can't misrepresent what happened between him and me. I guess he could still lie about the robbery."

"How about if we leave the horses down here in the bushes and walk up there," Julia said. "You talk to him first, Adam, and then we can join you and see if he changes his story."

"That might work," Adam said.

"Or it might backfire." Oliver frowned. "Can't think of a better plan, though."

"All right," Julia said. "If he's outside, it shouldn't take us long to locate him. But, Adam, you might have to go inside the headquarters and ask for him if he's not out where Oliver said. I mean, we can't let anyone in the office see Oliver."

"Let's do that." Adam dismounted and led Socks off the trail and into a stand of acacia that was thick enough to camouflage the animals from the mine. However, if someone rode along the trail, he doubted all three horses would keep quiet. "Let's do this quick," he said.

Oliver was right behind him, with his pinto. "Agreed." He and Julia tied up their horses, and they made their way back out to the trail.

Julia looked back. "I can see Bravo's spots."

"They'll be all right," Adam said. "Let's just be as quick as we can."

They walked cautiously upward toward the buildings. The stable lay behind and off to one side of the headquarters. A dozen of the company's mules milled about or dozed on their feet in the adjacent corral. A man came out of the stable, pushing a wheelbarrow full of manure. Oliver held up a hand and ducked low.

"That's Clew."

"He's cleaning out the barn," Adam said.

"Yeah. People from Ardell who work at headquarters leave their horses in the corral on the far side, or in the stable. During the hottest part of the day, there might be fifteen or twenty horses inside. Somebody has to clean up. And Clew makes sure the horses all get water once or twice during the day, too."

"Tell you what," Adam said. "You and Julia stay hidden, but get into the stable if you can. I'll get Socks and ride on up there like I'm just coming in from my trip alone. I'll take Clew inside and talk to him."

"All right," Oliver said. "While you get your horse, we'll sneak up there."

When Clew had dumped his load on the manure pile out back, he brought the wheelbarrow around again and left it outside the stable. He went inside and emerged with two horses, which he led toward the watering trough.

"Go on," Oliver said. "Julia and I can get inside while he's taking more horses out to drink."

Adam went back down the trail and off to the acacias. Socks snuffled a greeting. Untying his lead rope, Adam spoke to the other two horses. "Don't fret now. We won't be long." He sure hoped he was doing the right thing.

Julia waited, flattened against the end wall of the stable, while Oliver peered around the edge of the building. Horses were shifting about inside, and she heard Clew slap one and say, "Get over, you!"

A few seconds later, Clew's muttering grew fainter as he led some of the animals out of the stable. Oliver turned to her and jerked his head toward the front of the building. He scurried away, and she bent over and ran after him, around the corner and into the semidarkness. They huddled in the shadows together and looked outside. Clew was pumping more water with the pitcher pump over the company's well, while two horses guzzled it out of the trough.

Oliver touched her shoulder and beckoned for her to follow him. They plunged deeper inside.

"Here?" Julia pointed to an empty stall.

"He's probably going to put one of those nags back in there," Oliver said. He kept walking to the end of the building, where several saddles hung on racks. Beneath them were a couple of wooden barrels. Oliver rocked one and moved it out from the wall a foot or so. He nodded to her.

Julia went over and peeked behind the barrel. There weren't any snakes. She tried not to think about spiders and scorpions as she slid in behind it and crouched against the wall. Meanwhile, Oliver moved the other barrel out and hid behind it just as Clew brought in the horses he'd watered. He led two more from their straight stalls and walked them outside.

Julia had the sudden urge to laugh. This whole cloak-and-dagger escapade was ridiculous. "We should just march out there and talk to him," she whispered.

"Let's try it Adam's way," Oliver said.

A minute later they heard Adam's hail.

"Howdy, Sheriff," Clew replied.

Socks's steel shoes thudded on the trail as he trotted closer. "Can I talk to you for a minute?" Adam asked.

"Sure. Just let me put these critters away."

Julia peeked from behind the barrel. Having left Socks outside, Adam entered the stable in the wake of the horses Clew led.

"So, Clew," Adam said as the older man came out of the stall where Julia had suggested hiding, "have you seen Oliver Newman lately?"

Clew stood still and stared at him. "No, sir, Sheriff. I heared you took out after him. You mean you didn't find him? 'Cause that boy is innocent. I'm tellin' you, he's not a stage robber."

"What makes you so sure?" Adam asked.

Clew shrugged. "He's a good boy. Always was, even when they was out to Canyon Diablo. He always did what his pa said. Now, his sister, she was a handful, but she was a good kid, too."

Julia clapped a hand over her mouth to keep a giggle from escaping.

"So, Clew, where were you when the stagecoach was robbed?" Adam asked.

"I was right here, at the mine headquarters, same as I am ever' day. Not countin' Sunday, that is."

Oliver stood and walked out of the shadows. Surprised but not willing to be left out, Julia squeezed between the barrels and followed him.

"Good to see you, Clew."

The old man stared at him with a slack jaw then grinned and stuck out his hand. "Ollie! Man, where were you?" Clew peered past him toward the barrels and spotted Julia. "And your sister's with you. Ain't that fine?"

"We think so," Julia said.

"Thanks for helping me the other day." Oliver pumped his hand.

"You're welcome, boy."

Julia studied Clew's face critically, but she couldn't see anything that hinted he wasn't sincere.

"Now, Clew," Adam said, "getting back to the day the stage was robbed, is there anybody here who can vouch for you?"

Clew sobered and shot him a keen glance. "What do you mean, vouch for me?"

"Anyone who saw you working around here that day? At different times of day, I mean. Especially in the morning, before Oliver came back from the village."

Clew went completely still for a moment. "Sheriff, I don't like what you're getting at."

Oliver touched Clew's sleeve. "It's all right, now. Don't get upset. You've got to look at this from Adam's point of view. I was his best suspect. Well, I think I've convinced him I didn't do it. So now he's got to look at everyone else and see if he can tell who did."

"But..." Clew looked around at them. "You think I'd shoot Bub Hilliard? That's crazy. Bub was a good man."

"Yes, he was," Adam said. "But if he didn't know who you were, and if he was going to kill you, wouldn't you shoot first?"

"In self-defense, you mean?" Clew asked.

Julia decided it was time to speak up. "No, that's not what he means, Clew. Defending yourself when you're committing a robbery is not considered self-defense."

"But I didn't shoot nobody." Clew glanced toward the door, then to Oliver. "Tell him, Ollie. I was here in the mornin', when you left."

Oliver nodded. "That's right. You saddled Bravo for me."

"Sure. And I was right here when you came back."

"Yes," Adam said, "but a whole lot happened in between there. You were the one who told Oliver that he was suspected of robbing the stage."

"Well, yes, I admit that. I didn't want to see the boy get hurt."

Adam nodded. "I understand that—if you had nothing to do with it. But think about this, Clew: Wouldn't a guilty person try to throw suspicion on someone else?"

"Hold on just a minute there." Clew drew back as if he was about to swing at Adam.

Oliver leaped to grab his arm and hold him back. "Easy, Clew. Just tell us how it was."

The old man glared at Adam, and his breath came in short, shallow gulps. At last he shook Oliver off.

"All right, here's what happened that day. I went about my business. Ollie left on that paint horse of his. I made myself a pot of coffee along about midmorning, and then all—" He glanced at Julia, cleared his throat, and said, "Then things got crazy around here."

"How did you first hear about the robbery?" Adam asked.

"It was when you rode out here, Sheriff. I heared some of the other men talking about it. They said the stage was held up and our payroll got stolen. And Bub Hilliard was shot dead." Clew nodded firmly. "That's what I heard. It was all over the offices. I went in to do some sweepin' in there, and that's all I heard, wherever I turned. Folks was wantin' to know where Ollie was and why he wasn't at his desk for two or three hours past."

"What did you do?" Adam said.

"I kept on working. After a while, I went out to the guardhouse again. At dinnertime, some of the men from the office came out to get their horses so they could ride into Ardell, so I got 'em ready. That's when I heard them sayin' right out that they bet Ollie was the robber. Well, lookee here, mister, I ain't goin' to put up with that, no sir." Clew glared at Adam. "I stayed around here, watching for Oliver. And when he come back, I told him he was in a bad place for sure. That he'd better lie low until this thing blew over."

"And I appreciate it," Oliver said.

Adam nodded, but his expression looked a little pained. "I hear you, Clew, I really do, but see, there's a couple of things that I don't understand."

Julia decided Adam was trying to keep Clew from getting mad so he'd keep talking. Maybe he'd had some training for being a sheriff's deputy, or even back with the Rangers, that taught him how best to question a suspect.

"Now, you can see how it looks, can't you, Clew?" Adam said. "You were the one who told Oliver he was suspected of the robbery. And that's why Oliver ran away and hid—based only on what you told him."

"But it was the truth," Clew said with a stubborn jerk of his chin. "I truly believed Ollie was in danger. Not just from you, but the people in town was all het up. I couldn't stand by and see the boy get railroaded for something he didn't do."

"That's very loyal of you," Adam said.

Oliver nodded. "I consider you a true friend, Clew. You did a lot for me."

"Well, thanks," Clew said, "but the sheriff here don't sound like he believes me."

Adam winced. "Well, there's a couple of other things. See, when you were out here puttering around the stable, nobody else saw you, so no one can vouch for where you were during the robbery. And then there's this." He pulled the matchbook out of his pocket and held it out. "Do you recognize this?"

Clew looked down at it. His mouth twitched, making his whole beard tremble.

Julia wanted to reassure the old man, but she held her ground. What did she really know about Clew, anyway? And if she ruled him out as a suspect, who was left?

"That looks like a matchbook Ollie gave me," Clew said.

"And where is that now?" Adam asked. "Do you still have it?"

Clew patted his pockets and stared toward the doorway, his face grim. "I guess I musta lost it."

Adam put away the matchbook. "In that case, I'm sorry to have to do this, but you're under arrest. I'm going to take you back to the—"

"Maybe it's in my coat." Clew strode toward the wall where a coat hung on a peg amid bridles and tools.

"Hold it, Clew." Adam drew his revolver. "Stop right there."

Clew turned halfway around. His eyes widened in surprise. "You're pulling iron on me?"

"Take it easy. Just put your hands up."

Clew stuck both hands in the air, palms out. Oliver stirred uneasily but said nothing.

Adam said, "Julia, you go over and get Clew's coat. Turn out the pockets and see if you find anything."

Julia threw an apologetic glance at Oliver and walked past Clew to the wall. She lifted down the corduroy jacket hanging there. It was none too clean. A button was missing, and the cuffs were frayed. She thrust her hand into the right pocket and came out with a crumpled bandanna. She grimaced and shoved it back in. In the other pocket, her hand closed on something square. She pulled it out and opened her hand.

"Arizona, the forty-eighth state. It sure looks like the other one." She carried it over and handed it to Adam.

He stared down at it as though he couldn't believe his own eyes. Slowly he holstered his revolver and took out the matchbook he'd shown them earlier. He held them up side by side. They appeared to be identical.

"That's the one Oliver gave me," Clew said, gesturing toward the matchbook Julia had handed over then self-consciously returning his hands to their upward position.

Adam opened the matchbook from the robbery site. Only three of the paper matches were left. He closed it and opened Clew's book. A whole row remained.

"You didn't use many matches," he said.

Clew shrugged. "I used a few to light the fire. I'm sorry I didn't give it back, Oliver."

"Don't worry about it," Oliver said. "I don't think I told you to. It really didn't matter."

Adam looked exhausted. His whole face wilted. His shoulders slumped as he glanced at Clew, who still stood with his hands raised.

"You can put your hands down. And I'm sorry. I had to make sure."

Clew lowered his arms. "I understand."

Julia shivered and held out the jacket to Clew. "You'd better put this on. It's getting chilly, and you must feel it, now that you're not working."

"Thank you." Clew took it and shrugged into it.

"Why don't you come to supper at our house tonight," she said, casting a belated glance of question toward Oliver.

"Yeah, you do that," Oliver said. "If Julia and I aren't in jail."

Julia arched her eyebrows at Adam.

"I'll tell the folks you're innocent, Oliver," Adam said. "And. . . I'm truly sorry."

"Not your fault," Oliver said.

"Yes, it was. I got things all turned around in my mind, and—well, I don't like that. I should have trusted you. You, too, Julia." His eyes crinkled.

Julia wasn't sure she could trust her voice. And she didn't know as she should trust Adam either. His error in judgment had obviously upset him. He'd apologized last night. He'd even said he loved her—had loved her all this time. But that was when he'd seen that Clew might be the guilty party. What now? If he couldn't find the real killer, would his suspicion fall on her and Oliver again?

Part of her wanted to tear into him again, but another part of her wanted to hold him and comfort him. Until she reconciled those two parts, she'd better tread softly.

"Come on," she said to Oliver. "Let's go get the horses."

Chapter 13

As soon as Julia and Oliver headed down the trail to where they'd left their mounts, Adam had one of those feelings. What if they took their horses and rode off?

That was crazy, and he knew it. He looked at Clew Harrison. "I need to see if Mr. Gerry's in his office. Will you stay here while I'm inside, and tell Oliver and Julia where I am when they get back?"

"Sure," Clew said. "I've still got a few horses to tend."

Adam went into the headquarters building. A young man sat at the desk inside the front door.

"May I help you, Sheriff?"

"Thanks. I'd like to see Mr. Gerry."

"Just one moment, please."

The young man disappeared through a doorway and came back a minute later. Right behind him was Gerry. He held out his hand as he advanced toward Adam.

"Sheriff Scott! Glad you're back. I heard you were in pursuit of the stagecoach robber. What's the word?"

Adam shook Gerry's hand and stepped back. "I'm still looking for the outlaw. I wanted to ask you, sir, if anyone else besides Oliver Newman was absent from the mine on that day."

"Well, I— What do you mean? Have you not found Oliver?"

"I found him," Adam said. "And I think he's innocent. So now I have to look at who else could have committed the crime."

Gerry frowned. "I'm glad to hear that you found him—and that he didn't do it, of course. I've been worried about that young man. Where is he now?"

"He'll be traveling with me back to Ardell," Adam said. "I imagine he'll return to work soon. I wanted to stop in here and see you and assure you that it's all right to let him do that. But I also need to know if any other mine personnel were unaccounted for on the day of the robbery." Adam smiled and hoped it looked sincere. "Let's start with you, sir. Where were you that morning?"

Gerry's eyes narrowed. "Why, right here. What's your meaning, Sheriff?"

"I'm just trying to establish the whereabouts of people concerned in this matter. Other than Bub Hilliard, you lost the most in that robbery. I'm told all the money in the treasure box on the stagecoach belonged to the mine. So I'm asking you and some of your other associates, where were you when the robbery occurred?"

Gerry stared at him. "I can't believe this. Is this a game to you?"

"Just play along with me, sir," Adam said.

After a tense moment, Gerry shook his head. "All right. I believe I was right here all morning. You can ask Mr. Denham at the desk in the entry. He schedules appointments for me and makes note of visitors who come in to see me. At lunchtime, I went home and ate with my wife. That was shortly before you came here."

"Thank you," Adam said. "I'll speak to Mr. Denham."

He went out to the entry. To his surprise, he found Oliver, Julia, and Clew inside. Oliver was leaning over Denham's desk, talking to him.

"I thought you were waiting at the stable," he said to Oliver.

"I wanted the mine people to know I'm all right."

Adam frowned but could think of no reason to protest. "Mr. Denham, could you please check your records for me? On the day of the robbery, was Mr. Gerry here all morning? And if so, did he have any visitors?"

Denham paged through a book of lined paper on his desk. "It appears that he was, sir. He met with Mr. Cosgrove that morning, as is customary on Mondays, and after that he worked in his office.

He didn't have any visitors until after noon, and that would be you, sir. And a Mr. Brink, who came in from Flagstaff on the stagecoach that day."

"Thank you. And what about you?"

Denham blinked at him. "Me, sir?"

"Yes. Were you here all day?"

"Oh yes, sir. I ate dinner at my desk. Mr. Gerry took his usual hour to go home, though."

"Very good." Adam turned to the others. "Let's go into town. I can come back tomorrow and question the rest of the mine's personnel if I need to. We don't want to ride into town after dark."

They walked outside, and Adam squinted against the bright sunlight.

"So that pretty much clears Mr. Gerry," Oliver said.

"Are you sure?" Julia asked.

Her brother shrugged. "Well, yeah. Denham keeps track of everyone who comes into the building—visitors, I mean. It's not like he cares whether I'm there every minute, but if anyone who doesn't work there comes in, he writes it down. And I'd say he's pretty aware of Mr. Gerry's presence all the time. And everyone who works there sees Denham when they go in and out, so in that sense, we all vouch for him. He was there when I left. He was there when Adam came to see the boss. Half a dozen other men who work in that building can tell you he was there when they walked through the entrance, too."

"And yet you left, and he had no idea you weren't in your little chicken coop of an office," Adam said.

"Well, like I said, he doesn't have to know where I am every minute. No one does."

"And the fact that they were all surprised that you weren't in the building tells me that anyone who works there—at least the management chaps—could most likely slip out for an hour or two and not be missed. You stayed away longer, and that's what made it remarkable." Adam sighed, feeling rather useless. "Let's go."

"Sheriff, it's almost my time to quit work for the day," Clew said. "What do you want me to do this evening?"

"Do what you normally would, Clew. Just don't plan any out-of-town trips without telling me, all right?"

"You got it."

"Thank you for all your help," Julia told the old man.

"T'weren't nothin'. You still want me to come for supper?"

"Sure," Oliver said. "Come with us now if you're able."

Clew grinned at him. "Kin you wait just a minute? I'll get Ol' Blackie."

The others mounted and waited while the old man hurried to the corral for his horse. He was ready in just a couple of minutes.

"You know," Julia said as they guided their horses toward the road that led to Ardell, "you had that notion about me possibly helping the robber—"

"Forget that," Adam said quickly. The last thing he wanted was for her to bring that up and start fussing at him again.

"No, listen to me." Julia moved her horse up beside Socks. "The idea of an accomplice inside the stage isn't so very crazy. What if one of the other passengers was there for that purpose? If things got too dangerous, he could make himself known and keep the rest of us in line while his partner got away with the money. But the man outside had the situation in hand, so he didn't make a move."

Adam frowned at her. "You mean Hinze or Chesley, or that guy visiting Mr. Gerry? Brink—was that his name?"

"Any one of them could have been in on it," she said. "You fixed on me because you thought the man outside was Oliver. But what if you'd thought he was Denham, from the mine's headquarters? In that case, I suspect you'd have looked harder at either Chesley or Brink, because they're both connected to the mine."

Adam let that sink in.

"She's right," Oliver said, from his other side. "And if the robber was a ranch hand, you'd have suspected Ike Hinze."

"I can talk to them again, but I doubt I can get any more out of them than I did before."

"It would probably be a good idea to ask a few more questions," Oliver said. "For instance, did you ask Chesley why he was on the stage and not working in the mine that day?"

"Well, no." Adam felt about as low as a horseshoe nail.

Oliver grinned at him. "I can tell you."

Adam reined in his horse. "You can?"

"Sure. It was payroll day, remember? I had to add up every man's hours for the month. I remember that Joe Chesley's pay was docked because he'd been out for six days."

"What for?" Julia asked. "He looked healthy, though he slept most of the way from Flagstaff."

"His sister died. He'd been to the funeral. But he doesn't get paid for his time away."

"Huh," Adam said. "Well, he wasn't even armed, so I didn't really think he was in on the holdup."

"How do you know that?" Julia asked. "Just because he didn't pull out a gun doesn't mean he didn't have one."

"Well, that's true, but. . ."

"Did you search him?" she asked.

"No, I didn't search anybody."

"Maybe you should have."

Julia was starting to sound belligerent again, and Adam didn't like that.

"Calm down," Oliver said. "He had no reason to search any of you. Jules, you and Brink and Hinze all admitted you had guns, and each of you could testify that the other two had them. Adam wouldn't need to search you to know you were armed. If he'd had any indication that Chesley was involved, I'm sure he would have searched him, or at least questioned him more closely."

"All right," Adam said. "I admit I didn't do a very good job on the investigation that first day. Let's get into town."

They rode along in silence for about ten minutes. As they approached the outskirts of Ardell, Julia piped up again.

"I don't see how you can figure out who did it. There are too many people who can't prove where they were."

"You don't have to look at everybody," Oliver said.

"Don't I?" Adam asked. "I don't want to make the mistake I made before."

"No, but look at all the clues. Maybe talk to Chick again about what the robber looked like. Did he really look like me? Was he the same height and weight? What about the way he walked, or his voice? Were they like mine?"

"There's the matchbook, too," Julia said.

Adam gritted his teeth. "Let's face it—there's no proof the matchbook has anything to do with it."

"You said you found it right beside where the treasure box landed," Oliver reminded him. "It's pretty unlikely that it got there after the robbery, and if it had lain there too long, it wouldn't be in such good condition."

"Yeah," Julia said. "Maybe you should ask Chick and the other passengers if they've ever seen a matchbook like that. You could rule out one of them dropping it while they were helping get Bub into the coach."

"That sounds reasonable," Adam said. "Thanks." They were coming up on Main Street, and he thought about what he would say to the people. He'd promised to tell them that Oliver was innocent. He was firmly convinced now that Julia had nothing to do with the robbery, and that she arrived the day of the robbery purely by coincidence. But was he a hundred percent sure that Oliver wasn't in on it? He might be suggesting other people who could be guilty in order to throw suspicion off himself. Adam didn't like even the shadow of the thought. And yet, the question remained: If Oliver wasn't guilty of the crime, who was?

He felt drained, unwilling to again cast his best friend in the role of a thief and murderer, but too exhausted to work out an alternative tonight. Tomorrow he would follow up on the possibilities they'd talked about, and maybe put his doubts to rest. A good night's sleep was what he needed, and then he'd be ready to deal with this.

The chance of heading to bed early disappeared as soon as they reached the end of Main Street. Lucas Morley spotted them and yelled, loud enough for it to echo off the mountainside, "Sheriff! You brought him in!"

Folks began to stare, and soon shoppers were pouring out of businesses and gathering along the edge of the street. People who'd gone into their houses for supper came out to gawk at them. By the time they reached the jail, half the town seemed to be crowding them. Adam kept Socks close to Oliver's horse, and Julia and Clew followed close behind.

"Sheriff, where'd you find him?" somebody yelled.

"Why h'ain't you got him tied up?"

"Hey, we was wondering where Miss Julia got to. What's going on, Adam?"

Adam was going to ignore them all, but when somebody shouted, "When we gonna string that killer up?" he knew he couldn't do that. Julia's face was pinched, and she looked pale for a woman who'd spent the last two or three days out in the sun.

He leaned toward Oliver and said over the hubbub, "You and Julia get inside my office. I'll disperse the crowd."

He hoped he sounded more confident than he felt. Sam Dennis worked his way through the spectators and came to stand beside Socks.

"You need any help, Sheriff?"

"Thanks, Sam. Maybe you can help these three get inside and make sure they don't come to harm while I talk to the people."

"Sure," Sam said. "I can guard the prisoners for you."

Adam didn't try to correct his assumption. Sam was already at Julia's side, offering her a hand down. Adam watched long enough to make sure Oliver got to the ground and up the steps to the sheriff's office in one piece. Then he turned Socks around and faced the crowd.

"Settle down, folks." Most of them calmed down and waited for him to speak again. From his vantage point on Socks's back, he watched their faces. These people were angry. Some of them registered fear or frustration. Mostly they looked ready to tear someone limb from limb.

He glanced over his shoulder at the door to his office and the jail. Sam was leaning in the doorway, his hand hovering near the butt of his pistol. Oliver, Clew, and Julia had disappeared, apparently safe inside. It struck Adam how many of the men in the crowd were wearing sidearms. Normally you might see two or three walking around Ardell armed, but now nearly every man wore or carried a weapon. The robbery had done this to them.

"We don't need to wait for any judge, Sheriff Scott," called the owner of the Red Bear saloon.

"That's right," said somebody else on the fringe of the mob. "We can hoist Newman right now and be done with it."

"I got a rope in my wagon," said one of the ranchers.

"Did his sister try to help him escape?" came from another quarter—Adam was surprised that a woman said it.

He held up his hands. "Hold it, folks. Just calm down and hear me out."

The faces were stony hard, grotesque in their rage. If he had to, he'd lock the Newmans up overnight for safety. Sam would help him, but how many other people in this town were interested in finding out the truth? Most of them seemed to want vengeance, and they weren't too picky about justice.

"It's true I went after Oliver Newman, and I found him. I've heard his story, and I've compared it to the evidence I have. And frankly, I don't think he's our man. Now, I'm going inside to tend to business. If anybody's got any new evidence since I left town on Tuesday, you can come around and talk to me. But I'm not charging anyone with the crimes that took place on Monday until I've had a chance to sort through everything. Is that clear?"

The replies were mostly disgruntled mutterings. A few more men yelled comments.

"You know he's guilty, Sheriff."

"Why are you protecting him? He killed Bub Hilliard."

He recognized that speaker—Lucas Morley, the mercantile's owner.

"Now, Lucas, you can't know that. If you've got some evidence, like I said, bring it to me. But Oliver Newman has not been proven guilty of any crime. So quit that talk."

"Are you holding him for the judge?"

"If the evidence calls for it, I will hold him. But if it doesn't, then he'll go free. And I expect him to be able to walk these streets safely."

Adam dismounted, secured Socks to the hitching rail, and

checked the others' horses. A few people shuffled away, and he hoped they would all go about their business. Maybe if he wasn't there for them to heckle, the rest would leave.

"You all right to stand here a few more minutes, Sam?" he asked the livery owner.

Sam nodded. "Take your time, Sheriff. I'll yell if I need ya."

Adam went inside and shut the door.

Julia waited impatiently with Oliver and Clew. She hadn't seen the inside of the jail for two years. When Adam first took the job, she'd been over here a couple of times. During her absence, he hadn't added a thing to his office, unless it was an extra stool and new wanted posters. His desk and chair, with a small woodstove and a couple of shelves, completed the spartan furnishings. A doorway opened on the back room, where Adam lived now, according to Oliver's letters. He used to live with his uncle after his father's death, but apparently he wanted to stay closer to his work now. The cell held two narrow cots with straw ticks, quilts, and pillows. A washstand with a metal basin, pitcher, and cup stood near the far wall, with a galvanized bucket beside it.

She turned her back to the cell door, determined to forget where she was. Adam had better take care of this mess, and fast.

The door opened, and he walked in scowling. She could still hear people talking outside, and through the one small window, horses and pedestrians were visible, milling about.

"Why don't they just go home?" she asked.

"They're not satisfied." Adam took his hat off. He walked over to his desk and tossed the hat on it. With a weary sigh, he sank into his chair. "They think there's still a killer running around loose."

"Isn't there?"

"They think I'm it," Oliver said, and Adam didn't deny it.

"Them people are plumb crazy," Clew said.

"Maybe so, but I think you ought to stay here tonight," Adam said, eyeing Julia warily.

"Is that necessary?" Oliver asked.

"If you go home, I'd have to place a guard around your house."

"Well, in that case," Clew said, "I'm going to go get me some grub, and then I'm going home. I suggest you folks sleep on it, and mebbe tomorrow you'll think of something else, Sheriff." He stepped toward the door.

Adam sat straighter in his chair. "Don't you go far, Clew. I may need to talk to you again."

The old man looked back at him. "Sure thing. You know where my cabin is?"

"I do."

Clew nodded. "Reckon I'll stop at the Red Bear for some supper, and after that I'll be at home." He opened the door. "Howdy, Sam."

Dennis said something, and more voices could be heard, raised in comments that Julia couldn't distinguish. Clew backed into the room and shut the door.

"Sheriff, it don't look too good out there."

Adam got up and went to the window. "You're right. If anything, there's more people out there now than there were when I came in." He turned and eyed Julia and Oliver thoughtfully. "I'm sorry, but I think it would be best if I lock the two of you up for tonight—for your own safety. And that way, folks might settle down, knowing I had someone behind bars."

Julia caught her breath. "You said you believed us."

Adam hesitated then said, "I do. But I don't want folks bothering you in the night, and I don't want to see this crowd moving over to your house. Could you sleep with them outside, yelling that Oliver should be lynched?"

Julia gulped. "No."

Oliver said, "Guess not. But are you going to charge me with the robbery and shooting Bub?"

"No," Adam said firmly. "Unless more evidence is found, I'm not arresting you again. That was. . . Well, all right, I admit it. I made a big mistake out there, and I'm sorry. You'll have to trust me, Oliver. As a friend."

Julia could tell from the strained expression on Adam's face that he was struggling. He was right, they did have to trust him. And right now, she had more faith in him than she did in the fickle people of Ardell.

A shout from outside pierced the walls. "Sheriff, we want to talk to you."

Adam looked toward the door. "Sounds like I'll have to go out there again."

The door opened a foot, and Sam Dennis stuck his head in. "Adam, things are getting a little dicey out here, but Bob Tanner's come to help out."

"Good. I'll be out in a minute. Tell the people to hold on." When Sam shut the door, Adam turned back to Oliver. "I'm sorry it's this way, but I think you're better off in the cell."

"Bob Tanner," Julia said. "Isn't he the barber?"

"Yes. He rode with me the day of the robbery. He's a good fellow."

She nodded. "Will he and Sam be enough to help you keep the peace?"

"I don't know, Julia. I wish I did, but I can't predict what will happen."

What they did was up to her. Gazing at Adam, she made her decision. She walked over to the cell, and the door swung open at her touch. "Come on, Oliver. Adam is right. We're safer in here." She stepped inside and faced her brother.

Slowly, Oliver walked over and entered the cell.

"I promise you, I will do everything humanly possible to keep you safe," Adam said.

Oliver nodded, but his teeth were clenched and his face pale.

Julia put her arm around him. "It's going to be all right."

"Well, I'm not going in there," Clew said. "Nobody's mad at me."

"You don't have to," Adam said. "You can probably get through the crowd with no problem."

"All right, then." Clew paused. "Do you want me to come back and help you hold this place down, Sheriff?"

"Only if you want to, Clew. Go get something to eat."

Clew glanced at Julia and Oliver. "Good night, kids."

" 'Bye, Clew," Julia said, "and thank you."

When he'd slipped out the door, Adam came over and closed the cell door. "If you need anything, just say so. I'll stay here all night. If Bob and Sam want to stay, I'll be happy to have their company. But right now, I've got to go out there and convince the good people of this town to go home and stay there." He put the key in the lock.

"Hold it," Oliver said. "What if we need to get out?"

"You mean, like a trip to the outhouse?" Adam asked.

Oliver winced. "I was thinking more of someone touching a match to this place."

Julia caught her breath. She hadn't considered anything like that happening. They'd be trapped if it did.

"Don't worry," Adam said. "I've got two stout men now. We'll keep a good watch on the building."

"Adam," Julia said, before he could turn away.

"Yeah?"

"I'll be praying."

Adam looked deep into her eyes, and Julia felt the same flutter in her stomach that she'd felt last night when he held her outside the cave. Did he really love her? She wanted to believe that. And that he had Oliver's best interest at heart.

"Thanks," he said. "I'll pray, too." He turned the key in the lock of the cell door and nodded at them. "Just to keep out anyone who gets past me."

❧

Julia walked over to one of the cots and sat down. Oliver hovered near the door, until she said, "Come over here. Let's pray together."

He slowly walked to her bed and sat gingerly on the edge. "Think this thing will hold both of us?"

"Oh, I imagine Adam gets some pretty husky prisoners in here. Rowdy ones, too. He needs sturdy furnishings."

"Guess you're right." Oliver swallowed hard and rubbed his hands on his knees. "Are you scared, Jules?"

"Yes, in a way. If some of those men get liquored up, we may have some fireworks tonight."

"I wish we'd stayed at the Diné village."

"Well, it's too late to think about that." She patted his arm. "It's going to be all right."

"I hope so."

"Where's your gun?"

Oliver grimaced. "Adam's got it, I guess."

"Didn't he give it back when he untied you last night?"

"Nope. I didn't think of it. He's probably got it in his saddlebags."

"I saw your rifle in your room at home, but that won't do us any good."

"Yeah. Wish I'd taken it to the mine that day. I don't always take my revolver, but it was payroll day, so I had it along."

"That was a good thing," Julia said, "though I guess you didn't need it."

Oliver smiled. "I shot a snake on the way to Canyon Diablo. But I didn't figure I'd need a rifle on Diné land, and if I ran into trouble on the way—well, I don't know what I thought. Just that it would be too dangerous to go home and get it."

Julia nodded. "That's understandable. My gun's right here." She pulled her small pistol from the pocket of her wool jacket. "Adam didn't search me or ask for it. You can take it, if it'll make you feel better."

"Do you really trust Adam?" He reached for the gun.

Julia bit her bottom lip and nodded. "I do. I think he's on our side now. But I don't trust the other people out there."

"What about Sam Dennis and Bob Tanner?" Oliver asked.

"I think they've picked sides, and they'll stand by Adam. But you know them better than I do."

Oliver went to his cot and stuck the pistol under his pillow. "I hope they'll stay loyal to him. Maybe we should do that praying." He sat down beside her.

Julia bowed her head. A moment later, Oliver's hand touched hers. She turned her hand over and clasped his fingers.

"Dear Lord," Oliver said, "thank You for bringing Julia home. Now please, if it's not too much trouble, could You get us out of this mess?"

Outside, the clamor of voices rose again, and Julia could barely hear her brother's quiet petitions.

Chapter 14

"Listen to me," Adam yelled, but the men standing in the street continued to shout at him and each other.

"Lemme try," Sam Dennis said.

Before Adam quite understood his intent, Sam fired off a round from his revolver. A woman screamed, and then silence ruled the street.

"That's more like it," Sam said, returning his gun to his holster.

"People, please calm down," Adam said, before they could start up again. "I told you, I'm investigating every avenue I can on the robbery and the murder of Bub Hilliard."

"You wasn't even here for his funeral, Scott," Lucas Morley called.

"That's because I was tracking down a suspect." Adam's patience had worn thin, and he'd had about enough, but he couldn't go inside again and leave them seething out here.

"You've got him now, so let's get on with it," called one of the miners.

Adam realized with a start that the crowd had swelled as the mining crews finished their work for the day. A couple dozen men appeared to have come into town for some refreshment and found a near riot instead. If they went to the saloons and then came back to the jail, he was in trouble.

"Folks, I want to make it clear that while Oliver Newman is in my custody, he is not under arrest. I have no evidence to charge him with these crimes. So I'd appreciate it if you'd—"

"How come you've got him in the jail if he's innocent?" rancher Gib Weston yelled.

"Yeah," several others chorused.

Adam put his hands on his hips and surveyed them with mingled disgust and rage. "You have to ask me that? Look at you! I don't dare let Oliver go while you're all so worked up. I don't want another murder on my hands, you hear me? Let me do my job and find the man who shot Bub Hilliard. Go on home, now."

Bob Tanner stepped up beside him, holding his rifle up where all could see it. "The sheriff's right. You all are taking on like a bunch of five-year-olds. Now get out of here."

The people in the crowd lingered, eyeing them uncertainly.

Sam Dennis came up on Adam's other side. "Look, we don't know if Oliver Newman and his sister are guilty or not, but Bob and I are going to help the sheriff protect the prisoners."

"They're *not* prisoners," Adam said with an apprehensive glance Sam's way. "Folks, go home. Please. Let us handle this."

A man at the front of the crowd turned to his friend. "Come on, Chub, let's get over to the Red Bear. This ain't going nowhere."

"Thank you," Adam called after them.

"And don't come back," Tanner yelled.

The crowd began to thin, and Adam let out a deep sigh. "Thank you, fellas. You've got to understand, I locked the Newmans in the jail only for their safety. They are not under arrest, and no charges have been brought against them."

"Got it, Sheriff," Bob said.

"You want me to have Peewee take your horses up to the stable?" Sam asked.

Adam smiled. "Peewee" was Sam's son, and he was half again as big as Sam. "That would be a big help. Thanks. But my bay can go out back in my corral."

"We'll take care of it," Sam said.

"Now what do you want the two of us to do?" Bob asked.

"Well, if you don't mind, I'd like you to stay right here for at least a half hour, until we're sure those people aren't going to come back and work mischief. If all's quiet then, you could take turns going to get some supper, and maybe bring something back for Oliver and Miss Julia."

"What about you, Adam?" Sam asked.

"I'll get something eventually. Right now I'm going to take a turn around the building, and then I want to talk to the other passengers again. Ike Hinze and Joe Chesley, and that mining fella who came in on the stage to see Mr. Gerry. Then, if everything's quiet, I'll try to get some sleep."

"I saw Ike a few minutes ago," Tanner said. "He'd probably come help us if you wanted, though he's got a family out at the ranch to think of."

"Thanks," Adam said. "I'd like to catch up to him before he leaves town."

"Try the Gold Strike."

"Will do." The Gold Strike was another of Ardell's flourishing saloons, and the ranchers seemed to prefer that one, while a lot of the miners favored the Red Bear. Adam supposed it was time he let his presence be felt in all the saloons—he'd let the town alone for several nights in a row. He wasn't too keen on facing the erstwhile lynch mob, though.

He recalled the story about Canyon Diablo in its heyday. The first lawman there, when Hell Street was home to numerous saloons, gambling dens, and dance pavilions, had served a short time. He'd been sworn in at three in the afternoon and laid out for burial at eight o'clock. Ardell had never been as wild as Canyon Diablo had been in the 1880s, but even so, Adam paused at the bottom of the steps to the Gold Strike.

If You want me to find the killer, Lord, You're going to have to make sure I live through this night.

He squared his shoulders and walked in.

❧

“Are you awake?”

Oliver’s voice was quiet in the darkness. Julia turned her head toward his cot on the other side of the cell.

“Yes. I haven’t been to sleep.”

“Me either. I’m sorry, Jules.”

“For what? You didn’t do anything.” She rolled up on her side, but her brother was still just a dark lump under the blanket over there. The pale square of the window, striped by bars, didn’t help much.

“I shouldn’t have run off like that. Clew got me all scared, and I couldn’t see how it would look if I hid. I just thought I needed to keep my head down.”

“I know, and it’s all right.”

“But Adam lost three whole days looking for me, when he should have been investigating here in town. By now the robber is probably in Mexico.”

“More likely in some saloon in Flagstaff,” Julia said. “I’m the one who messed things up. I should have been nicer to Adam, but he made me furious.”

“He went by what he saw. I guess I *did* look suspicious. I acted like a guilty man.” Oliver stirred. “It’s quiet outside now. Maybe we can go home in the morning.”

“I hope so.”

“Jules?”

“Yeah?”

“You don’t hate Adam, do you?”

She rolled over on her side and squinted, but she still couldn’t see him.

"I don't hate him."

"Good."

She probably ought to say more, but how could she explain her tangled feelings about Adam? She'd done her best to shut him out of her heart, but he kept finding crevices and seeping in. If they got through this quagmire, and Adam didn't get himself killed, could she let her love for him grow again?

The door to the building opened softly. Julia tensed and peered into the darkness of the sheriff's office beyond the front bars of the cell.

"That you, Adam?" Oliver said.

"Yeah, it's me. Didn't mean to wake you up."

"We're not sleeping." Oliver's cot creaked.

Julia sat up and swung her legs over the side of her bed. "What's going on out there?"

"It's pretty quiet. The saloons are still open of course, and there's some card games going. It's about normal for this time of night."

"Are Sam and Bob still out there?" Oliver asked.

"Bob and Ike Hinze. I caught up with Ike down the street, and he offered to stay in town tonight and help us out. I sent Sam home and told him to come back at 2:00 a.m. If it's still quiet then, I'll let Bob go sleep until daylight."

"Did you talk to Ike about the robber?" Oliver asked.

"Yes, but he still says he didn't see him. He wasn't sure about the voice, either. Said it sounded a bit raspy, but it could have been anyone."

"That's not helpful," Julia said. Any man trying to disguise his voice might sound "a bit raspy."

Adam stood just outside the bars and peered in at them. "Well, I found Joe Chesley, too. He was even less helpful. But I can't say there was anything about either of them to make them look suspicious. Oh, and Chesley says he doesn't own a sidearm."

"How about the fellow in the suit—Brink?" Julia asked. "He had one, and he looked like he wouldn't hesitate to use it if he had to."

Adam shook his head. "He left yesterday. Stayed at the Placer two nights and took the stage back to Flagstaff. But Mr. Whitaker at the hotel said he went out to the mine twice, and he seemed like the genuine article. I can check with Leland Gerry again tomorrow and ask him what they talked about, but I don't think he's mixed up in the robbery."

"And Mr. Gerry's out of it," Julia said.

"Yes. I'm fairly certain of that. By the time he left for lunch, the robbery was already under way."

Julia let out a long sigh. Adam's investigation would have to look further afield. "Are you going to turn in?"

"Yeah, I've got a cot in the back room. I hope you both can rest."

Footsteps and rustling sounds followed. Julia thought he must have stopped by his desk.

"You can light the lantern if you want to," Oliver said.

"No need. And it might bring folks around again."

"What's the plan for morning?" Oliver asked. "Are you going out to the mine again first thing?"

"I reckon I'll go back down to where the robbery happened," Adam said. "I'll look around again, but I doubt I'll find anything I didn't find before."

"I looked, too, that first day," Julia said. "I didn't see anything either, except a mark where the box fell and an old whiskey bottle."

"Adam?" Oliver said.

"Yeah?"

"Maybe we could all pray together."

Julia held her breath. She wouldn't have had the courage to

suggest that. If Adam wouldn't pray with them, did it mean he still didn't completely trust them?

After a long moment, he walked over to the cell door. He struck a match, and it flared up, too bright in the darkness. Julia squeezed her eyes shut and turned away, but she could still see the orange burst for several seconds. During that time, Adam's keys jingled, and the lock turned.

"Come over here, Jules," Oliver said. She shoved her bedding aside and stood unsteadily, orienting herself to the window and the noise Adam made as he opened the door and entered the cell.

She took several hesitant steps with her arms extended in front of her. The cell wasn't very big, but it surprised her how long it took her to find Oliver.

"Hey," he said softly, and she touched his arm. He grasped her hand and pulled her down on the cot beside him. "C'mon over, Adam."

A moment later, he settled on the floor close to them. Julia took a deep breath. Adam had left the cell door open. If he thought they might overpower him and escape, he wouldn't have done that. It was a small concession, especially since two armed men still stood outside the office door, but it calmed her.

"Let's pray," Oliver said.

She bowed her head and clung to her brother's hand. Oliver's voice was quiet and soothing, his words passionate.

"Lord, may justice be done. May the killer be found out. And may You be glorified. Amen."

"Amen," Julia whispered.

Adam's amen was firmer than her own, and she took an extra helping of comfort from that.

"You could go to our house and sleep," Oliver told him. "It'd be quieter there."

"No, I need to be here when I have someone in the cell. Sometimes I just sit up all night in my chair."

"You don't need to do that." Julia noted that he hadn't said when he had prisoners.

"Well, I told Bob I was going to try to catch forty winks. You'd best do the same."

Fatigue washed over Julia. She was a little sore, too, from all the riding she'd done in the past four days. She squeezed Oliver's hand and stood. "Good night. I think I can sleep now."

She lay awake a little longer, listening to the small noises the men made as they settled in for the night—Adam in his desk chair, she thought, although she wasn't certain. From a distance, she caught muffled strains of "Camptown Races" from one of the saloons' pianos and occasionally heard voices or hoofbeats as people and horses passed the jail.

Sometime later, she was jerked awake by a quiet screech she soon placed as the opening of the stove door. The night had fallen chilly, and Adam was building a fire as quietly as possible. The last thing she remembered was his intent face bent over the glow of his infant blaze while he fed in more kindling.

Adam awoke with a start when he heard voices outside the office door. He sat straighter in his chair with a grimace. He should have lain down. Sleeping slumped over your desk was even worse than sleeping on the ground.

Gray light came through the barred window behind him and the smaller one high on the cell wall. He clambered to his feet and went to the door. Sam Dennis was huddled in the doorframe outside, sitting on the top step with his shotgun cradled in his arms. He swiveled his head as the door moved behind him and glanced up at Adam with alert but weary eyes.

"Mornin', Sheriff."

"Mornin' yourself," Adam said. "Nice and quiet?"

"Yup. Lucas Morley just went by, but he was cordial."

Adam nodded and looked out over the town. People were just beginning to stir. Lamplight shone from a couple of windows, but most of Ardell was still dark.

"It's cold out here. You should have come in to get warm."

"I'm all right. I sent Ike home though."

Adam nodded. " 'Preciate your staying. I'll make some coffee."

A lone horseman came up the street, silhouetted dark against the graying sky.

"I reckon that's Bob, coming to relieve me," Sam said. He stood and stretched his wiry arms, shotgun and all.

"Whyn't you go get some breakfast?" Adam said. "If it's still peaceful when you get back, I'll go do the same."

"Awright. I was going to bring Peewee back this morning, but if folks have settled down, I guess we don't need him."

Adam tiptoed back inside and went about replenishing the stove and filling his enameled coffeepot. By the time he had it fixed, the stove was ticking and Julia was sitting up on her cot, peering at him in the twilight of dawn.

"Good morning," he said. With her face flushed from sleep and her hair tumbling willy-nilly about her shoulders, she was adorable, like a child never scarred by the world. "Would you like to. . . uh. . .freshen up?" He felt his own cheeks flush, and he turned back to the stove and checked the fire as an excuse not to look at her. Usually he left the prisoners in the cell with the bucket, but with a lady. . .and she wasn't really a prisoner.

"Yes, thank you." Julia tugged at her skirt and swung her feet over the edge of the bed. She reached down for her boots.

He sauntered to the cell door and turned the key. She looked at him and sat up quickly, tossing her hair back. Their gaze held for a moment, until Oliver rolled over and opened his eyes.

"Uh. . ." Adam's pulse was galloping, but he opened the door and said to Julia, "It's out back."

"I figured. Do I need an escort?"

He glanced toward the closed front door. "Well, Bob's sitting on the steps. Do you feel safe going out there alone? It's pretty quiet this morning."

"Yes, I feel perfectly safe."

He swallowed hard. He'd feel better if he or one of the others at least went around the building and watched her get safely to the privy and back, but he had a feeling Julia might resent that.

"All right."

"You want to carry this?" Oliver said.

She turned around, and Adam looked over at him. Oliver was holding up her pistol. Adam stared at it. She'd had that gun in her bedroll in the cave, but once they'd made peace, he hadn't given it another thought.

"Do you have a problem with that, Sheriff?" she asked.

"No. You're not a prisoner. I told you that before."

"Right. I'm sure you would have searched us both if we were prisoners." She smiled mischievously.

Adam stood stock still as she retrieved the gun, put it in her pocket, and walked over to the door. When she opened it, Bob Tanner said cordially, "Morning, Miss Newman."

"Hello," she said. "Excuse me, Mr. Tanner. I'll be back in a short while."

Bob poked his head in at the doorway. "Everything in order, Adam?"

"Everything's fine. I'll be going out for some breakfast soon if it's all the same to you."

"Sure thing." Bob shut the door.

"You knew we had the pistol, right?" Oliver asked.

"Of course." Adam walked to the shelf and took down his tin cup without looking at him.

"Don't feel bad about forgetting."

"A mistake like that could get me killed." Adam poured a half inch of pale liquid into the cup and tasted it. It was still cold water, with a few coffee grounds floating in it.

"I know," Oliver said. "Like Pa. But Julia did tell you she had a gun the other night."

"And I knew she wouldn't use it on me," Adam said.

"So it's not a problem."

Adam slammed the empty cup down on his desk. "But I forgot. What if you two were desperados?"

"Take it easy, Adam. We're not criminals. You let go of the thought because it wasn't important."

Adam shook his finger at Oliver through the cell bars. "Your sister has me wound up like a clock, pal. Not that it means anything, but I'm just sayin'."

"As if nobody could tell."

Adam blew out an exasperated breath and stalked around his desk. He plopped down in the chair. "I can't help it. I still love her, Ollie."

"Does she know that?"

"I told her at the cave."

"What'd she say?"

"Not much. She drives me nutty, but she's still the finest woman that ever breathed Arizona air, and I think—I *know*—she was the best thing that ever happened to me. I never should have let her go."

"You couldn't stop her. Not short of leaving off being a lawman."

Adam thought about that for a long time. He'd been thinking about it for more than two years. Sometimes he'd nearly convinced himself to quit his job. Those were times when he felt all soft toward Julia and willing to do anything to win her back. Other times he just got angry. Why should she expect him to give up the job he loved? To stop doing the thing that he believed in. Did he dare say that he felt God called him to be a lawman?

Where did that leave him after his horrendous blunder this week—accusing his best friend of robbery and murder, and tracking him down like a chicken-stealing coyote?

He'd already apologized twice to Oliver. Saying it again wouldn't help things. Still, Adam felt guilty and stupid. How could he ever think a fine man like Oliver was capable of such crimes? And how could he find out who really committed them?

"Think that coffee's hot?" Oliver asked.

"Maybe." Adam stood and went into the back room. He had another cup on the shelf in there. As he turned to it, he glanced at the stage line's treasure box. He might as well give that back to Chick. They'd need a new lock, though. The robber's bullet had ruined that. He stooped and lifted the lid so he could examine the damage. He froze for a moment, and his heart seemed to stop then kick and go on. He stared down into the box at several piles of neatly stacked paper money.

Chapter 15

Adam inhaled carefully. That money had *not* been in the box when he brought it here Monday afternoon. He picked up the wooden box and walked slowly into his office.

"Ollie—"

"Hmm?" Oliver still sat on his cot, pulling on his boots.

"You're not going to believe this. I don't believe it myself."

As he spoke, the door opened and Julia walked in. She eyed him with speculation in those cool, blue eyes.

"Is that the chest from the robbery?"

"Yes." Adam's throat was so dry he could barely croak the word out.

Oliver had come to the cell door and watched him warily. "What is it, Adam?"

"The money's in here."

"What?" Julia strode toward him and stared into the treasure box. "All of it?"

"I don't know."

Oliver pulled the barred door open and walked out of the cell. "Let me see."

Adam set the box on his desk. Julia and Oliver stood over it like statues, looking at the money.

"That box was empty when I brought it in here the day of the robbery," Adam said.

"You're sure?" Oliver looked up at him, then back at the money.

"Of course I'm sure. It was lying on the ground open, out where the holdup happened. I picked it up and brought it here. It was absolutely empty."

“So. . .someone put the money back while you were away,” Julia said. “Was this building locked?”

“No.”

“But why would the robber do that?”

Oliver scratched his head. “Maybe he felt guilty, because of Bub.”

“Or maybe the robber didn’t put it here.” Julia raised her chin and looked at Adam. “Maybe someone else found the loot and put it back.”

Adam sat down in his chair. “What do I do now?”

“I suggest you count the money,” Oliver said.

“Good idea.” Adam reached into the box and took out the stacks of bills. He lined them up on his desk. “Will you count it after I do, Oliver?”

“Sure.” Oliver glanced toward the stove. “I smell coffee.”

“Oh, there’s another cup in the back room.” Adam pushed his chair back. “I was going to get it when I found the money in the box.”

“I’ll get it,” Julia said. “You two start counting.”

Ten minutes later, the two men sat back.

“So we’re agreed,” Adam said. “It’s three thousand dollars even.”

“Yup. A little more than half what was taken.” Oliver stacked the bills on the desktop.

“So what do you do with it?” Julia asked.

“I guess we should give it back to Mr. Gerry.” Adam wondered if there was a reason not to do that. “There’s no proof this was actually part of the money from the robbery, though.”

“Where else could it have come from?” Julia asked.

Oliver tapped the stack of bills nearest him. “The paper bands have HDM on them. The bank does that to indicate it goes to High Desert Mine—just so there’s no mix-up when they’re getting it ready, I guess. But it always has that when we get the payroll.”

"Good to know." Adam rose. "I guess I should take it out to Mr. Gerry and tell him how I got it. Will you ride to the mine with me?"

Oliver looked at his sister. "Do you mind, Jules? It might be good to have Adam with me the first time I see Mr. Gerry again."

"All right," she said. "But Mr. Gerry won't be there this early. Let's go home, and I'll make some breakfast. You come, too, Adam."

"Well. . . I guess I can send Bob Tanner home. And we'd best take the money with us."

"Put it in something else," Julia said. "You don't want to march down Main Street carrying that treasure box."

"All right, but let's hurry before more people are out and about. I don't want too many folks to see Oliver out on the street."

A half hour later, Julia served Adam and her brother breakfast. She'd fried up some bacon and potatoes, and Oliver had scrounged a few eggs. Not a bad meal on short notice.

"I'll go up to the livery and get your horse after we eat," Adam told Oliver. "I don't want people seeing you walking around by yourself yet. Somebody might remember that they thought you should hang."

Oliver didn't refuse, so he and Julia waited at the house while Adam went for their mounts.

"Guess we should unpack our stuff from the trip," Oliver said.

"It's not much. Just let me look at you, Ollie. I've hardly had a chance to this whole time. You haven't told me about Mama yet, either. I want to know more about her illness. I'll unpack my bedroll and our saddlebags while you're gone to the mine."

They sat down in the front room, and she looked him over closely. His eyelids drooped from fatigue, but other than that, he looked good.

"Do you think the people will accept the fact that you're innocent, now that the money is back?" she asked.

"I don't know. And only part of it was returned, don't forget that." Oliver leaned his head back against the antimacassar their mother had crocheted. "What do you think really happened, Jules?"

"I can't imagine. And if we never find out, I may go insane thinking about it." They sat in silence for a moment. "Well, I hope no one comes here wanting to do you in," she added.

Oliver straightened, his eyes troubled. "Do you want to ride to the mine with us?"

"No, thank you. I've had more than enough riding this week." Julia stood and walked over to stand before him. "Come on. I feel grubbier than I did when I got off the train in Flagstaff. I want a bath and a nap. Help me bring in some water while you wait for Adam?"

"Sure," Oliver said as he rose.

"Great. And later, I want to sit down and talk to you. We've missed so much, it'll take us weeks to catch up."

"I don't know about that. Things were pretty quiet before you came home."

"Ha. Don't you start blaming it on me. But seriously, Ollie, I'd like to go to the cemetery later." Tears threatened, and she blinked them back. Being here with Oliver and working in her mother's kitchen brought her sense of loss to new depths.

"Sure. I'll go up there with you anytime."

She could tell from his gentle tone that he understood perfectly.

"Good. As soon as you're back from the mine, then."

"Good morning, Mr. Gerry. The deputy sheriff's got something for you."

Leland Gerry stared at Oliver as he entered the boss's office and jumped to his feet. "Newman! Good to see you." He glanced beyond Oliver toward Adam. "Sheriff, what's this about?"

Adam strode forward and plopped a plump flour sack on Gerry's desk. "Part of your payroll money was returned."

"What?" Gerry's jaw dropped. "I don't understand."

"Neither do I, sir, but this money showed up unannounced at the jail, and I figure it belongs to you. It's not all that was stolen, but it should help alleviate your loss. There's three thousand dollars there."

Gerry sat down with a quiet thud. "This is fantastical. Do you know who did it?"

"Nope. I aim to find out." Adam hauled in a deep breath. "Maybe you'd count it now, sir, and write me a note saying you received it."

A short time later, after Mr. Gerry accepted the cash and told Oliver he could take the rest of the day off, Adam and Oliver rode back into town. They stopped when they reached Main Street.

"Guess I'll see you later," Adam said. "I'm going to catch a nap. Then I plan to start questioning people again. What are you going to do?"

"Julia wants to visit Mama's grave."

Adam nodded. Poor Julia. Because of his skewed thinking, she'd wasted the last four days when she and Oliver could have been comforting each other.

"Come around for supper if you want," Oliver said.

"Thanks. I'm not sure Julie would want to feed me again."

"She didn't look mad this morning."

"No, but when she has time to think things over, she'll likely still hate me."

"She doesn't hate you. She told me so."

Adam pressed his lips together. That was something. "I'll think about it."

"Do that," Oliver said.

Adam rode to the jail. He put Socks away in his corral at the back and went inside for a quick look around the empty building. He peeked into the treasure box in the back room, to make sure it was still empty. Satisfied that no one had left him any more surprises, he went outside and stepped into the quiet street.

Ardell wasn't much of a town. It used to be bigger and wilder, in the mining heyday. Now the High Desert Mine was the only big operation in the area, and it had bought up most of the promising ground, or the mineral rights to it. The town served the employees of the mine, as well as ranchers in the hills, but mostly people bypassed it. Ardell had no railroad, and the electric lines and telephones hadn't made it up here yet.

He yawned and walked down the street toward the boardinghouse. Mrs. Edson would be fixing dinner for her boarders. Maybe he'd stop in there around noon and get some of her good cooking. Of course, young Doctor Browning boarded at her place now. Adam wouldn't want to run into his uncle's rival. He ambled toward the corner.

Everything seemed quiet, as it should in mid-September. People were going about their business. He hoped he could keep them from going off half-cocked again when they learned that part of the stolen money had been returned. Of course, they would still want the murderer caught.

A poster on the front door of the haberdashery caught his eye. Leland Gerry for Senator. Adam was glad he wasn't running against Gerry—or running for any office. Why had those men in Phoenix asked him to, anyway? Probably because he had a name most folks in the area would recognize. But that wasn't the sort of thing he was good at. Gerry would do fine. He knew how to talk to businessmen and lawyers. He would probably like going to Washington and promoting his causes, whereas that life would strangle Adam. Even having to stay in Phoenix for a few months at a time would stifle him. Meetings and confabs and sessions—that was all he'd be doing if he took a seat in the legislature.

Besides, who would vote for him? Right now the people of his own town wouldn't vote for Adam Scott. The fickle citizens of Ardell would probably fire him and run him off the mountain if he didn't catch the killer soon.

He'd taken the route past the saloons on his way to the boardinghouse. It wasn't the shortest way, but he had time to spare, and it wouldn't hurt to peek inside the saloons—they stayed open twenty-four hours a day—and see who was already half soused. Piano music trilled from the Gold Strike, and he turned his steps toward it.

Ten yards ahead of him, someone shoved the door of the saloon outward. His uncle staggered out onto the small porch. The top two buttons of his shirt were open and he had no tie or hat, things he would never have left his house without six months ago. He gazed about with a dazed expression as the cold air hit him.

Adam pulled up short. The sight hit him hard in the stomach. He'd known Uncle Royce had slipped and was drinking more than he should, but when had he sunk to this level of degradation? The older man lurched forward, fetched up against a porch post, and fumbled in his pockets. He took out his pipe and took his time filling it with shaky hands. Finally he had the tobacco in it and tamped down to his satisfaction and took out a book of matches. He tried to light one, but couldn't. The distinguished and highly respected Dr. Scott was too drunk to light his pipe.

Struggling with disgust, pity, and grief, Adam gazed at him. Pity won out as he realized he'd neglected him. Uncle Royce needed someone to help him out a little, to look out for him, and to keep him accountable. He didn't have that since Aunt Alma died, and his medical practice had shrunk to where he saw very few patients. The saloon was his social outlet now.

With a mild shock, Adam realized his uncle hadn't been to church in months, so far as he knew. He dropped in to see the old man now and then, and had taken him out to supper once or twice a month. Maybe he should have moved in with him again after Aunt Alma's death. He used to stay with them when he was in the Rangers. He'd had no other place to call home between patrols.

But Adam had enjoyed his freedom, and he hated confrontation. Criminals were one thing, but people he knew—well, that was another story. Uncle Royce didn't want any advice, and he certainly didn't want anyone telling him that he was drinking too much. Adam had tried that once, and it only made him mad. Of course, his uncle had had several glasses of whiskey at the time. Adam had tried to find a time when his uncle was sober to talk the matter over seriously with him, but he had to admit he hadn't tried overly hard. And somehow that time had never come.

The matchbook fluttered from Uncle Royce's hand to the porch floor. Adam strode forward and mounted the steps.

"Here, let me get that for you."

Uncle Royce grunted. "What—Adam? Thank you."

He didn't sound *too* drunk.

"Let me walk you home," Adam said, reaching for the matchbook. He picked it up and stared down at the cover. ARIZONA, THE FORTY-EIGHTH STATE.

He'd given Uncle Royce some of the matchbooks.

He caught his breath and looked at his uncle. Why hadn't he thought of that? Maybe he had, but he'd disregarded it because Uncle Royce was too old and unsteady to rob a stagecoach single-handed—wasn't he?

Julia tied the strings of her best Sunday bonnet. She wanted to look nice for her first visit to Mama's grave, and besides, she might very well see the minister. Oliver waited patiently. They'd both bathed, and Oliver had shaved. Her brother looked quite handsome. Julia wondered why he didn't have a sweetheart.

She'd have to have a heart-to-heart with him later. He'd written last year that he had his eye on someone, but then he'd dropped the subject. She'd asked what happened, and he'd closed the topic without really telling her anything. She wondered now if the girl he'd fancied had died or moved away—or turned him down, which would be every bit as tragic in her mind.

A knock drew Oliver to the front entrance. Julia picked up her gloves and put them on, watching as her brother opened the door to their caller.

Adam stood there, panting as though he'd been running and still rather disheveled.

"Come with me, Oliver. Julia, you, too. I need you to go down the road with me."

Julia stepped forward. "What for?"

Adam wiped his cuff across his brow. "We need to go back to the place where the stage was held up."

"Why?" Julia asked. Adam's urgency had her heart thudding.

"Oh. Sorry." He looked from one to the other of them. "It's just that I—I found a new clue, and I think there's evidence out there. But I need you to help me find it, Julia."

"Me?"

"Yes." Adam huffed out a breath and lowered his head, staring at the floor for a moment. "I've got Socks, and I stopped by the livery and told Sam and Peewee to saddle two horses for you, pronto."

Julia looked at Oliver. He was clearly as puzzled as she was.

"If this evidence has been out there all week, will it still be there now?" she asked.

"I don't know."

"Well, what is it?" Oliver put on his hat as he spoke.

Adam's confidence seemed to have fled, and his shoulders drooped. "I–I'd rather not say until I'm sure. I don't want to make the same mistake that I made with you and Clew. When I'm sure. . ."

"Good enough for me," Oliver said. "Ready, Jules?"

"Not really. I changed out of my riding skirt."

"We'll wait," Adam said. "But hurry." She met his gaze with a glare, and he added, "Please."

Julia hurried up the stairs, removing her bonnet as she went, and took off her dress as soon as she reached her room. The frock was one she'd bought in Philadelphia, and she'd written to her mother and described it for her. The episode had prompted a wave of homesickness, and that returned today, as she realized anew that she'd never be able to share her simple pleasures with her mother again.

She laid the dress on her bed, determined to make the journey to the cemetery yet today. She hated to put on the dusty split skirt, but she saw no other alternative. At least she had a clean shirtwaist. Instead of the pretty hat from Philadelphia, she clapped on her riding hat again and exchanged her fine white gloves for old leather ones.

As she scurried down the stairs, Adam and Oliver both stood

at the bottom, watching her. She couldn't help but notice the light in Adam's eyes, even though she'd changed into her least attractive outfit. Well, he didn't look so bad either, though he still had nearly a week's growth of beard and the stains of travel on his worn clothing.

Julia was puffing by the time they reached the livery. Peewee and Sam had the horses ready. She got the dun again, and that was all right. She was getting rather fond of him.

They rode down the winding mountain road at a quick trot. When they arrived, Adam jumped to the ground.

"All right, Julia. Tell me again what you saw when you came out here. I'm talking about after the robbery—later that day."

"Nothing."

"That's not what you said before."

"Well. . ." She swung down from the saddle and looked around. She tried to remember what she'd told him, gave up, and concentrated instead on that afternoon. She'd been frightened, both because Oliver was missing and because Adam had implied that he might be mixed up in the robbery. She'd worried that Oliver was hurt and needed help. And she'd been frustrated because there seemed to be nothing she could do to change the situation.

"There was a mark on the ground, where Chick tossed down the strongbox." She scanned the dusty road. "I can't see it now." She walked hesitantly to the edge of the road, where she could see out over the valley, over the arroyos, and off toward the mesa in the distance. "I think it was right about here."

"And what else?"

She tried to remember, but shook her head.

"I know," Oliver said, still in the saddle. "Last night, when we were talking to Adam, you said you'd found a bottle."

"Oh, that's right. It was over there." She pointed to a jumble of large boulders on the other side of the road.

Adam walked over there with her, and Oliver dismounted and joined them.

"Was it lying in plain sight?" Adam asked.

"Nooo. . ." She walked between the rocks. "It was here somewhere. I didn't see it until I walked off the road. But it wasn't what I'd call hidden, either."

"I should have seen it." Adam's face looked as though he was in pain. "Where is it now?"

"I threw it in the bushes." She led him farther from the road, where the shrubbery began and the ground sloped upward. Beyond were a few piñon trees, but she stopped near some low, prickly juniper. "It's probably in here somewhere." She moved some branches aside with her foot.

"If it's still here, we'll find it," Oliver said. He and Adam began to search among the vegetation, between the boulders and the trees.

Halfheartedly, Julia poked around, too. She tried to recall exactly where she'd stood that day and how far the bottle had gone when she'd flung it.

She lifted the low branches of a clump of juniper to peer underneath it and jumped back with a little scream.

"What is it?" Oliver called.

Adam, somehow, was already at her side.

"Snake," she gasped.

Adam pushed her gently behind him and drew his revolver. "Where?"

"Under that bush."

"Here?" He pointed to the one she'd been investigating.

Julia nodded. Her heart pounded, and her mouth went all dry.

"Rattler?" Adam asked.

"I—I don't know. I didn't hear it rattle."

He said over his shoulder, "Get me a stick."

She looked around, but didn't see any loose sticks long enough to do any good.

Oliver walked over. "Whatcha got?"

"Snake in that juniper," Adam said. "I can't see it. Can you find a long stick?"

"How about your rifle?"

"Get it."

Oliver went over to the horses and pulled Adam's rifle from his scabbard.

"You want to poke or shoot?" Adam asked.

"I'll poke the bushes. You're a better shot than I am." Oliver leaned forward and used the end of the gun barrel to cautiously lift the branches. Adam crouched, peering into the foliage.

Julia stood a few steps behind them, her heart racing. She put her hands to her ears in anticipation of what was to come. A moment later, Adam fired several shots in quick succession. Oliver jumped back, and the two men stood still for a moment. Oliver reached out with the rifle and prodded at the juniper bush.

Julia lowered her hands. "Did you get it?"

Oliver held up a three-foot section of snake, holding it by the bulbous rattle on the tail end. "In spades. Good shooting, Adam."

"You shot its head clean off," Julia said.

Adam smiled and holstered his revolver. "You want to cook that up for supper?"

"No, thank you." Julia made a face at him. She'd eaten snake two or three times when they lived at Canyon Diablo, but it was by no means her favorite dish. She considered it food for the very poor or the very desperate.

Adam laughed and kicked about in the brush a little more.

"Come over here, Julie."

She approached warily. Adam reached down into the juniper and straightened, holding a bottle. He held it out to her.

"Is this the one?"

"Looks like it."

Adam nodded grimly. He turned it in his hands, stared at the label, and inhaled deeply. "My uncle is very particular about his whiskey. This is Kessler—his brand."

Chapter 16

Walking up the steps to his uncle's house was harder than watching Julia get on the stagecoach two years ago. Adam dreaded the confrontation. He paused on the porch. Maybe he could send to Flagstaff for the sheriff. But, no. He needed to face this himself.

He knocked on the door and wished he hadn't. No turning back now. Uncle Royce's words from Monday night flitted through his mind—*"I wondered when you'd come by."* Adam had thought he meant it as a gentle reproof because he hadn't visited for a while. But maybe that wasn't it at all. Maybe his uncle had expected him to put the clues together sooner.

The door opened, and he stood face-to-face with the old man. Neither of them spoke for a moment, and then Uncle Royce stepped back.

"You might as well come in."

Adam stepped into the waiting room.

His uncle shut the door and turned toward him. "So."

"Uncle Royce. . ." Adam didn't know what to say. Officially he knew, but before God, what was the truly right thing to say now?

His uncle raised his chin. "Might as well get it over with."

"I. . ." Adam squared his shoulders. Uncle Royce was acknowledging what he knew to be true, and now he had to go on. "I don't want to believe it."

"Well, it's true. I did it, and I'm glad you finally came. It's been eatin' at me."

A lump as big as a duck's egg swelled in Adam's throat. "I'm sorry. I should have known you needed help. Uncle Royce, I could've done something."

"No, you couldn't."

"Sure I could. I could have moved back in here with you, or at least given you some money now and then. I could have—"

Uncle Royce held up a hand. "Let's not bother with what we could have done. I was too stubborn to come to you, so. . .like I said, let's get on with it."

Adam studied him for a long moment. "Just tell me why you put part of the money back."

His uncle sighed. "When you came and told me Monday night that you were going after the killer, I realized you had no idea it was me. I feel so bad that I did that to Bub. I never intended. . . Well anyway, it happened. But I didn't need all that money. I knew I didn't need nearly that much. So I counted out how much I figured I'd need to see me through if you didn't ever figure it out. And I put the rest back while you were gone. I just. . .didn't need that much, Adam."

"To live on, you mean?"

"Yes. I give myself six months at most, but there are always contingencies. And you'd have some expenses connected with the funeral. Taxes I owe on this house, things like that. So I put back three thousand and kept the rest out. In case you didn't ever realize. . .but I knew you would. You're smarter than that."

"What do you mean, six months?"

"I have cancer, Adam. It's bad. I thought at first I might have a couple years, but it's pulled me down fast. This last month or so, the pain's increased. I can't get around like I used to."

"But if you. . ." He didn't even want to say it, and he swallowed hard. "If you're strong enough to hold up a stagecoach. . ."

"That didn't take much strength. Just nerve. I made sure nobody got too close to me and the passengers didn't see me. I was afraid Chick Lundy would recognize me, but I guess he was too distracted. And I made him drive on before I came out of the bushes."

Adam lowered his chin. The weight of his uncle's confession felt like a ton of rock pressing down on him. "I don't want to lock you up, Uncle Royce."

The old man held his hands out in front of him. "Do what you have to do, son."

Adam walked slowly out of the cemetery with Julia and Oliver on a chilly November day. The county sheriff waited out by the road, where folks from outside of town had tied up their teams. He rested a hand on Adam's shoulder.

"Well it's over now. You did all right, Scott."

Adam nodded. "Thank you, sir."

"I wish you well." The sheriff nodded to Oliver and Julia and walked over to his horse.

"Come on to the house, Adam," Julia said.

The wind tugged at her hair and the black silk and velvet hat, and she shivered. Adam drew her hand through the crook of his arm.

"Thanks. I'd like that."

"Some of the ladies asked me if they could send some food to the jailhouse, but I told them to leave it off with me, and I'd get it to you."

"You're not entertaining the whole town today, are you?" Adam asked.

"No. Just you. Folks don't want to come chitchat. They don't know what to say."

Adam sighed. "I don't know either."

As they reached the boardwalk along Main Street, Chick Lundy was climbing onto the stagecoach, but he hopped down again and came over to shake Adam's hand.

"I'm awful sorry about the old doc."

"Thanks, Chick," Adam said.

"I never thought it was him—but you know that. Still hard to believe. Every time I drive past that spot where Bub was shot, I shudder."

Adam nodded. "I'm just glad my uncle didn't have to go through a trial and all that."

"Well, if they'd been quicker to get things going at the court. . ." Chick shrugged. "Just as well." He pulled out his pocket watch. "I need to get moving. See you folks later." He nodded at Julia and Oliver and mounted to the driver's box.

Peewee Dennis climbed up beside him, hefting a shotgun. They both had revolvers strapped on. Chick had told Adam a few weeks back that he never took the reins anymore without at least two loaded guns. Between him and Peewee, they were loaded for bear, but so far there had been no further incidents along the route.

Julia tugged Adam along the sidewalk. "Come on, it's cold."

A minute later, the stagecoach rolled past them, on the way to Flagstaff. Adam waved to Peewee and Chick. If rumors were any indication, the stage wouldn't run to Ardell much longer. The High Desert Mine now owned two trucks, and Lucas Morley had brought the first automobile to town.

They walked on up the street. As they approached the crossroad, Oliver said, "Have you thought about moving into the doc's house?"

Adam shook his head. "Not yet." The thought of going into the empty house was too depressing. He didn't think he wanted to live there. "I expect I'll sell it."

The place that really seemed like home was the Newman house. That's where he'd always felt welcome, even during the painful time after Julia broke up with him. The family had never turned Adam away, whether he was happy, glum, bearing gifts, or flat broke. After Julia left, it was just Oliver and his mother, but their friendship had carried him through a lot of difficult times.

When they reached it, Oliver opened the front door.

"Come on in."

Adam let Julia go first and followed her inside. The house was peaceful, as always, and it smelled like fresh-baked bread.

"Make yourself at home, Adam. I'm going to go change my clothes." Oliver went up the stairs.

Julia took off her black hat and coat. Beneath it she wore a blue dress that made her eyes look more vivid than ever, and her upswept hair gave her an elegant, formal air, despite the work the wind had done at the cemetery. She looked more the Philadelphia society lady in Adam's eyes than a woman from an Arizona mountain town.

He took off his hat and jacket and hung them near the door.

"Come on out to the kitchen if you want," Julia said. "Oliver plans to go to work this afternoon, but he'll eat with us."

They walked through the parlor to the warm kitchen, and she headed straight for the stove.

"Let me build the fire up for you," he said.

"Thanks." She picked up the coffeepot that had been simmering on the back. "Want some coffee? You can sit and talk to me while I get dinner ready."

"Sure."

He raked up the coals in the firebox and put in three good-sized sticks of wood.

Julia poured him a mug of coffee, hot and strong, and set it on the table. She put the coffeepot back on the stove and took an apron off a hook near the back door. He watched her tie it around her waist.

She looked a little more approachable with the apron on, but still, she wasn't the girl he'd known back before he'd proposed to her and she'd said no. She seemed much quieter now, more serious and thoughtful. It wasn't only that they'd just come from his uncle's funeral.

She bustled about like her mother used to, taking dishes out of the icebox and the cupboards and putting them on the table. She put two pans on the stove and dished food into them. Every motion had a purpose.

Adam's throat ached. Where was the carefree girl who rode breakneck across the desert, wearing a split skirt and a man's hat? Was this Julia who couldn't risk loving a lawman—or Julia who'd go head-to-head with him and loved every second of it? Was she ready to transfer some of her fierce loyalty from her brother to him—or would she reject him once more and go back East? He'd wanted to ask Oliver if she would stay, but he hadn't dared.

She set a plate of sliced breads—two different kinds—on the table and looked over at him. "Folks have been quite generous. I'll fix you a box to take to the jail with you. There's probably enough jam to last you all winter." She turned back to the cupboard and brought out a dish of applesauce.

"Julie. . ."

She met his gaze and smiled. The lump of lead in Adam's chest began to melt.

"Seems like we haven't seen much of you lately," she said. "I hope you know you can come here anytime."

"Thanks." He'd been busy the last few weeks, nursing his uncle through his final illness and tending to the old man's affairs—not to mention busting up a gang of rustlers working the nearby ranches. It was true he hadn't seen much of Julia, though Oliver had sought him out several times at the jail or Uncle Royce's house.

In between Uncle Royce's arraignment and his death, Oliver had stayed with the old man at times when Adam needed to be away. Sometime, when his nerves weren't so raw, Adam would thank his friend properly.

The kitchen door opened, and Oliver walked in.

"Dinner ready?"

"Almost." Julia loaded their plates with food from the pans on the stove and laid two biscuits between the beans and the side meat. She sat down and bowed her head. Oliver asked the blessing, and they began to eat. Adam tried to keep his mind on the conversation. He asked Oliver a few questions about things at the mine. Julia said she was thinking of buying a horse from Sam Dennis.

Oliver quit after one plateful and a piece of pie. "I'd better get going."

"Don't you want more coffee?" Julia asked.

"No time. I told Mr. Gerry I'd be there by one. Tomorrow's payday, and I have a lot to do."

Adam stood and said something inane, and then Oliver was gone.

He was alone with Julia for the first time since the cave. He must have shown his anxiety, because Julia eyed him sharply.

"Are you all right?" she asked.

"Yeah, I. . ." He sat down, nodded, and took a sip of his coffee.

"More pie?" she asked.

Adam shook his head.

"What is it?"

He looked around the room for a moment then gazed at her. "I feel all hollow inside, Julie."

She walked over and touched his arm. "I'm so sorry."

"I reckon I'll ride out to meet the stagecoach tomorrow. They'll be carrying the payroll."

She nodded. "If you feel you have to do that, then do it."

That didn't sound like her, and he studied her warily. Did she actually agree with him that he should put himself at a higher risk in order to protect the payroll and the people on the stagecoach?

"Come on into the front room for a few minutes." She nodded toward his coffee cup. "Bring that if you want to."

He rose, and she untied her apron and tossed it over the back of her chair. He topped off his coffee and followed her into the front room. She sat down on the sofa, instead of in the rocker. The new item of furniture was Oliver's birthday gift to Julia. She'd protested at first and then gave in and picked out the sofa she liked best from the catalog.

Adam sat beside her, suddenly nervous at being this close to her.

"What are you thinking?" she asked.

"I'm glad it's over."

She nodded. "So am I. The poor man. He helped so many people over the years. It makes me sad that he didn't feel as though he had any friends when he needed help."

Adam sighed and leaned back on the cushions. "You know, Uncle Royce was a heavy drinker for several years now, and I think people noticed that."

"They probably couldn't help it."

He nodded. "I noticed, but I should have paid more attention. That's why he lost most of his patients, I'm sure. When the new doctor came, a lot of them quit going to Uncle Royce and went to Browning. I can't say as I blame them, really, but it's too bad in a way."

"Yes. That probably upset him to the point where he drank even more," Julia said.

"Uh-huh. And his income dwindled down to practically nothing. When most of his patients deserted him, he couldn't afford whiskey and pipe tobacco anymore. I wish I'd realized it sooner."

He looked up at her. "I just assumed he'd put enough by over the years. I could have helped him some. Not a lot, but— Well, I probably should have moved in with him when he asked me to, but I was afraid we'd be too crowded and get on each other's nerves. I didn't know he needed me."

"He was too proud to tell you. Do you think he decided to rob the stagecoach while he was inebriated?"

"Probably. After I arrested him, he told me he was so desperate he couldn't see any other way to get money. At the time, it seemed like a brilliant notion to him. He could stop the stage, get the payroll, disappear, and no one would be the wiser, so long as he made sure no one recognized him. He didn't intend to kill anyone." Adam shook his head. "Bub was a friend of his and had been a patient for years."

"So sad."

He took a sip of his coffee. "He said he hadn't really aimed when Bub fired at him. He just let off a round. He was amazed that he was able to hit anything."

Julia reached over and squeezed his wrist gently. "Are you going to be all right, Adam?"

"I think so." He looked long into her eyes.

"It's not your fault, you know."

"I feel like it is. And he suffered. . .toward the end." Tears formed in his eyes, and his face ached.

"Oliver told me some of it. I'm sorry you had to see that, but I'm glad he had you with him."

Adam nodded. His throat was too constricted for him to speak, but he understood what she meant.

They sat in silence for a long moment. At last he raised his cup and was able to take a swallow. He tried to pull his thoughts together.

"Julia."

"Yes?"

He looked over at her portrait, hanging on the opposite wall. She looked very grave in the photograph, as he supposed all schoolmarms should. Gazing at it was easier than looking at her. "Are you thinking about going away again?"

She hesitated so long, he had to sneak a glance at her.

"No," she whispered. "I'd like to stay here with Oliver."

His heart beat more normally then.

"When you went away. . ." He stopped. Was there any use in asking?

"Yes?"

"You were upset with me. You said. . ." He made himself turn and look into her eyes. "You said you could never marry a lawman."

She nodded. "I did say that. I meant it."

"Do you still feel that way? Because I don't feel the Lord wanting me to change to being something else, but. . .but I don't know as I can go on living without you."

Her smile was a bit shaky, and it was her turn to avoid eye contact. "Are you asking me to marry you, Adam?"

"Should I? Because I don't want to hear you say no again. I don't think I could stand it. So if you're going to say no, I'm not going to ask." He clenched his teeth and looked at the portrait. She was probably a very good teacher. Maybe he should just let her go.

After a long time, she stirred. "Why don't you go ahead and ask."

She wouldn't be that cruel, would she? To give him a drop of hope and then drown him in disappointment?

He turned his head just enough to see her from the corner of his eye. Slowly, she extended her hand to him, palm up. He took it and clasped it tight in his own.

"Julie!"

She smiled, but unshed tears stood in her eyes. Adam set his coffee cup down on the rug, slid to the floor, and knelt before her.

"Will you? Will you marry me, Julie?"

She either sobbed or laughed, he wasn't sure which, but she put her other hand up to his cheek.

"Yes. I will."

"Are you sure you want to be a lawman's wife?"

She nodded, looking into his eyes. "I want to be *your* wife, whatever that involves. And I'm ready now."

He leaned forward to kiss her, but it was too awkward, so he jumped up and pulled her to her feet.

"I love you."

"I love you, too, Adam."

He took her in his arms and kissed her. He'd do anything he could to make it easier for her—to make it so she didn't need to worry so much. But the fact that she knew he'd still be in danger and could live with that made all the difference. He held her close, unable to speak for a long time, knowing how much she was sacrificing for him.

The door behind him opened and they broke apart.

"Well, now." Oliver came in and shut the door. "Forgot the ledger I brought home last night. Excuse me."

Julia walked over to her brother and reached for his hands. "Ollie, we're getting married."

Oliver smiled and nodded at Adam. "It's about time."

Epilogue

On February 3, 1912, the town of Ardell turned out in fine style for the wedding of Deputy Sheriff Adam Scott and Miss Julia Newman. The Reverend Jan Kepler was happy to perform the ceremony in the church. Oliver served as best man, and Julia prevailed upon Edna Somers, Bub Hilliard's heartbroken fiancée, to serve as her bridesmaid.

She was glad she'd made that choice. Edna needed something to lift her spirits. The wedding preparations gave the two young women plenty to talk about. Julia had at first feared that planning another woman's nuptials when her own intended groom had been killed so unexpectedly would force Edna into deeper depression. Instead, they became fast friends, and the festivities proved a good distraction for Edna. Julia liked her so well that she began to toy with the idea of encouraging Oliver to call on Edna.

Despite the sub-zero temperatures on the mountain that day, the entire town—from the lofty Mr. Gerry to the poorest of the miners and ranchers—came out for the party held afterward in the church.

"Well, Scott!" Mr. Gerry slapped the groom on the back, nearly causing him to spill the cup of sweet cider he held. "Too bad you decided not to go into government. I'm headed for Phoenix next week. We could have traveled down together."

"I'm pleased for you, sir," Adam said, "but I think I'll be happier right here in Ardell. There are some good men running for office."

"That there are. Well, I wish you both the best, and I'll be counting on your vote."

Gerry ambled away, and Adam gave Julia a crooked smile.

"Guess we gave him a good campaigning opportunity."

"Yes." Julia cast a wary eye toward the refreshment tables, where the minister's wife and Mrs. Morley presided. "You're sure the miners haven't sneaked in some liquor? I'd hate to see this party get rowdy and the church torn apart."

"I've got Sam and Bob on the lookout," Adam said. "They're under orders to taste the cider every ten minutes to make sure it hasn't been spiked."

As Julia watched his two unofficial deputies, Sam poured a ladleful into his own cup and took a swallow.

"That could be a lot they drink before we're through."

"Oh, I think they can hold their cider." Adam laughed. "When do we cut the cake?"

Half an hour later, when folks had enjoyed their cake and the chatter was beginning to ebb, Leland Gerry again paused near them, stopping beside the table where Julia, Adam, and Oliver were seated.

"Oliver, I just wanted to tell you that I've approved a raise for you."

Oliver's eyes widened, and he hastily stood to face his employer. "Thank you, sir. I wasn't expecting that."

"No, I guess not. But you've done a good job, and I admit I've felt a little guilty for suspecting you of—well, you know—stealing the September payroll." Gerry laughed. "Pretty wild idea, eh?" He glanced at Adam. "Can't imagine where that rumor started."

"Think nothing of it, sir," Oliver said.

Julia wished she was sitting on that side of the table, where she could reach her brother to give him a gentle kick. Think nothing of it, indeed! Oliver might have been hanged.

Gerry passed something to Oliver and walked away to buttonhole someone else. Oliver looked down at the object in his hand

and laughed. He passed it to Adam, who held it up so that Julia could see it. The small matchbook was imprinted with the words, "Gerry for Senate."

Across the room, Edna was smiling as she spoke with Mrs. Kepler, but her gaze kept straying back to their table. Julia didn't think it was her bridal attire that drew Edna's attention.

She leaned toward her brother. "Oliver, I believe Edna could do with a cup of cider. Why don't you fetch one for her? Ask if she'd like to join us for a few minutes."

Oliver blinked at her but didn't move.

"Please?" Julia said. "She *is* my bridesmaid, and I'd like to hear her thoughts on how the ceremony went."

Slowly, Oliver stood and pushed back his chair. He touched his necktie and looked over at Edna. When she again glanced their way, Julia was certain their gazes met and held for a second or two. Oliver walked toward the refreshment table with a ghost of a smile on his face.

"I suppose you think you've accomplished something," Adam said.

"Whatever do you mean?"

"Oliver's mentioned to me how tragic a figure Miss Somers makes, and how well she's borne her grief."

"Has he now?" Julia eyed Oliver with satisfaction. "He hasn't said anything to me about her."

"He wouldn't. Of course, he wouldn't want to intrude where he wasn't wanted, but I suspect he admired her long before Bub proposed to her."

"Really? Why didn't Oliver court her?"

"Hmm, not shy exactly," Adam said, "but a little slow moving."

"Yes. I understand what you mean. And as soon as he saw that another man showed interest, he wouldn't want to interfere."

"Of course not. Your brother's almost too much of a gentleman."

Julia reached for his hand. "Don't say that."

"Why not?" Adam squeezed her hand and gazed into her eyes as though he really had no interest in the topic.

"Because a man can never be too much of a gentleman, can he?" She was gratified to see Edna accept the cup of cider from Oliver. The two began to talk, and after a moment they walked together to the table. Oliver pulled out a chair for Edna.

"Oliver tells me you're setting out for the Four Corners in the morning," Edna said as she sat down.

"That's the plan," Adam said. "I hope it's not too cold. I hate to ask Julia to ride that far if it's freezing."

"We'll be fine," Julia said.

"It sounds like an exciting trip, but more arduous than I'd want to make this time of year," Edna said. "Do you think a lot of people will go to watch the monument set in place?"

"I don't expect too many will." Adam looked over at Julia. "It's so far out in the middle of nowhere."

"And in the middle of Indian lands," Oliver said.

"Well, I think it's romantic that they're setting the monument on Valentine's Day, and that you'll be there on your honeymoon." Edna smiled at Julia. "Your trousseau must be unique."

Julia chuckled. "I've been working on it since Adam proposed in November. As soon as I heard about the Four Corners monument, I knew I wanted to see it, and Adam told me that the new permanent one would be put in place as soon as President Taft signs the documents for statehood."

"I think they'd go ahead with the monument even if he didn't sign it," Adam said, "but it looks like a sure thing this time."

"I hope so," Oliver said. "That was pretty low of him to veto our statehood last summer."

Julia shook her head. "If we have to vote one more time—"

"We?" Adam arched his eyebrows. "I wasn't aware that you ladies were voting."

Julia grimaced, but Edna laughed at him.

"Don't you worry, Sheriff. It won't be long before we women have as much say in Arizona affairs as you do."

"Well, New Mexico's statehood was approved in January," Adam noted. "I don't see how they could turn us down now."

Julia smiled at him. "Me either. I can't wait to see the spot where the four states meet."

"Yes," Oliver said with a bit of a smirk, "you can stand in Colorado and kiss Adam in Utah."

"Or each put your feet in different states and hold hands over the center," Edna said. "That's surely a wonderful way to celebrate the day."

"Well, I can think of ways to celebrate here," Oliver ventured.

"Can you?" Adam shot Julia an amused glance.

Oliver cleared his throat. "Well, yes. I thought perhaps we could have dinner at the Placer in comfort, Miss Somers, while they're freezing their toes off at the Four Corners."

Edna blushed a becoming pink. "Why, thank you, Mr. Newman. I'd be honored."

"Oh, it won't be as cold up there as it is here in the mountains," Adam said.

Julia thought she might just burst with happiness today, between at last being Mrs. Adam Scott and hearing her brother ask a lovely lady to have dinner with him. But if she said anything too direct, Oliver wouldn't like it. Adam squeezed her hand. She'd make do with that for now.

"Excuse me," Mrs. Kepler said, and Julia turned to look up at her.

"Yes?"

"We ladies wondered if you plan to toss your bouquet."

Julia picked up the spray of tissue flowers Edna had made for her, since they couldn't get any real ones up here in February.

"I'll do that right now." She knew who she'd aim for when she threw the posy.

February 14, 1912

Julia and Adam stood in a circle of people surrounding the spot where the new bronze monument would rest. The concrete pad had been prepared in warmer days, and it was now ready to receive the bronze marker that would show the demarcation of the boundaries of Arizona, New Mexico, Colorado, and Utah.

The spectators were swathed in heavy clothing, ranging from elegant furs to plain, thick woolens. Elders of the Diné and Ute tribes living in the area represented their people in their ceremonial dress. Off to the sides, two large fires were kept burning so that people could warm themselves.

It seemed to Julia they waited a long time, and she was glad that the temperature was fairly warm—ten degrees or so above the freezing point. Several government officials made speeches, describing the first survey of the area in 1868 and Robbins's survey in 1875, when a sandstone marker was moved to this location. In 1899, a new stone had replaced the broken marker. The one being placed today was meant to be a permanent monument.

At last a rider came galloping toward them along the road that led to Cortez, Colorado, forty miles away.

"It's official," he yelled. "Taft signed the proclamation at ten o'clock Washington time. With a gold pen."

The spectators set off a loud cheer, and several men drew their pistols and fired into the air. Photographers were ready with their cameras as the crew moved the bronze marker forward and settled it into position.

Adam threw his arms around Julia and kissed her.

She grinned at him and looked around surreptitiously, but no one seemed to care what they did. Everyone shouted and made noise any way they could. One man had brought along some firecrackers and set them off. The popping and cracking went on for some time, and Adam tugged Julia away from it.

"Come on. Let's get over into New Mexico. It might be quieter there."

She laughed and walked a few yards with him. As the noise continued around them, she stood on tiptoe and brushed his lips with hers. "I believe I want to kiss you in all four states."

"I'd be happy to oblige you, ma'am," Adam said. They made a circle around the monument and ended up back in Arizona. He gazed down into her eyes. "Happy, Julie?"

"Oh, yes. I'm so glad I can have Arizona and you, too."

Susan Page Davis is the author of more than sixty Christian novels and novellas, which have sold more than 1.5 million copies. Her historical novels have won numerous awards, including the Carol Award, the Will Rogers Medallion for Western Fiction, and the Inspirational Readers' Choice Contest. She has also been a finalist in the More than Magic Contest and Willa Literary Awards. She lives in western Kentucky with her husband. She's the mother of six and grandmother of ten. Visit her website at: www.susanpagedavis.com.

Honor Bound

BY COLLEEN L. REECE

Chapter 1

The door to the playroom swung inward. Honor Brooks looked up from the table where she and six-year-old Heather had been making letters.

"Miss Brooks, Heather"—Ben Stone beamed as he looked down at his daughter and her governess—"how would you like to go to the Grand Canyon?"

Honor was speechless. Heather was not. "Daddy, Daddy!" She flung herself into her father's arms. "Are we really going?"

"We certainly are," Laurene Stone indolently posed in the doorway. "Since President Wilson signed it into a National Park it's really quite the place to go." Her usually petulant face showed a spark of interest. "I understand El Tovar Hotel is sumptuous. Several of my friends are going for the summer, and Ben needs time away from his law practice." Her cool eyes were almost fond as they swept over gray-clad Honor. "It will be good for you, too. You can take Heather out in the fresh air and sunshine."

"That's very kind of you." Honor blushed.

"It will take about a month to get ready. I'll have all new clothing, of course. You're good with a needle, Honor. Would you like to remodel some of my present gowns for yourself?" A look of dismay crossed the carefully made-up face. "You weren't planning to go into mourning, were you?"

"Laurene!" Honor had never heard Ben Stone thunder before. Was this how he talked to lying witnesses in the courtroom?

Now Laurene had the grace to blush. "I didn't mean to be rude, or anything. It's just that the Canyon and all—your brother wouldn't want you to wear black, would he? And being with Heather every day—"

Honor lost the rest of the explanation as a small hand slipped into hers. Heather stood with one finger in her mouth, her earlier joy of the news about their trip gone, showing clearly how the scene was affecting her.

"You're right, Mrs. Stone. Keith would never want me to wear black." She even managed a wan smile. "Your gowns are lovely, and I believe I can make suitable garments from them."

"There!" Laurene turned triumphantly to her husband. She pulled a bell rope and waited as a maid responded. "Sally, have Jimson bring down the trunk of clothes by my closet."

Heather crossed to her mother but looked back at Honor, eyes still anxious. "They're really pretty. You'll look nice in them."

Honor forced herself to smile at Heather. "I'm sure I shall."

"Don't wear yourself out sewing, Miss Brooks."

The concern in her employer's voice unnerved Honor, but Sally was already draping gowns over every available chair—garnet satin, dark blue crepe, deep green, lovely amber—yards of gorgeous material trimmed with real lace. Some were far too décolleté for Honor's taste, but they could be remodeled until even their original owner would not recognize them!

Last of all Laurene ordered Sally to open a satin-lined box.

"Oh!" Honor's dark blue eyes opened wide. Never had she seen such a beautiful frock. The white lace and satin were pearl-beaded—with even a small purse to match.

"Hardly." But Honor still fingered the frock, and a rich blush filled her face at the memory of a dark-haired soldier who had once briefly entered her life and then gone away.

When they had all left, Honor sat still, reliving another day when Ben Stone had entered the playroom. She had looked up that day, too—and the world had gone black as she saw the concern in her employer's face and the yellow telegram in his hand.

"Run along downstairs for a little while, please, Heather." He had waited as his daughter scampered out. "Miss Brooks—Honor—"

She had shoved back a lock of golden-brown hair and a wave of faintness with one motion. "It's Keith, isn't it?"

Now she bit her lip, feeling the sickening taste of blood, trying to control her shaking hands. She resolutely clamped down the lid on the memory of that day, as she had done dozens of times since. Keith was dead. She must go on.

You can't run away from it.

Had the words been whispered by her own heart, or were they merely the remains of the torture she had gone through these last weeks? Automatically her fingers lifted the heavy dresses, fitted them on hangers. One by one she carried them to her own room and placed them in the large wardrobe.

It was no use. All the gowns in the world could not stop her memories. She threw herself on the bed, letting the tears come. Would the pain never end?

There had been no trace of Ben Stone's usual courtroom crispness in his voice that day. But he had not attempted to soften the long-expected blow. "Yes. The War Department has confirmed his death." He had caught her as she swayed, helped her lean against the table. "He fell bravely, fighting for his country."

"That's comforting." Was that her own voice—bitter, harsh? "It's just that—all this time, when there was no word except he was missing—even since the war ended—" She could not go on.

"I know." Mr. Stone's face was sympathetic. "Evidently the War Department found someone who had actually seen Keith killed. There is no doubt." He cleared his throat. "They buried him in France, but if you want his body brought back home, I'll see to it.

And Honor, don't worry about expense. You've come to be part of our family. Everything will be taken care of."

Another tear fell, splashing against her clenched hands, as she remembered the kindness of the considerate employer for whom she had worked the past two years.

Thinking a walk would help, she tied a heavy hood over the bright brown hair so like her brother Keith's. She caught back a cry of pain. It couldn't be possible Keith had died somewhere in France. When the Armistice Day bells rang on November 11, 1918, she had expected Keith home soon. He hadn't come. Months passed. A War Department telegram informed Honor, his only living relative, that Keith was missing in action.

A fresh wave of torture filled her as she remembered the long days, sleepless nights. Missing in action—dead or alive, no one knew. Yet deep inside was the assurance Keith would return. Surely God wouldn't let Keith die when he was all she had left!

Honor's face darkened. She couldn't think of God, not now. Snatching up a long cape that covered her dress to the hem, she wrapped it around her and fled into the early afternoon. She was unconscious of the stares from passersby. The long cloak was out of place in the late spring softness of San Francisco. Yet huddled in its depths Honor still felt cold, outside and inside.

Memories threatened to drown her: moving to Granny's cottage when both parents were killed in the great earthquake—she had been eleven, Keith six; teaching her little brother to read before he went to school; learning to rely on Granny for warmth and love.

Honor shuddered. Keith would answer her call no more. Why had he lied about his age to serve his country? Had God punished that lie with death on the battlefield? No! Her inner rebellion could not accept that. Keith had accepted Christ as his Savior when he was small. She could almost see his happy face becoming clouded over as he pleaded, "Honor, believe on the Lord."

She had scoffed in the lofty way her twelve years allowed. "If God really loved us, He wouldn't have let Mama and Daddy die."

Wisdom shone in the little boy's eyes. "The Bible says God loved us enough to send His own Son to die. God must have felt just as bad as we did about Mama and Daddy. Don't you listen when Granny tells us about Jesus and reads the verses?"

It hadn't been the last time Keith worried over her. Throughout their growing-up years he kept trying to win her to the Lord he loved. But Honor would not give up her stubbornness, even when Granny had died a few days before the Armistice. She clung to the idea that Keith would be back. When he came there would be time enough to talk about whether God loved her.

Her fingers clenched as a terrible thought crossed her mind: *If I had accepted Christ, would Keith be alive now?*

No! Granny had taught them they were responsible for their own actions. God would hold them accountable for what they did—Honor's lips twisted—or for what they failed to do. Although others could be hurt by their actions, salvation was a one-to-one transaction between God and every person on earth.

Her remembrance left weakness. There had been an unpaid mortgage. The little home had been sold. The day had come when Honor's pocketbook and tiny cupboard in her dingy rented room were empty. She had tried to pray at first, but nothing got better. If God still knew she was alive, it didn't seem to matter to Him. Only the thought of Keith's homecoming had kept her moving down the street looking in every window for a HELP WANTED sign.

It was through an old family friend that Honor had met Ben Stone, a lawyer who wanted someone to give his four-year-old daughter the time and attention his wife was unable to give. Heather walked into the library of the Stones' mansion and into Honor's heart at the same moment.

Laurene Stone seemed to be glad to be rid of even the minimal care she had been giving the child, and within a week Heather and Honor had become inseparable. The flaxen-haired little girl trotted after Honor eagerly and never argued when told to do something. Was it because of mutual loneliness? Laurene always seemed to have enough energy for balls and parties, but none for Heather. As a result, the child automatically turned to Honor's welcoming love. Honor believed that Mrs. Stone's only real problem was being spoiled, but she had little contact with her and poured out all the love she had on Heather.

Ben Stone had been as good as his word. It was several weeks before Keith's body could be shipped home, but Mr. Stone had done everything in his power to speed the process.

For Honor the waiting was even worse than when she had waited for Keith to come laughing in the door. Now her waiting was without hope. She was truly alone. Only Heather could reach through her suffering.

One night as she tucked the child in bed, Heather, rosy from splashing in the ornate marble tub, said, "I'm sorry your brother died. Daddy said he was a soldier." The beautiful face was wistful. "I never had a brother. Aren't you glad you did, even though he died?"

It caught Honor unprepared. Thoughts whirled through her feverish brain. Heather's face was turned up, expectantly waiting for an answer. What she said now might be of lasting value or damage to the child.

"Yes, Heather. I am glad I had a brother."

Heather's wide-open eyes indicated she was in the mood for

confidences. "Tell me about him, when he was little like me."

Haltingly at first, then buoyed by her listener's interest, Honor uncovered some of the buried memories she had put aside because of their painfulness. It got easier as she went along. When Heather's reluctant eyelids finally stayed closed and Honor had slipped to her adjoining room, she lay awake for a time. It *was* better to remember, even painfully, than to try to forget. Heather's final sleepy comment still hung in the air. "I bet Keith'd be happy now he's gone to know you still have me."

A trickle of comfort touched her. It was true. She had a place to live, the love of Heather, the admiration of Mr. Stone. She wasn't totally alone.

The child's love had helped her through the hard memorial service, the final laying of Keith to rest in the soil of the country he loved and for which he had given his life. Yet in the weeks following the burial, Honor was unable to pick up the shattered pieces and go on. She grew thin, pale, nervous. Even Heather wanted to know if she was sick. Honor told stories of her own childhood to amuse Heather and comfort herself, but continued to toss restlessly at night.

Alarmed, the Stones sent for a specialist, who checked her over. Honor overheard him tell them, "Shock. She carried on so long, but when hope was taken away, her body rebelled. She needs to get where there is a better climate. I don't like the sound of that cough she's developed."

Nothing more had been said until the Stones had come into the playroom today with the incredible announcement of a vacation to the Grand Canyon.

Honor suddenly realized she was chilly. Afternoon had given way to evening while she journeyed to the past. She hastily returned to the mansion and went in search of Heather.

The little girl was bubbling over with happiness. "Daddy said we're going in a great big car. There's going to be sand and mountains and all kinds of things to see! Aren't you excited, Honor?"

Honor led her small charge to the nursery, where Heather had her meals. "Of course I am. Keith—" her voice faltered then firmly went on, "Keith and I always thought it would be a good place to visit."

With uncanny insight, Heather read the meaning behind Honor's words. "Since your brother can't take you, we will. I heard Mama tell Daddy you need to go—"

Honor's heart lifted. She wouldn't have thought Laurene cared about even a high-class servant that much. But Heather's continuing monologue shattered her illusions. "—and that we needed a vacation anyway, and this summer was the time to go while everyone thought it so smart."

Yet even those revelations could not completely dim Honor's anticipation. She lay in bed that night staring at the ceiling. She had always wanted to visit the Grand Canyon. She had read every book she could get her hands on, secretly hoping in her childish dreams she could visit a big cattle ranch someday, yet knowing the possibility was slight.

A rich blush crept up from the high-ruffled neck of her cambric nightgown, touching her thin cheeks with color. She had even daydreamed of being mistress of such a ranch.

The excitement of the proposed exodus provided Honor with strength. Within a week she was working on the frocks Laurene had discarded. She and Heather took long walks past the great stores of the city, noting a knot of velvet here, a trick of gores there, that set apart the stylish frock from the ordinary. Honor's skillful needle faithfully transposed those tricks into her growing wardrobe. Heather learned to sew along with Honor's alterations, and doll clothes emerged for her favorites.

One evening Honor wore her new dark blue dress down to dinner. Most evenings she had dinner in the nursery with Heather, but on occasion she was pressed into service when an absent dinner guest made an uneven number. Her glowing cheeks were attractive and her eyes shone.

She wasn't prepared for Mrs. Stone's reaction. "Why, Honor, where did you get that lovely dress?" Astonishment narrowed Laurene's eyes. "That can't be—"

"It is." Honor laughed and whirled. "I wondered if you would recognize it."

"You certainly did a nice job!" Laurene peered at her more closely. "That fichu—it's just like the one on the Paris dress I found in a darling shop. If you don't mind, I may let you help me with my wardrobe at the canyon. I'd just as soon not bother with Sally."

"I'd be happy to help." Honor's sincere smile brought an answering glimmer to her employer's wife's eyes. Honor treasured the extra sign of friendliness. Laurene wasn't one to praise other women, especially one so insignificant as the governess.

It seemed only a few days passed, and suddenly it was time to leave. The house would be cared for by Sally and Jimson in their absence. Honor had a final glimpse of the mansion as they stowed themselves in the big touring car Mr. Stone had purchased especially for the trip. A strange desire to flee back to the security of the walls that had housed her for so many weeks and months touched Honor briefly and was gone. Ahead lay—what? Why should she suddenly long for her own room?

It was a long trip. By the time they arrived Laurene was tired, and she ordered Honor to see that Heather had a snack and was put to bed. Honor's heart beat quickly as she obeyed, anxious for her first sight of the canyon. She had already thrilled to the massiveness of El Tovar Hotel, built just after the turn of the century. Its native boulders and pine logs were different from anything she could have imagined, yet perfect for the setting. Grateful she could be alone for that all-important first sight of the canyon, she reassured Heather, promising she would get to do all the wonderful things the canyon offered while they were there.

Honor deliberately did not look into the canyon until she found a secluded spot a good distance away from the hotel. She kept her eyes fixed on a distant point on the far wall.

Her trembling fingers caught the twisted trunk of an old tree as she finally peered into a rent that could have been created only by the hand of God. She gazed down on mountaintops—and they were a mile high! No wonder writers described the canyon as indescribable. Nothing on earth could have prepared her for it. It was beautiful, awful, magnificent, terrible.

How long she stood gripping the tree she never knew. She turned away, only to look back once. Every movement of light and shadow changed the canyon from red to purple, light to dark. It was impossible to grasp with the human mind—a never-ending, shifting panorama.

Honor tottered back, sinking down on the needle-covered ground. The sorrow of the past months had been drawn from her by the sheer force of what lay before her. She shuddered. God had created all this and still sent His Son to die to save sinners—the God Granny said was waiting for her to accept Him. She tried to laugh and failed miserably. She deliberately brought up her losses: parents, Granny, Keith, home. No. Even such a God could not find place in her life after taking away everything precious. She could stand no more.

Yet after a simple dinner with Heather she again slipped into the evening's dimness. She watched until no light was left to reveal the canyon's secrets, an uneasy peace fighting with something inside clamoring for recognition. What if God really was calling her to accept His Son? Granny had talked time and again of those who were "under conviction" for their sins. Was this what she had meant, this terrible tearing apart inside? Part of her longed to fling herself to the ground and cry for mercy, while her head told her it was insane. More than likely it was just the effect of her illness and shock coupled with the beauty of this place.

Without warning a handsome face laughed in the still night air before her, leaving her drained. "I need someone," she whispered.

She laughed bitterly. First God and then a wraith from the past. If this was what happened when she came to Arizona, she'd better run back to San Francisco and find another job. Still, the new idea tormented her. She needed someone to love and honor, to cherish, to fill her life. Overhead the bright Arizona stars seemed close enough to pick.

She had attended many weddings, seeing innermost feeling and glimpsing what love between man and woman could be. She could even remember how her parents had been. It kept her from being attracted to a cheaper form of excitement. She would not accept second best. *Someday he will come*, she thought.

She caught her breath. Was this the recognition for which she had been brought to Arizona? In her soul, the searing certainty it was not shook her. What of the far greater truth she had so steadfastly denied?

Refusing to answer, she hurried toward the main entrance of El Tovar and dashed across the lobby. She heard a group clattering down the stairs before she saw them. The next instant she lay sprawled on the floor.

Honor looked up into the devastatingly handsome face of a dark-haired, dark-eyed man, who was apologizing and helping her up.

"I say! I've knocked you down with my clumsiness. I should have been watching where I was going."

His face changed. Delight, incredulity, and recognition mingled in rapid succession. "Honor? Honor Brooks?"

From her unladylike position Honor saw what her mind could not accept—the man who had knocked her flat was her soldier from long ago—Phillip Travis.

Phillip! He had come into her life like a whirlwind years ago, appearing with a small group of soldiers who came to church one night. He had made a special point to talk with her afterward.

It was the beginning of a tremulous, butterfly world. Phillip's home was *Casa del Sol*, "House of the Sun," near Flagstaff, Arizona. Dark and handsome, he fit the storybook image of the knight in shining armor who would one day sweep her off her feet and carry her to his ranch to live happily ever after.

Honor's mouth twisted in a slight twinge of the pain she had suffered when he went overseas, promising to write and disappearing as suddenly as he had come. She had wondered if he, too, had fallen in France. It seemed inconceivable he would not have written, if he were able, after spending every free moment with her and Granny.

She could still remember his farewell. "Honor, I don't know if I'll be back. But would you wait for me? When I come home, will you marry me?"

Alarm had brushed gentle wings against her spirit and reason. "We hardly know each other!"

His gaze was compelling. Taking both her hands in his, he drew her unwillingly toward him, overriding the strange combination of longing and reluctance she felt.

"You can't tell me you don't care."

Honor had tried, but there was a biding-my-time look in his smile. "We will have time when I come home." She had felt her heart pound as he promised, "I'll write."

Chapter 2

Phillip drew her to her feet. "I'm sorry. I'm terribly sorry. You aren't hurt, are you?" He held her off with both hands, still clutching her wrists as she mutely shook her head. "Come in for dinner with us. We just arrived, and the dining room is still open."

Some of Honor's composure returned. "I have already eaten, Mr. Travis. Besides—" she glanced down at her white shirtwaist and plain dark skirt. "—I'm not dressed for dinner."

"You look fine." He turned to a girl in the party. "Babs, tell Honor—Miss Brooks—she looks fine."

He didn't seem to catch the scowl on the pretty redhead's face as her social breeding forced her to respond. "Of course. Do come in for a cup of coffee, at least."

Phillip led her to a table. "Everyone, this is Honor Brooks." His ardent gaze made her uncomfortable. "She is the girl I told you all about, the one from San Francisco. Or did I? Anyway, now that I've found her again, I won't let her get away so easily!"

In spite of herself, Honor blushed. He made it sound as if she had once escaped him when the opposite had been true. He was the one who had promised to write and never followed through.

The blush didn't escape Phillip. "A girl who blushes in this day and age? Will wonders never cease!" He waved a lazy arm toward his friends. "Mark, Cecile, Jon, Patti; you've already met Babs." There was something in his voice demanding recognition, but Honor had never heard of them before.

Phillip surveyed her with keen eyes. "When did you come? You've never been here before, have you?"

Honor was aware of her position in the split second before answering. She was also aware of how painfully crumpled her shirtwaist must be and how her hair was falling all over the place. "I'm here with Mr. and Mrs. Stone. He is an attorney in San Francisco."

Phillip's eyes widened in admiration. "I'll say he is! Everyone has heard of Ben Stone. I didn't know you knew him."

"I am his daughter's governess." Honor didn't miss the glance of scorn from Babs. Her chin came up. "After Granny died and when Keith didn't come home from France—" Suddenly the cloud of smoke around the table got to her. What was she doing here with this group of people? She had no part in their way of life. Phillip was the only one not smoking. Drinks were being poured.

She stumbled to her feet, throat thick from emotion and smoke. "Thank you for the coffee. I'll excuse myself now."

"Oh, I say, Miss Brooks!" Phillip trailed her to the door. "I'm sorry—about your grandmother and Keith, that is. I didn't know."

His sympathy was so sincere that she found herself smiling up at him through the gathering mist. "Thank you, and good night."

"You aren't going to run off from me, are you?" he demanded. "Not just when we've found each other again?"

Honor's heart leaped in spite of herself. The memory of his charm hadn't done him justice. Phillip Travis held an appeal for her that couldn't be denied. But what was he doing in such a crowd? Evidently he knew them well; they were his friends. He hadn't been like that in San Francisco. There had been no mention of smoking or drinking. He had called at her home and taken her to church. Sometimes they had taken long walks. Had he changed so much, or had she been wrong about him?

Phillip totally misunderstood her silence. "It isn't because you're working, is it?" He grinned. "I always thought I'd try it. They tell me it's fascinating." A hoot of derision came from the table they had just left, and Honor's face flamed. This was no place for her. Evidently Phillip was a member of the "pleasure seekers," or "parasites," as Mr. Stone classified such people.

"Thank you for the coffee." Before Phillip could detain her she slipped away, but not before overhearing Babs cattily remark, "That girl walks like royalty."

Honor couldn't help smiling grimly to herself. Why not? Her family might not have been rich, but they were honorable. Why shouldn't she walk proudly?

Yet as she prepared for bed with a last glance out the window toward the canyon, her heart beat faster. Phillip was so handsome. There had been gentleness in his touch and voice as he spoke of Granny and Keith. For a moment it overruled the indolent arrogance she had sensed in him, an arrogance that was not in keeping with the long-held image in her heart. Did he still own the ranch, Casa del Sol? Her face cleared a bit. That might explain it. Perhaps he was an important man here in northern Arizona.

She remembered stumbling home, anxious to tell Granny about Phillip's proposal. She could still see the troubled look in the blue eyes, the lined face surrounded by curly white hair.

"Is he a Christian, Honor?"

"Who cares? I'm not, either."

Granny's gnarled hands lay still in her aproned lap. "I pray every day you will be."

Remorse filled her, mingled with anger. "I thought you liked Phillip!"

"He is courteous, charming, and utterly godless."

"That's not fair!" Honor's white face had waved battle flags of color. "After all, I met him in church."

Granny suddenly looked old. "Anyone can go to church, Honor. If he hasn't trusted the Lord Jesus Christ in his heart, his going to church doesn't mean anything." Granny's next words ran like a prophecy. "I believe that someday you will accept our Lord, who has waited for you so long. I don't know what it's going to take to make you see you can't outrun God. When you do, if you are married to an unbeliever, your life will be misery." She softly quoted, " 'Be ye not unequally yoked together with unbelievers: for—' "

" '—for what fellowship hath righteousness with unrighteousness? and what communion hath light with darkness?' " Honor finished bitterly, noting the surprise in Granny's eyes. "Oh, yes, Granny, I know 2 Corinthians 6:14—you've made sure I know scripture well. Too bad it just 'didn't take.' " She ignored the pain in Granny's face. "I'm going to wait for Phillip Travis. Besides, if God does catch up with me, there's no reason He can't catch Phillip, too."

In the following weeks, when no letter had come, Granny never mentioned Phillip. Neither did Honor. A new fear had touched her. If Phillip were dead she would never know. Should she write Casa del Sol? No. Phillip had not gone home before being shipped overseas. They wouldn't know she existed. Phillip had said he had one brother and seemed disinclined to say more, so she hadn't questioned him.

So long ago! Almost another lifetime. In the years since she first met Phillip she had been too busy and harried to meet other eligible men. Since coming to the Stones she had never gone to church. Granny was gone. She would not be a hypocrite. It couldn't be that her half promise to wait for Phillip had haunted her, could it?

In weakness of spirit, Honor faced it squarely. Ridiculous as it might seem, she had been bound to Phillip Travis. Until she knew for sure he was dead, she had not been able to accept another in his place.

Finally the excitement of the trip and the fresh air did its work. Honor could stay awake no longer.

ꝏ

She was awakened by a broad ray of sunlight crossing her room and Heather standing by her bedside.

"Miss Honor, just see!"

Heather's face was barely visible above the largest bouquet of flowers she had ever seen, eyes sparkling as Honor protested, "There must be a mistake! No one would be sending me flowers."

"It says H-O-N-O-R," Heather pointed out proudly, glad to show off her newly-gained ability to recognize letters.

Honor took the flowers from her small charge and put them on the table. American Beauty roses, a wealth of them, catching the sunlight into their depths, filled the room with fragrance.

"Great Scott!" Laurene Stone had wandered into Honor's room. "Where did those come from?" She looked at Honor suspiciously.

"I don't know." Honor's clear gaze met Mrs. Stone's. "Oh, here's a card."

Have breakfast with me, or I will
think you haven't forgiven me
for running you down. I'll be in
the lobby whenever you're ready.
Phillip

Honor could feel her face heating as she silently passed the note to Mrs. Stone.

"Who is Phillip?"

"Phillip Travis. He knocked me down when I was coming upstairs last night. I met him a few years ago when he was stationed in San Francisco."

"Phillip Travis! Not the one who owns that fabulous ranch here in Arizona with some Spanish name meaning sun?" New respect shone in Mrs. Stone's face. "How did you ever meet *him*?"

"He came to church with a group of soldiers. I suppose they were lonely for home." A reminiscent smile curved Honor's finely carved lips.

"Well, what are you waiting for? Get ready and meet him for breakfast."

Honor's memories faded. "I can't do that! He's here with a group. Besides"—she smiled at Heather—"we have all kinds of things to do today."

"He can join us for breakfast. I'm sure Ben will enjoy meeting him. Get Heather ready, and we'll meet downstairs as soon as possible." Mrs. Stone ended the discussion by sweeping out the door.

Honor stared openmouthed after her employer's wife. Well! It certainly made a difference whom she knew. Mischief briefly touched her face, but she busied herself arraying Heather in a charming red dress then quickly got ready herself. She hesitated, trying to decide what to wear, then firmly pushed aside the party dresses and settled for another shirtwaist, sparkling white and crisp. Her brown hair had been brushed and shone by the time she and Heather descended the stairs.

The Stones were already there, seated in a sunny corner. So was Phillip. Honor couldn't help the soft color that mounted to her hairline as she joined them.

Laurene Stone showed no traces of ill health this morning. "Honor, as you can see we went ahead and introduced ourselves. It's so important making good contacts right away when one goes into a strange land."

Honor disciplined a laugh at Mrs. Stone's implications. She didn't dare look at Phillip. But a few minutes later she raised her head. "Thank you for the roses, Mr. Travis." In the time since she had learned Phillip really was an important person, she had also decided it had better be "Mr. Travis." She had no right to presume on former friendship.

Phillip would have none of it. "Make it Phillip, all of you." His glance included the Stones but returned to Honor. "Perhaps I'd better introduce myself a little more, Mrs. Stone. My brother and I own a cattle ranch just north of Flagstaff. He actually does most of the work, but I—"

"A real ranch? With cowboys?" Heather broke her usual silence around strangers, with a frankly hero-worshipping look.

"Real cowboys." His smile at the little girl was endearing. The next moment he leaned toward her. "Miss Heather, how would you like to visit that ranch when you leave here?"

"Oh, Daddy, Mama, could we?"

"Really, Mr. Travis—Phillip." Ben Stone's face was dark with annoyance. "We have barely met. Heather shouldn't have hinted."

"I didn't hint, Daddy. He 'vited us." Heather's lip trembled, and her clear eyes filled with tears.

"That's right." Phillip had never been more charming. "I really mean it. Casa del Sol is a sprawling hacienda with room for a dozen people. We love company. Our housekeeper, Mama Rosa, likes nothing better than cooking for a houseful."

Honor was amazed at how quickly Mr. Stone capitulated. "If it isn't an imposition. I really have always wanted to visit a working cattle ranch." He grinned. "My doctor told us to get out-of-doors. I'm sure he'd approve!"

"Then it's settled. Whenever you're ready to leave the canyon, let me know. I'll go on ahead and get ready for you." He turned back to Heather. "We even have ponies just your size."

She smiled delightedly as he added, "Oh, by the way, you must take the mule trip into the canyon while you're here."

"Not I!" Laurene Stone threw her hands up in mock horror. "I'm going to spend my time right here in this lodge. Some of our San Francisco friends are coming, and we already have bridge games arranged. The rest of you can take care of the outdoor life." She lifted one shoulder daintily. "I'm sure my husband and Honor will want to go. I can keep Heather with me."

"Oh, Mama!" Heather's face fell with disappointment. "Can't I ride a mule?"

Again Honor was impressed by Phillip Travis's quick evaluation of the situation. He leaned across to Heather once more. "Those mules are pretty big, Heather. How about riding down the trail with me? I've been several times, and it's always a little lonely on the mule's back. You can fit in the saddle just in front of me."

Mr. Stone looked worried. "Are these donkeys safe?"

"Not donkeys, sir. Mules. Our donkeys are smaller and known as burros, or 'Arizona Nightingales.' " Phillip laughed. "You won't believe it when you hear them bray. The mules that go down in the canyon are trained beyond belief. The trainers flap slickers at them, do everything in the world to startle them before they are even allowed on the trail.

"You know, the little burros have been given a rather unique legend." An unusual softness crept into his voice. "It is said Jesus put a cross on the back of each burro as a reward for service. The old prospectors believe it. If you look at a burro's shoulders, you'll see that cross. Some are plainer than others, but there is a more or less distinct marking on every burro's back."

He paused, smiling again. "Our burros have saved countless lives. They are not only good pets but also a prospector's best friend. They are also sturdy. Now *mules* are different—ornery. Wait until you get on a trail edge and your mule decides to reach over the side to chomp grass. I do believe the good Lord created them with a sense of humor!"

Honor's eyes sparkled. Had she been wrong about Phillip and his friends? He spoke so easily of the legend and the good Lord's creation. He was quite a man. The man for her? The thought was enough to fill her face with a shine and set her heart pounding.

The rest of the meal passed swiftly. Heather's laughter rang out at the witty remarks of Phillip, who seemed to take delight in talking with her. When they finished he said, "I don't want to intrude, but since I do know the canyon, would you consider taking me on as a guide?"

Even Honor was touched by the wistfulness in his question, and the keen glance of Mr. Stone seemed to be weighing Phillip's sincerity.

"I really mean it. My crowd has been here so often the thrill is gone. It will be like seeing it for the first time, showing you everything there is to see."

"We would be happy to have you with us for whatever time you have free," Mr. Stone told him.

"Then I'll be with you all the time!" His dark eyes twinkled. "Just wait and see!"

Phillip became the perfect host. First he introduced Laurene to several avid card players he knew. By the time her San Francisco friends arrived, she was already part of a well-established circle that widened to include them. Her reaction to the Grand Canyon had been a shiver and, "What a terrible hole in the ground!" Then she settled into a daily routine of sleeping late, breakfasting in bed, and meeting with friends for cards, followed by a leisurely preparation and donning of exquisite gowns for dinner each night.

Ben Stone lost his paleness in the hours he spent outdoors. Sometimes with just Heather, more often as part of the foursome with Honor and Phillip, he radiated happiness. Once when Honor found him alone on the canyon rim as sunset threw mocking banners into the sky to reflect on the panorama before them, she tried to thank him.

"I am the one in debt, Honor." He waved into the ever-changing shadows of night creeping toward the canyon. "I didn't realize how I needed to get away—until I used you as an excuse to come!" A look of reverence shown through his level gaze. "No one could look on such a scene and not believe in a Creator, could they?"

"No, Mr. Stone." But he had already turned back to the canyon, now murky in its depths, leaving Honor feeling she had been forgotten.

Honor was free for a time each afternoon when Heather took a nap and after she had gone to bed. Phillip gradually filled those moments until it became a usual thing for him to be waiting when she came down. Several days after they arrived he asked her if she would walk with him. Something in his look stirred her. The afternoon was bright. Birds called, and squirrels ran along the canyon edge, looking for bits of dropped food.

Honor's hand trembled as she dressed carefully and brushed her bright hair into waves. Was the pale blue dress too fussy? When she had told Phillip the clothes were "made over," he had covered his surprise by commenting how clever she was with a needle.

As they skirted the outcroppings of rock to find a quiet place in full view of the canyon but not the hotel, Honor noted how quiet Phillip had grown. Was there some significance in this particular invitation?

"Honor, will you be my girl?"

She was speechless.

"I mean it." He doggedly forced her to look at him, compelling with his eyes. "You know I was in love with you in San Francisco.

I even asked you if you would wait for me. Don't you remember?"

She could only remain silent, unspoken words dying on her lips.

"I know I treated you shabbily, going off and not writing after I promised. But Honor, I've had a lot of time since then to consider." He looked deep into her eyes. "I love you, Honor." Without asking permission he caught her close and tried to kiss her.

She sprang back. "Why did you do that? Why did you have to spoil everything?" Vexation steadied her trembling lips. "We barely know each other!"

"Don't you believe in love at first sight?"

She wanted to shout no, but couldn't do it. She remembered the feeling she had had when they first met, the same feeling that had intensified beyond belief since meeting him again at the canyon. "How can I take you seriously? You don't even know me, not really."

"I know you well enough to know I'm going to get ahead of Mark and Jon." His jaw set stubbornly. "I saw how they watched you, even the night you came. I'm putting my bid in first."

"I'm not up for grabs, you know."

His mouth twisted in an odd smile. "You think I don't know that? I'm twenty-nine years old, Honor Brooks. I've known a lot of women. You think I can't tell the difference between real and imitation? You're what my grandmother calls 'a real lady.' There aren't many of them around these days." He pushed back a lock of hair. "I don't want second best."

From the corridors of memory came Honor's own words, *I'll never settle for second best*. It brought hot blood to her face. "I'm sorry, Phillip. You have your friends. I'm here working a vacation job. I'm not looking for a summer romance."

"And you think I am?" A surge of color filled his own face.

He gritted his teeth, obviously trying to control anger as he gazed across the canyon, seeming to find in its depths strength to calm himself. "What right have you to judge me? I've waited all my life for a girl like you—and that's what you are, a girl, in spite of being almost twenty-four, as you told me. I'll wager you haven't lived those twenty-four years without getting some knowledge of human nature. I fell for you when I first met you. Then with the war and all, you slipped back into memory." His voice deepened. "Then I came here—and found you. When I picked you up from the floor I fell for you—hard. I'd begun to think I'd never find the girl I wanted to marry. Sure, I've had all kinds of girls and women, even considered marrying a few of them, but never did. Men have ideal women, too, you know." The mobile mouth curved in a smile. "If you can honestly tell me you felt nothing when I picked you up, I'll apologize and get lost."

Honor couldn't speak. Only the strength of his hold kept her from falling. When he had spoken of wondering if the "right" person would ever appear, she had identified with him in a quick rush of sympathy. Was her heart trying to tell her something? Was she stubbornly refusing to listen? Had Phillip really been searching—for her?

"You can't do it, can you? Then think about this." Gently he drew her to him, kissing her on the lips. Startled, she broke from him like a shy fawn and fled back the way they had come, only to be followed by his exultant cry, "I'm going to marry you, Miss Honor Brooks—and you're going to like it!"

When she reached her room she was breathless. Tears stood in her eyes, brilliant, refusing to fall. Futilely she bathed her hot face, demanded of her image, "How did he dare?" Yet the gentle touch of his kiss stayed on her lips even after she had furiously scrubbed them. The walls of the room she had found so charming now closed in on her. She must get free. She caught up her sweater and slipped out, carefully checking the lobby to make sure she was unseen. In her walks between El Tovar and the canyon rim, Honor had noticed a secluded spot. She headed for it. Would the canyon reach out to her, slow her whirling emotions?

"What if he meant it?" Honor gazed into the chasm, unaware of anything except the lingering pressure of Phillip's lips on her own. "I love him!"

A cloud flitted across the sun, sending a curious mist to the canyon. To Honor's excited fancy Granny's face seemed to float there with accusing eyes. Her warning about marrying any unbeliever rang in Honor's heart. With it came the memory of Phillip as he had been that first night in the dining room—surrounded by smoke and the tangy odor of liquor. Her heart quailed. In spite of not acknowledging Christ as Lord, Honor abhorred cheapness, and to her, smoking and drinking fell in that category.

"But Phillip was not smoking or drinking," she protested brokenly. The mist disappeared, and her rebellion burst its bonds. All Honor's accumulated misery during the hard years gathered in one great force, just as the massive clouds overhead mustered forces to batter the earth. She sprang to her feet. "I will not give him up! I know now I loved Phillip even when he told me good-bye. It's been there all the time. That's why I have felt bound."

A crack of lightning followed by a burst of cannonlike thunder halted the words, striking fear into her heart. She would not bow before it. "Where were You when I gave You a chance, God? Where was the love You told of in those verses I learned when I promised to try and know You better if You'd spare Keith? Or when I begged for a job and only got one by chance? Everything I've ever loved has been taken away. I will not give up Phillip!"

She raised her face in defiance, as if to challenge the very storm itself. It had increased in intensity, pelting the earth with raindrops the size of hailstones, kicking up dust and turning it to red mud. "If Granny was right, if misery is ahead—" she caught her breath at the possibility and again hardened her voice "—I'll pay the price for the happiness I'll have in between."

She sank to the ground, not heeding the violent storm soaking her, turning her into a muddy, crumpled figure. For better or worse, she had chosen. Why should another verse learned years before haunt her at this moment? It was Joshua 24:15—"*Choose you this day whom ye will serve. . .but as for me and my house, we will serve the Lord.*" She impatiently refused to admit her slight hesitation, replacing it with Phillip's laughing face. He would ask her again to marry him. Next time there would be no hesitation. After all, hadn't he said he'd known all kinds of girls and women?

Some of her triumph faded. Had he kissed those others the way he did her? She would never tell him he was the only one who had kissed her, but she was glad. She had kept her promise and waited; he had come differently than expected. With a smile, she returned to the present. If she had wanted solitude at the canyon, she had it. No one would be out in this storm.

But she had been wrong. A dark shape hurried toward her. "Honor! I've looked everywhere for you." His voice was filled with fear, for her, she knew. Suddenly all her troubles were gone. Phillip had come for her.

"I'm here, Phillip. You've found me."

He peered into her face, seeing the way it was turned to him.

"Honor!" The next moment she was caught close in an embrace that deepened as she sighed and relaxed against him. Surely it must be right when she felt so happy. She lifted her mouth, and in the storm on the canyon's edge, returned Phillip's kiss. She didn't care if the storm never let up. She had fought so long against the fact of her family's death. It was sheer heaven to lean on someone stronger.

This time it was Phillip who broke away. "Honor—you care. To kiss me like that—a girl like you—it must mean you care." He caught her in his arms, carrying her slight frame, running back through the rain as if he would never let her go.

"Put me down, Phillip! What will they all say?" She struggled furiously, but he rained more kisses on her wet mouth and hair.

"Who cares? We'll just announce our engagement at dinner tonight." He set her down just inside the door, still with his arms around her, his face lit up with triumph.

"Engagement!" A cold chill went through her. "Phillip, you're mad. We can't announce an engagement now."

Doubt crept into his face, and his reply was cynical. "Then you're like the rest of them? Lead a man on and toss him aside?"

It hit her cruelly. "Phillip! Of course I'm not like that. It's just too soon—no one would ever understand. I'm not sure I understand myself." She blushed. "What would the Stones think?"

His face softened, and he took both her hands in his. "It's all right, Honor. I'm sorry." One lock of wet hair dangled in front of his eyes, making him look like a truant schoolboy. "You're absolutely right. We'll wait and announce it at the end of your vacation here."

"We'll see." She knew her color heightened under his ardent gaze. "Now if you don't mind, I'd like to get into some other clothes."

Phillip threw back his head and laughed. "You look like a drowned squirrel. Run along, my dear, and meet me back down here when you've changed."

The glow and tingle of Honor's skin wasn't all caused by her stinging shower. Phillip loved her. Phillip Travis loved her! She raced through her dressing. She mustn't wait one minute longer than necessary. She wanted every bit of time with him she could find. To think, a few weeks ago she had been a poor, forsaken person feeling sorry for herself. Today she was loved—and loved in return. Memories of her parents' happy years glorified her feeling for Phillip.

"Tell me about your home," she urged as they sat together on a big couch in the lobby later. They had eluded his friends, who were going to a dance. Phillip had wickedly whispered, "I don't want any man's arms around you but mine." Honor's heart had pounded. Dancing was another thing she didn't do.

Now Phillip relaxed against the couch and stared into the huge fireplace with its dancing flames. "I suppose the story goes back to my great-grandfather. He married a wealthy Spanish girl, and they acquired Casa del Sol."

"House of the Sun," she translated.

"You know Spanish?" He sounded surprised.

"No, I—I remembered." She wouldn't tell him how she had treasured that phrase all the long, lonely months after he went away.

"Funny, I love it even though I'm not there much. Too busy having a good time. Now that you'll be there with me. . ." His look said volumes.

Honor hastily changed the subject. "Phillip, Babs looked at me tonight as if she hated me."

"Babs and I grew up together, had a lot of fun. I even would have married her a few years ago. She turned me down cold. Now if she wants me back it's just too bad."

She was shocked by his callousness but soothed as he added, "Babs and I are alike—too selfish, demanding. I won't be that way with you." There was an air of humility about him that Honor sensed was foreign to his nature.

"I'm glad you told me, Phillip. Now let's forget it. If she didn't care a few years ago, she probably doesn't care now." But when Honor entered her room that night, lips still tingling from Phillip's good-night kiss, she gasped in dismay.

Seated in a chair by the window, Babs waited, enmity in every fold of her exquisite green gown.

"Do come in." Her voice was mocking. "It *is* your room."

"What are you doing here?" Honor barely had breath to ask. She had been shaken to turn from Phillip and suddenly meet the girl he had once loved.

"I thought we should perhaps have a little talk. You seem to be occupied during the day and evening, so I came here." She motioned insolently to the bed. "You might as well sit down; I intend to be here for some time."

Honor wondered if her shaking knees would carry her that far. "If you are going to tell me all about you and Phillip, you don't need to bother. I already know. He told me."

"Did he indeed! I doubt that he told you *all* about us." The green eyes glittered like algae in a lake, murky and treacherous. "Did he tell you that we have been engaged for years?" She held out a long white hand with bloodred nails. A huge emerald winked a wicked eye from the third finger.

Chapter 3

Honor felt as if she had been stabbed. "Engaged?"

"Of course." Was pity mixed with anger in the other's eyes? "Don't be a little fool. Every time we go on a jaunt Phillip finds a girl. Not always one like you, I'll have to admit. But when vacation's over, he forgets. Didn't he do just that when he left you in San Francisco?" She hardened again. "He knows we will marry when I get ready. Maybe even soon."

"I don't believe you." The sinking feeling in Honor's heart belied her words.

"I suggest you think about it. Don't rush into anything. Once Phillip gets away from the canyon and you, well, he will laugh at his romantic little interlude." Babs rose, magnificently stretching to full height like a sleek cat. "Let him go. It's for your own good."

Strength born of fear flowed through Honor as she remembered little things about Phillip. She must defend herself—and him. "Phillip will be going first. He has asked the Stones and me to visit Casa del Sol. Even if they have to leave, Phillip says Mama Rosa will chaperone me."

"You can bet your sweet life on that!"

Honor ignored the bitter interruption. "We won't get married until we have time to know each other. When we do, I'll be Mrs. Phillip Travis, and nothing can change it!"

"I wouldn't count on it." Babs glided to the door. "I wonder what Phillip's brother will say about you." Her laugh brought color to Honor's face. "He's a hundred years older than Phillip in outlook."

"That's why Phillip is going first." Honor wished she had bitten her tongue when she saw the triumph on Babs's face. "Phillip is sincere—"

"I thought so." The redhead pounced on the first half of Honor's statement. "As far as sincere—Phillip wouldn't recognize the meaning of the word if it bit him on his handsome nose. If you expect sincerity, you'd better run as far and fast as you can from Phillip Travis." Babs's eyes shifted then fixed their cold stare on Honor. "You're one of those do-gooders, aren't you? Then don't deliberately walk into a lion's den." She must have caught Honor's look of surprise. "I went to church—a long time ago, before I met Phillip. Don't think you can change him."

Honor felt herself stiffen. "I'm sure your advice is well meant, but I believe I know what the real Phillip Travis is like. I am going to marry him someday."

Honor could see emotions warring in Babs's face—pity, disgust, hatred, contempt. Pity won. "Then, my dear little governess, may the gods have mercy on you. You'll need it."

The door opened and closed behind her, leaving Honor alone—more alone than she had been even waiting for Keith to come home. The storm in the canyon was as nothing compared to the storm in her heart. Incredible as it seemed, Babs did love Phillip. Then why hadn't she married him when she had the chance? Honor shivered, remembering the callous way Phillip had spoken of Babs. What if he were to say the same about her? No! Her shocked, white face in the mirror denied the traitorous thought. Phillip loved her. Yet hadn't he loved Babs when he once asked her to marry him?

Minutes ticked into hours, and the questions did not cease. Once Honor thought of digging out the Bible Granny had given her so long ago, but discarded the idea. She had made her choice, forfeited her right to expect God's help. She might not be a Christian, but she did know scripture, and God didn't bless those who deliberately turned away from Him. With the first touch of dawn she slipped to the stairs. She would get away from her accusing walls.

As she descended the stairs she heard the clink of silver and laughter from those who were preparing the dining room for breakfast. For a moment she envied the happy workers who came from all over the United States to work with the summer crowds at the canyon. The next moment she slipped outside and ran to the canyon's edge.

"It's unbelievable!" A small squirrel eyed her in alarm and scuttled away. Honor's eyes were no longer heavy. The early morning canyon mists had driven away need for sleep.

How could it be so different, bathed in the almost-ethereal glow of morning? She had seen it in daylight, darkness, storm. Now it had changed completely. No wonder she had read that she wouldn't *see* the canyon but *experience* it.

Honor pulled her cape closer against the chill morning air, watching lazy patches of mist yield to the insistent sun. A tug within reminded her of the struggle from the night before. Some of the beauty dimmed. Why couldn't she put aside the childhood teachings now she had made her choice? Must they forever haunt her?

The sun burst over the canyon wall after sending heralding streaks to announce its arrival. "If only Keith were here!" she cried to the warming rays. But Keith wasn't here. He would never see the canyon. Her face hardened. If he had come back, perhaps she could have accepted the Lord he believed in so strongly. But not now. She had her life to live, and the splendor around her showed that the world could still be beautiful. She would find strength for whatever might come, but not through Christ.

"Good morning, my darling."

Honor whirled from the canyon, feeling betraying color

flooding her face. Phillip was standing a few feet away. His appearance shocked her. Where was the frightening man Babs had described? This was Phillip, eyes soft, hand outstretched—the same Phillip who had come for her in the storm the day before.

"I thought I would find you here." He led her a little apart from the other sightseers, seeking privacy beneath the spreading branches of a tall, gnarled tree. "You're even more beautiful in the morning sunlight than you are drenched from a storm!"

Relief filled Honor until she would have fallen if he had not held her arm. Still, she could not speak. It was the same as coming from the storm into a lighted room—protected, safe, secure. She raised her face to his.

"You're the sweetest girl on earth, Honor." His husky whisper brought her back.

"And you're the most wonderful man." She was rewarded by a look of almost humility in his face.

"I don't deserve you, you know."

Honor felt a strange surge of power and covered it by agreeing. "Of course not!"

Phillip's expression changed to match her gaiety. "You rascal! Let's get some breakfast. We're signed up for the mule trip into the canyon, and it will be leaving soon."

"We are what?" Honor's eyes filled with horror. "You won't get me on any mule going down there!" Her scornful finger indicated a narrow, winding path leading down along the gigantic rock walls, melting into infinity around a bend.

"Of course I will. Ben and Heather can hardly wait to get started. I thought you were excited about going."

"I was," she confessed in a small voice, "until I saw the trail."

"You'll be fine." Phillip innocently added, "Even Babs went last year, and you know she isn't about to go in any danger."

She eyed him suspiciously then relented. "If I fall in the canyon it will be on your conscience."

"You don't really think I'd ever take you where it was unsafe, do you?" Phillip's gaze settled her more than anything else could have done. "You'll be as safe as home in your rocking chair. Ben will be right behind you; Heather and I will be in front of you."

But when breakfast was over and they were ready to go she couldn't help trying once more, appealing to Phillip when the others weren't listening. "Are you sure you want me to go? What if I faint?" She didn't tell him she had never fainted in her entire life. "I'd slow down the whole group."

"Look at me!" Heather piped up, already seated on the mule Phillip would ride. She looked so tiny Honor had another qualm. "She'll be all right, won't she?"

"With me here?" Phillip just smiled. "Simple as riding a rocker." He helped her mount a shaggy beast who turned and looked her over then disinterestedly went back to cropping the sparse grass by the trail. She found herself patting his shoulders timidly, wishing he were a little burro with a cross, instead of just an ornery mule.

"We won't stay overnight this time," Phillip told her. "Next time, after we're married—"

"Next time!" Honor glared. "If you think there will be a—"

"As I was saying. . ." He flashed his famous grin. "They are talking of building a real accommodation in the bottom of the canyon. Phantom Ranch, I think it will be called. But this time we'll just stop for lunch then climb back out this afternoon. We go down several thousand feet. It will be hot." He looked approvingly at her lightweight jacket, which could be removed. "It's going to be a real pleasure educating you in all the things you've never done before, Honor."

Honor's face flamed. Would she always blindly follow his lead, trailing along as she was now trailing on her mule? Her natural common sense and good humor took over.

So what if she did? She'd lead him, too, though in more subtle ways. She clutched her reins, eyes sparkling, and looked straight ahead.

"Don't look down," the guide warned as they rounded a hairpin curve what seemed like eons later. Honor had slid off her jacket, and the warm sun hit her back with its rays.

"Close your eyes if you like, and don't be scared," Phillip called.

What now? Honor had swallowed her heart countless times already. One by one the mules ahead slowed then doubled back on themselves to disappear around the hairpin bend. Closer and closer Honor came until she reached the edge of eternity. Her eyes were fixed straight ahead as she had been told—until Old Baldy's neck shot downward, over the edge of the rim. Involuntarily Honor glanced down, following the line of ears with her gaze, and froze. It was terrible. It was grand. It was the worst thing that had ever happened to her.

"You're doin' fine, miss." The guide's brown face split into a white smile. "Forgot to tell you. Old Baldy always like to crop a little grass right here." He didn't seem to notice how the reins were being held in a death grip that whitened her knuckles. "Just let him eat a bit and he'll make the turn just fine."

Honor couldn't have answered if her life had depended on it—and maybe it did. She just sat. Old Baldy finished his leisurely munching, turned, and followed the others. The weakness seeping through her almost unseated Honor, but with trembling fingers she managed to clutch the reins and smile weakly. She had kept herself from screaming. Now she even managed to smile at Heather.

From that point on, nothing frightened Honor. She had faced the worst with silence. Even the splash of Old Baldy's hooves as he forged through a creek at the bottom of the canyon didn't daunt her. When she fell off her mule into Phillip's arms, it was triumphantly. He need never know the last mile of trail had been managed by sheer determination.

"Well, Honor, wasn't it worth it?"

She gazed around her, really seeing the canyon bottom for the first time. The valley floor lay before her, an oasis of lush greenness. The burbling Colorado River ran red and sluggish. She was glad she had not had to cross that!

"It's—" She couldn't find words.

Phillip tenderly smoothed back clinging tendrils of damp hair from her hot face. "I know. That's why I come here."

Again she was aware of depths within him that did not ordinarily show. Her heart gave a great leap of joy. Surely he would understand and accept the way of life she had chosen, once they were married and she was able to tell him the happiness she had found in it.

"I feel like a glutton," Honor confessed later as she surveyed the shambles of her plate. "I didn't realize anyone could be so hungry!"

"Remarkable how fresh air and exercise can work up an appetite, isn't it?" The grizzled guide had seated himself next to Honor. "Nothing ever tastes so good as outdoor food. Say, if you're going to be around long, you should plan on some of the other canyon trips. You did a good job today. I'd say you could even tackle some of the rough trails."

"Rough trails! You mean this one isn't?" Honor was astonished.

"Of course not. This one's for beginners and tenderfeet." The guide turned away and didn't catch Honor's expression.

Phillip did, and laughed. "Don't look so shocked, Honor. This is Arizona."

All the way through the rest time and back up the canyon

she thought of what Phillip had said. Arizona. It was everything she had dreamed of and more. Soft color stole to her hairline. "Phillip, when—when we're married, would you show me Arizona? All of it?"

"Fervently." The meaning in his one word sent a glow through her. What a change it was, being cared for and protected. The contrast between these past few days and her bleak life since the death of her parents brought a quick rush of emotion to Honor. How could she doubt Phillip in any way when he was so ready to please her?

By the time they got back it was growing a bit dusky. This time Honor didn't fall off Old Baldy; she had to be helped off. "What's wrong with my legs?"

"You're going to be pretty stiff, young lady," the guide warned her. "Take a hot bath and get to bed early. You'll be hobbling a bit tomorrow."

The dire prediction came true. Not only was she hobbling, but Honor also found it took her three tries to get out of bed! Only Phillip's note telling her he'd wait and have breakfast when she did spurred her on.

"Miss Honor, are you going to marry Mr. Travis?" Heather's face was innocent in front of the huge bow in her blond hair.

Before Honor could reply, Phillip said, "I certainly hope so."

"Well!" Mrs. Stone looked as if the breath had been knocked from her. "Why haven't you told us, Honor?"

Phillip came to her rescue, adroitly drawing attention away from the scarlet cheeks above her high-necked white shirtwaist. "She was afraid you'd think it a little sudden."

"Isn't it?"

Honor caught Ben Stone's frown and found her tongue. "I

knew Phillip years ago. He was in San Francisco. . . ." She sounded incoherent even to herself. "I guess I never forgot him, and—" Mrs. Stone cut her off by congratulating Phillip. But Mr. Stone whispered, "Are you happy, Honor?"

"Yes." Joy suffused her face with even more color. "He's everything I ever wanted." Was that a disappointed look in her employer's eyes? Honor pushed the thought aside. How could anyone be disappointed with Phillip?

There was something she must determine now the engagement had been announced. Later, in their favorite spot by the canyon, Honor watched Phillip teasing a frisky squirrel, wondering how to approach him.

"What are you thinking?" he demanded.

It was the perfect opening. "How glad I am I found you again."

A dark flush stained his face. "Was it you who found me? I thought I found you."

"What difference does it make?"

"None, to me." His arms reached for her, but she leaned back.

"Phillip, do—" her voice trembled "—do you care dreadfully for drinking and all that?"

He sat up abruptly and stared at her. "What are you? A preacher?"

It was her turn to flush. "No. I just wondered." She took a deep breath. "I just don't believe in those things." Her voice was small. "I don't know how well I'll fit in your world—or you in mine."

"I'm a heathen, Honor." He didn't catch her involuntary look of dismay. A steel hand seemed to squeeze her heart. She had known he was no Christian and accepted it. But this—

"Do you believe in God?"

"Doesn't everyone?" He waved an indolent hand toward the canyon. "It took a Master Plan to build that."

Honor turned her head to hide her feelings, scarcely able to sort them out. Why did she feel disappointed about his statement? What did she have to lose when she had already put God aside?

"I don't care about drinking when I have you. You can do with me what you like. I'm weak with the crowd. You're seeing the best of me here."

In spite of the heat waves bouncing off the colorful canyon walls, Honor felt a chill trickle down her spine. "You have everything, Phillip. Why follow the crowd?"

A somber shadow crossed his face. "Because of my brother. If he weren't so competent maybe I would be stronger. He thinks it's easier to do everything himself than wait for me to do it. He's right." The shadow deepened. "Don't get me wrong. I love him more than anyone on earth except you, but if he would shove me out and tell me to sink or swim I would be better off."

"What a terrible thing to say!"

"Is it?" Phillip's face contorted. "Let's forget it, kiddo. We'll be happy like they are." He pointed to a bird singing his heart out to his mate.

Honor's throat constricted as she matched the change of mood. Now was no time to preach. Deep inside, resentment of the way Phillip's brother treated him began to grow. Was he an ogre? Even Babs had said he was a hundred years older in outlook. He must be an old fogy, set in his ways. She could just see him: burly; a little uncouth, perhaps, in spite of being the charming Phillip's brother.

Her lips set. She would not build up dislike before meeting him. But once she was established at Casa del Sol she intended to have a little talk with Phillip's brother.

Chapter 4

Incredible as it seemed, summer was nearly over. Mr. Stone reluctantly told them at breakfast one morning, "My business is piling up back home." He looked across at Phillip. "I don't want to rush you, but if you still want us to visit your ranch, it will have to be soon."

Phillip rose to the occasion gracefully. "Of course I do! I'll go ahead myself, maybe even leave today. We'll be waiting for you when you come." The look he gave Honor brought flags flying in her cheeks. That afternoon while Heather napped, Phillip led Honor to their private spot by the canyon's edge.

"It's only the beginning, you know." He looked deep into her eyes, and she bit back the impulse to deny it. Ever since she had known he was to leave and go ahead without her a strange feeling—was it premonition?—had filled her. Perhaps it was because she had overheard Babs say, "About time we were leaving, old thing. It's getting a little tiresome here this time. I'll ride with you, of course."

Phillip evidently didn't sense how lost Honor felt. He was going on about what a wonderful time they'd have at Casa del Sol and how she would love being mistress of the ranch.

"Phillip—" Must her voice shake? Something terrifying gripped her, as if she stood on a high pinnacle, ready to be swept away forever. "Do you really think I can make you happy?"

His eyes warmed. Taking both her hands in his own he drew her close, forcing her to look directly into his eyes. "I am the one who should be asking that." The humility so strange to his nature surfaced again. "You are everything I ever wanted, and much more than I deserve. Fate has been kind."

Honor's own eyes brimmed. If Phillip felt like that, helping him find happiness away from his wild companions should not be such a mountainous task.

Then he was gone. A final kiss, a careless wave, and Phillip Travis disappeared around the bend, leaving a strangely silent canyon.

At first Honor felt bereft. Then she sternly snapped out of it. She was here to be with Heather and was touched when Heather said, "I like Mr. Travis. He was a'f'ly nice about taking us places." She skipped alongside Honor on the trail to the rim, and her hand slid confidingly into Honor's. "But it's nice just us, isn't it? Like it was back home."

Compunction filled Honor. Had she neglected her duties to Heather because of Phillip? She silently shook her head. *No*, her times with Phillip alone had been while Heather slept or was otherwise occupied. She hugged the little girl hard, knowing how much she would miss her. "Yes, it is."

Heather stopped short under a huge pine, feet planted firmly in the needle-carpeted ground. "You won't be going home with us, will you? Mama says that you'll stay at that ranch." Her bright little face clouded over. "What am I going to do without you?"

Honor had dreaded the moment but was prepared. "I talked with your mama and daddy. Heather, they've decided to let you go to school this fall. You'll be six, and it's time. You're going to have a wonderful time. You already know your letters so you'll be ahead of some of the others. There will be other boys and girls and—"

"You mean it?" A smile crept onto Heather's face, chasing away her tears. "Oh, Miss Honor, that's next best to having you!" She clapped her hands and bounced in glee. "But first we get to go to the ranch and ride ponies. Mr. Travis promised."

But Heather was doomed to disappointment.

Ben Stone's face was filled with distress as he came into the dining room, where the rest of their party waited for him so they could start dinner. "A case is coming up, and I must go back tomorrow. I didn't think it would be until later, but I must get home—right away."

"But the ranch," Heather wailed. "What about our visit—and Honor?"

Mr. Stone sighed. "Honor can go ahead with her plans. I believe it's only a matter of weeks until she is being married. I'll hire a car and driver to take her to Casa del Sol."

"But won't you need me on the way back to San Francisco?"

"My dear!" Ben Stone didn't catch his wife's look at the involuntary endearment. Neither did he see her eyes narrow, noticing how beautiful Honor had grown during her stay at the canyon. He was too intent on expressing gratitude. "We are in your debt. You will be well chaperoned by Mama Rosa. Perhaps we can visit another time."

Laurene's words fell like hard, cold rocks, every trace of former friendliness gone. "My husband," she emphasized the words, "is right. I am perfectly capable of handling Heather on the way home."

Honor was shocked at the fury in her face, then comprehension came. The woman was *jealous*! It was all Honor could do to quietly stand. "I'll start packing, right away. I really am not hungry." She escaped with face burning, humiliated by the unjust accusation in Mrs. Stone's eyes.

Her last night at the canyon was filled with troubled dreams, darkness, hands reaching out. She awoke bathed in perspiration, calling out, "Phillip!" Was something wrong at the ranch? Could Phillip have been hurt? She had never given much heed to dreams, but this one left her unnerved.

The driver Mr. Stone hired was taciturn. While the tires nibbled away the miles, Honor had time to reflect. Bitterness toward Mrs. Stone gradually was replaced by pity. What a terrible way to live, suspecting even a hired governess of trying to capture a loved one! She determinedly put the thoughts aside. It was a glorious time to be in Arizona. Already the leaves were beginning to show color. She could picture the bold and golden way the land would look later.

"Take the road toward Kendrick Peak," Phillip had instructed. "About five miles out there is a sign pointing north. Just stay on the road to Casa del Sol. We've had it graded."

His casual directions should have prepared her. They hadn't. She saw the turnoff then the sign boldly blazoned over an arched entrance and cut into a wooden frame, almost as if in a trance. They drove down an endless, tree-lined lane. Honor marveled, even pinching herself to be sure it was real. It was.

Finally they swung around a gentle curve and stopped. The driver unloaded her bags, murmured a quick good-bye and was gone, leaving her staring ahead. Before her lay the mansion, reminiscent of old Spanish dons. Phillip had said it was a Spanish hacienda. He hadn't told her how the warm cream walls and the red tile roof nestled into the hills as if it had been created there. He hadn't told her that it was built around a courtyard. Through an open iron gate, she glimpsed a fountain, flowers, even singing birds. Weakly she leaned against the lacy ironwork. It was too much. How could she ever belong to such a kingdom?

Memory of Babs's taunt flashed through her mind. Honor's chin came up. She would fit in. She would show them all. She and Phillip loved each other, and it was all that was important. It steadied her, but as she slowly approached the great carved door her heart fluttered. Would Phillip seem a little unapproachable here in his own setting?

"May I help you?" Liquid brown eyes in a round face above a spotless white apron looked at her curiously as the door opened.

"Mama Rosa!" Honor impulsively held out her hand, taking the older woman's hand in her own.

"You know me?" The puzzle had not left the housekeeper's face.

"Oh, yes. Phillip has told me all about you."

"Oh. Felipe. You are his friend? Come in. You are welcome."

"I am—" What check chained her from adding, "his fiancée"? "I am his friend," Honor substituted. "Is Phillip here?" She looked expectantly around the great hall, subconsciously noting the dark wood against cream walls, the high vaulted ceilings.

"No, he has gone—"

Honor felt his presence before he spoke from behind her. "I'll handle this, Mama Rosa."

The Mexican woman opened her lips to protest, but Honor was already whirling toward the doorway behind her. "Phillip!" Her greeting fell to a whisper. *"What has happened to you?"* Her horrified eyes took in the bloodstained bandage around his head, the way he leaned against the wall for support. "Darling, my dream was true. You're hurt!"

"It's all right." He caught her in mid-flight, before she could throw her arms around him. "Mama Rosa, can you get me something for this? That ornery colt Juan and I were working with stumbled and threw me against the corner of the fence."

Mama Rosa came to life and scuttled away, but Honor clung to Phillip. "You must sit down." She spied a blanket-covered couch against the opposite wall and half led him there. "Oh, Phillip, I just knew something terrible had happened. That's why I got here so early."

The man on the couch looked at her wearily. "You call me Phillip. I don't seem to have had the pleasure of meeting you."

Honor stared at him, unable to believe her own ears. "Not know me! You mean you don't remember the canyon—or anything?"

He passed his hand over his eyes. "I don't seem to. Would you mind terribly? Could we talk later?"

Her face reflected how stricken her soul was, but she only said slowly, "You mean the blow on the head has erased everything—you really don't know who I am?"

Her agony must have shown. The dull eyes looked sympathetic. "I'm sorry." He turned toward Mama Rosa, who had come in with a basin and antiseptic. "Mama Rosa, give this young lady a room. What did you say your name was?"

"Honor Brooks."

Phillip staggered to his feet. "I'll talk with you later, Miss Brooks. Wait here until Mama finishes with me, and she'll show you where to go." He lurched against her, then with Mama as guide, disappeared into another room, leaving Honor alone.

She sank to the couch, automatically smoothing the blanket. What a horrible thing to have happen! What should she do? Phillip looked so ghastly with that bloody bandage on his head, not at all like the man she had known. Yet a great sympathy went through her. How must he feel, being hurt and entering his home to find a perfect stranger there, one who called him "darling" and insisted he knew her?

She sprang to her feet. Why was she standing there doing nothing? Couldn't she help? But before she could more than take a step in the direction he had gone, Mama Rosa came back. "Come with me, please." She led the way up a curved staircase and into a room at the right. "You will stay here."

"But how is he?"

Mama Rosa's impassive face widened in a smile. "He is fine. It is nothing for him to be thrown. Now he needs rest. He will see you after siesta." She threw back the covers of the huge bed so in keeping with the other decor. "Rest. I will tell you when to come." The smile came again. "But first I bring you a tamale."

"Thank you, Mama Rosa." The door closed behind her. Honor smiled. Even in his pain Phillip must have thought of her. The plate Mama Rosa brought contained not only tamales but a taco as well, bearing little resemblance to the pale imitations Honor had eaten in San Francisco. She drank glasses of ice water to get the heat from her mouth then threw herself on the bed. If siesta was the custom here, she was all for it.

After her sleepless night, the good food and warm room had done its work well. She slept until slanting afternoon sun rays filled the room. She had only stirred enough to torpidly reach for her shoes when Mama Rosa tapped at the partly open door. "Come now."

Honor ran a brush through her hair and followed the Mexican woman down a long hall, carpeted in red, to the open door of a huge room. "You go in there." Mama Rosa stood aside.

Why should she feel strangely unwilling to cross the threshold? For a moment she hesitated, then the rich voice she had learned to love called, "Come in."

She stepped inside, glancing quickly toward Phillip. He was not lying down as she had expected. He was seated behind the most massive desk she had ever seen. This must be the study. It had all the stark necessities of a business office: typewriter, file cabinets, everything needed to proclaim it the utilitarian room it was. Honor bit back her disappointment. Even if he didn't remember her, did he have to fortify himself behind that desk? It was as she had feared and more. He was not only unapproachable; he was totally remote from anything connected with her.

She could delay looking at him no longer. To her relief the bandage had given way to a smaller patch near his hairline. He still looked pale, but it could be the filtered light through the heavy drapes.

Phillip leaned toward her, motioning her to a chair at the end of the desk. "Miss Brooks, this must come as quite a shock to you. You don't know how sorry I am."

"It is a shock, Phillip." Could that strained voice really be hers? "After the past few weeks, all our plans—" she faltered. How could she talk to the stone-faced man across the desk?

The measured glance softened. Abruptly Phillip rose and walked to her. "I believe we should go somewhere a little more relaxed. You were right. I remember nothing of you, but I want to know." His kindness nearly broke her control. She stumbled a bit, and he caught her arm as they walked downstairs and into the courtyard. Blinded by tears, she was only barely aware of its beauty. His strong hold was all that mattered.

"Now." He seated her on a garden bench, pillowed with cushions, sheltered by a great cottonwood tree. "Tell me all about us."

For a moment Honor was speechless. "But—how can I tell you—it's like talking with a stranger! Oh, Phillip, can't you remember any of it?" A new thought struck her. "Not even knowing me in San Francisco?"

"San Francisco!" For a moment hope flared but died as Phillip shook his head. "No. I remember nothing of the sort." He must have sensed her distress. "Talk to me not as a stranger but as a friend. I promise not to interrupt."

It was the most bizarre assignment Honor could have been given. To tell Phillip, beloved yet not knowing her, how they met—everything!

Honor was aware of the strong clasp of his hand as she leaned back on the bench. Hastily she sketched in their meeting and friendship in San Francisco. She skipped over the sorrow during Granny's and Keith's deaths and looking for a job, and went into how the Stones hired her and brought her to the Grand Canyon. Now and then he smiled, giving her courage to go on. After all, this man had fallen in love with her and proposed, even inviting her to Casa del Sol. Why should she fear him simply because he could not remember through no fault of his own?

When she reached the part about meeting again at the canyon she was breathless, glad for the lengthening shadows hiding his face and her own. "I ran for the door, crossed the lobby, started upstairs. I could hear laughing voices. The next moment I was on the floor, staring up stupidly. You had been talking with Babs and the rest of them. You picked me up, recognized me." A soft glow filled her face. "You said, 'I say, I've knocked you down with my clumsiness. I should have been looking where I was going.'"

There was a muffled sound of protest from Phillip. She continued, "It was the beginning of—of an old acquaintance."

"And love?" His stern voice gave her the shivers.

"Yes," she whispered. "What we felt in San Francisco when you asked me to wait for you all came back. As the days passed, and we spent time together at the canyon. . ." Her voice trailed off. She returned to the present with an effort. "You invited the Stones and me to visit Casa del Sol. You wanted to prepare your brother before we arrived. I have to confess, I am anxious to meet him. He's grown to be something of an ogre in my mind." She laughed nervously.

As if galvanized into action, Phillip leaped to his feet to tower over her. She was instantly contrite. "I'm sorry! It's just that I want him to like me. When will I meet him?"

"Soon enough. Go on. The Stones couldn't make it?"

"No. He was called home. Is this bringing anything back to you?" She could hear him breathing hard.

He shook his head and said, "I promised not to interrupt, but I have to tell you I know this isn't easy for you. Believe me, it's the only way."

She gave a little cry and put her other hand over his. "I'm so glad you understand! Last night I dreamed of strange, troubled hands reaching toward me. I woke up feeling something terrible had happened to you. That's why I came early."

He released her hands and drew her closer. "I don't think it's terrible. I think perhaps it's the best thing that ever happened."

"What a strange remark! Are you sure your head is all right?"

"It's fine." He stood, propelled to his feet with almost catlike grace. "Honor, we must have dinner. You can finish telling me the story later. We'll build a fire in the fireplace."

After the delicious dinner Mama Rosa served on a tray in her room, Honor followed the housekeeper downstairs to what evidently was the library. It was all she had pictured, with its blazing fire. Again she was grateful for the darkness.

"Honor, the one thing you haven't told me is how you feel. Are you in love with me? Did you promise to marry me?"

Her shining hair curtained her downcast face. "Yes."

She could hear the sharp intake of breath before Phillip answered. "And you're the kind of girl who would never go back on a promise." It was not a question, but a statement. It brought Honor's eyes to his.

"I am bound by my word." For one frightening moment she was back on the canyon's edge, facing the storm overhead and the tumult in her heart. It was almost as if she were being given a second chance to reconsider. Phillip didn't remember her. What if he never did? What if she was deliberately deluding herself into thinking she could be queen of this near-palace? The immensity of the very room in which they sat increased her doubts. What was she, a child's governess, doing in this place?

"Well?"

Even as she opened her mouth to break the chains binding her to this unknown Phillip, memory of her position came. Granny, Keith, home—all gone.

Even the security of her position with the Stones was gone. She could not go back. What did it matter if he didn't know her now? When he remembered, he would still be her beloved, the man who was kind to Heather, who openly confessed a past dark with unsaid choices but who also reached forward to a brighter future here on the ranch with her to strengthen him.

"You really think Phillip Travis is the husband you need?"

Had he divined her thoughts, or was his memory returning? "Yes." Once it was said, it was easier. "We will share our lives, create a home, have children—just as we planned." It was all she could get out for now.

Phillip broke away, turned to the fire and moodily stared into the flames. "Go home, Honor. Back to San Francisco. You will never find happiness here."

His command roused a demon of opposition she hadn't known lay within. "Never! You asked me to marry you. I accepted. Surely you will remember in a few days."

"Have you ever been in love before?" He swung to face her.

"Once." She could feel a reminiscent smile turn to laughter as she confessed. "A certain soldier came to San Francisco—he asked me to wait for him." She sobered. "When he didn't write, I shut my heart and wouldn't admit how it hurt."

"Phillip Travis?"

"Yes."

He gripped her shoulders. "Are you prepared to deal with drinking, sometimes to excess? With other women?"

Her confidence turned to fear. "But—but you said I was the one you'd waited for all your life. You said drinking didn't mean anything when I was with you."

"And you still want to marry me?" Disbelief filled his eyes. "Even knowing those protestations might not be true?" His face slowly iced over. "Or do you expect me to change?"

"I—I hope you will!" Stung by the agony inside she cried, "Why do you downgrade yourself? I know there is a part of you that wants more from life than idleness." She faced him squarely and had the satisfaction of seeing him drop his eyes.

"Did we talk about this at the canyon?"

She had to be honest. "Some. You told me I was seeing the best of you there, alone, away from temptation. I want to help you, Phillip."

"What else did we talk about?"

"Everything. Your desire to be more a part of the ranch, to convince your brother—" She broke off.

She wasn't prepared for the fury in the blazing eyes threatening to scorch her, or his low reply, "Forget about my brother!"

"Phillip!"

He ignored her cry. His eyes turned to black coals. "If you expect to have all your childish fantasies come true, you better keep moving. Phillip Travis is not a knight on a white horse."

She swayed, unconsciously putting up her hands in protest. "Why do you keep referring to yourself so? Or are you pretending? Maybe you do remember." Horror filled her. "That's it, isn't it? You do remember and are regretting getting entangled with a governess." Her face felt tight, her lips parched. "You have changed. Did Babs convince you I wasn't worthy? When you prate to me of worth, is it me you are thinking of, *or yourself*?"

He sidestepped the question and gripped her shoulders again until she knew there would be bruises in the morning. "Is there nothing I can say that will make you go away?"

"Only that you never want to see me again." One final time she felt on the brink, but she ignored the bridge and plunged in. "Nothing else on earth can make me leave you."

Phillip's face twisted, a groan escaped his tightly clenched lips. "Then stay—and may heaven protect you!"

Even through her victory the bitter drop remained. She had forfeited the right to expect God's protection—for Phillip. Shaken, she pushed down the thought and lightened the atmosphere. "I expect you to show me Arizona. Not just Casa del Sol but the White Mountains and the Oak Creek Canyon and—"

"And just when are we getting married in all this?"

Honor caught her breath. "Oh, not until you remember everything, and you will."

"I am already getting a clearer picture of the past from what you have said."

Joy skyrocketed inside her as she lifted her face and put her arms around him in a gesture both loving and protective. "Then let's do as we planned. We can ride and talk and learn to really know each other!" She was amazed at her own boldness and dropped her arms hastily. "Phillip, you seem almost a different person here in your own home, almost a stranger."

She could feel his surprise as he asked, "Which man do you love? The vacationer at the canyon, or the rancher in his home?"

"Since it will be my home, too, it will have to be the rancher—" She never finished. Slowly he crushed her to him, seeking her lips with his own. Her arms crept around his neck as she returned his kiss. "Why, Phillip, you really are a stranger! You have never kissed me like that before." She pulled back and stared at him.

"A man in his castle is a different creature than on any other ground." A curious glint filled his eyes, and the lips that had claimed hers turned upward into a smile she did not understand. But when he held out his arms again, she flew to them like a homing pigeon. Stranger or not, Phillip Travis was the man she loved.

Chapter 5

Somewhere in the darkness a horse softly whinnied. Honor turned in the heavily carved bed then ran to the window. Why would anyone be out now? Moonlight sneaked through her slightly parted drapes to touch a clock on the wall. One thirty.

Her eyes widened as she pushed the heavy drapes open. A tall rider was swinging easily onto the back of a white horse that gleamed in the moonlight. His upturned face brought a gasp to Honor's lips. Phillip! The prancing horse daintily stepped away from the corral and down the path. Honor could hear the rhythm of hooves as horse and rider gradually increased speed once away from the hacienda.

"How strange! I didn't think Phillip would be the type to go riding at midnight." A thrill shot through Honor as she shivered her way back to bed. The night was crisp, and fresh air streamed through the partly opened window. She breathed deep and hugged her knees. It all smelled so clean, pines and flowers. How could she be so fortunate?

A smile lit her face in the darkness, sending a glow through her. The next instant it vanished in a frown. How different Phillip was in his own home! Why had he ordered her back to San Francisco? She could feel her heartbeat quicken. He could not be the selfish person he had described, or he wouldn't be putting her ahead of himself. Even though he seemed firmer and stronger here at Casa del Sol, he must have been thinking of her happiness, afraid he could not fill her expectations. A protective wave of love for him replaced her other feelings. She would help him be what she believed he could be—in spite of his own protestations. No one could feel about the canyon the way Phillip did and yet be narrow-minded enough not to recognize a better way of life than that of his friends.

The weakness of her reasoning hit her immediately. She refused to listen to the voice inside. She had chosen. She would not turn back. She would become mistress of Casa del Sol. The high ceilings of the spacious room echoed her whisper, "Is it all a dream?" She pinched her arm hard then rubbed the aching spot. No. She really was here. In her wildest dreams she had only imagined visiting a large ranch someday. Now she would be part of it, and when Phillip's brother came—Honor's face flamed in the darkness. Where was he? She hadn't even thought to ask. How could she have blurted out as she had about Phillip's brother being an ogre? Phillip must think her gauche if not downright rude. She set her chin resolutely. When he did come, she would make him like her. Much of her happiness depended on the unknown stranger.

Now that she had seen Casa del Sol she should be able to conjure up a better image of Phillip's brother than an ogre! He must be industrious. Phillip had confessed indolence, and the ranch still prospered. Her fingers interlaced as she promised the night wind, "Phillip is going to learn to work. He will be happier. I'll start by asking to see the ranch. He can't help learning when he sees how interested I am."

Honor shivered. "Learning! Will I ever learn everything there is to know about this place? Will I ever really be comfortable with Mama Rosa? She will have to teach me." She laughed nervously. "Nothing in my background has fitted me for this!"

Memory of the mule trip and resulting stiffness brought a rueful twist to her good intentions. "I'll have to learn to ride. Not on that magnificent white animal I just saw. Maybe there's a pony."

Her thoughts returned to the absent brother. No picture would come. Sleepy from her mental gymnastics, she turned over, wondering where Phillip had gone.

A gentle tapping roused her. The brilliance of the sun pouring through the drapes she had left open hurt her eyes for a moment.

"Come in." She pulled the sheet up under her chin, stealing a glance at the clock. Ten! She had slept away half the morning of her first day at Casa del Sol.

"I brought your breakfast." Rosa's brown face above the tray was as impassive as it had been the day before.

Honor smiled warmly, noting it brought a response. The muscles in Rosa's face relaxed. "Good morning, Rosa. What a beautiful day!" She slipped from bed and into a robe and slippers then ran to the window again. She looked down, amazed at the pang that shot through her when she discovered the corral was empty.

"Where are the horses? And Phillip? I heard him ride out last night."

Rosa's gaze was startled and there was a slight breathiness in her reply. "Felipe is not here."

"And his brother?"

"Señor is not here, either."

Honor whirled. "You sound—" She broke off. It was not for her to comment on how Rosa sounded. "This looks delicious, but I can never eat it all!"

For the first time Rosa actually smiled. "You will eat. Casa del Sol makes you hungry." She fussed about, buttering the hot biscuits, rearranging the silver. "The peaches come from our own trees. The bacon is from our hogs. The honey is from our hives."

"Rosa." Honor put her hand on the sturdy brown one. "I'm going to marry Phillip, but I don't know anything about running a place such as this! I can cook, but not like this. Will you teach me all I should know?"

The smile became a beam then faded. "It will be for Señor to say."

"Señor?" Honor was puzzled, then light broke. "Oh, you mean Phillip's brother." Something of her fear of the unknown Señor showed in her flat voice.

"Sí." Rosa moved toward the door. "Call when you have eaten." She indicated an old-fashioned bellpull. Dignified, with no trace of the softer nature she had shown only moments before, Rosa opened the door and glided through.

"Very much the controlling influence of Casa del Sol," Honor told the empty room. "She changed when I mentioned my new brother-to-be. She calls him Señor. He must be *uno grande hombre.*" Honor laughed at her own mixture of English and Spanish. "If I'm going to use any Spanish I'd better learn more than I know now!"

The breakfast was delicious, and when she had finished Honor bathed and dressed, this time in a simple blue gown. She would carry her own tray downstairs. Perhaps Rosa would be a little friendlier. But it wasn't Rosa Honor found when she located the kitchen after opening three doors to other rooms. Phillip sat at the gleaming white-topped table so out of keeping with the rest of the house.

"Good morning, Phillip." The pleats in her skirt swung as she started toward him.

He motioned her back. "Don't get too close. I've been with the horses and am not fit to be around beautiful ladies."

Color flowed freely into her face. He sounded like a little boy. "I saw you ride out last night. Where did you go?"

"I had a lot to think of." Laughter fled from his voice. His dark eyes held her as he pushed back his chair abruptly. "How about a ride this morning? You have breakfasted, haven't you?"

"So much I probably won't be able to get on a horse!"

Her fears were unfounded. Phillip led out a pinto pony a half hour later. Clad in knickers and boots, with her khaki skirt and a sombrero borrowed from Rosa's daughter, Carlotta, she managed to get in the saddle with one gentle boost from Phillip. Her pony, Jingles, had an easy gait. Phillip said Jingles was a single-footer. It was almost like riding a rocking horse!

Honor reined him in at the top of a cedar-covered ridge. "Does it never end?" Her eyes ranged from the red and white shorthorns grazing the valley floor to the already snowcapped mountains to the north. Casa del Sol's roof shone red in the sunlight, warming the gray sage and green pines and cedars surrounding it.

"It is a responsibility," Phillip said. "A trust from my grandfather and father." Honor sensed he spoke more to himself than to her. "Dozens of families depend on us and the way this ranch is run. Not just our cowboys and other workers. We furnish meat for a lot of Arizona."

"I believe it. It's almost too much for one family."

"That's what my brother says." Phillip's eyes were somber.

A strange feeling dimmed the sun streaming down on them. He couldn't mean his brother was considering selling the ranch! Not just when she had determined to make Phillip a part of it. She started to speak, thought better of it, and said, "I just hope I can be—"

She never finished the sentence. A man on a horse was racing toward them, a yellow paper in his hand.

Honor looked at Phillip. His face was the color of parchment. He spurred his horse, and the white stallion leaped forward. Flying hooves ate the distance between the two men. Honor started to follow. She was struck by the rigidity of Phillip's figure as he took the yellow paper and read it. She automatically hesitated, and Phillip turned back toward her. As he shortened the space between them she couldn't help admiring the ease with which he rode.

The parchment color had left his face, replaced by a dark flush. "Honor, would you marry me right away? Before the end of the week?"

"But we agreed—"

"I know. I just don't feel that way any longer. You don't want a big fancy wedding, do you?"

"No, Phillip." She had a terrifying sense of something lurking ahead, some unknown danger. "I just want a simple ceremony. But I wanted more time, time for you to remember. . ." Her voice gave way.

"I know." He touched his mount's side lightly with his heels, bringing him alongside Jingles. "I'll take care of you, Honor. I'll make sure you don't come to any harm. Won't you do as I ask?"

Honor's eyes dropped to the yellow page still in Phillip's hand. Sudden understanding filled her.

Phillip's eyes followed her gaze. "Yes, it's from my brother. He will be home sometime next week."

Honor couldn't bear the way his head drooped, as if in shame. A great wave of love and understanding again flooded her. Phillip needed her. He dreaded the homecoming, what might happen. Would there be violent objections? The same protective warmth that had stirred the night before crept into her veins. If disappointment mingled with it, she valiantly pushed it back. Did it really matter if she knew this white-faced man weeks, months, or years? Again she squelched the *yes!* her conscience was shouting. If Phillip needed her so much, how could she refuse? "The only white dress I have is one I made from a discard of Mrs. Stone's wardrobe."

"You don't think that matters!" He swept her into his arms. It was enough to eliminate any lingering doubt she might have had.

On the way home Honor was quiet. Phillip did not attempt to intrude on her thoughts. It wasn't until he helped her down that he said, "Honor, no matter what happens, you won't ever despise me, will you?"

He knows I know he is weak. Honor bit back a betraying rush of tears. "I will love you as long as I live."

Phillip did not kiss her again. Instead he held her close to his rapidly beating heart. "It's the only way. When you understand, when—"

"I already understand." She placed gloved fingers over his lips.

"Rest a bit before lunch, Honor. This Arizona weather is far different from what you are used to in San Francisco."

"I noticed I had a little trouble breathing."

"We're several thousand feet high. You'll adjust in a few days."

Honor ran upstairs. In just a few days she would be Phillip's wife—for better or worse. Why did that phrase have to pop up? She whirled into her room.

Carlotta, in school skirt and middy blouse, looked up from folding back the bedspread. Her Spanish ancestry showed in her shining dark hair and eyes. "How do you like Casa del Sol?"

"I don't know if I can ever be worthy of it."

She repeated the words later that week to Phillip. They had ridden through the soft twilight to a different knoll above the valley. "This place—can I ever be worthy of it?"

"Worthy? You? It is I—" He broke off, unseeing eyes tracing the pattern of a bubbling stream in the valley that was only a silver thread from their viewpoint.

"You will be worthy, too, Phillip. When your brother comes, we'll show him that you really want to be a part of the ranch. He will respect your feelings."

Phillip's dark eyes flashed. "The ogre, as you nicknamed him?"

Honor turned beet red. "I'm sorry for that. I really didn't mean it. It's just that I want us to be happy here." The wistfulness in her voice brought a squeeze from Phillip's hand that threatened to crush her fingers, even in the sturdy riding gloves Carlotta had furnished.

"I pray you will never be anything here but happy."

"Just to think that a few weeks ago Mr. Stone was telling me not to come down here and marry some Arizonan!" She laughed.

"Would you rather have waited and asked him to the wedding?"

Honor felt the tension in the question. "No. He would never understand how I could be so sure so quickly, when all my life I've been waiting." Her fiery color intensified until it matched the jutting rocks near where they had stopped. "I'm not sure I understand myself."

"You aren't regretting it?"

There was no hesitation. "No, Phillip. I will never regret marrying you tomorrow."

"You're the sweetest thing on earth." He leaned across from his horse Sol's back to kiss her, almost reverently. "I will do everything in my power to keep you from regretting it." His eyes were like glittering obsidian in a chalky face. "Honor, will you promise to trust me, no matter what?"

"I will."

Even later, as she dressed for her last hours as a single woman, Honor thought of the scene on the little plateau. Tomorrow she would take her wedding vows. But her real vow had been taken on that little plateau overlooking Casa del Sol.

"This time tomorrow I'll be your wife." Honor's eyes were pools of happiness as Phillip walked her to her door that night. The moonlit night threw patterns of fantastic beauty across the upper hall.

"Yes." Why did Phillip seem distracted?

"You—you aren't regretting?"

She felt him start in the dimness. "I regret nothing." He captured her, kissing her the way he had done that first night she arrived at Casa del Sol. Honor's doubts fled before the intensity of his love. It was a long time before she broke away.

"Good night, Phillip." She slipped through the heavy door, closing it behind her. Just before it shut out all sounds, somewhere in the hacienda a bell rang. The telephone? What if Philip's brother—she laughed at her own fancies. How melodramatic to think a disapproving man would appear on the doorstep at the eleventh hour to stop her wedding!

At last Honor had time to think.

Tomorrow Juan and Rosa and Carlotta would go to Flagstaff for her wedding with Phillip. Carlotta would be her bridesmaid. Phillip had said earlier this evening he had arranged for them to be married by a minister.

Her heart swelled. How thoughtful! He had instinctively known how she would want it. But a horrendous thought marred her happiness.

What if Phillip's brother should be in Flagstaff?

She punched her pillow then buried her face in its cooling depths. She must get over this obsession about the man! All she knew about him was the little Phillip had told her.

Again Honor heard hooves in the night and ran to her window. Again she saw the tall dark-haired man mount an unsaddled white horse, one she now knew as Sol. Was he nervous about tomorrow? The thought was strangely comforting. She had been so sure she'd never sleep. Now she dove into bed and moments later was unconscious.

"Señorita, you are beautiful!" There was no disapproving silence about Rosa this morning. "Señora Dolores would be proud to have you marry her son!"

Honor's eyes filled. Early this morning a large box had arrived with a note from Phillip:

I know you have a white dress to be married in.
I hope you will wear this with it.

There had been no signature, but inside had been the most exquisitely wrought lace mantilla Honor had ever seen or imagined. Slightly yellowed with age, it only brought out the highlights of her skin.

"I don't know how to wear it," she confessed to Carlotta.

"We will help you," the beautiful bridesmaid promised, her dark face picking up color from the soft, rosy gown she wore. Now as Honor faced herself in the mirror, it was not only her own image she saw but the joy on the faces of Rosa and Carlotta. Turning impulsively she threw her arms around them both, heedless of the priceless mantilla. "I am so glad I came to Arizona!"

"We are glad, too! You and Señor will be very happy." Carlotta's eyes danced.

"We will help you dress and arrange the mantilla when we get to Flagstaff," Rosa promised as they disrobed her and carefully packed her dress and mantilla in boxes. "Bad luck for bridegroom to see you in dress before wedding."

"Mamacita believes in old customs." Carlotta laughed, but there was genuine respect and love in her voice.

"I think I do, too." Honor danced to the window, still in her long white slip. "Was there ever a more beautiful day for a bride? I'm a fall person. You know, my birthday is next week."

Rosa beamed. "Why did you not wait and be married on your birthday?"

"Phillip didn't want to wait so long." Her voice was muffled in her slip as she quickly drew on a simple dress for the drive into Flagstaff. "I think he's a little bit afraid of his brother coming home and stopping the wedding."

In the absolute silence that fell Honor pulled the top triumphantly over her head and settled it. Only then did she realize how still it had become. She was instantly contrite! "I shouldn't have said that! It is just that I want us all to be happy, and I wish he *would* come!"

Rosa's somber glance reminded Honor of the way she had responded when Honor first came. Quietly she gathered up the slip and packed it then turned toward the door. "Señor Travis is a fine man." She slipped out, leaving Honor staring.

"It's all right." Carlotta seemed anxious to bridge the uncomfortable moment. "Mamacita thinks the sun doesn't come up or go down without first consulting Señor!"

Honor laughed in spite of feeling guilty, picturing the sun bowing daily before Casa del Sol and asking permission to rise and set! "Just where is he now?" Honor inquired as she ran a brush through her hair.

"Oh, here and there." Carlotta sounded vague, disinclined to discuss his whereabouts. "Where are you going for your honeymoon—or do you know?"

"Right here. Where could there be anything more glorious?" She spun about and frowned. "When we were at the canyon we talked about going back after we were married. Carlotta, it's so strange. He still doesn't seem to remember a lot of what happened at the canyon."

"Why is it important?" The liquid brown eyes shifted.

Honor turned back to the window, noting how the golden leaves fluttered—cottonwood, aspen, birch. She had learned to love them all. "He just seems so much older here. Different. More mature."

The watching eyes reflected breathlessness in Carlotta's question. "Which do you love more? The canyon man, or this one?"

Honor's face glowed. "I love the man who owns Casa del Sol. More than anything in the world."

"Then I suggest you come with me and marry him." The laughing invitation from the doorway brought consternation to Carlotta's face until she saw Honor light up and bow. "I'll do just that."

"You like my invitation, Señorita?" The watching dark eyes were suddenly sober.

"I love your invitation, Señor." She turned to Carlotta. "Coming?"

"No. Mamacita and Papa and I will take our own car. You will want to come back alone." Her flashing smile added to her beauty.

"That's right, Carlotta. I'm going to want my wife all to myself for a few hours."

Honor could feel a tiny pulse beating in her throat. "You'll bring everything, Carlotta?"

"Everything."

Carlotta was as good as her word. A few hours later she carefully lifted the priceless mantilla to Honor's head. But it was for Rosa to carefully adjust its folds so it cascaded to Honor's shoulders. Something in Honor's eyes seem to touch the good woman's heart. "Be happy, Señorita." She pressed her warm brown cheek to Honor's paler one, feeling the clutch of nervous fingers before Honor laughed.

"It is time." Carlotta threw open the door of the little room next to the chapel.

How could Phillip have arranged so much in such a short time? The small chapel seemed smothered with autumn leaves, dark fir branches. Fall flowers of every color perfumed the room. The measured tones of the "Wedding March" from *Lohengrin* softly pulsated, keeping time to Honor's beating heart.

Honor clutched her bouquet of old-fashioned flowers. They must have been especially chosen by Phillip from those she admired most in his courtyard. Late roses, even a few tiny forget-me-nots. It was a shame for such a perfect wedding to be seen by so few.

Carlotta's rosy skirt swished to a standstill. It was Honor's turn. Shakily, she started down the long aisle, seeing nothing except Phillip waiting for her.

The wedding ceremony was a little blurred. Only one thing really stood out in the kaleidoscope of Honor's memory. When the minister turned to Phillip he said, "Do you, James Travis, take this woman. . ."

Honor gasped, feeling as if inchworms were measuring her spine. The next moment Phillip's strong had tightened reassuringly on her own. His face was pale, but the dark eyes were steady. Honor wondered how the minister could have made such a mistake. Obviously it was all right, or Phillip would have stopped the service for a correction. Her surprise soon settled down. Of course—James must be Phillip's first name and necessary for legal documents. Her unanswered musings were drowned in the "I do" that rang from the arched beams of the little chapel.

Honor's own response was quieter. Two words, so little to signify passing her life into James Phillip Travis's keeping until death did them part. She blinked back mist that hid the scene for a moment, realizing as never before how truly irrevocable that promise was.

"I pronounce you man and wife. What God hath joined together, let no man put asunder." In spite of her joy, Honor shivered. How could any man or woman break promises as solemn as the vows in the wedding service?

Phillip turned to her. His lips found hers, lingering as if loath to let her go. She could feel his resignation when he finally released her. Her heart responded. Their first kiss as man and wife; holy, beautiful. If only everyone would just go away and leave them alone! But it was not to be. From somewhere a photographer appeared.

"I thought you would want pictures," her new husband explained. "But not during the actual ceremony. I've seen too many weddings interrupted by photographers. Would you mind posing with me, Mrs. Travis?"

"Not a bit, Mr. Travis." Excitement like a skyrocket trembled within her as she laughed and smiled. Phillip had even arranged for a wedding cake in a nearby restaurant's private room. "We want pictures for our children." He watched her color rise as she stammered.

"It's a bit hard to talk to a brand-new husband, isn't it?" She finally gave up small-talk efforts in total honesty. "It's also time for us to go home."

"Home!" Something golden glowed within Honor. "House of the Sun. May it ever prove to be so for us."

"And when the shadows come?"

She looked resolutely into his face. "We will know the sun is always there. Shadows pass, the sun returns."

"You darling!" The ardent look in his eyes stirred her. But he only said, "Wouldn't you like to change into something else for the drive back? That mantilla must be heavy."

Honor thought for a moment. "I'll take the mantilla off but leave my gown on. I won't ever have another wedding day, so I want to look beautiful on this one."

He gently lifted the mantilla from her hair and handed it to Mama Rosa, voice sober. "Put it away, Mama. I'm taking Honor home."

"Vaya con Dios." The beautiful Spanish blessing rested on them

as Phillip helped her into the big touring car. She waved and smiled as they backed and turned.

"What does it mean, Phillip? Something about God, I know that."

"Go with God."

"How fitting. Vaya con Dios," she repeated the words then turned back to him. "Phillip, it will take all the days of our lives to learn what there is to know about each other."

The Willys swerved, righted itself, then slowly inched ahead. Honor vaguely noticed and wondered at a honking carload of people next to them, waiting for a wagon ahead to pass, but paid little attention to them. Phillip's hands were white on the wheel. "Honor, there's something I have to tell you, as soon as we get home—"

His sentence was never finished. From the open Stutz next to them a wild whoop went up. Staring across at the other car, Honor was stunned. A tall dark-haired man was wildly waving—and he was an exact replica of Phillip!

She opened her lips to speak then glanced at Phillip. He had gone a curious color, as if all the blood had drained from his face under the tan. His lips twisted. The pain in his face caught at her heart. Again she tried to speak, but nothing came from her frozen throat. Was Phillip that much afraid of his brother? It must be he in the other car, but why hadn't Phillip told her they were twins?

Her calculations, slowed by shock, were shattered when the other man called, his mocking voice clearly audible in the late fall air. "Well, Honor, James—what have you two been up to? And Honor in a white dress, even!"

Honor reeled back against the seat. It was the same voice she had heard on the floor of El Tovar Hotel. There was no mistaking it—the man in that car was Phillip Travis! Arm about Babs, laughing with the others Honor knew from the canyon, he was in curious contrast to the man gripping the steering wheel of the car she was in—the man she had just promised to love, honor, and cherish for as long as she lived.

"That's Phillip." Her voice broke in a sob, pleading for understanding just as that same something that had haunted her during the wedding magnified. "But then, who, what—he called you James. You aren't, you can't be—" She couldn't get another sound past the mountain that seemed to have closed off her throat.

Her words seemed to release her companion from the trance he had fallen into, almost as if a wicked spell had been called out in that laughing, accusing voice from the other car.

He turned to her for an instant then shot ahead and around the corner out of sight of the pointing, laughing hecklers. A crooked smile touched his ashen lips, a mocking salute recognized by her stumbling question. "Meet James Travis, Señora. Once again the lovely princess has married the ogre."

Chapter 6

"*You?* It can't be true." Honor flexed stiff lips, sliding far away from him, as if he really were an ogre. Flecks of memory darted to her. "Then—" Her laugh was slightly hysterical. "Of course. That's why you didn't remember anything from the canyon. *Because you never were there with me!*"

His silence was maddening. Honor swallowed hard. It must be a nightmare. Her perfect wedding, and now this? Impossible! The man beside her who had been so gentle, so loving—an impostor. She could feel herself shrinking into nothingness. In self-defense she lashed out. "How could you do such a thing? Telling me you were Phillip? Making me fall in love with you?"

"But, my dear," James seemed grimly amused, "*you* were the one to call me Phillip. If you remember, I never once told you I was Phillip. Why should I? If you will remember a little more, I tried to send you away. I told you the truth. I told you Phillip Travis could never make you happy. I also told you that your childish longing for someone to come along on a white horse did not fit Phillip."

Honor moistened her parched lips with the tip of her tongue. In minutes the companionable man she had known since she arrived at the ranch had changed into a stranger. "Then I was right. You were a stranger when I arrived at Casa del Sol. You were nothing like Phillip."

"Thank you." This time he laughed aloud. "That's the finest compliment you could give me."

"But why?" She had to break through his calm. "Why did you marry me?"

"There was no other choice." His laughing mask slipped. In its place was a deadly serious man. "I had to protect you from my dear brother. I tried to send you away, and you wouldn't go. I tried to tell you about him, and you wouldn't listen. So—"

"So you passed yourself off as Phillip and hurried up the wedding before he came!" She fumbled for the door handle as they neared another corner. "I'm getting out of here, and now!"

"You aren't going anywhere." The strong arm she knew so well reached across, pinning her against the seat, infuriating her more. "Don't ever try and run away from me. This world isn't big enough for you to hide in."

"Who are you to tell me what I shall and shall not do?" Honor wrenched free and sat trembling as he picked up speed and headed onto the open road, leaving Flagstaff behind.

"I just happen to be your husband."

"Not for long! As soon as I can get help you won't be." Her voice gathered assurance. "Phillip will never stand for this. He will come to Casa del Sol for me."

"He will be welcome to so long as he remembers you are my wife."

"Your wife? Are you insane? Do you think I'd stay with you after what you have done?"

"Of course." Could that really be surprise in his face as he shot a keen glance at her. "You told me you were truthful and steadfast. You told me you never broke a vow. You also promised to love, honor, and cherish me until death parted us. How can you be ready so soon to break those vows?"

If sheer fury could kill, James Travis would have died on the spot. "You don't by any stretch of imagination think those vows are valid under these circumstances! I believe you are insane! I was right. You *are* an ogre!"

To her amazement, James threw his head back and laughed.

Didn't any of this bother him at all? She would show him! She would get away at the first opportunity!

The slow, mocking voice went on. "Really, Honor, don't you believe in fate, or God, or something? I would have bet you do. How do you know this wasn't all planned?"

"How dare you? Isn't it enough that you have ruined my life? How can you mock God?" A tiny drum beat in her brain. *Isn't that what you've done?*

James whipped the car into a leafy lane out of sight of the main road, killed the motor, and turned to her. His face was as white as her own. The hands he placed on her shoulders dug in. "Ruined your life! Shall I tell you what your life would be like with your precious Phillip?"

"No! You have no right to malign your brother!"

The steel fingers bit deeper. It was all Honor could do to keep from crying out.

"It is not maligning to tell you the truth. You think you know Phillip Travis. You know nothing of him! You know only the front he puts on when he meets a new girl or woman. Do you think you are the first to be invited to Casa del Sol? No, not the first, nor the last. Babs is the only one he might ever be true to. When she is convinced of that, she will marry him. In the meantime, it is a succession of girls and women; summer, winter, fall, spring—season makes no difference. Phillip has the art of loving and leaving perfected to the highest degree." He gave her a little shake, his eyes burning like freshly stirred embers.

"Why didn't he meet you as he promised? Why didn't he come? I can tell you. Once he left the Grand Canyon you were only a dim memory." She flinched, and he shook her again. "Wake up, Honor. Do you think a man like Phillip could be true to you? Do you really think a man who loves women and carousing could settle down and make the kind of home you want, the kind of home you will have at Casa del Sol?"

"He promised to stop drinking! He said he didn't even want to drink when he was with me."

Slowly the fingers loosened. Terrible pity filled James's eyes as he pulled a newspaper from his pocket. "I hoped you would never have to see this."

Wordlessly, Honor took it. Blazoned across the front was a picture, unmistakably Phillip. His hair hung in his eyes, his mouth was slack. Underneath was the caption: LOCAL RANCHER SPENDS NIGHT IN JAIL FOR DISORDERLY CONDUCT.

The newspaper fell from Honor's nerveless fingers. "How could you be so cruel?"

"Is it more cruel to tell you the truth, or to let you marry him and find out for yourself?"

"But what am I to do?" All the old lack of self-confidence, of being totally alone, rushed over her. "You were joking when you said you expected me to stay, weren't you?"

James gripped her again, face chiseled in determination. "I never meant anything so much in my entire life."

She wrenched free. "To make the perfect touch, I suppose you're going to swear by all that's holy to you—or is anything?—that you fell in love with me at first sight and used this excuse to marry me."

Matching color burned in his face. "Why not? Didn't you do much the same with Phillip?" Speechless with fury, Honor couldn't reply. But James was not through. "Since you obviously wouldn't believe it, I won't swear undying love."

She hated him for the laughter underlying his thrust. "I wouldn't believe anything any Travis told me. You certainly planned it well. Why"—a new wave of indignation shot through her—"even Carlotta, Rosa—how could you get them to agree to such a monstrous plot? I should have known." Her eyes widened. "Rosa—she called Phillip 'Felipe.' She calls you 'Señor.' Why didn't I notice?"

"You were too busy deluding yourself about Phillip."

Honor buried her face in her hands, biting back a sob. She would not show weakness, not now.

"Cheer up, Honor. Things could be worse." James suddenly abandoned his lightness. "Don't hold it against Rosa and Carlotta. They knew you would be better off married to me, even hating me, than facing the inevitable humiliation you would find as Phillip's wife." His laugh sounded strained. "Who knows? We may even learn to love each other in time."

When Honor found her voice it came out in hard syllables, like crystal tears bouncing on a glassy surface. "That has to be the most ridiculous remark I have ever heard in my entire life. Love you? Never!"

"Never is a long time."

"You—you—" Her fury increased to the snapping point. In the midst of it a snatch of conversation with Carlotta burned red-hot in her mind. *"Which do you love more? The canyon man, or this one?"*

Her own reply now stood to accuse her. *"I love the man who owns Casa del Sol—more than anything in the world."*

"I demand you take me to the ranch so I can pack and go."

James laughed outright. "Wives don't leave their husbands so soon after the ceremony, my dear. Besides, I saw Phillip and his bunch pass the main road. They will be there to meet us. No one forced you to marry me, you know. If you remember, you even insisted!" He laughed again. "What a coup! Even Phillip will enjoy my trick. I'm sure the photographer will put our pictures in the paper. Perhaps there can be some more headlines about the Travis family: 'Young Beautiful Bride Marries Wrong Twin.' How exciting! Something you can tell our children and grandchildren." Before Honor could find her tongue, he added casually, "It's lucky for me you are such an honorable person. Why, another woman might even do as you threatened and leave me. But not you." His face was blandly innocent as he put his foot on the gas and shot forward. "You are bound. Honor bound." She could have strangled him for his laugh. "You will go in looking like the bride you are."

Honor turned her back on him.

Never had miles gone by so slowly. All the glory of the day had gone. Even the red streaks heralding sunset failed to rouse Honor. James's laughing words had gone deep. In spite of everything he had done, she had promised, given her word. But how could she stay at Casa del Sol hating James as she now did? The love she had felt for Phillip was gone, obliterated by the sight of his drunken face in the newspaper. Deep inside a question formed: What if the love she had thought was for Phillip had really been for James at the ranch? She stepped on it, hard. She would never forgive him. Better to break her word than to remain where she had known so much happiness that had now turned to bitterness.

James must have read her thoughts. "Until you get over being upset, you needn't worry about my being around. I have work on the range and won't be in. You'll be treated as a special guest, nothing more."

Honor could feel color creeping up from the high neck of her wedding dress.

"I don't want a wife who still fancies herself in love with my twin brother. Until you get us sorted out in your mind you'll be just what I said, a special guest, nothing more."

Honor sank back against the seat, speechless again. What an unpredictable man! Yet his words had given birth to hope. What if she took him up on it? What if she stayed at Casa del Sol, let time help her decide what to do? She was in no condition to make any decisions right now. Too much had happened. She had been taken from joy to despair to disillusionment.

"You give your word?"

"I do." His warm hand shook her icy fingers in a businesslike grip as he swung into the cutoff toward Casa del Sol, as if a corporation merger had just been signed. "Now, let's show everyone what the partnership of Travis and Brooks-Travis can do. If they once find out you didn't know you married the wrong twin, this crowd will never let it be forgotten."

Wonder of wonders, Honor laughed. If she could just concentrate on getting through one thing at a time it would provide what she needed—a quiet place to think. But first she had to face that crowd—including Phillip. Phillip! How could such a terrible thing ever have happened? In love with one man, married to his twin brother who expected her to keep her vows. She shoved the thought aside. Now was not the time to think about it. She had to go in that house and face them all with a smile on her lips. With an involuntary shudder, she braced herself as James came to a stop, vaulted over the side of the low car, and before she knew what was happening scooped her up in his arms.

"Put me down," she ordered furiously, but he only grinned.

"It's what they'll expect! Hold still." With a mighty kick he shoved open the door, which had been left standing ajar, and strode into the big hall. To Honor it seemed there were a million people there.

"Just what are you all doing here on my honeymoon?" There was no welcome in James's voice, just righteous indignation. He set Honor on her feet but kept a supporting arm around her. Did he know she would have fallen if he had just put her down?

An indolent figure detached itself from the group. "We came

to wish the bride and groom all happiness," said Phillip, smiling as only he could smile. For one instant Honor fought the pain of what might have been, only to have it replaced with relief when he lifted high the glass he was holding.

"Get that booze out of here!" Honor wasn't prepared for James's roar. "You know I don't allow it in this house."

"What's all the shouting about, James?" Babs had crossed to them. "It's just a little drink. We brought our own." The emerald on her finger winked wickedly.

"You're welcome to visit for a little while, but you can't bring that stuff in here."

For one long moment brother faced brother. Honor would never forget it. Seen against the clear and clean-cut features of James, Phillip was a rather smudged carbon copy. Her heart suddenly knew the truth of her words to Carlotta. She had fallen for the strength in Phillip that belonged to his twin. No wonder she had been so relieved to find him different at his ranch than when with the crowd. It was a good thing they paid no attention to her. Would her face give it away?

I must never let James know. He wouldn't, couldn't say he had fallen in love with me. He must never know how right he was. But determination was born. She would make him love her until he was glad he had married her—not to protect her from Phillip, but because he loved her. Hot color spurted into her face, leaving her breathless.

Honor's attention returned to the brothers. Phillip's eyes fell first. "Oh, all right." He carelessly set his drink down, followed by the others. To create a diversion, Honor deliberately stepped forward. "Hello, Phillip." Her quiet voice turned all eyes toward her, slim, smiling, more beautiful in her white gown than they had seen her. Desire rose in Phillip's face, but this time Honor was prepared. She had seen his falseness. Scales had dropped from her vision.

"I'm sorry you weren't able to attend our wedding." Suddenly she knew it was true. She was free forever of Phillip Travis.

Phillip couldn't seem to answer. It was red-haired Babs who mocked, "Some little trick, Miss Honor Brooks. So Phillip wasn't here when you arrived? He had—other things on his mind."

"It didn't matter. James welcomed me."

Babs drew in a sharp breath. "I'll say he did! You pulled a real trick in getting old James to the altar. I wonder what Lucille's going to say?" Yet behind her baiting Honor sensed genuine relief in Babs's face, an almost-approval of what had happened. Did she care for Phillip that much?

James broke the uncomfortable silence. "Now if you really must go, I believe Mrs. Travis would like to change."

"The old 'here's your hat, what's your hurry' routine," Babs mocked. "Come on, Phillip. We aren't wanted—or needed here." But the glance she threw over her shoulder at Honor was one of gratitude. "You'll just have to put up with me since your lady love prefers your twin." Over Phillip's protests she dragged him away, but not before he called back, "I'll be home soon."

Honor sighed with relief as the heavy door closed behind them. Slowly she turned to find James watching.

"You did very well, my dear." He stepped nearer, and her heart pounded. Surely he could hear it! She wouldn't have expected his next comment. "How would you like to go for a short ride?"

Honor stared at him then said, "Why, I'd like that. Let me get changed." She ran up the stairs thinking to herself, *When I get to bed tonight I'll probably cry or scream. Now all I can do is go riding with a husband who married me to protect me!*

By the time she had changed, James had Sol and Jingles ready. Silently he helped her mount. She laughed a little at her awkwardness. "I'll be a tenderfoot for some time, I'm afraid."

"Then you'll stay?" Was that restrained eagerness in his voice or her own wishful thinking?

"For a time. It seems a shame to miss out on a real ranch vacation just because of something so trivial as a mistaken-identity wedding." Before he could answer she had prodded Jingles with her heels and was racing down the road.

"Honor, wait!"

What imp of perversity caused her to dig in her heels more? "Come on, Jingles, let's go!" Ignoring the pounding of Sol behind them, she urged her pony forward. Faster, faster, until—Jingles stumbled, went down. Honor felt herself sailing through the air, then blackness enveloped her. A sharp pain stabbed her right shoulder. She cried out and knew nothing more until she lifted heavy lids to find herself cradled in James's arms. She tried to struggle, but the pain in her shoulder was too much.

"Lie still." She felt the swing of a horse. James must have taken her on Sol.

"Jingles threw me. He must have stepped in a hole." She incoherently tried to explain.

"That's why I called. You don't run horses at night or in half-light." His voice was cold and hard. "Jingles hurt his leg pretty bad. I may have to shoot him."

Honor twisted until she could look in his face. "Oh, no!"

Pain crossed the features above her, still visible in the ruby sunset. "I'll call the vet. If it's only sprained, we can use hot compresses to get the swelling down. If it's broken—"

"It's my fault!" The first tears of the whole amazing day slipped from beneath her tightly closed lids. "If you have to shoot Jingles, it's my fault."

He didn't soften the blow. "Yes, it is. If you won't listen to people who know more about ranching than you do, maybe you'd better just stay in the house. Casa del Sol is a beautiful place. It is also a dangerous place. There are wild animals. There are rattlesnakes in the rocks."

Honor shivered, feeling small. "I'm sorry."

He slid to his feet, still carrying her, leaving Sol with his reins dragging. "I'll get you in the house and call the vet."

"Señora!" Even through her remorse and pain Honor caught the change in Rosa's greeting. She was Señora now, mistress of Casa del Sol.

"Mrs. Travis has had a bad fall. I'm taking her to her room, Mama Rosa. Bring liniment. Her shoulder is sprained." For all the feeling in James's voice she might have been of less importance than the barn, Honor thought fleetingly. Mama Rosa and Carlotta worked with swift fingers, undressing her, getting her shoulder bathed and dressed with a stinging liniment.

"You will feel better tomorrow. What a way to start a honeymoon!" Carlotta grinned impishly before slipping out the big door, leaving it slightly ajar.

Honeymoon! Honor tried to sit up and failed. She was just too tired to move, physically and emotionally. She threw herself back on the pillow, heedless of the pain in her shoulder. Had she ever lived through such a day? Her wedding day, the day she had dreamed of since she was a child, and especially since she met Phillip. What a travesty! Slow tears seeped into her puffy pillow. It might as well have been a rock. She could no longer put off facing what she had done.

Through her pain and misery came Granny's stern, sad voice, *"I don't know what it's going to take to make you see you can't outrun God. When you do, if you are married to an unbeliever, your life will be misery."*

A final spurt of rebelliousness brought a protest to her lips, but it died before she could even whisper. No. She couldn't blame God any longer. She had insisted on idolizing Phillip Travis even against her own nagging doubts and the repeated warnings she had been given.

The dimly lit room receded to be replaced first by the scene at the canyon then later here at Casa del Sol—that momentary, on-the-brink warning. It was not the chill evening breeze from her partly opened window that turned Honor cold. It was memory of her response to God's pleadings—and she knew they had been just that. Instead of listening to the scriptures that had been planted in her brain, she had been swayed by the beauty of the canyon, the thrill of Phillip's attention, the false assurance that all would be well.

Tossing from one side of the great bed to the other, she faced it head-on. God had not done this to her. She had brought it on herself because she refused to listen to God's call. A new, sharper thrust filled her heart. She struggled to pray, to ask forgiveness, help, peace. *"My spirit will not always strive with men."* She remembered the words from Genesis. Why did her prayers only ascend to the ceiling? Was she repenting more for the way things had turned out than for being a sinner? Was she really better off married to a man who obviously despised her than to Phillip? And was what she thought love for James really only clutching for security, strength, someone to stand between her and a world grown harsh?

Her weary brain refused to answer. James must have dropped a sleeping powder in the warm milk he had brought. Even if she could find God and be forgiven for a life of rebellion, she would still have the consequences of her mutiny—either a broken marriage relationship or an unbelieving husband.

Chapter 7

James Travis kept his promise. In the month following their wedding, Honor saw little of him. Evidently he had meant just what he said. There was no time for leisure. He had a huge ranch to run and did just that.

Honor found she was a special guest as James had promised, nothing more. When he was in for meals, he was quietly courteous, asking if she was enjoying learning to know the ranch. Most of the time he was gone.

Once she curiously asked, "Do you stay in what Mama Rosa calls 'line shacks' when you are out on the range?"

His smile was sardonic, leaving her feeling she had blundered again. "Sometimes. I can't very well stay in the bunkhouse when the hands think this is still our honeymoon."

His thrust had gone home and silenced her.

To Honor, who had been busy all her life, that month was dreamlike. At first it was enough just to rest and sort things out. Yet that very sorting out left her more confused and miserable than ever. It had been as she feared. God's forgiveness would not extend to making everything rosy between James and her. Would they ever be anything except courteous strangers? Neither did she feel God had forgiven her.

She grew thin, worried. In spite of the time she spent with Rosa learning to prepare the spicy Mexican dishes, there wasn't enough to keep her busy. James had forbidden her to ride alone. Sometimes in the evening he took her out, always a stern shadow, an impeccable escort, and as remote as Kendrick Peak.

James unexpectedly appeared at lunch one day. "Would you

like to take a drive this afternoon?"

She hid her surprise. "Why, yes. Can you spare the time?" She hadn't meant to sound sarcastic, but it came out that way.

James's expression changed. "I believe it can be arranged."

Nothing more was said until they were seated in the Willys. Honor nervously adjusted a veil. The snowline on the mountains was steadily encroaching upon the valley. No wonder! It was definitely fall. Every leaf flaunted red or gold winter dress in a King Midas world.

"Where are we going?"

"Do you have to ask a question as if I were still an ogre?" James sounded irritated.

"Aren't you?" Instantly repentant, she laid one gloved hand over his strong one on the wheel, her most unself-conscious gesture since their marriage.

"Don't touch me while I'm driving!"

She snatched her hand back as if it had been burned, more hurt than she would admit even to herself, and made herself small against the door on the passenger side, turning her back on James so he could not read her expression.

"We're going to see an old friend of mine. His name is Judge Bell. I call him Daddy, and have since my own father died."

Something in his voice reached even through Honor's misery. "You really care about him, don't you?"

"I love him and his wife. They're real people."

Honor sneaked a glance at the forbidding face behind the wheel. A ghost of a smile had replaced some of the irritation.

"Judge Bell grew up knowing he was going to be a minister. When he got in his teens he was mixed up in some kind of unpleasantness—he's never said what. He was innocent, but since his comrades were guilty, it looked as if he would be sentenced along with them. The judge in the case was known to be harsh. He was always fair, but the boys knew there was little hope.

"Evidently the judge listened and was impressed by the boy's sincerity. He dismissed the charges against Daddy. Daddy was so impressed he prayed about it, he said, and decided he could do as much good as a Christian judge as if he became a minister. He did. He spent over fifty years as a judge before he retired. Now his heart isn't strong enough for the grueling hours required in his former work."

"What does he do now?"

James laughed. "If you have a picture in your mind of a broken-down man, you're in for a shock. He ministers. He gives love and comfort to the poor, the dying, even to—" He broke off suddenly, giving her a piercing glance that brought red to her face.

"And you think he can bring comfort to me?"

"I hope so." James swung the big touring car into a small lane. "Honor, I want to talk to you."

Why should his simple statement send shudders up her spine?

"I know you aren't happy. I can't expect you to be, I suppose. Daddy said I did a terrible thing, marrying you as I did."

"He knows?"

"Of course." James's mouth twisted. "I rode over the night after we were married and told him." Bitterness filled his face. "So you don't have to play any games with him. He can see right through you."

I hope not.

Had she spoken the words aloud?

No. James went on uninterrupted. "You'll like him and his wife. They live what they believe." He shot her another quick glance. "By the way, what does that God you believe in—or do you?—think about our marriage?"

She chose to answer his first question first. "Yes, I believe in God. I always have. I just never did anything about it—until now." Her voice trailed off.

"Are you a Christian?"

"No." She swallowed a lump in her throat, feeling constricted almost to the point of being unable to breathe. "But I want to be, James, I want to be!" Forgetting the estrangement between them, she turned to face him directly. "From the time I was small I blamed God for everything that went wrong. Granny tried to tell me everyone who lives on earth is subject to natural consequences, but I wouldn't listen." Her troubled face reflected her struggles. "I'm afraid I waited and rebelled too long."

"Ridiculous! What have you ever done that was so terrible? You haven't killed or anything like that. You have lived a good life."

Honor shook her head. "I've sinned most of all by refusing to listen to the Holy Spirit sent to show me what God wants—and by turning my back on the gift of eternal life and salvation through acceptance of God's only Son." She turned away, eyes desolate.

James cleared his throat. "I can't help you with that, but Judge Bell can." He changed the subject. "You didn't tell me what your God thought of our marriage." His lips curved downward. "You think God punished you for not accepting Him by letting you marry an ogre?"

"I can't blame God for what I insisted on." Her lips quivered.

With a muttered imprecation James started the car and drove in silence to a small white cottage with a picket fence, leaving Honor to stare at the blurring countryside they passed.

If ever there was a case of love at first sight it was between Honor and the Bells. "Why, you remind me of my father!" Honor's spontaneous remark was met with warmth like flames of an open fire.

"Come in, come in, children." Motherly Mrs. Bell and the equally welcoming judge threw wide the door, but after only a few moments the judge said, "Run along, James. I'll be wanting to talk with your lassie alone."

"Well!" Mrs. Bell's crinkling eyes belied her pretended hurt. "We've been dismissed, James, my boy. We'll go out and get our doughnuts ready for when they've finished."

After they left, Honor waited for Judge Bell to speak. When he did it was to ask her to call him Daddy.

"You know what happened?" She couldn't hide her trembling fingers.

"Aye. But I wonder if you do?"

It was the last thing Honor had expected. "Wh–what do you mean?"

"Did the laddie tell you why?"

A shake of the head was all she could manage.

"I thought not." The soft burr in Daddy Bell's Scottish voice soothed her as nothing had done for weeks. She leaned forward.

"Did—did he tell *you* why?"

"He told me more than he realized. After you had mistaken him for Phillip and went upstairs he paced his library for hours. He ran the gamut of emotions from wanting to horsewhip Phillip to wishing he had never been born twin to such a philanderer.

"He had tried to send you away. He had tried to warn you what Phillip was and you refused to believe. If he'd told you he was Phillip's brother, you would have had more reason to distrust him."

Honor flushed, remembering how she had referred to the absent brother as the ogre.

"Early in life James and Phillip's father had given James charge over his brother, a brother's-keeper responsibility. When Phillip refused direction, James became bitter. When you appeared, it was the last bit of evidence of Phillip's nature to convict him.

"James could see you would never break your vow. He decided to marry you. It had taken an entire night to decide, and he could no longer stand the confines of the library. He saddled Sol, rode here, and caught me just as I was coming in from a call. He—"

Honor could stand no more. Her eyes flew open. "He *told* you what he was going to do?"

"Of course not. Much as I love the laddie, he knew I'd not stand by for such a thing."

The crisp tone brought a wave of color to Honor's face. "I'm sorry. It's just that it's all been such a shock."

"I understand. Lassie"—Daddy Bell's eyes were kind—"did you not know down in your heart Phillip Travis was no man for you?"

It was the final touch. Honor put her face in her hands. "I knew. God even tried to warn me."

A light came to the old man's eyes. "You are a follower?"

"Any following I've done is after my own way."

"And now you're sorry."

"With all my heart." Honor slipped to the hand-braided rug at his feet. "Not just for choosing Phillip over God, but for everything. For not listening to Granny and my brother and. . ." Her voice dropped until it was barely audible. ". . .and the Holy Spirit."

She heard grave concern in his voice as he asked, "Lassie, did you not know the Spirit's calling?"

"That's what is so terrible. I deliberately chose Phillip Travis over God!" She scarcely heard his quick intake of breath. "Now when I try to pray, it's as if God has turned His back on me—just as I did on Him."

"Look at me."

There was something magnificent in Daddy Bell's voice reminiscent of days when he tempered justice with mercy. Honor fixed her gaze on his face.

"Do you recognize now how much of a sinner you are? Do you freely acknowledge it and believe Jesus died to save you from those sins? Do you accept Him into your heart and life forever?"

"Yes!"

The soft cry in the still room seemed magnified in Honor's ears. Daddy Bell's admonition, "Tell Him so," brought a rush of feeling as Honor stammered, "I'm a sinner, God. Forgive me. I accept the gift of Your Son and salvation through Him." She could not go on. The month of sleepless nights had taken its toll, but the next instant she felt weariness leave. In its place was peace—not the false assurance that she could work things out, but the knowledge that no matter what came, God was there to strengthen her. Along with the peace was knowledge—she was free, forgiven. But it did not mean every trouble was over. She was just what Granny had said she would be: wedded to one who scorned the Christ, or at best ignored Him, just as she had done.

Another memory found its way to her lips. "I said, when Granny warned me, that if God ever caught up to me, there was no reason He couldn't catch Phillip, too." Her regret struck deep. "How blind, willful, sinful I was!"

Daddy Bell's hands were warm on her own. "It's over, lassie. I won't try and excuse you in any way for what you have done. You must live with it. Neither will I excuse James." His shrewd eyes searched her. "I will say I doubt the laddie married you entirely to save you from Phillip."

"He despises me as a weakling." Honor couldn't hold back tears. "How can you say he might care?"

"It has been my business to know men."

Daddy Bell's words echoed in Honor's mind as James and Mrs. Bell came in, to be told the news of Honor's acceptance of Christ.

Mrs. Bell appeared delighted. James did not. On the way home he spoke of it. "I suppose now you're a Christian you'll be even more bitter about me." He didn't give her a chance to reply but quickly added, "What does God say about Christian wives with husbands like me?"

She sought sarcasm and found none. Was he serious? She would respond as if he was. "In 1 Corinthians 7:14 it says, 'For the unbelieving husband is sanctified by the wife, and—'"

"The Bible doesn't say that!" James shot her a glance that was totally unreadable.

"See for yourself. It's right there."

"If I had a Bible, I might just do that."

Honor rode quietly all the way home. When they reached the sprawling hacienda she climbed from the car without waiting for his assistance, only saying, "Thank you for taking me." She dashed upstairs, threw open the big trunk she had brought from San Francisco, and delved clear to the bottom. For a moment she held close the precious Book she unearthed. She would need it now more than ever. As a child of God she must study.

With a sigh she touched the worn cover regretfully then lifted her chin. Daddy Bell would get her another Bible. In the meantime...

James looked shocked when she appeared, out of breath, at the bottom of the stairs. "What on earth—"

"Here." She steadied her voice, forcing casualness into it she did not feel. "I have been wondering what to give you...whether to give you this." She held it out.

"A Bible?"

The trancelike state he seemed to have gone into released a spirit she hadn't known existed. "It's perfectly proper to accept, Mr. Travis. Even if we weren't married, a Bible is always considered an acceptable gift."

She retreated up two steps, away from the disturbing dark eyes. "Don't forget to read it—especially 1 Corinthians." Her sense of mischief faded. "And John, especially verse 3:16." She could not go on so blindly ran upstairs, remembering how he stood staring at her. She gently closed her door and dropped to her knees by the side of the bed. How easy it was to tell someone else to read the best-known of all verses, "*For God so loved the world, that he gave his only begotten Son, that whosoever believeth in him should not perish, but have everlasting life.*" But how hard it had been to accept it!

Tears drenched the beautiful spread. If only she had accepted that verse and invited Jesus into her heart, asking for forgiveness for her sins long ago when Keith did, how different things would be now! She would not be in love with a husband who cared nothing for her and even less for the Lord she had suddenly discovered was more precious to her than anything else on earth.

Chapter 8

That was only the first of Honor's visits to the Bell cottage. James took time from his duties on the ranch to teach Honor to drive, and once she was competent, she traveled to the little home near Kendrick Peak often. Each visit produced growth in her Christian walk.

One particularly beautiful afternoon she said, "Daddy, all the scriptures I have known practically forever mean something now. Is it because I am reading with my heart?"

"Aye, lassie." The wise eyes lit with an inner glow. "Faith is the key to unlock the mysteries of the universe."

Inevitably their talks included James. Daddy was firm in the belief that James would come to know God as other than a Mastermind. "He's a pantheist, you know." He intercepted Honor's questioning glance. "One who equates God with nature and the laws of the universe."

"Is it wrong to see God in nature? At the canyon I felt something of this." Honor's face was wistful, remembering the beauty and magnificence of the place.

"There is nothing wrong with seeing God as Creator of this earth's glory so long as you don't lose sight of God—the Father, the Son, and the Holy Spirit, who brought salvation to this world."

"And James only sees the creating force." A shadow crossed her face. "Daddy, who is Lucille Lawson?"

The old man looked surprised at the change of subject. "Why, she's a twice-divorced woman who"—he looked shamefaced, and Honor could see him carefully choosing words—"who had designs on James and his ranch." He peered at her more closely. "How did you hear of her?"

"Her name was mentioned by Babs and the crowd the day I was married. I also saw it on an envelope in the library."

"She's not your kind—or James's."

Honor spread her hands wide. "Who is?" Her honest eyes met Daddy's. "He is such a mass of contradictions. Laughing one moment, locked behind a granite wall the next. I know he doesn't drink or go in for that sort of thing." Her face shadowed. "Because of my stubbornness here I am married to him. I'm learning the terrible results of sin. If I hadn't insisted on my own way, James would be free."

"Are you sure he wants to be?" The quiet voice cut through her depression.

"How can he help it? He laughed when he told me how he even arranged with Juan to come dashing out with the telegram supposedly telling Phillip was coming. It did say that, but James had already known Phillip was due soon." She stopped, trouble chasing away the joy that always came through her learning sessions with Daddy. "Such a quixotic gesture! He seems honorable enough, except for that—"

"Would you have thought of yourself as honorable before meeting Phillip Travis?"

"I would have then."

"Yet you chose not only to marry Phillip but to deny every teaching you have been given," Daddy gently reminded. "I cannot say why James did such a thing. When he came to me after the wedding and told me, I was stunned. I cried out in protest, asked how he could deliberately plot and arrange this marriage."

Honor held her breath in the little pause that followed.

The judge's face was stern. "He told me that even though you persisted in believing nothing but the best of Phillip, he couldn't stand to see you crushed under his brother's boots like a frail flower."

"I really thought Phillip would change, especially after coming to Casa del Sol."

She couldn't believe the way Daddy's big hand balled into a fist and struck the shining edge of a piecrust table. "Lassie, any girl or woman who marries a man in hopes of reforming him is doomed to a living hell on earth! If it is not in a man to live clean and honorably before marriage, only rarely will he do it after."

"Yet you refuse to see my marriage to James as a tragedy." Honor regretted the words as soon as they came out.

Daddy Bell's face settled into deep lines. "I would have given anything on earth to prevent it. Now it is done; you can only go on from here."

"I know." She stood and restlessly walked toward the window. "Even when I was being married I sensed something wrong. I refused to admit how weak Phillip was. He needed me. Since accepting Christ I have begun to see the awfulness of what God saved me from, and it is from my own actions."

"It always is."

Honor turned back toward him. "It's just that I don't know how to approach him. I don't know if he reads the Bible I gave him. Even if he does, he never mentions it."

"You've stayed in spite of everything. Are you going to continue to honor your vows?"

Honor looked deep into the searching eyes. "I must. I promised before God and man, gave my word." She bit her lips to steady them. "Unless he sends me away."

"And do you want to stay, lassie?" Before she could answer, his face crimsoned. "Forgive me." He held out both hands to Honor. "I have no right to ask such a thing."

He deliberately changed the subject. "The only good whatsoever I can see coming from such a beginning lies in your heart, and in the life James has led since childhood. He hates anything smacking of cheapness."

Honor nodded, and Daddy continued, "He also believes in God but has not yet met Him face-to-face. He cannot admit he is a sinner and claim forgiveness through Jesus' death on Calvary."

"Will he ever?"

"He must!" Daddy dropped her hands to bring his fist down against the arm of the chair. "He knows the way. But it may take a long, hard road of traveling before James Travis accepts the gift of salvation through our Lord Jesus."

"Just as it was a long, hard road for me."

Daddy sighed. "Yes. I cannot condone in any way what the two of you have done. Neither is there any time for crying over the past. You must go forward and leave what will be in God's hands."

"You will pray for us?" It was through a blur that Honor saw his benedictory smile.

"I have been—since James came with the news. Live your faith so he can see it is real. Your refusing to break your vows will be a witness."

Mrs. Bell's round, smiling face appeared in the doorway. "Honor, one of these days I'll teach you to make some of my special recipes. James loves them." In the general conversation following, Honor's depression could not help vanishing. She laughed. "It will be a real accomplishment when I can equal your doughnuts!"

"Anything worth knowing is worth working at," Daddy reminded, leaving Honor with a parting word. She knew it was not to doughnuts but to her own life and walk with God that he referred.

Several days later she told Rosa, "It's good to be back in the kitchen." Her floury hands stilled on the big board where she was practicing making tortillas. "I haven't had a chance since Granny died, and I'm really a homemaker at heart."

"It is good. Señor's woman should be home, not off working for others." Rosa snorted. "Flagstaff women are leaving homes and children. Pah! They should stay home where they belong."

Honor hid a smile. What would Rosa, happy with her pots and pans, think of San Francisco, where women were flocking to offices! "Where do the cowhands eat?" she asked.

"The cookhouse." Rosa's white smile widened. "I show you when everyone is gone. Cookie likes my pies but no visitors."

It took weeks for Honor to discover how big her new home really was. James began to take her around more, as if she truly were a special guest. She could almost forget the unusual marriage at the sight of the birds, coyotes, a startled deer.

"Honor," he asked on one of the expeditions, "are you unhappy here?"

"No." Before he could reply, she remounted the pony who had replaced Jingles. Although her favorite pinto would recover, he wasn't to be ridden for a time. When she was in the saddle she looked down. "When I forget about—about that ceremony, I am not unhappy."

"I'm glad." He covered her rapidly tanning hands with his own. Something in the dark eyes flickered, making her wonder if Daddy Bell could be right. Was her husband beginning to care for her? It was the first time he had touched her since their wedding day.

Breathless, unwilling to acknowledge what she either saw or

imagined, Honor touched her horse with her heels. "Race you back to the ranch!" The spell was broken. She felt the wind in her face and, exulting, cried out encouragement to her pony. She felt rather than saw when James caught up with her. The longer stride of Sol easily overtook her pony.

"Faster, faster," she urged, but always he was there beside them, laughing above the wind she created with her momentum. Neck and neck they raced to the corral. At the last moment Sol leaped ahead and left Honor and her mount to come in second.

"You could at least have let me win," she complained as she slid from the saddle, refusing his help. "Seems it would be the polite thing to do!" Her disheveled hair surrounded the hat that had slid back until it was only held by the cord around her throat. Strangely stirred inside, she felt the need to pick a quarrel of some kind to relieve the tension, even if it was only over a silly race.

"Is that what you want—to be let to win?"

If the quizzical question had a hidden meaning, she chose to ignore it. Stepping close, hands on hips in an easy Western pose, she glared at him. "I intend to beat you fair and square, Mr. Man. And I'll do it with honor."

Her pretended indignation slipped at what she saw in his face. The combination of tenderness and kindness almost proved her undoing. Quickly she turned back to her horse. "I'm going to begin by showing you how well I can unsaddle my horse and rub him down." Her deft hands that had practiced hours in secret for this very moment made short work of lifting the heavy saddle. She staggered a bit but triumphantly got it where it belonged and went on to groom down her horse in the best way possible.

"Say, you're going to make a pretty good rancher's wife after all!" He took one step toward her, a new admiration showing.

Honor's heart flipped over. The intensity of her own emotion almost overwhelmed her, but the feeling was interrupted.

"Really, darling, it takes more than being able to rub down a horse to be wife of the heir of Casa del Sol!"

Honor whirled toward the speaker. Soigné, every shining blond hair in place, green eyes smiling maliciously, the woman was everything Honor was not at that moment! Acutely aware of her own appearance, Honor flushed deeply. Who was this woman?

"Hello, Lucille." James's voice was flat, unemotional.

So this is Lucille! Honor boiled as the woman tucked her hand in James's arm and smiled up into his face. "I understand congratulations are in order. This must be the little bride?" She lifted highly painted lips and kissed James square on the mouth. Honor had the satisfaction of seeing him recoil.

"Always dramatic, aren't you, Lucille? What brings you out here?"

"Curiosity." The boldness of her statement left Honor speechless. "I ran into Phillip. He told me he was carefully staying away from the ranch for a while—until the honeymoon was over."

So that was why Phillip hadn't come as promised. Honor's mind ran double track, wondering why Lucille had come.

"Mrs. Lawson is an old friend," James explained. "Lucille, my wife, Honor."

"Honor!" The heavily made-up eyes widened. "How quaint!"

It was too much. Honor's good nature had been strained. "Yes, isn't it? But then, I'm a bit quaint myself. Perhaps that is why James married me." She saw his jaw drop, and smiled sweetly at their guest. "I must excuse myself and tell Mama Rosa there will be a guest for dinner. You will stay, won't you?"

"I'll stay." With the tables turned, Lucille sounded grim.

"Then I'll see you later."

"Do you dress for dinner?"

Honor thought rapidly then disarmingly touched her rumpled clothing. "Doesn't it look like we need to dress for dinner?" She walked steadily toward the house before Lucille could answer. This was one time she felt she needed to dress for dinner. The horrible truth dawned on her—she had no evening gown except the white dress she had been married in!

Giggling nervously at the hastily contrived trap that had caught her, she burst into the house. "Mama Rosa! Come quick!"

"Señora, what is it?" An alarmed brown face peered from the doorway, closely followed by Carlotta's anxious one.

"A Mrs. Lawson has arrived—"

"Her!" Carlotta's sniff was a masterpiece. "Mrs. La-De-Dah in person!"

"Exactly." Honor felt herself relaxing under their understanding. "She was hateful, wondered about dressing for dinner. I told her yes. But I don't have anything except my wedding gown!"

"Wear it," Carlotta advised. "Wait!" She dashed into the open courtyard and returned triumphantly with a handful of late roses. "Mama can put up your hair and tuck a flower in it." Her skillful fingers were twining the flowers even as she spoke, carefully removing thorns, fashioning a beautiful corsage. "This goes on your left shoulder."

When Honor was dressed, her two faithful friends stepped back in admiration. "Beautiful!" Carlotta clapped her hands, but Mama Rosa only smiled and said, "Señor will be proud."

He was. Honor could see it in his eyes when she descended the curving staircase. Lucille Lawson stood close, shivering in a backless ice-green gown.

"Why, Mrs. Lawson, come in where it's warm! That hall of ours does stay cold." Honor threw open the door to the library. "James, why did you leave her standing out there?" She didn't wait for an answer. "Tell me, are you here for long?"

Slightly disconcerted but unwilling to allow anyone else to steal the stage for even a minute, the green eyes matching her gown hardened. "I really don't know. That is, when I came to Phoenix—I've been shopping in New Yawk, you know—well, I just heard about the wedding and rushed right out here with a gift." She handed a heavy box to Honor.

For one moment Honor felt like throwing it into the fireplace, but then her own breeding replaced the urge with a quiet smile. "It was kind of you to think of us. James, will you open it, or shall I?"

"Go ahead." If the tone of his voice was an indication, they were in for cold weather during Mrs. Lawson's stay.

Honor hesitated, noting the expensive label on the box. She wanted nothing from this woman, especially her gifts. Why had she come, just when things might have improved with James? Keeping her face bland she lifted the contents of the package. "Oh!" She dropped it back in its wrappings, unable to conceal her distaste. James came to her rescue, holding up the platter surrounded with heavily carved silver snakes.

"Lucille, that has to be the ugliest thing I have ever seen."

"Why, Jimmy!" She pouted. "It's solid silver. I thought you'd like it—to remember me by."

His voice was grimmer than Honor had ever heard it. "Then if it's solid silver I'm afraid we'll have to say thank you and return it. We couldn't possibly accept a present so valuable. *Or inappropriate*," he muttered just loud enough for Honor to catch.

"Sorry, darling." Steel blades unsheathed themselves in her green eyes. "Just thought I'd bring you a reminder of all our past—associations."

"What is that supposed to mean?" James Travis caught her by the shoulders, swinging her around to face him. "You know there's never been anything between us."

"Oh?" She pointed a woman-to-woman glance at Honor, who stood frozen in place. "Of course, darling, if you say so."

"I do say so. To be brutally frank, you've been a nightmare. There hasn't been a time you haven't followed me and tried to give the impression of some hidden relationship between us."

"Poor boy." She stroked his cheek with a white hand she had managed to free. Honor stood like a statue, wondering. *How can she do it? I would be scared to death if James looked at me like that! There's almost murder in his eyes!*

"Don't touch me!" James loosened her so she nearly fell. He jerked the bell rope nearby. Honor could hear it pealing in the distance. Time stood suspended until Juan appeared, almost running. "Señor?"

"Mrs. Lawson won't be staying for dinner. Please show her out, Juan."

Honor gasped as Lucille Lawson went a dull, murderous red. It was her turn to shoot hateful sparks into the air. "So, it's true! This baby-faced little thing has you snared. You think she'll ever have brains enough to be mistress of Casa del Sol? The way I hear it, she fell in Phillip's arms like an overripe apple, got herself invited down here." She spun back to Honor. "What happened? Did you find bigger game?"

"That's enough!" James seized her by the arm and propelled her to the door, only stopping to scoop up the offending silver gift. The eyes of the carved snakes glittered in the dim light. "Get out and take your snakes with you!"

Honor heard their footsteps across the tiled floor of the hall then the dull thud as the heavy door banged into place. She dropped in a chair, exhausted by the scene, frantically searching for something to say when James returned.

He came back, breathing hard. Without a word he crossed to the fireplace and poked its already blazing contents into a minor inferno.

"Well?" She hadn't known her voice could be so weak and trembly.

"Well, what?" The anger in his eyes was directed at her now.

"Well, Mrs. Lawson—she—" Honor was unable to go on.

"She's a troublemaker and always has been."

Honor waited, but he didn't go on. How could he so casually dismiss that vicious woman? Gnawing doubt crept into her heart. "She must have had something to base all that on. It's hard to imagine any woman bursting into a honeymoon. . ." She turned fiery red but forced herself to continue. "Unless she had been given some kind of reason to expect—"

James towered over her, tall, terrible, as she had seen him earlier. "She has never been given any reason to expect anything!" Honor's sigh of relief was almost lost in his fury. "The only mistake I ever made was in treating her as a human being and not telling her to get lost every time she hung around." He laughed bitterly. "You're my wife. In spite of everything, I shouldn't have had to tell you that. Do you believe me?"

She was so startled by his abrupt question she could only stammer, "I—I—"

His laugh was even more bitter. "It doesn't really matter. Think what you like. I don't care either way."

"Then since you don't care, I won't bother to answer." Honor rose, her heart dropping like lead. He didn't care, at all. She managed a dignified exit until she got just to the doorway of the library. "Why did she have to come? This afternoon I thought maybe we could be friends. . . ." Her words died on her lips.

"Friends?" James looked at her as if she had dropped in from outer space. "I'm afraid not. Friends are people who trust you." He brushed past her, arrogantly striding toward the door. "I don't believe I care for any dinner. I'm going out on Sol."

Again she heard footsteps cross the tile floor, the same thud of the big door closing. This time she did not try to think of something to say. She was seething with fury.

"You come to dinner now?" Mama Rosa peered into the library. "Juan say Mrs. Lawson is gone. But where is Señor?"

The innocent question brought even more fury to Honor. "I don't know and don't care. I don't want any dinner." She ran for the staircase, trailing the white dress she had put on so eagerly such a short time before. "Señor can go where he pleases. I don't care what he does!" Passing Mama with her shocked face, Honor pelted up the stairs, bolted her door, and fell on the bed.

"Let him go! Let him go riding. I don't care if he never comes back. Why should he take it out on me? Just because I couldn't instantly say I had full trust in him! How could he expect me to trust him, after what he pulled with our wedding?" The next instant she was on her knees, crying her heart out. "Oh, God, what am I going to do?"

Hours later she heard Sol's rhythmic gait. She had learned to distinguish it from that of the other horses. Carefully she slipped to the window, watching as she had watched other times. Even from this distance she could see James's restrained fury. Angry with her? Or Lucille? Or both? Did he regret the mad impulse that had caused him to marry her in a quixotic plan to save her from his brother?

Cold air struck her the same time fear hit. Perhaps now he would realize how insane it had all been and send her away. The new thought paralyzed her and sent her shivering back to the big bed. Wave after wave of fear went through her. He would send her away. She would never see him again. Too numb to pray, still her heart pleaded, "*No, don't let it happen! I love him.*" But only the cold night wind answered by its frosty breath. Half frozen, she finally stumbled from bed and closed the window. No use trying to sleep. She touched a match to the always-laid fire in her tiny fireplace and cuddled in front of it wrapped in a robe and the comforter from the bed. Gradually the little fire warmed her.

As the heaviest frost of the season turned every branch and twig into a carrier of white rime that sparkled in the first rays of dawn, she wrestled with her problem. Body warm, heart still a chunk of ice, she at last slipped into bed, too worn out to think anymore.

The next day Phillip Travis came home.

Chapter 9

"Home is the sailor, home from the sea,' and all that." Phillip Travis's debonair manner disappeared as he slumped into a chair. Honor had been trying to read in the library without much success. Every footstep on the tiled hall floor brought her heart to her throat. She expected James to come in, look at her coldly, and order her to go.

Her relief was so great that she welcomed Phillip more warmly that she would have thought possible. "Hello! We've been wondering when you would come."

"Oh?" The dark eyes were wary. "Wouldn't have thought you'd care one way or the other now that you're all hitched up with James."

Choosing her words carefully, Honor insisted, "We will always care about you, Phillip." Her gentle voice attested to the truth of her words.

"Sure you will. That's why you came down here and married James within a week of the time we were engaged."

"I can explain that—" But Honor stopped short. She couldn't explain. It would be too humiliating.

Phillip didn't seem to notice. He was staring moodily into the roaring fire that was always kept going now that the weather had turned colder. "I might have known. You were always good to me. It's really better this way." He grinned crookedly at her shocked expression. "I mean it. I'm a rotten guy. James can make you happy."

It was the last thing on earth she would have expected from him. "You—you really mean that?"

"Sure." He looked surprised. "Even at the canyon I knew it

wouldn't last." He caught her disillusionment and leaned forward. "I'm just no good, Honor. At least not for a girl like you. I even wish I could be, but not all the time."

From somewhere deep inside Honor was given insight, as she had been at the canyon. "Phillip, if you have even a desire to change, God will help you if you will only—"

"Don't preach, Honor." But there was no anger in his voice. "Funny, I'm James's twin, and *he* isn't always drunk or gambling." Again there was a note of wistfulness. "But of course, he has the ranch to look after."

"And you? What do you have to look after?"

For one moment she thought she had probed too deeply, but Phillip only stared at her then lazily yawned. "Me, I guess." He yawned again. "A long time ago I thought I'd have Babs to look after, but she had other ideas."

Eyes steady, forcing him to look at her, Honor said, "I believe Babs cares for you more than you know."

There was a quick flare of hope in his eyes, replaced by dullness. "Too late. I don't care about her."

"Don't you, Phillip?" Without giving him a chance to answer, Honor stood. "Why don't you invite Babs for a visit? Give her a chance to be something other than your 'good-time' date. You might be surprised."

"At least it would be something different. I'm about fed up with the social whirl. Maybe I will give her a call." He slumped back and closed his eyes, but Honor thoughtfully went to her room. Did she dare? She did. She would dare anything to help that troubled man downstairs. Her original love for him had died, but there was another reason to help him now. He was James's brother, weak, perhaps foolish, but still James's brother—and hers, if she stayed.

Gently she picked up the phone and rang. "Operator? Please

give me the number of Barbara Merrill in Flagstaff." She didn't want to let Phillip see her searching for the number. "Babs, this is Honor Brooks-Travis." She could hear unfriendliness and suspicion in the other woman's voice, but rushed on, "I believe Phillip may be going to call and invite you here. You will be welcome. Phillip needs you."

There was a long pause, along with the thudding of Honor's heart, then Babs's slightly thawed voice said, "Thanks." Was that a husky note?

Honor cradled the phone. Had James been right when he said Babs was waiting for Phillip to prove he could be true? It was odd, out of keeping with her own sheltered life. Such games and social ploys were out of her sphere. Babs seemed to be sophisticated. Was it possible she wanted a lasting marriage? Honor would have judged her as someone to try again if the first time didn't work.

Soberly Honor donned her riding outfit. It didn't pay to judge. But how strange it would be if it turned out Babs was one of the first she would be called to witness to about her recent experience in acceptance of Christ! Her heart sank. What a task! Yet if God gave her the task, He would send strength to do it.

Babs had sounded almost thunderstruck when she hung up. The next few days might be quite interesting!

When Honor got downstairs, Phillip was waiting. This time his lazy manner failed to hide his eagerness. "I called Babs. She's coming and will be here for dinner." Suddenly he dropped his pose. "I don't blame you for throwing me down after you met James. We can at least be friends, can't we?"

Without her own volition Honor parroted James's words to her from the afternoon before. "Friends are people who trust you."

"I trust you, Honor." Phillip stepped closer, looking up to her on the second stair above him. "I don't know why you married

James in such a hurry, but it's all right."

"Oh, Phillip." Blindly she reached out a hand to be caught in the white ones shaped like James's hands but so different in color and texture from the working hands she had learned to love!

"What a touching scene." The sarcasm in James's voice effectively separated the two on the stairs. "Welcoming the prodigal home, Honor? Don't overdo it." He brushed past them rudely. Honor clung to the banister rail in order to keep from being upset.

"Just a minute!"

Honor had never seen such determination in Phillip's eyes. It must have startled James. He swung around, looking back down with intense dislike in his face.

"Honor was kind enough to suggest that I ask Babs for a visit. I told her Babs was coming and asked Honor to be my friend. That's why she gave me her hand."

"My wife needs no explanation of her actions to me by you or anyone—especially by you." James's face was granite, his eyes flint. "If Babs is coming I would suggest you remember she is your guest. My wife will make her welcome, of course." Had there been the slightest emphasis on the words *my wife*?

Phillip started up the stairs. "Why, you—"

"Phillip, no!" With a horror of scenes, Honor caught his arm. He mustn't fight his own brother on her account! She had longed to bring peace to this house, not contention. "You must not fight! Either of you." She scornfully looked at James. "Phillip told you the truth. If you don't want to believe him, that's your problem."

"Then since it doesn't matter, I won't commit myself. We'll be dressing for dinner, I suppose, in Babs's honor?"

Tears of fury stung Honor's eyes. He had parried her plea for trust as effectively as she had done the day before. "Yes, we will dress for dinner." She turned her back squarely on him. "Phillip, I don't seem to have the proper clothing for Casa del Sol and its visitors. Perhaps you and Babs will drive in with me to Flagstaff one day this week. I'm sure Babs can tell me where to buy."

Only the sneaking admiration in Phillip's eyes held her together. Had she been expected to knuckle under? Perhaps as Phillip had done—too often? With a weaker personality it must have been much easier just to take the line of least resistance.

"I'll give you a check when you want to go shopping."

Resisting an impulse to kick him in the shins or say something even more sarcastic than he had done, Honor counted to ten and turned. She would not lose her belief in a soft answer's turning away wrath simply because this man infuriated and goaded her beyond belief. Her voice was low and even. "That won't be necessary." She even managed a smile. "After all, brides provide their own trousseaus."

She thought he would protest. His face had thunderclouded to a scowl. At the last moment he changed tactics, stepping aside and sweeping her a low bow. "As you say, my dear." For the first time since the wedding he turned and caught her to him, kissing her lightly on the forehead. "Sorry I was cross. Why don't you have a ride before dinner? There's plenty of time." As if forgetting why he had been going upstairs, James trod heavily down and across the hall, leaving the door ajar behind him.

Phillip smiled. "You've got him befuddled, Honor. He wants to believe in you but isn't too sure about me." He grinned, yet an anxious look crept into his face. "I suppose I should be flattered, but I really don't want to cause trouble between you two. He's the biggest thing in my life. I've always wanted to be more like him."

Honor again caught the cry for help. "There's no reason you can't be, Phillip. If you would only believe in yourself—and in God."

"I really can't see myself in that role." He shook his head.

"I can—with all my heart." Her fervent exclamation scored, and a bit awkwardly Phillip asked, "How about that ride? We certainly have James's blessing."

Honor swallowed a lump in her throat. James's change of direction had been superb showmanship, nothing more. The kiss had not held tenderness, as had his kisses before their wedding. It had all been for Phillip's benefit. Dashing back disappointment, she forced gaiety. "Of course! How long has it been since you've really ridden here? I bet I know more about Casa del Sol than you do!"

"We'll see about that!"

But an hour later Phillip had to admit defeat. "You're right. You really do know more. I guess I've been too busy indoors to remember how grand it is." His sweeping hand took in the still-yellow aspens, towering firs and pines, and distance-softened rolling hills leading to mountains dusted by early snow. "You think Babs will like it?"

Honor whirled toward him. "Phillip, I want to know right now—why did you pay all that attention to me, build up promises? You know you've never really loved anyone but Babs!"

She didn't think he would answer, and when he did it was in a shamed voice. "I know. But you were different, sweet. When Babs turned me down I made up my mind I'd never let her hurt me again. She—" He stopped, forced himself to look at Honor. "When I was at the canyon I really did think maybe I could make it with you."

"It was a terrible thing to do, Phillip."

Her gently accusing voice brought color even to his ears. "I know—now. But it all turned out all right. You married James. You could have searched the world over and never found a better man."

"Does your brother know how much you care about him?"

"Don't be ridiculous!" The mood was broken. "Men don't go

around telling each other stuff like that."

"You're the one who is ridiculous. He's your brother. If you had let him know a long time ago how you feel, a lot of the trouble between you could have been solved before it began."

"Maybe you're right." But it was too serious for Phillip. "Come on—race you to the ranch!"

❧

"Didn't think you could do it," he teased as he reined in beside her. "A tenderfoot like you beating an old hand like me?"

"An old hand like you had better do more riding. You're getting rusty. Next time I'll beat you worse!" Honor swung from the saddle and prepared to remove it.

"Hey, let one of the hands do that."

"What? A good rancher takes care of his own, or her own, horse. Get that saddle off and your mount rubbed down."

"That's telling him," a soft voice applauded. Babs Merrill leaned against the door laughing at them, even more beautiful than when Honor had seen her before.

"Babs, welcome!" Honor stepped toward her, a smile lighting her face. "I won't offer to shake hands—mine are pretty dirty!"

"That won't stop me." Phillip took the well-groomed hands in his own grimy ones. Honor saw the look in his eyes and turned her back. Who would have thought she wouldn't have minded? She busied herself with her horse, glad for the activity to keep pace with her galloping thoughts. She really didn't mind. She only hoped Phillip could find happiness. Would Babs ever be interested in learning about God? How much happier they could be if they knew Him! She closed her lips tight. She wouldn't preach.

She didn't have to. After the leisurely dinner interspersed with laughter, Babs excused herself and went upstairs. Wondering, Honor followed to see if there was anything needed in the ornate guest suite. Babs's room door was open, but she wasn't there. Strange. Honor glanced in the open door of the guest suite bathroom. No Babs. Her own door stood open. Had Babs gone there?

Babs was sitting on Honor's bed when Honor entered. "Why did you invite me here? Another of your do-gooder deeds?" But her voice held only a flick of her usual sarcasm. "Why did you say Phillip needed me?"

"Because it's true." Honor saw the doubt mixed with hope in green eyes gone suddenly soft. The long, slender fingers trembled. Honor knew what she must do. "Babs, you were right at the canyon. Phillip saw me as a summer romance."

"And you?"

"Much more." She could be candid, open, without fear of hurt. "I was lonely. I saw everything in Phillip I'd ever wanted. Yet I also knew it would take a miracle for us to ever be happy. I wanted to believe Phillip had a longing inside for something more than his present way of life. I felt I had something to offer him." She fell silent for a moment. "Babs, I still do."

Honor saw Babs stiffen, resentment oozing from every pore.

"Wait! Not what you think, Babs! I'm married to James. I have no love for Phillip at all."

"So you didn't marry James for his money!" Babs had the grace to flush. "Maybe I've misjudged you. You're really in love with him, aren't you?"

Honor was speechless that this woman of the world could so easily shatter her defenses.

"Honor, forgive me. But what did you mean, you still have something to offer Phillip?"

Honor's tongue was released. "I have the Lord Jesus Christ to offer Phillip. A better friend, a finer companion than anyone on earth could ever be. He's there for the taking."

Babs looked disappointed. "Oh, you mean religion."

"Not exactly." Honor's face glowed with determination. She had been given a chance to witness without preaching. She would do just that. "Religion encompasses many things. But the belief in and acceptance of Jesus Christ as your Savior is much more! God sent His only Son to earth that we might know Him and have eternal life."

"You really believe that? Why?"

Honor thought for a moment. "Babs, I was only a child when my parents were killed in the San Francisco earthquake. But I had my brother, Keith, to look after and Granny to lean on. Then Keith died somewhere in France. Granny followed. I was left alone, so alone I wished I could die, too." Tears glittered but did not fall. "For a time I was numb, uncaring. Then I knew my life had to count for something. Their work was over; mine was not."

"You mean this God of yours took away the pain?" Babs was frankly disbelieving, but at least she was listening.

"No, Babs." Honor faced her guest steadily. "The pain is there, but God has given me extra strength so I can live with it." She was encouraged by Babs's face, the almost reluctant fascination.

"Haven't you ever stayed awake at night, Babs, wondering what life is all about? Haven't you ever been so lonely you would have gladly traded everything you have to have one friend close enough to share your deepest feelings with? Haven't you ever been let down so badly, even by Phillip, you wondered if life was worth living?" She could see her shot had struck home. "God doesn't let people down. I know that now. He sent His Son to show us the best and only way to live." She broke off. What she said could be crucial at this point. She prayed silently for guidance.

Babs was no longer cynical or laughing. "Then you believe God controls everything in your life and that it's all for a purpose?"

Honor hesitated, choosing her words carefully. "Only when we accept that we are under God's control. So long as we go our way, feeling *we* are in charge, we step out from under His protection. . . ." She searched for a parable. "If we were walking together down the street under an umbrella and I deliberately chose to step out from under it, I would be subject to the storm."

"But Christians still have storms in their lives." Babs's green eyes were more speculative than antagonistic. "Why doesn't God take better care of those who worship Him?"

For an instant Honor thought of James's lightly asking how she knew it wasn't God's will for her to marry him instead of Phillip. A spasm of regret chased shadows into her eyes. "Sometimes God does send trials, Judge Bell says. I really think, though, that most of the time we bring them to ourselves when we refuse to follow Him."

Babs slowly rose. "Glad I came." So few words in response to the message of salvation.

Honor's heart sank as she hesitated then said, "Babs, it wasn't until after my wedding I stopped rebelling against God and accepted Christ. I can honestly say it's made all the difference in the world. If you want real happiness you will seek God and help Phillip do the same." There! It was out.

Babs looked amazed. "I'd have thought you were—" Her face flushed. "I won't say it. I'll think about it, Honor."

"Don't wait too long." Honor could feel the strain in her voice. "Good night, Babs." Prey to her own emotions, Honor still rejoiced. At least some of the bitterness and suspicion Babs carried for her had gone. Would she consider what Honor had said? Troubled by her own flippant remarks to James, desiring to share the Lord she had ignored so long, and concerned over wondering if she could ever become the kind of witness she wanted to be, she restlessly wandered around her room then donned her riding habit for the second time that day. Jingles was much better now. Maybe she could either lead him or ride a little on the path near the house.

Cautiously she slipped downstairs and out the door, noting it was ajar. How strange Juan had not locked it as usual! Was someone else prowling? She laughed at her groundless fears. Why get panicky over an unlocked door?

The moon was bright as she walked toward the corral, keeping her head turned back over her shoulder. Why should she feel as if she had been observed slipping from the house? Intent on watching the front door she ran smack into a solid, tall figure in riding clothes.

"Phillip!"

There was a slight sound then the man pushed back his sombrero and grinned sardonically. "Sorry to disappoint you, Mrs. Travis. Not Phillip. Just your husband." James Travis stood bareheaded bcfore her.

How maddening! Now what did he believe about her? Honor wasn't long in finding out.

"Why did you invite Babs here? As a cover? Seems like you could wait a bit before sneaking out to meet Phillip!"

"I did not come out to meet Phillip!"

"Oh?" She could see his lip curl even in the moonlight. "Then what, may I ask, are you doing running around the ranch in the middle of the night?"

Her voice quivered. "Maybe you can't understand how hard it is for me to be here." Mistaking his silence for disbelief, she stumbled on. "How would you like to live in a place where you were watched, mistrusted? How would you like to have someone spying on you all the time, waiting for you to make a mistake?"

"I was not spying. I have every right to be here. I live at Casa del Sol—or haven't you noticed?"

"I've noticed. I've noticed how everyone around here jumps without even asking how high when you speak. Phillip—"

"So you're still in love with him!"

She ignored the savage way he cut the air with his riding crop. "I am not in love with him! That doesn't mean I can't see what you are too blind to notice. Phillip worships you, wishes with all his heart and soul he could be like you! He envies your strength, longs to be able to take control as you do—"

"And covets my wife."

"He does not! You were right: he never loved anyone but Babs. I was a passing fancy, like all the rest." She paused for breath. "I hope Phillip and Babs marry and get as far away from you as possible. You don't know how to love anyone but yourself!"

It was curious what strange tricks moonlight could play. For an instant she could have sworn a terrible pain crossed the face above her. There was something deadly in his voice as he softly asked, "Oh? Have you so soon forgotten?" She was inexorably being drawn to him. Her cry of protest was smothered by his kiss, gentle at first, then demanding. When he lifted his face from hers she was exhausted.

"Good night, Mrs. Travis." With giant strides he was at the corral. Before Honor could move he had cut out Sol, leaped to his bare back, and disappeared around the bend in the moonlight.

Chapter 10

As she had done so many times before, Honor stood by her window, gazing down with unseeing eyes. The autumn leaves that used to greet her were gone. They had been replaced with a soft white mantle that had come during the night. She had seldom seen snow in San Francisco. Even if it did fall, the shining veil soon melted, leaving no trace of its coming. Here it meant stillness beyond belief. Every twig proudly bore its new winter garb, shining in the sun that had come out to beam on the scene.

Two laughing figures ran into view, hand in hand. Babs's scarlet coat was a brilliant spot against the all-white background. Honor smiled in sympathy as Babs's silvery laugh ran out. The change in their redheaded guest in the weeks since she had come to visit Casa del Sol was incredible. And Phillip! Honor couldn't stem the tide of warmth flooding her. Gradually Phillip Travis was growing up after all the years of childish self-indulgence.

"Come on out, Honor!"

She shook her head but called from her window. "I have something else to do. Maybe later."

"Sissy!" Babs's upturned, laughing face glowed. She snatched a handful of snow and threw it upward as Honor slammed down the window. If only she could be out there with them! If only James. . . But her husband was more unapproachable than ever. She had thought after the night by the corral things might get better. He was courteous, nothing more. He treated her exactly the way he treated Babs. If he noticed Phillip's and Babs's speculative gazes he ignored them.

Only once had he unbent. Phillip had insisted on being given more responsibility around the ranch. Reluctantly James had assigned him work, and it had been done well. James had sought out Honor.

"I just wanted to say I appreciate your telling me how Phillip feels." His voice was husky. "I believe he and Babs will marry and live on the ranch. I also believe they can be happy here." James had wheeled and left the room before Honor could reply.

"Hey, Honor!" Phillip's call drew her back to the window. He was lugging a huge old-fashioned sled that he must have discovered in the barn. "We're going to the big hill out back. Want to come?"

Honor's determination not to be a third party weakened. Babs was smiling and beckoning. It was too much. In a spirit of gay recklessness she threw wide her window. "Be right down!" In moments she was bundled into a heavy winter coat James had brought home from a trip to Flagstaff and sent to her by Carlotta. She snuggled in its warmth. Dark green evergreen spires tipped with snow enticed. Why worry on a day like this?

It was the most glorious day she could remember. The snow was perfect, packing down the way it had on sled hills when she was a child. Each time she raced downhill was a thrill. Sometimes alone, or with Babs—sometimes all three of them. The great *whoosh!* across the surface, growing speed, pelting down, and the final slowing and long uphill climb.

"I've never been happier," Babs confided as she and Honor pulled the big sled up the long hill after a particularly exhilarating slide. Her cheeks were redder than her coat, with no need for paint.

"It shows." Honor smiled at the other girl.

"I know." Babs's teeth gleamed. "Phillip asked me last night to marry him, on one condition." Honor could feel herself begin to tense as Babs continued. "He wants to live on the ranch. No more playboy stuff. He certainly has changed since we came here."

"What about you, Babs?"

"Me, too." She grinned impishly at Honor. "Thanks to you. When I saw how much Phillip appreciated your simplicity I decided to take stock of myself. That's why I spent so many hours alone at the South Rim."

Honor scarcely dared breathe. "And?"

"And I decided you weren't for real." She laughed at the disappointment in Honor's face. "Don't look so shocked. That was then. Since I've been here I know it's real. Someday maybe I'll even have you introduce me to your Friend." There was no mistaking her meaning.

Honor's heart swelled. It was worth all the pain and trouble she had gone through to hear Babs say that. "Don't wait too long."

"I won't." Babs twisted the emerald, now worn on her left hand. "I want to talk to Phillip about some things, and—"

"Hurry with the sled, you two! Winter will be over before you get here!" Further confidences were broken, but Babs's warm smile as she broke free and ran the few remaining steps up the hill promised other talks.

Honor trudged slowly, filled with her own thoughts. So Babs and Phillip would marry. A flick of pain at the thought of her own shadowy romance brought a lump to her throat, but she pushed it back. Phillip and Babs were arguing when she reached them.

"Aw, Babs, it's nothing. I've gone down that other side a hundred times when I was a kid." He pointed opposite the well-beaten path they had been using to a sharper decline, dotted with green trees.

"You aren't a kid. You don't know what might be under all that snow." Babs looked worried.

"I just want one trip down there."

"Please, Phillip, don't go." Honor added her entreaty to Babs's. "James has warned me so many times about the dangers on the ranch—"

"Dangers!" Phillip drew himself up in a ridiculous pose. "I know this ranch as well as I know my own bedroom." He flung himself to the awkward sled and with his feet pushed the conveyance toward the edge of the bank.

"Stop!" The hail came from a tall man running toward them, his face a thundercloud in its command. "Don't push off that sled!"

Honor saw the opposition roused in Phillip by James's curt order.

"Sorry, brother! I get first ride." With a mighty shove he pushed over the edge and started down before James could reach him. "This is the life!" His voice floated back to them, only to be drowned out. The sled must have hit a hidden snag. For one terrible moment it seemed to stand on end. Phillip was thrown downhill, sliding, arms flailing in a vain effort to stop his momentum. To the horrified gaze of the onlookers he gathered speed in spite of his efforts, smashed into a great tree, and crumpled into a heap.

"Phillip!" Heedless of his own safety, James started down the hill. His great boots sank into the snow as he went, leaving giant stride marks. Clutching at every outstretched branch, he slipped, slid, and by sheer determination stopped where Phillip lay horribly crumpled.

Babs was the first to come to her senses. "Quick! We'll get help!" She grabbed Honor's arm, shaking her back to reality. "We've got to get back to the house and call a doctor. Or at least get Juan and Rosa. They'll know what to do." Cupping her hands around her mouth she called to James, "We're going for help."

Fear lent wings to their feet as they raced back to the house.

They burst into the kitchen. "Rosa, Phillip's hurt. Where's Juan?"

Concern didn't detract from Rosa's swift actions. "Out shoveling." She threw open the door and called to him, waving her arms imperatively. "Juan! Quickly, Felipe is hurt!"

In moments Juan, Babs, and Honor were huddled in the big Willys as it churned through the snow down a little-used road that would bring them out only a few hundred feet below the brothers. "I'm so thankful for this heavy car," Honor breathed.

Juan braked, stopped, and was out of the car and up the separating distance, closely followed by the two girls. James looked up to answer the unspoken question trembling on their lips. "He's hurt—badly." He pressed his scarf against Phillip's head. Honor could see bright bloodstains on the snow. "We've got to get him to a doctor."

"Rosa is calling one now." Honor found her voice, but James shook his head. "We can't wait for a doctor. We'll take him to Flagstaff immediately."

Honor's involuntary protest died under the look of anguish in James's eyes. "But how—" she faltered.

"The roads are clear." Already Juan and James were lifting Phillip carefully, inching their way down to the car. "We'll get him in the back where he can lie down. Mama Rosa will know what to do until we get to Flagstaff."

It was a nightmare Honor would never forget. The seemingly endless procession to the house, the fitting of all of them in and still leaving room for Phillip to half lie down.

"Can you drive?" James whirled toward Honor. "I want Juan to help me steady Phillip."

"Not in snow and ice." She shivered. "I only learned here this fall."

"I can." Babs's lips were white but determined. Already she was slipping into the driver's seat. Mama Rosa stayed with the two men, pressing compresses hard on the wound spurting blood. Carlotta huddled between Babs and Honor in the front seat. There had been no question but that they would all go. *It's a family*, Honor thought. *My family.* But there was no time to explore such thoughts.

The road to Flagstaff was icy and had not been sanded. In spite of Babs's skillful handling of the car, it still slid now and then.

Once Babs looked across at Honor. "Now's the time to call on that God you told me about." There was no mockery in her words.

"I am." Honor's lips moved silently.

Mile after mile they traveled as fast as Babs dared. When they reached the outskirts of Flagstaff, Honor breathed normally again, but it wasn't until they were in the emergency waiting room with Phillip on his way to surgery that some of the tenseness left her.

"He's cut badly on his head," the doctor told them after the first cursory examination. "He doesn't appear to have lost too much blood. No bones appear to be broken, but. . ." He hesitated. ". . . there is always the danger of internal bleeding."

If James Travis's face could have gone whiter, it did. Babs stifled a little moan, and Honor reached for her hand to grip it hard. "Don't, Babs. God will take care of Phillip. I know He will." Something in her level look steadied Babs, who clung to her.

But James couldn't hold back bitter words. "If there really is a God, why did He let Phillip get hurt in the first place?"

Honor's heart sank. James would never understand. "God didn't force Phillip to go down that hill." James didn't speak but turned away, leaving Honor shaken. In spite of everything, she had hoped they could make their marriage work. But if James had no use for God, how could it ever be?

It seemed hours before the doctor returned. His face was grave. "He will live." His words were almost lost in the gasps of relief, but the doctor's face didn't lighten. "He will live, but. . ." He looked around the little group, at James last of all. "The head wound is close to his eyes. We found a piece of bone depressed into the brain. The surgeons are working with it now. Until it is over and he wakens we just won't know."

"Just won't know what?" James's face blazed.

The doctor's face wrinkled in sympathy. "Whether he will ever see again."

Honor felt the shock ripple around the circle.

"Blind!" James repeated stupidly.

"There is that possibility." The doctor gripped James's arm. "We are doing everything humanly possible, and—"

"You said humanly possible. What else could be done?" James's ashen face frightened Honor.

The doctor didn't waver. "There is a power higher than man." With another strong pressure on James's arm he turned and left them. This time there was no mockery in James's voice. "Honor?" He turned toward her, stumbling a bit. "Honor? You know that higher power. Will you do something?" The pleading in his eyes hurt Honor.

"I have been praying ever since the accident."

Babs seemed to come to life. "Honor, if I promised God to live as He wants, would He save Phillip's sight?"

Honor's lips felt stiff. "You can't bargain with God. All we can do is pray—and wait."

"She's right." Judge Bell stood in the doorway, panting as if he had been running. Babs instinctively turned toward the kindness in his face.

"There, lassie, we must trust our Father in heaven—"

"Trust Him! I don't even know Him!" James's face contorted in agony. "All this time, you tried to tell me, and I wouldn't listen. Daddy, is Phillip's accident a punishment because I haven't believed?"

Honor stood rooted in sorrow. She remembered asking the same question.

"No." There was something magnificent about the judge. "God punishes us for our own sins, not those of others."

James's face was chalky. He went on as if he had not heard. "I should have been an example. Why haven't I been what I should have been? Phillip is weak, and I knew it." He raised dull eyes toward Honor. "If I had believed in Christ and told Phillip how important it was, maybe he wouldn't be such a mess. Maybe he wouldn't even be lying there now." His harsh laugh grated in the shocked silence. "I contributed to his weakness."

Honor could not bear his suffering. She turned away.

James looked at Daddy Bell. "You told me I would have to face God, to answer for laughing at the idea I wasn't in total control. But did it have to come this way? Did anyone ever sin as I have, deliberately choosing to ignore everything that really matters in life?"

"Come, laddie." Daddy Bell placed his arm around James as if he had been a child. "We'll fight this out together."

Honor and Babs stood frozen as the two men, one bent with the ministry of years, the other from his growing recognition of sin and careless ignorance of sacred things, slowly walked down the long hall and disappeared behind a door marked CHAPEL.

Honor could not speak. Even when Babs moaned and sank into a chair, Honor remained standing straight, looking down the hall. It suddenly seemed a great gulf separating her from James. What happened now would literally save her husband's life or leave him empty, unfulfilled, bitter.

"Oh, God, let him accept Your Son that he might be forgiven."

It was all she could whisper. If only she could be at his side! She could not. It would be for Judge Bell to make clear the only path that did not lead to spiritual death. Then James must make the decision, not to attempt a bargain with God for his brother's sight, but to seal himself as God's child, forgiven and willing to obey.

Was all of life a fight? Sickness, health. . .good, evil. . .God, Satan. . . In spite of her studies the thoughts left Honor helpless.

What was happening in the little chapel? Was James listening with his heart instead of with his head, as so many educated minds seemed to do? Could the prejudices and false images he had built be shattered? Yes! Hadn't God done exactly that for her?

A little cry from Babs snapped Honor from her trancelike state. There was work to do here. God would help James. She would cling to that hope and silently pray. Her other prayers for Phillip and Babs mingled together in one great plea to God.

For hours she and Babs sat together. The waiting room was mercifully empty of others. Only fear kept them company, and after a time, even it was blunted by sheer exhaustion. At first Honor tried to keep up a conversation with Babs, but it was useless. Babs's eyes were fixed on the door to the emergency room. Was she remembering all the laughing days they had spent carelessly going their pleasure-mad way? Was she remembering moments at the canyon when she had gone away from the others to evaluate? Or was she even remembering days long ago, before Phillip, days when she said she had gone to Sunday school?

Honor's brain whirled. The broken woman next to her was a far cry from the worldly creature who had once infuriated a rebellious girl by telling her the truth about Phillip. Impulsively Honor laid her hand over Babs's clenched ones.

The green eyes swung to her briefly. A small tremor of her lips betrayed tightly held emotion, and her hands opened to clasp the one extended in friendship. There was a gentle pressure of the cold fingers that slowly warmed, then the icy face gave way to pain, unashamed.

An eon of time seemed to have passed before the chapel door swung open. Honor held her breath. What would be the results of what had happened in the little room?

"James has found his God." Daddy's tired face still radiated.

With a little cry Honor ran to them. "It wasn't just to save Phillip?"

James went white to the lips, and Honor wished fervently she had bitten her tongue to hold back the words.

"No. It wasn't for Phillip." He looked past her, eyes dulled instead of expectant as they had been before. "I read your Bible, Honor. At first, it was with scorn. How could anyone believe any tale so simple?" His dark eyes were almost black in their intensity. "You had circled a place." He fumbled in the Bible she knew so well, found the marked passage. "John 3:16: 'For God so loved the world, that he gave his only begotten Son, that whosoever believeth in him should not perish, but have everlasting life.' " He closed the Book, almost reverently. "I still wouldn't admit the feeling I had when I read it." A spasm of pain crossed his face. "Daddy Bell made me reread it. Then I knew. *Whosoever* meant me, and everyone. Every man, woman, and child on earth must bow before God, admit they are sinners, and realize the fact of the Lord Jesus Christ's death in their place so that they might have forgiveness, mercy, salvation. I only wish I had listened and accepted it all years ago." The last words were almost a whisper.

For an ecstatic moment Honor felt faint from joy and relief. Her prayers had been answered—James was saved! Now there was nothing to stand between them! Now they could. . . The thought died. Just because James had accepted Christ didn't mean he loved the woman he'd married under such bizarre circumstances.

"I intend to set straight everything I have done to wrong others." James's voice broke into her mind.

Honor bit her lip. He must mean her. He would feel the only way to make things right was to release her. Could she stand the pain still ahead? Would she never stop paying for her rebellion and willfulness, even though she was forgiven?

And James—he would carry forever the memory of the way he had married his twin's fiancée in an underhanded way. Both would pay in being freed by law from unfulfilled vows, bound in God's sight—and in their own. Granny's warning, Keith's pleadings—all had led to this, and there was no one to blame but herself.

She breathed raggedly. It was not the time to explore their relationship, with Phillip still in danger, nor was it in the days following. Babs haunted the hospital. For even though the doctors were hopeful, there was nothing to do but wait.

Chapter 11

One thing that came about from all the trouble was a new closeness between Babs and Honor. From distrust, to wariness, and at last to the acceptance of Honor's hand at the hospital that terrible night, Babs took slow steps toward trusting another woman. Honor sensed the struggle. How terrible to have lived among those where self-preservation ruled out real friendship!

One evening Babs said, "Honor, the hardest thing in the world for me is to admit I'm wrong, but if I'd admitted to myself at the canyon what I knew you were, I'd never have said all those terrible things."

Honor looked up from mending a blouse she'd brought to the hospital. "They were all true. I didn't realize how true until I came here and accepted Christ. I'm glad you said what you did, although it made me angry. Even though I couldn't accept it at the time, I thought of it later and admitted you were right."

"Even if Phillip is blind, I'm going to marry him."

Honor dropped her mending. "Will he?"

"I'm not letting him go again—ever." There was nothing of the sophisticate in the determination in Babs's face. "It's not from pity. I've always loved him. I just couldn't trust him not to find another pretty face, and now he may not be able to even see those faces."

"Stop it!" Honor dropped the blouse and shook Babs hard. "The doctor says he has every reason to believe Phillip will be all right."

"Then why doesn't he regain total consciousness?" The cry echoed doubts in Honor's own mind. "Honor, I have to have something to hang on to, like you have. Would God really forgive me and send peace?"

"If you confess yourself a sinner."

"You'll never know how great a sinner." The admission was low.

"I don't want to. It's between you and God. That's why Jesus died on the cross, to save you forever from all that. He took your place, Babs."

"But what do I do?"

"Just repent, and then accept it. Salvation is a free gift. You gain eternal life. You gain Christ and the Holy Spirit and peace from God. You are free, Babs, free from every ugly thing in your past." Honor breathed a prayer and took Babs's ice-cold hands in her own. "Just tell Him you are sorry for all your sins, and accept the gift of His Son and salvation."

"I—" The opening of the door from Phillip's room cut her short.

"He is awake." The doctor's smile warmed Honor's heart.

Babs remained frozen in place for one second then gave a low cry and ran into the room.

"It's all right," the doctor told Honor. "The first thing he said was, 'Where's Babs?'"

Babs didn't stay long in Phillip's room. When she came back she was radiant. "He complained of a headache, but he can see!"

Honor felt as if the strain that had been holding her up suddenly gave way. She stumbled into a chair, trying to form words for the praise and gladness in her heart. Phillip would not be blind! *Please,* her heart whispered, *cure Phillip and Babs of a different kind of blindness, and help them find You.* What would Babs have said if the door had not opened just when it did? She had been close, so close!

The question haunted Honor for the next week. During that week Phillip was pronounced fit and sent home. What a far cry from that terrible trip they had made taking him to the hospital!

The touring car with James, Honor, Phillip, and Babs swung into the driveway to be greeted with Christmas garnish. Decorations were everywhere. The Hernandez family had spread sweet-smelling boughs, bright ribbons, every kind of decoration they could imagine.

"Some welcome home." Phillip sounded subdued. "I could have been—"

"Thank God you aren't," James spoke softly.

"You? Thanking God?"

But the old mocking light died from Phillip's face as James replied, "I have discovered what a fool I have been in discounting the only thing in the world that really matters."

Phillip swung to Babs, standing close in the lightly falling snow. "I suppose next you'll be telling me you feel the same."

Honor's fingers clenched until they were white, even under their warm wool mitten covering. The group of four stood motionless. Could Babs sense she was at a crossroads?

"I—" Her pleading gaze at Honor lifted to Phillip's handsome face. "I am glad to be home." She broke free of the group and hurried through the massive front door.

Honor's disappointment spilled over. She had to turn away from the two men to hide her telltale face. Babs had been so close! It was all she could do to pretend gaiety at the Mexican meal Rosa and Carlotta had prepared to welcome Phillip home. Once she met James's searching eyes, and a faltering smile hovered on her lips. Later he whispered, "Don't forget—God reached even me."

In the library before the fire after dinner Phillip paced restlessly and finally whirled toward Babs. "Well, are you going to marry me on Christmas Eve?"

Babs gasped then recovered something of her old haughtiness.

"I am not." Before anyone could move she added, "But I will marry you on Christmas Day."

"This is our cue for an exit." James motioned Honor out of the room.

"Well, it looks as if things are going to work out for Phillip and Babs." Honor stopped at the foot of the great staircase and smiled at James.

His face didn't light up the way she had expected. For one moment he seemed to be looking over her head and into the future. Somber, brooding, his answer chilled her. "Yes, things have turned out for them. What about us?"

Before she could speak, he was gone.

As she slowly mounted the stairs to her room, again she felt alone—only this time God was there to help her bear the pain. Yet even that pain gave way before another disappointment the same night. After tossing and turning for what seemed like hours she was startled to hear her door slowly opening.

"Honor?" Babs glided to the bed.

"Babs!" Surprise choked off Honor's voice. "Are you ill?"

"No."

The snow outside had stopped earlier. Now a pale moon targeted the red-haired woman through Honor's partly uncurtained window. Yet even the dim light failed to hide her agitation. Her hands were icy as one brushed against Honor's face.

"Honor? I have to talk with you."

Sleep fled. "What is wrong, Babs?"

"I tried to tell Phillip about what you said about God."

"And?" Honor held her breath.

"He laughed. Not so much as he would have done before the accident, but he still laughed."

Honor's heart ached for the desolate sound in her friend's voice.

"What about you, Babs? You know it's all true, don't you?"

"Yes." Babs's face turned even paler. "But I can't accept it." As if she felt Honor's shock she brokenly added, "I've waited years for Phillip to notice me in a real way. Nothing must spoil that!"

Her cry echoed Honor's heart, a duplicate of her own cry at the canyon's edge what seemed like eons ago. "You are choosing Phillip instead of God?"

"I must." The icy hands clutched the warm one Honor held out. "Phillip has already changed more than I ever thought possible. We're going to make our home here. He's going to give up drinking and all that. Isn't it enough?" Her voice was anguished.

"No, Babs." The inflexibility of the two words wilted Babs.

Honor couldn't keep despair from her voice as she cried out, "The greatest sin in the world is not accepting the free gift of salvation through the Lord Jesus Christ. All the being good in the world, all the good deeds won't save you or anyone. Please, Babs." Her voice rose. "Don't turn your back on Him. Don't crucify the Lord again by your refusal to accept Him!"

Babs slowly withdrew her hands from Honor's desperate clutch. Her eyes held fear, regret, pain. She rose from the bed where she'd been seated to tower over Honor. "I have no choice. I can never give up Phillip."

For one wild moment Honor wondered—should she tell Babs she, too, had once made that same choice and with what tragic results? Slowly she shook her head. Now was not the time for that. Instead she said, "Babs, I had to come to Christ just as I would have done before. But instead of it being easy and natural, there were years of pain and bitterness in between. We have to learn the same lessons, whether we do it God's way or our own, and our way is hard."

"Someday, if Phillip can accept, I will, too." Babs slipped out.

The tears on Honor's pillow that night were not for herself.

Christmas and the wedding rushed toward them. Soon it was Christmas Eve. Babs had not mentioned her decision since that night. Neither had Honor, who now lay sleepless. When God directed her to speak she would. Until then, she could only pray.

At least she could be thankful for the change in Phillip. He was becoming more like his brother every day. He had accepted his future at Casa del Sol, relishing it. The brothers spent time planning how to make it more efficient. Phillip had come up with some surprisingly good ideas. "Just because I wasn't running this place doesn't mean I never thought about it." The casual remark didn't hide his pleasure at their compliments.

Suddenly Honor could stand the confines of her room no longer. James's inscrutable eyes watched her from every corner. She would slip down to the library and find something to read. James still had her Bible, but she had noticed a big one downstairs with more references than the small one Daddy Bell had given her.

Before she could reconsider, Honor thrust her arms into a heavy turquoise quilted robe and matching slippers. She ran lightly down the stairs, struggled with the heavy doors, then crept inside. Fumbling for the light switch, she was immobilized by the tall, dark figure rising from the couch, etched against glowing flames in the fireplace.

"James?"

"At least you didn't call me Phillip. Do come into my parlor, dear little fly."

Why did he still have the power to hurt her? Or was it weariness in his voice instead of sarcasm? She ran her hand lightly over her hair. "I couldn't sleep. I came for a book."

He came a step nearer. "And just why couldn't you sleep?"

She could feel it coming—the floods of feeling behind the dam of control she had built so carefully. If she answered, that last line of defense would crumble under the onslaught.

"I asked why you couldn't sleep."

His insistence was the final undoing. "How could you expect me to sleep—under the circumstances?"

"You mean because Phillip is marrying Babs tomorrow?" She had never felt as flayed as she did by his accusation.

"Don't be completely stupid!" She hadn't known she could blaze so. All the long nights of wondering, of loving him hopelessly burst forth. "It's you, James Travis. Are you too insane to see it?"

A disbelieving look crept over his face. "Just what is that supposed to mean?"

The ice in his voice drowned all determination to tell him the truth. Honor fell back on the old original reason. "You really think any woman in my position could be happy? Married to a man who did it to protect her from his own brother?" She could feel his scrutiny even when she dropped her eyes to study the pattern one nervous, slippered foot was making on the floor.

"Oh, that." His voice went lifeless. For a moment he turned to the fire. The lights from the Christmas tree shone on his face, softening it into vulnerability. Honor knew she would never forget the way he looked. To hide the weakness threatening to paralyze her, she walked to the window, noting the heavy frost patterns and that it had begun to snow again.

"Honor, would you come sit down, please?" There was no spark in the request. Slowly she turned and crossed to the fire, carefully avoiding him.

"Honor, when I was in the chapel at the hospital and finally quit trying to outrun God, I made a promise." Something in the gravity of his tone chilled her. "You had said people couldn't bargain with God. I didn't. I did tell Him that when it was all over I'd do what I could to make up to you for marrying you."

For one wild moment Honor's heart leaped. Did he mean that he had learned to care? She was frozen anew by his next words. Face half in shadow, he poked the fire again. "I have put it off, hoping something would happen to change things. Maybe I was even hoping for a miracle. I planned to wait until after the wedding tomorrow." He threw the poker down with a little crash. "I can't wait any longer."

In spite of the warm room Honor shivered with premonition. Could God hear the silent prayer unconsciously going up for help?

"I can't go on the way things are. It's too hard having you here, knowing you despise me."

Shocked, she opened her mouth to protest, only to have the words die on her lips as he said, "I want you to go away. The day after the wedding I'll take you to Flagstaff. We can get the marriage annulled. I'll settle enough finances on you so you can be independent, but I won't keep you here any longer."

Sheer fury overrode Honor's sense of loss. Very slowly she rose to her feet, glaring up at the man who was her husband yet was not her husband. "So now that you've married me, you'll just pack me off the way you'd discard an old pair of shoes." She failed to understand what was in James's eyes. "Well, let me tell you something, Mr. Travis. I won't be shipped off and have money settled on me! I'm not leaving Casa del Sol. You don't have to like it, but you married me for better or for worse. I'm legally your wife. There's nothing you can do about it unless you want the whole story spread across the front page of every newspaper in Arizona."

She paused for breath then went on. "Have you ever once considered that I don't want to go?"

"I have considered it." His face was still in shadow, but the words came out individually, like small, hard ice cubes hitting a tile floor.

"I know you would rather live in misery than break a promise. Now that I have stopped running from God I appreciate it even more. But the promise you made was made falsely. I can't hold you to it."

"So you intend to dispose of me quite properly."

For one moment she felt she had gone too far. There was a quick flash in the set face. "I told you. I can't go on like we are now." In one stride he came close, gripping her by the shoulders, forcing her to look up at him. "If you stay at Casa del Sol it can no longer be as a guest, Honor Travis. It will be as my wife, living with me in holy matrimony the way God intended man and woman to live." His look seared her very soul. "Will you stay under those circumstances? Or will you go to Flagstaff the day after tomorrow, as I suggested?"

Honor's knees felt weak. "You mean—you mean you want me to stay as your wife?"

"Want you! I have wanted you since the day I looked up to see you standing in the hall of my home." His grip tightened. "If ever a man wanted a woman, I want you. You have brought sunlight and laughter. You have brought healing between Phillip and me. You have brought everything a man could ever want. Most of all, you have brought God into this house." His voice had dropped almost to a whisper. "Yes, I want you here—but not as a guest."

Honor was speechless, shaken by his passion. "Then all the time—even when you married me—it wasn't just because you pitied me?"

"No, Honor. It was because I loved you. I didn't know it myself at first. I tried to tell myself it was to save you from Phillip. It wasn't. I fell in love with you the day you came."

Honor's senses were reeling. "But—the day we were married, when I said you probably would say you'd fallen in love with me. . ." Her voice failed.

"Would you have believed me?"

"Not then."

"And now?" The clock ticked off seconds, repeating his question: *And now? And now?*

She was not quite ready to give in. "You said friends were people who trusted you." She moistened her suddenly dry lips. "You said—"

An amused look cut off her stumbling speech. "I said a lot of things—some in self-defense. What I am telling you now is the truth. I love you, Honor, as I have never loved any other woman. I will never love anyone else, even if you go away."

"Then I had better stay."

"You know my conditions."

"I know."

But James wasn't satisfied. He held her off at arm's length. "Are you staying because you promised—because you don't want to break vows you consider holy, even taken under the circumstances ours were made? Or is it possible that Phillip was right?"

It was becoming increasingly difficult for her to meet his searching gaze. "I don't know what Phillip said."

"Phillip told me weeks ago you had never loved him. You had fallen in love with what you thought he was."

Honor didn't answer. Her mind flashed back to the canyon; her rationalizing what Phillip might someday be; her determination to cling to him even at the expense of her own relationship with God.

"Well?"

Her eyes grew soft, but she bravely faced him. "Phillip was right." She hurried on, disturbed by the light filling his dark face. "Carlotta asked me which man I loved. You heard her—and my answer."

Color crept into James's face. "It is the only hope I had these past weeks."

Honor wasn't finished. Her clear eyes confirmed her truthfulness. "I was attracted to Phillip, you know that. In San Francisco, at the canyon.

"When I came here to Casa del Sol I had to revamp my opinion. Where was the charming, idle man I knew? My fiancé was no longer the laughing Phillip Travis, but 'Señor'—admired, respected, a big man doing a big job. It was hard to put the two together!

"James, I ran ahead of God, went on with the wedding, hoped for the best." Her throat was thick with unshed tears. "I have paid. Learning to know you, feeling I was a duty—" She felt heat creep into her cheeks. "But at least God didn't allow me to actually marry the wrong man."

She faltered as James gently pulled her closer. "You really care, Honor? You aren't just bound by your vows?"

A flash of mischief crossed her face. "All my childhood heroes rode white horses, just as you do." The hope and disbelief warring in his face were too much. She discarded her pretense. "I am bound, but not only by my vows. I am bound by the love I have for you—love that is second only to my love for the Lord."

Somewhere in the hall the clock struck twelve. Christmas Eve was over; Christmas Day had begun.

Honor closed her eyes and crept closer into her husband's arms, feeling the solid strength of James Travis. For one magnificent moment she seemed to see down the aisle of years—laughing, weeping, loving, sharing, together—loving life with Christ the Son as head of Casa del Sol.

Colleen L. Reece was born and raised in a small western Washington logging town. She learned to read by kerosene lamplight and dreamed of someday writing a book. God has multiplied Colleen's "someday" book into more than 150 titles that have sold six million copies. Colleen was twice voted Heartsong Presents' Favorite Author and later inducted into *Heartsong Presents'* Hall of Fame. Several of her books have appeared on the CBA Bestseller list.

If You Liked This Book, You'll Also Like…

Love's Story by Dianne Christner
Venture into this classic historical romance set in California from bestselling author Dianne Christner. As a female journalist, Meredith has something to prove with her big story on forest conservation. But when her heart becomes entangled, will she risk her career? Also includes a bonus story, *Strong as the Redwood* by Kristin Billerbeck.

Paperback / 978-1-63409-901-1 / $9.99

The Lilac Year by Janet Spaeth
Travel to the northern prairie wilderness where this historical romance from author Janet Spaeth is set. Mariah is searching for her nephew and a quick way to leave the frontier when she meets homesteader Ben Harris. Also includes the bonus sequel, *Rose Kelly*.

Paperback / 978-1-63409-908-0 / $9.99

Wildflower Harvest by Colleen L. Reece
Enjoy an inspiring historical romance set in Wyoming territory from author Colleen L. Reece. Dr. Adam Birchfield risks losing love in order to keep searching for his brother. Also includes the bonus story, *Desert Rose* in which a woman falls in love with a man through his letters.

Paperback / 978-1-63409-907-3 / $9.99

Find These and More from Barbour Publishing
at Your Favorite Bookstore
www.barbourbooks.com